Praise for the Novels

Christina Boyd

THEN COMES WINTER "As a connoisseur of Jane Austen-inspired short stories, I think *Then Comes Winter* is a confection that Janeites will wholeheartedly enjoy." —Laurel Ann Nattress, *Jane Austen Made Me Do It: Original Stories Inspired by Literature's Most Astute Observer of the Human Heart*

"...a delectable treat just perfect for holiday time and lovers of all things Jane Austen...there is something for everyone in this endearing collection." —Brenna Aubrey, *USA Today* Bestselling Author

SUN-KISSED: EFFUSIONS OF SUMMER "...exquisite romance, sparkling dialogue, much hoped-for happy ending and a few surprising twists along the way." —Joana Starnes, author of *The Unthinkable Triangle* and others

"As in any anthology, some stories worked better than others for me, but the standard of them all was excellent." —*Babblings of a Bookworm*

Linda Gonschior

REFLECTIONS "Well done, Ms. Gonschior, for daring to throw our beloved characters in a modern, yet not so uncommon situation." —*Austenprose*

"...heart-wrenching and intensely emotional..." —*Austenesque Reviews*

A TARNISHED IMAGE "Definitely a satisfying conclusion to the story." —*Amazon reviewer*

Suzan Lauder

ALIAS THOMAS BENNET "...a pretty entertaining, dynamic, and lively content, wrapped in an aura of mystery and intrigue." —*Warmisunque's Austen, Reviews of Fanfic Authors*

"...a real treat for fans of Austen-inspired fiction, and cannot praise its originality enough." —*Diary of an Eccentric*

Lory Lilian

REMEMBRANCE OF THE PAST "The love story between Darcy and Elizabeth is arrestingly beautiful and tender…" —*Austenesque Reviews*

RAINY DAYS "This book was my first introduction to Lory Lilian, and she is becoming a fast favourite!" —*My Kids Led Me Back to Pride & Prejudice*

HIS UNCLE'S FAVORITE "Loved the new twist…" —*So Little Time*

THE PERFECT MATCH "…it suited my tastes quite perfectly!" —*Austenesque Reviews*

Beau North

LONGBOURN'S SONGBIRD "Many books have paid homage to Jane Austen's *Pride & Prejudice*, but Beau North's tribute delivers a breath of fresh air with her unique setting and feisty heroine." —*Goodreads reviewer*

"Debut author Beau North may have transported Austen's characters and plot across the ocean to the American south and 135 years into the future, but the lyrical transfer is creative and engaging." —*Austenprose*

Then Comes Winter

Meryton Press
Oysterville, WA

THEN COMES WINTER

Copyright © 2015 by the authors of each story in this anthology

ISBN: 978-1-68131-003-9

Cover design by Zorylee Diaz-Lupitou with images from 123RF
Layout by Ellen Pickels

Then Comes Winter

Introduction

"Then comes Winter, with bluster and snow,
that brings to our cheeks the ruddy glow…
                    —Gertrude Tooley Buckingham, *The Four Seasons*

ANYONE WHO KNOWS ME KNOWS THAT WINTER IS MY THIRD—IF NOT
fourth—favorite season. I don't believe I am alone in this either. It's cold.
It's wet. The days are short. And did I mention it's cold? I suspect few would
disagree that there is anything as divine as a sun-kissed nose in a book while
one's toes are in warm sand.

But, "What good is the warmth of summer without the cold of winter
to give it sweetness." (John Steinbeck)

Then of course, winter also heralds the magic of the holiday season, so I
suppose we must forgive the cold. The season brings out joyous moments,
charitable intentions, childhood memories…fireside kisses, snowflake kisses,
mistletoe kisses, New Year's kisses. And I adore Bob Hope's words, "My idea
of Christmas, whether old-fashioned or modern, is very simple: loving others.
Come to think of it, why do we wait for Christmas to do that?" Why, indeed.

If you are like me and long for a toasty snuggle on a cold winter's night,
this compilation of original short stories inspired by the magic of the holiday
season—and more than a nod to Jane Austen—was fancied as a sublime
wintertime treat. On the heels of the summer anthology, *Sun-kissed: Effusions
of Summer*, and in concert with some of Meryton Press's most popular authors,
this romantic anthology introduces several promising writers. With a robust
mix of contemporary and Regency musings, *Then Comes Winter* rekindles
passion with equal wit, wonder, and romance.

"He who marvels at the beauty of the world in summer will find equal cause
for wonder and admiration in winter. … In winter the stars seem to have
rekindled their fires, the moon achieves a fuller triumph, and the heavens
wear a look of a more exalted simplicity."
                    —John Burroughs, *The Snow-Walkers*

                    —Christina Boyd

N.B. In the spirit of the collective and for consistency throughout,
this anthology adheres to modern U.S. spelling.

"Dare not say that man forgets sooner than woman,
that his love has an earlier death. I have loved none but you."
—Jane Austen, *Persuasion*

Holiday Mix Tape

. . . .

by Beau North and Brooke West

A Side: Half Agony
Track 1: Being Always Approachable

October 17, 2014

Anne felt the *beep, beep, beep* of the machines burrow between her eyes like a living thing. She rubbed her temples in what she knew would be a futile attempt to ward off a migraine. She got them sometimes, flashes of electricity in her mind like a lightning storm followed by pain— thick and redolent, inescapable like summertime humidity. The only relief came when she dug the heels of her hands into her temples, pressing her skull with all her might.

In the bed, her father was coming out of anesthesia, his complexion chalky under his ever-present tan. With his eyes closed and mouth slightly slack, Walter Elliot actually looked his age for once. Anne felt a moment of tenderness towards him. For most of her life, he'd made the pretense of being a good parent without doing any actual parenting, but Anne could remember a time before her mother died when he was a genuine person.

"How long are we supposed to wait? I haven't eaten in hours," her sister said, still flipping through the latest issue of *In Shape*.

9

"There's a vending machine down the hall and a cafeteria downstairs. You can eat anytime you like."

"You know I can't handle processed food. I can't believe you'd even suggest it. What do you think landed Daddy in here in the first place?"

"Liz, this is Portland, not Green Acres. There's bound to be somewhere you can eat that Gwyneth Paltrow approves of."

Liz was about to protest when they noticed Walter stirring from his sleep. She put her magazine aside and took his well-manicured hand in her own. Anne felt some of the tension that was knotting her up dissipate. She knew a cardiac catheterization was a standard procedure, but she had worried nonetheless.

"Daddy? How do you feel?" Liz asked.

"Thirsty. Have you been here the whole time, Elizabeth?"

"I haven't left your side."

Technically, Liz was telling the truth. She hadn't left their father's side for the twenty-five minutes she'd been there. But Anne was the one who'd gotten up at 5:30 in the morning to drive Walter to the hospital. Rather than let her irritation show, Anne left the room, telling Liz she was going to grab a cup of coffee. She stopped at the nurse's station to let them know her father was awake. Outside, the rain pelted hard against the window. Anne walked over and rested her aching head against the cool glass. She'd always found the gloomy Northwest weather to be soothing. For a moment, Anne studied her reflection in the rain-darkened window. The circles under her eyes spoke of sleepless nights, the hunched-in curve of her shoulders making her seem much older than her years.

"Excuse me, Ms. Elliot?"

Anne turned around, her heart sinking. It hadn't taken them long to find Walter's room. The girl appeared polished despite having just come out of the rain. Anne looked past the young woman's wine-colored pantsuit and nude heels, miraculously untouched by rain, to the small recording device in her hand.

"I'm Rebecca Freemont from the *Observer*. I hoped I could ask you a few questions about your father's condition and the allegations regarding his misuse of campaign funds."

Anne wished, not for the first time, that they'd been able to afford a security detail, but when your father has gambled away the family fortune, such expenses were always the first to go.

"I have nothing to say on either count," Anne said, stepping around the reporter, who was young enough to be one of her students. *Not a moment's peace*, she thought as she rejoined her father and sister who were laughing and joking as though nothing was wrong.

"More reporters," Anne announced. "The vultures are circling."

Liz scowled at her, or tried to. Liz's face moved oddly since she had started all the Botox. She was still a beautiful woman, though Anne worried that her sister was beginning the transition from "beautiful" to "well-preserved." Their relationship was often a contentious one, but Anne loved her sister the way a woman might love a pair of beautiful but uncomfortable heels.

"Anne, do you seriously want to discuss this now?"

"You're right, Liz. I'm sorry, Dad."

Walter waved her off. "You're right though, Annie. Vultures. Get a card next time so I'll know who to sue."

Anne sighed. "I don't think it works that way, Dad."

Ignoring her, Walter and Elizabeth fell back into their own conversation about spending the holidays in the Glen Ellen house down in Sonoma. The family attorney, Alan Shepard, had found tenants for the Elliot family manor in Kellynch Park. Anne hoped the rental income would stave off some of her father's debt. She planned to meet with Alan the next day to go over the details of the lease.

Anne slumped back into her seat and resumed rubbing her temples. She just had to get through the day.

Track 2: When Pain Is Over

From: sophia.croft@mailhub.net
To: wentworth@bandwagon.org
Subject: No Excuses!

Hi Eric, Henry wanted to thank you for the retirement gift. You are too generous, Brother. Now that we're back on the West Coast, you have to come visit us. We found the perfect piece of land, and Henry has got a lot of ideas for the new house. Ground breaks as soon as we close! In the meantime, we are renting an amazing house near Kellynch Park. Do you remember Senator Walter Elliot? Yes, THAT one who's in the news right now. We are renting that big old house of his in Kellynch Park; word is the senator is hiding from the press somewhere in California. We met one of his daughters. She's married to that economist I've seen on Bloomberg: Charles Musgrove, I think. They live just across the park. Henry and I both want you here for the holidays now that we have plenty of room! Don't think David isn't getting one of these guilt trips either; he absolutely is.

Call us and let us know when you've got your flight booked. Love ya, Eric.

—Soph

Eric sat back in his chair, hating that the very mention of Senator Elliot's daughter still made his pulse race. Yes, that was a name he remembered all too well. His heart hammered in his chest as he pulled up his browser and typed "Charles Musgrove." He recalled Musgrove from that summer he spent in Portland with his brother. From what Eric remembered, Musgrove was a soft-spoken young man who was smart but lacking social graces. He'd been carrying a torch for the Senator's middle daughter.

Anne, he reminded himself. Anne Elliot. Flaky, fickle Anne. No doubt, she'd married Charles Musgrove. *After all*, Eric thought bitterly, *I wasn't good enough for her.*

He found Charles Musgrove's website easily enough. His cursor hovered over the link while he argued with himself. What good would this do? What did it matter if she was married now? Did he expect she wouldn't be after all this time? He clicked the link that brought up the "About" page.

A picture popped up, showing a blandly smiling man with a nervous-looking woman and four children. Eric felt all the air leave him in a rush.

It's not her. He sighed, unsure whether he was relieved or not. The frail-looking woman in the picture did bear a resemblance to his old heartbreak. Eric realized with a start that she was Anne's younger sister, whose name he'd forgotten. She'd only been a teenager when he and Anne were an item.

He opened another tab despite his better judgment. He'd spent the better part of a decade trying to forget Anne Elliot and the pain she'd caused him. *Weak, flighty woman.* He hadn't thought of her in over a year, not since the unexpected death of Phoebe Hargrove, his friend James Benwick's fiancée. Eric had spent the long months after her death trying to keep his friend in the land of the living. He wanted to explain to James that the pain would fade bit by bit until one day he wouldn't remember what it was like anymore to know her, to love her.

BEAU NORTH AND BROOKE WEST

But he hadn't said a word. For one, Anne Elliot was still alive. For another, Eric couldn't say he'd entirely forgotten. His fingers hovered over the keyboard for a moment before typing "Anne Elliot Kellynch Park Portland."

He found a page under the Portland State University directory for an Anne Elliot, Professor of Creative Writing and author of a novel, *Perpetual Estrangement*. There was no picture. He tried Google and Facebook, but it was clear that Anne Elliot had kept out of the public eye, unlike her father—perhaps because of her father.

Eric pushed away from his desk and wandered into his walk-in closet. In the very back corner, he shifted aside a stack of folded sweats. Buried at the very bottom was an old shoebox. He grabbed it and put it on the bed, eyeing it warily. *What are you afraid of?*

With a sigh, he opened the box. Inside was a jumble of photos, letters, and mementos: a ticket stub from the Timbers game, a matchbook from the night they spent at the Mark Spencer Hotel, the mixed CD she made him. Eric felt a dangerous curiosity kindle inside him. This little ritual hit him like a punch to the gut. *God, how I loved her once.* What had become of the person with whom he made these memories?

He left the box open on his bed and went back to his computer, sending his sister a brief reply.

From: wentworth@bandwagon.org
To: sophia.croft@mailhub.net
Subject: RE: No Excuses!

Sophie —
I wouldn't miss it. Let you know the details, dates, etc. when I have them. Tell Henry to lock up the good stuff.

Eric

Track 3: No Hearts So in Unison

June 2006

"I KNOW THIS ISN'T REALLY YOUR THING," DAVID SAID APOLOGETICALLY AS they climbed the brick steps leading up the manor. "I just have to make an appearance—do some elbow rubbing."

"I'm not sure you're using that expression right." Eric laughed. "Honestly, it's fine. Just promise me we'll get some real food when we leave here."

"Deal," David agreed readily.

"Whose party is this again?"

"Senator Walter Elliot. I interned for him last semester."

Eric made a big show of smoothing his shirt. "Right. So, rubbing some pretty prestigious elbows tonight, then."

"You don't have to make it sound so dirty," David said just before a white-jacketed attendant swung open the door. David handed over his invitation, and they were ushered inside.

Eric scanned the room, straightening his cuffs and his shoulders, transforming his naturally serious features into an intentional mask of affability. David nudged Eric gently. "I see the bar in the next room over. Shall we?"

Eric followed, content to engage the wives and nephews of those whom they met on their way to the bar where Senator Elliot held court. Eric heard the deep, full laugh of the senator over the din of the party before they were halfway to him.

David wasted no time in gaining the senator's attention. "Senator Elliot, what a pleasure. Thank you for your invitation." David had to speak loudly to be heard over the noise in the room, stretching his hand in between the senator and a rather beige man holding a glass of chardonnay.

"David, how good of you to come." The senator greeted them warmly as he shook his former intern's hand. "Now, don't worry. I know it seems extravagant to invite my interns, but not all of your lot are here. I only invite the bright ones, my boy—only the bright ones," he repeated as he raised his glass towards David.

"Where's your drink, son? Charles!" Senator Elliot barked at the beige man, startling him. "Get David here a scotch." He looked at the glass in his own hand with nothing more than amber-tinted ice cubes rattling inside. "Bring two!"

"Better make it three," David said as he gestured to Eric. The senator raised his eyebrows very slightly, clearly seeing Eric for the first time. "Let me introduce my brother Eric Wentworth, who has just gotten his BA from Auburn and is about to have his first deployment in the Corps. Eric, Senator Walter Elliot."

"It's an honor, sir." Eric offered the senator his outstretched hand. "You host quite a party." The senator shook Eric's hand with a dazzling smile, a politician's smile.

"You should thank my assistant," he responded in a steely tone that didn't match the expression on his face. The senator turned back to David just as the drinks arrived. "There we are," the senator boomed.

"Now that we're all squared away, I've got a few rounds to make. Boys. Gentlemen," he corrected, "enjoy your evening." He beamed at the pair before turning to clap a nearby man on the shoulder with a laugh.

Eric sipped his scotch quietly, smiling at David over his glass. David half-shrugged in apology, understanding the gentle criticism in his brother's eyes.

"Yeah, he's kind of a…" David faltered.

"He's a peacock, David," Eric said with a chuckle. "All loud and strutting. He's got a fake tan and smile to match." In a more serious tone, Eric added, "He didn't seem all that impressed with me."

Dave sighed. "He likes to collect what *he* thinks are important people." David looked at his younger brother with affection. "He's just not always such a good judge of people. He's not the worst of them, though—not by a long shot. Walter Elliot might be vain and arrogant, but at least he's got *some* brains. Speaking of brains, I see that zombie Senator Cleary. Come on, this'll be fun."

Eric began to consider that his idea of *fun* was well removed from his brother's. For nearly an hour, they shook hands with everyone they encountered, mostly older white men, all of whom seemed surprised to meet them. Eric wondered whether it was because of their youth or their dark skin.

Finally wearied by the repetitious polite greetings, he took the first opportunity to excuse himself and wander off, telling his brother he was going in search of a bathroom. The further from the party Eric got, the more relaxed he felt. He roamed the cavernous, vaulted hallways until the music and chatter of the party were a low murmur. *Might as well find a bathroom while I'm here*, he told himself, trying the first door that looked promising.

He wondered whether stepping through the door had transported him into another house. Unlike the formal coldness of the rest of the house, this room was warm and comfortable. The walls were a peaceful aquamarine—the exact color of sea glass—decorated with old movie posters. He spotted at least two of Eric Joyner's Robot-and-Donut prints, one framed and the other propped up on a battered sewing table. At his feet was a rough semicircle of vinyl albums, CDs, little towers of DVDs and books. Thom Yorke's ethereal voice floated out of the older but expensive

CD boom box on the floor, where a young woman sat cross-legged and blinked up at him in bewilderment. Eric felt a strange falling sensation at the sight of her. He couldn't decide whether her eyes were blue like the walls or a stormy grey; they seemed to shift with the slight tilt of her head. Her light brown hair was piled on top of her head in a messy bun, held in place with two pencils.

"I...I'm sorry," he stammered as he realized he'd just invaded someone's bedroom. "I must have taken a wrong turn at Albuquerque."

Her eyes widened slightly as a laugh escaped her.

"Are you lost?"

He nodded, wondering why his mouth was so dry all of a sudden. "I thought this was a bathroom."

She studied him a moment. "Help me up, and I'll show you the way."

He stepped carefully around the items piled on the floor. "Interesting collection," he said. "Kate Bush, Public Enemy, Violent Femmes...very eclectic." He took her outstretched hand and pulled her to her feet. Up close, he could see a dusting of freckles across the bridge of her nose. Her eyes weren't grey like his but a placid blue.

"Yeah, well, variety is the spice of life and all that," she said as she put a little space between them, giving Eric a full view of her cutoff jeans and worn Sonic Youth T-shirt. He noted with interest that her toenails were painted in a black-and-white checkerboard pattern.

"This way." She led him towards the door. Eric had the delirious notion that he wanted to stay in that room, or at least in her company.

"Uh. I didn't actually need the bathroom. I just..."

"...wanted to get away from my father's party?"

He nodded, smiling awkwardly at her. She returned it with a wry little smile of her own.

"What's your name?"

"Eric. Um, Frederick Wentworth."

"I'm Anne." She put her hand out for him to shake. He took it in his own, liking the way her pale skin contrasted with his.

"Are you hungry, Frederick Wentworth?"

"Starving."

She ushered him through another series of corridors to a massive kitchen bustling with activity. Chafing dishes were set up on the long center island where trays were loaded up with finger food and carried back to the party. The waiters, so polite and formal in the midst of the senator's guests, were a noisy, raucous bunch when among their own.

Anne navigated her way around the party staff with what appeared to be practiced ease, disappearing into a walk-in pantry and coming out a minute later with armloads of junk food.

She tilted her head towards the French doors that led outside from the breakfast nook and dumped half of her haul into his arms. "Follow me."

Arms laden, Eric followed behind her, half-trying not to stare at the sway of her hips as she walked. She led him through a garden to a patio with loungers and an outdoor table. He sat down across from her, realizing that during the day the patio likely had a fantastic view of the Willamette River. Now all he could see were the lights of the city below and the breeze gently moving the honeysuckle vines behind Anne Elliot's seat, making the air sweet with perfume.

"You still live at home?" he asked.

"Isn't that obvious?" Everything she said carried a hint of archness that Eric found irresistible.

"What I meant to ask was: Are you in school?"

She grabbed three cookies out of the package and made them disappear in a few bites. He was impressed and charmed by this.

"I was at Berklee," she said. "Then my mom got sick, and I trans-ferred to PSU."

Eric almost asked about her mother then remembered David telling him that the senator's wife died after a battle with cancer the previous year. Instead, he asked whether she was a musician.

"Not exactly. I like to mix and produce; that's what I wanted to do. But PSU doesn't have much by way of a music program, so I ended up enrolling in the creative writing track. I decided just to plow through for my MFA."

She chewed her lip as she looked down at the half-empty bag of chips in her lap. When she looked up at him again, he saw such a naked vulnerability in her, it was all Eric could do to stay on his side of the table. He wanted to wrap his arms around her, protect her.

"I do deejay sometimes," she admitted, smiling through her evident grief.

Eric grinned. He'd just met her, and he was already lost. "Will I get to hear you sometime?"

Track 4: The Age of Emotion

October 18, 2014

ANNE STARTED TO STAND, REMEMBERED HERSELF, AND SAT DOWN AGAIN. It had become a habit of hers to flee the room whenever certain topics and certain people come up in conversation. She looked across the desk at Alan Shepard and asked him if he would repeat what he just said.

"The tenants I found for the Kellynch house: Sophie Croft and her husband?" Shepard, a small, stork-like man with a shaved head and perpetually watery eyes, was bouncing slightly in his seat with barely contained glee. "You've seen her show on the *Food Channel*?"

Anne nodded mutely. She was trying to find her voice, to say "not them," but she could not. She had no real reason to deny them. She'd never met Henry or Sophie Croft; she had only heard about them secondhand.

"She's opening a restaurant called SoCo in The Pearl," Shepard told her. "Southern fusion or some such."

Anne cleared her throat, trying to pretend that her whole world wasn't tipping over. "When can they move in?"

"First of November. Does that give you enough time to get everything you need out?"

Anne mumbled her assent while Shepard prattled on about moving companies and cleaning services, painters, and handymen. November. Just in time for the holidays. She startled as she realized Sophie Croft would likely host Thanksgiving at Kellynch and that *he* might be there. How would it be for him to come back to the place he suffered such a bitter disappointment at her hands? She wondered whether he ever forgave her. A small, resigned part of her hoped maybe he hadn't.

Track 5: The Natural Sequel of an Unnatural Beginning

July 2006

THEY LAY TANGLED TOGETHER ON THE FLOOR OF HIS ROOM IN HIS BROTHER'S apartment. Anne much preferred the hours spent there with Eric and his brother to her family's home in Kellynch Park, where every small detail still stung with the memory of her mother. She was content in that moment to lie wrapped around Eric like a vine, listening to the steady sound of his heart as he twined her hair between his fingers.

"You send me falling, you know," he said, breaking the silence. "Over cliffs and off of mountains. The tallest buildings."

Her heart beat faster at his admission. They'd only known each other for a month, but she knew that she loved him as sure as she knew her own name.

She kissed the warm skin of his chest before responding, emotion making her voice waver.

"I don't fall with you."

"No?"

She looked up at him. "No. I jump."

His strong arms circled her, pulling her closer to him, leaning over to kiss her.

She broke their kiss to roll on top of him. Her hair fell around her face, framing it, as she looked at him. Her eyes were blue fire, and Eric couldn't breathe in the heat of it. He stopped caressing her, his hands holding her hips, and let the feeling of loving her settle into his body, mooring him to the floorboards below. "Anne." He reached out, touching the tendrils of hair swaying between them.

Anne leaned forward to his lips, holding his gaze with hers. The world seemed to tip, and she was sliding off the edge of it into Eric, her heartbeat marking time before their lips touched and their world swirled into a gorgeous, ecstatic chaos.

They didn't feel the hard floor underneath, and they didn't hear when the Portishead CD stopped playing. They only had room for each other, and by the end of it, Anne felt as if she and Eric had become locked in a feedback loop—an *ouroboros*—each one falling eternally into the other.

Track 6: His Ceremonious Grace

November 26, 2014

"Are you sure you don't want to come with us?" Liz asked again.

Anne crossed her arms over her chest, digging her fingers into the soft flesh of her biceps. She didn't tell Liz that she could never make herself go back to the house in Glen Ellen where they spent the last happy Thanksgiving together as a family.

"I'm sure you and Dad will have a great time." Anne reached out and gave Liz's arm a squeeze. "I really can't go anywhere until the plumbing is fixed at my house and…I think Mary needs me more than you and Dad do."

The sisters shared a knowing look and a little laugh. They stood outside of Mary's house in the affluent Uppercross neighborhood. The weather had turned misty, and the damp chill settled into Anne's bones in a way that she loved.

"See you in the new year," Liz said as she pulled her into a brief but affectionate hug before heading over to the town car where their father was waiting. Anne waved goodbye, watching the car disappear down the avenue. Rather than go back inside, she pulled the hood of her jacket up and started walking.

The Uppercross neighborhood bordered the southernmost tip of Kellynch Park, and over the years, Anne learned to shortcut through the woods when visiting her sister rather than drive the long, meandering bypass road. Unaware of the path she took, she merely walked with her head bent, her hands stuffed into her pockets, and her eyes trained on the ground. The rain did nothing to dampen the earthy scents of late autumn—fallen leaves and wood smoke and the ever present smell of cedar. She thought of the house in Glen Ellen, feeling a little sting of regret for not going back. Her mother loved that house and the little town—loved the sloped green hills like enormous shoulders slouching against the sun and the rusty reds and browns of the autumn grapevines. *I must have loved it too*, Anne realized.

"Anne?"

The familiarity of the man's honeyed voice struck her like a ceremonial gong, resonating through her bones and springing her out of her memories and back into the park. She looked up and saw that she'd walked almost the entire way to her father's house, now in the care of the Crofts. A tide of nausea, elation, and pure panic threatened to overwhelm her. *Just don't get sick*, she told herself. With her heart sinking to her shoes, she turned, peeking from the hood of her raincoat.

Her first instinct was to laugh at the umbrella in his hand, white with a smattering of pink polka dots and a girlish ruffle around the edge. A tiny, impossibly scruffy white dog sniffed around his feet, tethered to a hot pink leash.

"Is it Eric?" she asked shakily. Not that she needed to ask. He looked much the same as he did the last time she saw him: straight backed and well built, his grey eyes still startling against his cocoa skin. His dark hair was shorter than she's ever seen it, shaved down nearly to the scalp. An unfamiliar scar tugged at the edge of his jaw. She thought that, if anything, he'd grown into his looks and was now more beautiful than ever. Recollections she's denied herself for years broke against her like a tidal wave; she felt herself sucked in and buffeted by them. For a moment, she allowed herself to languish in them, remembering the exact feel of her arms around his trim waist, the fervid smoothness of his skin under her hands, the raspberry splash of the birthmark just above his left hipbone.

"Yeah," he said stiffly. "It's Eric."

"Hello," she said simply, and then, almost as an afterthought, "welcome back."

"It's been a long time."

"Eight years," she replied with a nod, training her eyes to the space just under his ear. She couldn't quite meet his eyes.

"I'm surprised you remember me." His voice was frosty. Anne shivered, suddenly wishing she were inside, warm and dry and far away from this old heartbreak. She wanted to laugh at the notion that she could ever forget him.

"I almost didn't recognize you," he said. "You…well, you look so different."

"Time changes everyone." She looked at him. "Except you, it would seem."

He frowned slightly, a small crease appearing between his eyes.

"I should get back to my sister's," she said, attempting to feign a smile and failing. "It was good to see you, Eric. Happy Thanksgiving."

After a moment, he nodded and walked back into the house, the little white dog prancing happily beside him. Anne watched the polka-dot umbrella move away from her until it disappeared inside the house. All the air escaped her in one nervous, painful rush. She told herself the worst was over as she turned and began the trek back to Mary's house. Pulling her hood off, she let the rain soak into her hair and eyelashes, washing her tears away.

Track 7: Forced into Prudence

August 2006

WALTER PACED THE ROOM, HIS VOICE RAISED, OCCASIONALLY POINTING furiously at his middle daughter. Anne knew this was the time to be small and meek, to be *Anne*, but she couldn't—not with everything at stake. Remembering Eric and their promise to each other gave her the strength to sit with her spine straight, boldly meeting her father's eye.

"You are *twenty years old!* You are too young to get married, and *that is final!*"

"Dad, I'm young, but you know I'm mature…" She didn't say what she was thinking: that she was quite possibly the most mature person in the Elliot family. "And Eric is steady. He's a writer and a Marine—an officer—that's not *nothing*!"

"Well, it's not *something*, either!" her father shouted. "It's barely anything, Anne. Not enough for an Elliot."

"What is this? The 1820s? Are money and prestige all that should matter?"

"Anne, that's not what I'm saying."

"Then what are you saying, Dad? Do you think Mom loved you when she agreed to marry you?" Anne's voice rose. She knew that it was dangerous to bring up her mother like that, but she couldn't stop herself. "How would you feel if Mom married you just for your family's money, your pedigree, your vacation home?"

Walter's face went slack at the mention of his dead wife. "I know your mother loved me," he responded softly. "It's just—" Walter stopped, closed his eyes, and exhaled deeply. "It's a bad idea. You know how dangerous it is over there. Do you know how many soldiers come back every day in a bag or missing limbs? Do you actually think that's what I want for you?"

Anne felt herself rising to her feet, her hands balled up in fists at her side. "Don't you dare say that!"

Her father sighed and put a hand on her shoulder, guiding her back down to the couch.

"I hope for the best, Annie, but it's not a good situation. I know you might not think so now, but I only want what's best for you."

"Best for *me*, or best for your re-election?" She couldn't disguise the zip of satisfaction she felt at seeing her father recoil slightly as though she'd slapped him.

"I suppose I earned that," Walter relented. "If you won't listen to me, so be it. But think on this…you were right to bring up your mother. What would she say if she were here? Do you think she would support you in this?"

Anne couldn't argue this point. It wasn't the first time the thought had occurred to her. Her mother had married young and never expressed remorse at her choice but always impressed on Anne how important it was to not rush these decisions. Determined to have what she wanted, Anne tried many times to shut out that little nagging voice of doubt but found that she couldn't—not while it spoke with her mother's voice.

Track 8: Calm Waters

November 26, 2014

Eric came back inside through the mudroom off the kitchen entrance, where his sister was waiting for him. Her dog, Lady Russell, danced happily at her feet until she produced a treat from the pocket of her apron.

Eric was removing his muddy shoes when she asked him, "Who were you talking to out there?" She watched carefully, waiting to see whether her suspicions were confirmed.

He removed a paperback novel from his coat pocket and shook it off, wiping his hand across it to remove any droplets of rain. He'd been reading it just before he spotted her trudging up the path, her shoulders hunched under some unseen weight.

"*That* was Anne Elliot." He avoided meeting his sister's eye as he hung up his rain jacket. "Her family owns this house."

"Is she the one who—?"

"Yes," Eric said curtly.

"What happened there?"

"Her father didn't want her marrying some poor, black Marine from South Georgia." While almost a decade has passed, Eric could still hear the bitterness in his voice.

"She hardly needs her father's approval *now*." The stubborn set of his jaw told her she wouldn't get any more information out of him. She switched gears. "I need to get going on the dough for the rolls tomorrow. Do you want to come give me a hand in the kitchen?"

"Sure, let me go throw on a T-shirt and I'll come help."

He stopped to give her an apologetic peck on the cheek before heading upstairs to the guest room. She waited until she heard his heavy footfall going up the stairs before picking up the book with which he'd been so careful.

Perpetual Estrangement, by Anne Elliot. Sophie bit back a knowing smile and returned the book where he left it, a plan already taking shape in her mind.

Track 9: How Quick Come the Reasons

August 2006

When asked, David Wentworth was always quick to admit that his family was the most important thing to him, and nine out of ten times, it was true.

David wondered whether he wasn't partially responsible for his brother's stubborn and resentful personality. As the youngest of the family, Eric usually got what he wanted, mostly because neither David nor Sophie—nor even their parents—could put up with Eric when he didn't have his way.

"Where did you find *that* bottle? I don't even keep that much booze around! Do you have a replicator around here?"

Eric shook his head. "Replicator can't get you drunk, dummy."

"Dork. I haven't watched Star Trek in years."

"Yep, that's me." Eric nodded and poured himself another drink. David picked up the bottle, making a gagging sound as he read the label.

"This is pomegranate liqueur that someone left here."

"I bet it's good with Sprite." Eric splashed a tiny bit of soda in his glass. David shuddered, thinking of how wretched his brother was going to feel in the morning.

"And you call yourself a Marine." Eric's expression hardened. Though he didn't realize it yet, David was seeing a glimpse of the man his brother would become.

"Like *that's* supposed to impress anyone," Eric mumbled, his lips pursing in distaste as he sipped his ad hoc cocktail.

"Maybe she just needs time," David suggested. "She never said she wanted to break up. She just wants to put the brakes on the whole married thing."

"She doesn't want me now." Eric put the drink down as far away as he could reach. "She won't want me later. I'm looking at an eighteen-month deployment and who knows what after. A lot can happen in a year and a half."

"A lot can stay the same too, though. You should just...you know, stay frosty."

Eric put his head in his hands. "You don't understand. Wait until a girl does this to you."

"I like *guys*, Eric." David watched his brother's reaction. He'd only just gotten the nerve to tell him.

Eric paused for a beat. "Oh. Well, wait until a guy does this to you, and then *you* try to stay frosty." He dropped his arms and looked up at his brother at last. "Thanks for telling me, man."

"Thanks for listening. If only you listened to *everything* I had to say."

"Not this time, Dave. I am just *done*. Between her crazy family and this... maybe I'm better off."

"Hmm." David nodded, certain that his brother has just made an enormous mistake.

Track 10: Time Will Explain

December 1, 2014

ANNE LOOKED UP FROM HER LAPTOP AT THE SOUND OF THE DOORBELL AND considered not answering it. She knew it could very well be another reporter. *Or it very well could be someone else*, she thought. With a sigh, she got up and moved the curtain aside before hastily unlocking the door and swinging it open.

"Mrs. Croft! What can I do for you?"

The woman standing on her porch appeared to be in her mid-forties, elegant and stylish but with an approachable air. Her red winter coat set off her dark skin beautifully. She held the most perfect pecan pie Anne had ever seen.

"Are you Anne Elliot?" Anne thought the pull of her Georgia accent seemed less noticeable in person than it was on camera.

"I am. Would you like to come in?"

Sophie Croft smiled and stepped inside. "Why yes, thank you. I went to your sister's house but you'd already decamped."

"I was staying with my family while I was having my plumbing refitted here." She swept her hand around, indicating her tidy little bungalow. "I'm sorry, Mrs. Croft, but is there a problem at the house? Mr. Shepard left me some numbers if you need maintenance or repairs."

The older woman handed her the pie. The plate was warm in Anne's hands, her mouth watered at the smell wafting from it.

"Please, call me Sophie. The house is lovely. We are enjoying it thoroughly. That's part of the reason I sought you out. I'm having a holiday party in a few weeks, and I'd like for you to come. I understand you already know my brothers."

Anne felt the blood drain from her face. "Uh, well, it's been a while but... they left an impression."

Sophie looked as though she expected this answer. "I thought they might like to see some familiar faces since this party will mostly be the people from my new restaurant and a few of my husband's friends who live in the area. I've also invited your sister Mary and her husband."

Anne swallowed the lump rising in her throat. Her encounter with Eric Wentworth the day before Thanksgiving had burned itself into her waking thoughts. She regretted the distance that had grown between them, remembering how good it always felt to make him smile. *Maybe there's a chance you might make him smile again,* a little voice whispered in her mind. Not daring to hope, Anne addressed her guest.

"Would you like some coffee, Sophie?"

Sophie Croft watched all of this play across Anne's face and believed it was further proof that her path forward was the right one. After needling David for every detail on Eric's old love, Sophie was determined to see the woman for herself. Anne Elliot seemed more to her liking than she expected. Not an overt beauty, but there was a solemn strength in her bearing and an open kindness in her intelligent eyes that Sophie approved. Eric's solitary life and perpetual bachelorhood had always been a source of anxiety for her. Now she considered that she may have found a solution at last.

She gave the younger woman her most winning television smile. "I'd love some coffee, Anne."

B Side: Half Hope
Track 11: Worse than Strangers

December 15, 2014

THE SIGHT OF HER FAMILY HOME FULLY DECORATED FOR THE HOLIDAY PARTY caused a twinge of longing in Anne's chest. She couldn't remember seeing the home so beautifully decked out, even in her mother's day. The Crofts' decorations were tasteful and vibrant. Her mother's decorations, Anne remembered, tended to be more WASPy and staid. The arched doorways were festooned with pine boughs and red ribbons. White candles burned in colorful sconces on every surface, giving the room a cheerful glow.

A small crowd gathered, more than thirty people but less than fifty, the low murmur of their conversations punctuated every so often with a peal of laughter. Anne was pleased to hear Billie Holliday rather than the traditional Christmas music she's been forced to endure from every supermarket she's stepped foot into since Halloween.

Following behind her sister Mary and Mary's husband Charles, Anne shook hands with Henry Croft and received a good-natured hug from Sophie, who called to someone over her shoulder. A familiar-looking man bounced towards them. When he grinned broadly at her, Anne's memory made the connection.

"David, how nice to see you again," she exclaimed. "I'm not sure if you remember me; it's Anne Elliot." David laughed and pulled her into a brief hug.

"Oh, I remember you, Trouble." He grinned down at her. David always liked her best of all the girls his brother dated.

David Wentworth was taller than his brother was, his features more closely resembling Sophie's than Eric's—except his smile. Anne was mortified to feel the pink heat of a blush spreading across her face at his old nickname for her, remembering the reason behind it. David, who was only steps ahead of her father, had caught her and Eric in flagrante delicto. They'd scrambled away before Walter could see, and David had smoothly covered at the cost of teasing them without mercy for weeks after.

"No one has called me that in years," she muttered under her breath, playfully slapping his arm.

He grinned and gave her a knowing wink. "Come on," he said, taking her arm. "I want to introduce you to my Steven."

She let David steer her away from Charles and Mary as he introduced her to his partner, a man so ridiculously handsome, Anne found herself at a loss for words. His brown hair fell in a graceful swoop that looked effortless but probably took considerable prep. His deep blue eyes lit up when he smiled, which softened the line of his square jaw perfectly. He took her hand and, rather than shaking it, lifted it to his lips, kissing her knuckles.

"Good Lord!" Anne blurted out without thinking, making David and Steven both laugh. They fell into an easy and light conversation, and she was pleased to feel herself relaxing in their company. They were making pleasant small talk when she noticed Eric enter the room.

She felt the electricity of his presence the moment he appeared, his self-assured confidence giving the impression that he owned the room and everything in it. She was further rattled to see him approach their group, his eyes locked with his brother's and wearing a smile that made her legs wobble. A throbbing pulse began just below her navel. She felt it race through her body, down to the pads of her fingertips. She had to ball her hands into fists in an effort to control the sudden, maddening urge to touch him.

There was a potent intensity to him now that had yet to surface in the young man she'd once known. Gone was the affable uncertainty that had so endeared him to her when they first met, replaced with a sanguine masculinity that made him seem like another person altogether, a thought that violently unmoored her from the small measure of confidence she'd managed to gain since Sophie Croft showed up at her door with a pie and an invitation.

Eric joined their rough circle, giving his brother a hug and Steven a warm handshake. One look at him and Anne considered sending a thank-you card to his tailor. His suit was a rich navy color that made his grey eyes impossibly blue. His crisp, white shirt was worn without a tie and open at the neck. She felt drab by comparison in her plum-colored halter dress. He was beautiful, and clearly, he knew it.

She couldn't help but notice the way his smile slid from his face as he looked at her. He acknowledged her presence with cool eyes and a wordless nod. Anne attempted to smile but fell short. As if sensing her discomfort, David put his arm around her shoulders and pulled her close to him.

"Give him some time," he whispered. "He'll come around."

Anne laughed bitterly. "You bet," she muttered. Someone handed her a glass of champagne, and she took it gratefully, sipping more quickly than she normally would.

"I didn't think you liked champagne."

She almost jumped at hearing Eric address her. His expression was guarded, his words flat. She couldn't tell whether he was chastising her or attempting a feeble conversation. "I don't mind it so much now," she admitted. "Tastes change." As soon as the words left her mouth, she knew it was the wrong thing to say. Eric's eyes clouded over, and his shoulders tensed. He opened his mouth as if he wanted to speak, but they were interrupted by two pretty young women in dangerously short dresses.

"Anne!" Lucy Musgrove and her sister Etta rushed over, their faces glowing with excitement. "We didn't know you'd be here too!"

Anne hugged Charles Musgrove's twin sisters, who had recently turned twenty-one and were determined to make the most of it. "I might say the same to you two!"

"We both work at SoCo," Etta explained, her eyes glued to the men surrounding them. "We're servers. Mrs. Croft invited all of her employees."

"Who are your friends, Anne?" Lucy asked, looking boldly at Eric.

"Lucy and Etta, meet David, Steven, and Eric."

"Frederick," he corrected. Anne watched as he gave Lucy a winning smile, a smile that used to belong to her. He smiled at her like that right before he kissed her for the first time. She'd always loved first kisses, the singular thrill of lips touching for the first time. For her, those first few seconds were like a match being struck, or they were until Frederick Wentworth. The first time he kissed her, it set her world on fire. Anne forced herself to placidly sip her champagne when what she wanted was to grab the nearest bottle and call a cab home.

"Are you from here, Eric?" Etta asked, smiling coquettishly.

"No, I live in Los Angeles."

"Oh, awesome!" Lucy said. "L.A. is like, celebrity heaven, you know?"

Anne could see Eric struggling not to laugh at this statement and had to work hard not to laugh herself.

He coughed a bit and said, "Uh, sure. It's not quite my scene, but it's good enough for now."

"Are you on TV? You look like you could be," Lucy said.

"He was on MSNBC last week," David said, earning a dirty look from Eric. "What was that one about again?"

"The VA backlog," Eric said with a heavy sigh. "I'm the West Regional correspondent for the AP. And I sometimes cover Veterans Affairs."

"Ohmigod, were you in the service?" Etta asked, eyes wide.

Eric cleared his throat, clearly uncomfortable. His eyes flicked to Anne's for a moment. She took another, rather large sip of champagne to cover her own discomfort.

"Marines," he said finally.

"That's so awesome!" Lucy said. David chuckled and excused himself, putting an arm around Steven's waist and leading him away. Anne watched them go, wishing she could follow when she noticed a man observing their group.

His untidy blondish hair and a slight scruff of beard made him look slightly out of place in the well-groomed crowd. If it weren't for the perfectly pressed shirt and black-framed glasses, he'd pass for any West Coast surfer. He gave her a lopsided smile that she couldn't help but return. Taking this as encouragement, he worked his way over to their little group and leaned down so that only Anne could hear him speak.

"Thank goodness you're here."

Anne blinked, puzzled. His green eyes danced with amusement. It occurred to her that he was very good looking in an off-kilter sort of way.

"Do I know you?" she asked.

"Not yet. I'm Will." He offered her his hand, which she took in a handshake.

"I'm Anne. Why are you glad I'm here?"

"Because I'm *dying* to have an intelligent conversation that doesn't revolve around molecular gastronomy or proper braising techniques."

Anne laughed softly. "Not an industry professional, I take it?"

He shook his head. "I work for Somerset Media. We own the Food Channel."

"And all the shop talk is making you hungry?" Anne ventured.

"Ha! Why is everyone in Oregon obsessed with mushrooms? That's weird, right?"

"We do take our fungus pretty seriously." She considered him for a moment. "How did you know *I* wasn't an industry person?"

He grinned crookedly at her, all schoolboy charm but for the gleam of mischief in his eyes.

"I rolled the dice," he admitted. "I just really wanted to talk to you. You look like the kind of person who doesn't drop 'awesome' into conversation much," he looked pointedly at Lucy and Etta, who were still aggressively flirting with Eric.

"You got me," Anne said with a chuckle. "I teach creative writing at PSU."

His face lit up. "Oh, that's awesome!" They exchanged a startled look before mutually erupting into a fit of laughter, neither noticing the sour turn of Eric's mouth at the sound.

"Would you like to have dinner with me sometime?" Will asked her.

Without thinking, she looked at Eric, who suddenly appeared very interested in their conversation.

"Um…maybe some other time," she stammered, panicking. It felt like a cosmic joke that the first time she got asked out in almost a year happened in front of Frederick Wentworth.

Will frowned a bit, trying to hide his obvious disappointment. "Sure, whatever," he said. He handed her a small, glossy business card. "Here's my number if you change your mind and want to grab a cup of coffee."

Anne nodded, stashing the card in the pocket of her dress.

Lucy handed her empty glass to a passing waiter and grabbed her bejeweled clutch from the table.

"If you'll excuse me for a just sec," she said to the group but placing her hand on Eric's arm, "I just need to freshen up in the powder room." She turned to walk towards the back of the house when Eric's voice stopped her.

"Not that way," he said a little too loudly, making everyone look at him.

"That takes you to—" He halted and glanced at Anne, his face reddening. "The bathroom is over there, past the stairs," he said without looking at anyone.

Lucy strutted off, an extra sway in her hips, but Eric wasn't watching her. Anne suspected that Eric was about to give away to the group that he had once wandered in that direction and found his way into Anne's bedroom for the first time. The memory of his sudden entrance in her life made her want to reach for his hand, to regain some connection with him. She realized that she'd been staring at him for a few moments when he looked up, making eye contact. No longer cool and distant, he appeared curiously discomfited. Without thinking, Anne gave him a small smile, equal measures teasing, sad, and hopeful. To her surprise, he managed a self-deprecating but genuine half-smile in return.

Track 12: Clever, Well-Informed People

December 13, 2014

ANNE GATHERED UP WHAT SHE NEEDED FROM HER OFFICE, EXHAUSTED BUT relieved to have all of her finals graded a few days ahead of schedule. She was in the midst of her usual post-semester purge—recycling stacks of paper and making sure she wasn't leaving any half-finished candy bars on her desk or under it—when her desk phone rang, making her jump.

"Professor Elliot's office," she answered cautiously. Her father's scandal had made her phone more active than ever that semester; as a result, she'd gotten into the habit of letting all her calls roll to voice mail.

"Anne Elliot? It's Will Ellis. We met at Sophie Croft's party?"

Anne frowned at the oversized Miles Davis poster on the wall over her desk. "I remember you, Will. How did you get my number?"

"PSU has an online directory," he said with a little laugh.

"Oh, right."

"Hey, I just wanted to say sorry if I came on a little strong at the party. I hope I didn't make you uncomfortable."

Anne relaxed a little. "Oh, that's okay. It was just a little unexpected.

There was just weirdness because…" She thought again of Eric's apparent interest in her conversation with Will.

"Because that male underwear model is your ex? It was kind of obvious."

Anne laughed a little. "He's a reporter, but yeah, good call."

"Are you guys still…friendly?"

"Well that was the second time we'd seen each other in almost a decade so I think I can safely say not so much."

"Wow! Yeah, I can see now how that would have made it extra awkward. Look, I'll be honest. I think you're an interesting person, and I'd like to get to know you. It doesn't have to be anything; we could just hang out."

"Hang out?" Anne asked dubiously.

"Yeah, you know…as friends."

She thought before answering. "I wouldn't mind being friends."

"Great!" Will's enthusiasm was obvious. Anne smiled at the sound of it. "And to test you right away, I'd like to ask if you'd like to go to the movies with me tomorrow night."

"Hmm. I don't know…"

"You can bring a date if you like," he offered, making Anne laugh.

"I don't think that'll happen."

"Good, me either. For some reason the ladies remain resistant to my charms."

"Maybe because you call them 'the ladies?'"

"Fair enough. Come on, it'll be fun. And just to prove how much this *isn't* a date, the movie I want to see is *Die Hard*."

"The Bruce Willis movie?"

"The Hollywood Theater has a screening every year. It's my favorite Christmas movie."

Anne laughed and said, "Okay. *Die Hard* it is."

Track 13: Never Underestimate the Power of a Well-Written Letter
December 13, 2014

BY THE TIME ERIC FINISHED READING *PERPETUAL ESTRANGEMENT*, HE WAS no longer suspicious that it was about them; he was absolutely certain. His hands trembled as he touched the last page, the last line.

And yet, I hope.

"Oh hell, Anne." He sat up on the sofa, realization hitting him like a sledgehammer to his chest. He still loved her.

"Holy shit," he muttered.

David looked up from his phone. "You okay, man?"

"Yes. No. I don't know."

"Well, thanks for clearing *that* up. Wanna talk about it?"

"I'm an idiot."

"Ho-lee Moses, you just figured it out, didn't you? Anne?"

Eric nodded.

"Yep," David said with a chuckle. "You're an idiot, all right."

Eric narrowed his eyes at his brother. "Why didn't you say something sooner?"

"Pfft. Would you have listened?"

"Hell no."

David shrugged. "There ya go."

Eric launched himself off the couch, running from the room.

"Where are you going?"

Eric looked at his watch. He was meeting some old friends for drinks later, but he needed to talk to Sophie first. If anyone could see a way clear through the mess he'd made, it would be his sister. "To make things right," he said before leaving the room.

Track 14: The Madness of His Resentment

December 14, 2015

ANNE ENJOYED SEEING *DIE HARD* IN THE THEATER MORE THAN SHE'D EXpected. She remembered her father watching it on cable when she was a kid, but it never appealed to her then. Now, surrounded by people shouting the lines and cheering on John McClane, she felt herself being caught up in the experience.

She allowed herself to enjoy spending time with Will. She found him easy to talk to, especially when not under the eye of Eric Wentworth.

"That was a lot of fun," she told Will as everyone began milling out of the theater onto the rainy sidewalk.

Will grinned and wiped the rain off his glasses before pulling the hood of his jacket up. "Told ya you'd have fun. Are you hungry? There's a terrific pub two blocks down. They have a Welsh rarebit that's out of this world." Anne found herself charmed by the way he used his hands to pantomime his speech.

"Ah, you've discovered my greatest weakness," she said with a laugh, pulling her own hood up. "Bread and cheese."

He gave her his boyish smile and bumped his shoulder against hers. "Come on, let's walk."

She followed, trying to match his long strides as they hurried down Forty-Second Street against the rain.

"Are you spending Christmas with your family?" he asked.

"My younger sister Mary. She has four little ones, and they can be kind of a handful."

"I can imagine. Are your parents still around?"

She eyed him closely, suddenly wary. Could it be he didn't know who she was?

"My dad is still around. My mom passed away when I was in college."

"Oh jeez, I'm sorry. That must have been rough. Was it just you and your kid sister then?"

"No, I have an older sister, too: Liz. She lives in the Bay Area. Dad's staying with her for now."

"Do you guys get along?"

"In our own weird way. Liz is very into the Bay Area lifestyle. She worships at the Church of Crossfit. She's into macrobiotic eating and bimonthly colonics. You know the type. 'You'll pry my Lululemon from my cold dead hands.'"

Will snickered at this but Anne remained quiet. "Sorry, I didn't mean to pry," he said.

At first, Anne just shrugged. She quickly realized how that lackluster response must come across to Will. She offered him a smile, deciding not to let the unpleasantness of her family's history throw a pall over the evening. "It's okay," she said as genuinely as she could manage.

Their destination was a squat brick building, painted black with gold letters that stood out against the awning: The Moon and Sixpence.

Based on the exterior and the name, Anne expected the inside to look like a scene out of a Stevie Nicks video with Persian rugs, doves in cages, and filmy scarves draped everywhere. She was pleased when it turned out to be a standard English pub, complete with darts in the corner.

"Come on, let's see what's on tap."

Will put his hand flat against the small of her back and guided her through the crowd of Thursday-night drinkers. They were reading the drink specials off a large chalkboard mounted on the wall when a familiar squeal caught their attention.

"I thought that was you!" Lucy Musgrove rushed over and pulled Anne into a hug that reeked of cherry cider.

"Hey, Lou, did you meet Will at the party?" Anne asked.

"I don't think so…hey, I'm Lucy!" To Anne's amusement, she gave Will a hug, which seemed to baffle him.

Lucy grinned widely at both of them. "My date's at the bar getting drinks. Oh, wait, here he comes now. Eric! Look who I found!"

"It's not a date," Anne blurted, fighting a swell of panic when Eric appeared with a mug of coffee in one hand and an ice water in the other. He handed Lucy the water, which she pouted at. His eyes met Anne's, and a mutual jolt seemed to pass through them.

Once the initial shock of the moment passed, he appeared more relaxed and comfortable, less formal than he was at his sister's party. It was obvious to Anne that, while he wasn't drunk, he'd had a few drinks. Anne felt the caress of his eyes on her body and had to wrap her fingers around the chair behind her to keep herself upright. The slightest uptick of the corner of his mouth betrayed him biting back a smile. He put a hand out to Will.

"Eric Wentworth. I don't think we met the other night."

Will took Eric's hand in his own. "Um, hi man. I'm Will. Will Ellis," he said, frowning slightly through the greeting. Anne could feel the mild tension between the two men.

"It's so weird you're here, Anne," Lucy said, making a face as she sipped her ice water. "We were just talking about you."

For a second, Eric looked like he'd rather be anywhere else in the world before his cool confidence settled over him once more.

"As a matter of fact, we were," he said. "I was telling Lucy that I read your novel."

Anne reeled, feeling like a stone skipping across the water. *Perpetual Estrangement* wasn't just a novel to her; it was *their* story. She knew he must have realized that. She cleared her throat and asked what he thought.

"I liked it," he said, looking into her eyes. "Not sure about the ending though."

"No?"

"Yeah, I wish it had ended differently. Have you thought about a sequel?"

Anne blinked, unsure whether she should take his words at face value or he was asking about *them*. His expression was earnest, his posture rigid as though he was holding his breath. *Is this happening?*

"Um…I have. A lot lately." She laughed nervously. "But I worry that maybe too much has changed, too much time has passed." Anne watched him carefully, trying to catch her breath as the world fell away, waiting for him to respond.

"Come on, Eric," Lucy interrupted, wrapping her arms around his bicep. "Let's let Anne and Will get back to their date."

"It's not a date," Anne said again in a rush of pent up breath.

"We get it," Will said with an embarrassed laugh. "Not a date."

"Why don't you join us?" Eric asked, a sincerity in his voice she never thought she'd hear again. "I'm with some friends I'd like you to meet." He didn't look at Will or Lucy when he said this; his eyes were for her alone.

"Um, okay." She remembered that she wasn't there alone and looked at Will. "If that's okay with you?"

Will seemed uncomfortable but agreed. They followed Eric to the front of the pub, Lucy still clinging to his arm like an intoxicated barnacle. He led them to a table where two men were sitting with pints of beer. One was clean-shaven, his hair still military-short, dressed in jeans and a black T-shirt that showed off a well-sculpted chest. A crutch was propped beside his chair, the kind with the band that held the forearm. He looked at her with openly friendly curiosity. The other man couldn't have been more different. His hair was longer than even Will's and very dirty. His face was covered in a patchy beard, and his eyes didn't lift from the dark beer in his glass as Anne took a seat beside him.

Eric clapped the clean-shaven man on the shoulder and said, "Let me introduce you to my friend Harry Harville. He's got half the legs I do but he's still twice the man I am. And this rough-looking son of a bitch is Jim Benwick. Guys, this is Anne Elliot and Will Ellis. Lucy you've already met."

"So this is the famous Anne Elliot?" Harry Harville asked.

Eric chuffed him on the shoulder playfully with a warning. "Mind your damn manners, Marine."

Anne nodded, torn between curiosity and mortification that this man knew of her. What might Eric have said about her? She noticed that Jim

Benwick was now looking at her too. She shifted uncomfortably under all the scrutiny.

"You're the writer," Jim said. Anne felt her face grow warm. *How many people did he tell about that damn book?*

"Mostly, I just teach Creative Writing at PSU. The book was…kind of a fluke. Catharsis thing." Her feeling that everything she said about her novel now was a secret communication to Eric made it difficult for her to focus on the other people around her.

Jim's eyes lit up, interested now. "Yeah, I get that. I envy you that you found…a way through it."

"Ha, I don't know about that," Anne said nervously, willing herself not to look at Eric.

"I'd like to read it," Jim said. "Eric said it's really good."

"He's just being nice."

"What's it about?" Jim asked.

"Music. Love. Loss. The usual stuff."

Jim nodded and turned his head for a second. Anne thought he might be wiping his eyes.

"So, music, huh?" He turned back, less enthused than he was a second ago. "What do you like?"

"She likes everything," Eric piped up. "Or, at least, she used to."

Anne realized everyone at the table was looking at her. "I still like every-thing. Lately, I'm kind of in love with hip-hop coming out of the Midwest. Doomtree, Atmosphere, Lupe Fiasco—stuff like that."

Eric leaned over and asked, "Do you still spin?"

"Waaaaait a second." Lucy spoke up. "Are you telling me *Anne* used to deejay?"

"I guess that answers my question," Eric said. "Why'd you quit? You were something special."

Anne shrugged. "I guess I outgrew hanging out in clubs until three in the morning."

"That's too bad."

Anne took the pint that Will placed in her hands, an amber-red ale. She looked over at Lucy. "I guess we all outgrow things."

Eric's eyes pulled hers away, demanding she notice him. "And some things, we never grow out of."

Track 15: Some Lines of Feeling

December 24, 2014

NOT FOR THE FIRST TIME, ANNE WONDERED WHETHER ANYONE COULD drink too much chamomile tea. She watched her sister Mary prepare another cup, ignoring her three young sons as they ran wild through the kitchen. Mary's daughter, Eliza, sat at the table, coloring.

Anne gathered up her nephews and reminded them that Christmas was only a day away and that Santa was still watching them, and that even if he wasn't, *she was* still watching them. They shuffled out of the kitchen, considerably quieter though no less excited.

"*Thank* you," Mary said as she sipped her tea. "I just don't have it in me today. I didn't sleep a wink last night."

"How can I help?" Knowing her sister as she did, Anne expected that nothing would be done when she got there.

"I'm tempted to throw it all out and order pizzas for tomorrow," Mary groused. "I *told* Charles I needed help, but where is he?"

"Okay, you sit down and keep me company while I get everything ready." Anne directed Mary to sit down at the kitchen island and began pulling out pots and pans. "Here, peel these potatoes while you sit."

Mary complied easily, chattering away and drinking cup after cup of tea as Anne chopped, minced, sautéed, and baked. Anne nodded and spoke in all the right places as she worked, knowing that, more than anything, Mary just needed someone to talk to. Her hands almost slipped while dicing onions when Mary mentioned that her sister-in-law Lucy was bringing her new boyfriend. *Could she mean Eric?* She thought they'd reestablished a tenuous connection the night at the pub, but he *had* been there with Lucy when she arrived.

"Have you met him yet?" Anne asked, recovering quickly.

"Not yet. She tells me that he was in the Navy or something."

"Marines," Anne said hoarsely, hoping her sister would think her watery eyes were due to the onions. *So much for a sequel, I guess.* "Mary, would you make a cup of that tea for me?"

"She also told me *you* had a date with some shaggy man," Mary said as she prepared Anne's cup of tea.

"It wasn't a date!" Anne protested, more heatedly than she intended to. "We just saw a movie and grabbed a drink after."

"Last I checked that was the very definition of a date, Anne."

Anne heaved a put-upon sigh and sipped her tea, wondering what excuse she could give not to sit through this dinner. She knew the limits of her endurance, and watching Eric Wentworth court sweet, vapid Lucy Musgrove was well beyond those limits.

Anne heard the front door whip open then slam shut. Mary winced at the sound.

"Mary?" Charles called from the foyer. Mary clutched her mug with both hands and clenched her jaw, saying nothing. They could hear boxes dropping on the polished marble floor and shopping bags crinkling against each other.

Mary caught Anne's eye and stage whispered, "Always shopping at the last minute," her irritation with her husband plain.

"Mary?" His voice sounded farther away, like he's heading toward the stairs. Mary stayed silent.

Anne took a deep breath, plastered a smile on her face, and called back to Charles, "We're in the kitchen!"

Charles bustled around the corner, out of breath and disheveled, his sweater rucked up to his ribs on the left side. Anne knew well enough that was not out of the ordinary for her brother-in-law, who happened to be that peculiar sort of person who managed to have an innate brilliance and razor-sharp intellect while being utterly clueless about the world around him. They'd almost always had an easy companionship, excepting a brief infatuation on his part during college, which Anne firmly but politely discouraged.

"Oh good, I'm glad you're here, Anne," he huffed. "Can you come help me with a gift-wrapping emergency? I'd ask Mary, but it *might* spoil the surprise to have her wrap her own gift."

"Sure," Anne said as she handed Mary a whisk. "Here, make sure this gravy doesn't stick."

He led her back to his study, but instead of a present, he handed her a tablet. "Here, read this."

Anne looked down at the article posted by BlastNet, a Web site she recognized as a click-bait e-tabloid. Volleys of shock and dismay rolled through her as she began to read.

DISGRACED SENATOR'S BROKEN HOME
By William Ellis

Senator Walter Elliot, recently embroiled in allegations of misusing campaign funds, may be exposed in the public's eye for the first time in his career, but he is no stranger to deceit and scandal. Having lost his wife years ago, Senator Elliot has failed to keep three daughters in line, often with disastrous results.

The late Patricia Elliot was the only source of stability and reason in the Elliot household, sources close to the family say. Although it is reported that Mrs. Elliot suffered from a chronic illness, her sudden death was viewed with suspicion in some circles. No allegations were ever made against her husband. This suspicion was fueled by the fact that, shortly after Mrs. Elliot's funeral, the senator elevated an intern at his office to be his executive assistant in D.C. This fortunate clerk, Miss Olivia Clay, is reputed to have spent time with various wealthy bachelors and widowers before landing with the senator. Not surprisingly, Miss Clay ceased her employment with the senator several months ago—about the time the recent allegations came to light.

The loss of their mother must have hit the Elliot girls hard, as each one spun out of control in her own way. The eldest, Elizabeth, subscribes to the inclusionary Silicon Valley lifestyle and is truly an example of white privilege, unlike many of Senator Elliot's former constituents. Her extravagant "wellness" retreats are a burden on the family fortune, leaving the other sisters to make their way as they are able.

In true, middle-child fashion, Anne Elliot was involved briefly with a Marine of mixed heritage, shocking her father's white politician's conscience. The couple fell apart, however, after Anne sank into a seedy nightclub scene, and she struck out to try her hand at an honest job when deejaying proved insufficient to meet her considerable expenses. Her former college friends speculate that she may have been following her father's desire for power and influence as her paramour, Frederick Wentworth, is the brother of renowned Food Channel star Sophie Croft. Sources have seen the two together at recent social events, leading onlookers to speculate that the Elliot wild child is searching for a way to secure her future in the wake of her father's financial ruin.

The youngest, Mary, took the traditional route of marrying a rich man and follows her father's lead in living a life palatable to the public eye—until you peel back the layers and scrutinize it closely. Living the Northwest America bourgeois dream, Mary Musgrove has everything a woman of privilege could want: a successful husband, darling children, a beautiful home, and a doctor with a thick prescription pad. The Elliots have hidden Mary's instability and addiction to try and preserve the senator's public image.

And where is Walter Elliot as his children struggle and fail so spectacularly? Cheating and stealing his way through Congress, with nary a thought to spare for his wayward family. Surely, the way a man keeps his own home is a reflection of how he will keep the public's. Senator Walter Elliot: a man unable to control the impulses of his daughters and at the whim of his own criminal greed. Is this the kind of man we need in Washington?

The photo on the left was from her father's press conference where he answered the allegations surrounding his misuse of campaign funds. The photo on the right was a family photo, taken at Christmas, on the front steps of the house in Glen Ellen. Anne couldn't look at her mother's beaming smile without feeling that it was accusing her, judging her. Her stomach clenched painfully. She skimmed the article, feeling sicker with every word.

"He took everything I said out of context," she protested weakly.

"I know that," Charles said reassuringly.

"My father is going to hit the roof when he sees this. Never mind Liz and Mary."

"I know; it's why I showed you first. You can help with damage control."

"I think I've done enough damage." Anne sighed, feeling very tired. "I suppose it was too much to hope that we have a quiet Christmas this year."

Charles's smile was sympathetic. "Just a bit."

Anne rejoined her sister in the kitchen, trying to act natural, but she felt the weight of the article like a boot between her shoulder blades, pinning her down. She poured herself a generous glass of white wine despite the fact that she loathed the taste. It settled her nerves better than chamomile tea ever could.

To Anne's confusion, it wasn't Eric Wentworth who arrived on Lucy Musgrove's arm but Jim Benwick. Since the night they met at The Moon and Sixpence, he had shaved and tamed his hair but still retained a sort of wounded bad-boy air. Anne could definitely see the appeal.

Her shock must have been written all over her face when they walked in the door. Lucy kissed her cheek before floating off to pour herself a glass of wine, leaving Anne and Jim alone.

"So…you and Lucy, huh?" she said. Jim's eyes followed Lucy as she walked away, his smile so adoring that even Anne felt herself swoon a little.

"Yeah, she's pretty amazing." As if remembering where he was, he honed in on Anne. "You know that night we met, she wasn't actually on a date with Eric. From what he said, she just sort of tagged along, but he never invited her."

Anne's mouth became drier than the Santa Anas in summer. "I see."

"He wanted me to make that clear," Jim said with a knowing smile. "He *also* was very curious as to whether or not you'd be going to Sophie's New Year's Eve party at SoCo."

For a moment, her spirits soared until she remembered the article and crashed back down to earth. *The fallout is yet to come.* She shifted her gaze and said, "Perhaps," knowing full well she would not.

Track 16: Not Wise Yet

January 30, 2014

ANNE WAS RAIDING THE BEN & JERRY'S SECTION IN THE FROZEN FOODS aisle when she heard a familiar voice behind her.

"Are you about to feed an army? And why only ice cream?"

Anne looked down at her basket, which was overflowing with junk food. She turned around and saw David Wentworth watching her with concern.

"I got Fig Newtons too. Those are good for you, right?"

"What's wrong, Trouble? You're not buying twelve pints of banana split ice cream because everything is right with the world."

Anne felt herself quivering with rage again and looked at David, her jaw so tight she couldn't manage to speak. David plucked her basket from her hands and sailed towards the checkout lines.

"Come on," he called out behind him. "We are taking these back to your place and diving in. Just promise you won't tell Steven."

David paid for Anne's basket—her ice cream total was nine pints, not the twelve he assumed—without any protest from Anne. He didn't say a word as they walked the three blocks back to Anne's house. Only when she began angrily stuffing pints of ice cream into the freezer did he finally say, "Okay, out with it! The tension is aging me."

Anne slammed the freezer door. "That…that…*ass* Will Ellis is what's wrong."

Understanding dawned in David's eyes. "Ah, I see."

Anne ripped the lid off a pint of ice cream and dug in. "You saw the article?" she asked around a mouthful.

"I saw it. For heaven's sake, slow down. You're going to give yourself brain freeze. It hurts just watching you."

"Brain freeze be damned," she said, eating another enormous spoonful.

"What happened, Annie?"

Anne didn't know if it was the use of her father's pet name for her or the sharp spike of brain freeze behind her eye, but she dropped her spoon in the sink.

"I've been...making notes for a new book," she said. David smiled at her back, feeling a spark of hope that Eric had begun to right this very old wrong. "I was down the block at the coffee shop working on it. I had my headphones on and was in the zone, so I didn't see him come in."

She recounted Will's putting his palm on her back between her shoulders and the sympathetic smile he gave her.

"He actually *touched* you?" David asked, aghast. "After the stunt he pulled?" He whistled low. "Talk about gumption."

"I couldn't have been more sickened if a six-foot cockroach had asked me to dance. 'What the hell do you think you're doing?' I asked him. And do you know what he did? He *smiled*. Can you believe that?"

Anne walked out of the kitchen, animatedly giving David the whole story. "'I get it,' he tells me. 'I'm sorry about all of that. But for what it's worth, I really do like you, Anne,' he said." She whirled towards David. "I wanted to slap that smile right off his stupid, charming face."

A short bark of a laugh escaped David as he watched her fume.

"The barista even came over—apparently it was quite the scene—and was about to ask Will to leave, but I just grabbed my stuff and bolted. I swear that bastard started to come after me. I said if he knows what's good for him, he'll forget he ever met me. So next you'll probably see some new article about how unhinged and violent I am." Anne slumped into the seat across from him, her head in her hands. "I can't believe I let this happen."

"Look, this isn't on you. Snakes are hard to spot." He hesitated before asking, "How are you holding up? Any fallout from your family?"

"They're all predictably furious, but I think they blame him more than me. I hope so at least."

David watched her carefully as he asked, "Have you talked to Eric?"

Anne closed her eyes as though the light in the room hurt. "No. I have not."

"You are aware your phone is off? Say, if someone wanted to talk to you about…anything. Maybe a certain someone has already been trying to get hold of you…How would they reach you?"

A little huff escaped Anne. "It's not just off. I threw it into the river."

David laughed and shook his head. "You *are* Trouble. Adulthood hasn't changed that."

"After the fifth crying phone call from Mary, asking how I could do this to them, I just couldn't take it anymore."

"So I take it you're not going to Sophie's party tomorrow night?"

Anne wiped the tears that coursed down her face. Will Ellis's words rang in her head: *"…leading onlookers to speculate that the Elliot wild child is searching for a way to secure her future in the wake of her father's financial ruin." What did Eric think of that little tidbit?* she wondered.

"I've made such a fine mess of my life, David. I'm in no shape to face your brother."

With a rueful shake of his head, David pulled her into a hug, rubbing her back as she cried.

"Trouble," he said once more.

Track 17: He Could Not Be Unfeeling

December 31, 2014

ERIC PACED THE LENGTH OF THE RESTAURANT, HIS ANXIETY RATTLING HIM down to his bones. Every time the maître d' ushered in a new guest, Eric felt his heart leap. He checked his watch again. It was forty minutes to midnight, and Anne still hadn't shown.

He spotted David and Steven in the crowd and, after sparing a moment to be both delighted and disgusted by how perfect and happy they looked, made his way towards them.

"Hey," Eric said to his brother. "Have you heard from Anne?"

David's eyes shifted while Steven looked on in sympathy. "Hmm? Oh, I think I heard she's staying home."

"*Damn it!* Sophie still has her address, right?" Eric knew how frantic he must look, and for once, he didn't care, having lost enough to his pride already. He'd spent eight years comforting himself with the certainty that he was better off without her weak and fickle love. Too late, he realized that he was the weak one. *He* was the one who bailed on *her*. Eric tried to imagine how difficult it must have been for her to do the right thing all those years ago. *Of course, she was right. We were just kids.*

Steven sighed. "Tell him, David."

David looked reluctantly over at his brother. "I don't know if it's such a good idea, Eric. She's in pretty rough shape. I'm not sure she could withstand you knocking her down again."

"God, poor Anne," Eric lamented. "She's doomed to have men like Will Ellis in her life"—then more quietly—"men like *me*."

"Sounds like you still got it bad," Sophie said, making him jump.

"I love her, Soph," he said simply. "I'll never deserve her, but God, do I love her."

Sophie gave him a shrewd look. "I believe you." She turned and pointed at David. "You two, give him a ride then get your fancy butts back here for the ball drop."

"You know I never miss a ball drop," Steven said glibly as he grabbed Eric's elbow and led him away.

Sophie looked at David. "I'm not *even* going to ask what that means."

Track 18: Our Fate Rather Than Our Merit

December 31, 2014

WHEN HE APPROACHED THE HOUSE, ERIC WONDERED WHETHER HE WAS about to interrupt a party. Music flowed from the partially opened windows, sounding like a pinging pulse. He could see her through the filmy curtains, standing at a dual turntable setup with a mixing board and a laptop. He watched as she worked, a low thump like a wet heartbeat joining the pulsing sound. Her hair was pulled up in a messy knot; she nodded as she moved to the beats she was creating.

Eric felt his heart pounding harder by the second as he climbed the front steps. Sweat dampened his palms as he raised the knocker on the door and rapped it three times.

The music stopped suddenly. "Anne, it's me!" he called out. "I just want to talk!"

He heard her padding towards the door, the locks sliding open. She threw the door wide and looked at him. His breath caught; he was never prepared for how beautiful she was. Little tendrils of her fine brown hair had come loose and floated gracefully around her face. Her blue eyes were immeasurably sad, like she was waiting for him to explode. Burning behind the dull sadness was a hunger he recognized. A desire to touch and to be touched. A desire for him.

Without the strain of keeping up appearances in public, Eric felt like they finally had a chance to be honest with each other, to put aside years of separation and misunderstanding and truly see each other again—not the reporter or the professor, not the foolhardy young lovers, but the man and the woman. As he looked at the woman he loved, Eric realized there was nothing to say, nothing that needed to be said. He stepped forward, silently asking her permission. Anne started to move back into the house, making room for him to enter, but he moved faster, boldly taking her face in his hands. The first physical contact they'd had in eight years burned through him, searing his nerves in a delicious fire, anchoring him to her as if by an electrical current.

"I lied," he said. "I don't want to talk."

Anne gasped lightly and grabbed his forearms, completing the circuit. The touch of her hands took the wind out of him. He couldn't have spoken a word then if he tried. He brought her face to his slowly, and the room tilted around him as if he was falling through the floor with her and floating to the ceiling at the same time. For one crazy second, he thought he might miss her lips. It felt like eternity, and he watched her eyes the whole time, fearful of seeing any hesitation or uncertainty. But the instant their lips touched, she responded to him, her mouth pliant and yielding to his. The kiss deepened, each desperate to feel the other, to give, to love, to explore. Her hands wound their way around his waist, grabbing handfuls of his shirt underneath his jacket. He shrugged off the cumbersome garment, wanting nothing more than to feel his skin against hers.

"Eric." She laughed against his mouth, a sound so welcome he didn't even realize it was missing before. "Let me get the door."

He gave her a little room but refused to break his body's contact with hers as she leaned past him, closing and locking the front door. It was then that he noticed the tattoo on the back of her neck for the first time.

"What's this?" he asked, moving the strands of her hair out of the way. Two words in simple, looping script looked back at him: semper fidelis. Always faithful. He could feel himself start to tremble as the meaning hit him.

"Anne…all this time…"

She turned around to face him, her lips gently touching the corner of his mouth as she whispered, "It's always been you, Eric."

He took her in his arms, enveloping her, joyfully and hopelessly lost in her, neither of them aware that they had just rung in the first of many New Years together.

Bonus Track

December 24, 2015

"ARE YOU READY FOR THIS?" ERIC ASKED HER FOR WHAT MIGHT BE THE hundredth time. She gave him a shaky smile and gripped his hand in response.

"I *want* to do this," she insisted as the cab pulled to a stop in front of the sprawling house, tucked into the slope of a hill. The lights in the windows shone in welcome. Anne got out of the car, careful of the wrapped package in her lap. Eric got their bags and paid the driver, and then it was the two of them, looking small in front of the home's grand entrance.

The house was as lovely as she remembered. Even after all the years that had passed, she still felt her mother's presence strongest here. "It's weird," she said. "All this time I avoided this place because I thought all the good memories would hurt."

"They don't?" he asked.

"A little. But…they're *good* memories. Why would I run from that?"

She felt his hands, warm and reassuring on her shoulders. He kissed the top of her head. "Why do any of us run from what's good?"

She turned and gave him a brief but heartfelt kiss before pressing the doorbell.

"What's that for?" he asked, a wide, moonstruck grin on his face.

Her eyes sparkled in the soft light from the windows. "No reason at all."

Before he could say anything else, the door swung open. Walter Elliot appeared astonished but not unhappy to see them. Anne smiled and held her gift out to him.

"Merry Christmas, Dad."

* *

BEAU NORTH is the author of *Longbourn's Songbird* and the founder of the podcast and website Rhymes With Nerdy. She lives in Portland,

Oregon, with her husband. You can connect with Beau on Twitter @BeauNorth or at beaunorth.merytonpress.com.

. . . .

BROOKE WEST is a novice silversmith, proficient yogi, and expert cat-wrangler. She lives in South Carolina with her son, fiancé, and three cats. Find Brooke on Twitter @WordyWest.

"We have all a better guide in ourselves, if we would attend to it, than any other person can be." —Jane Austen, *Mansfield Park*

Becoming Fanny

by Melanie Stanford

QUIZ: Which Broadway Musical Should You Star In?
RESULT: *West Side Story*

I love to do quizzes. Not the school kind, but the kind that tell you who you were in a past life (an artist), what Hogwarts house you belong in (Hufflepuff), and which fashion decade is your favorite (the 50s).

I always try to be as honest as I can, and sometimes I know what answer I'll get. When I did the "What is Your High School Stereotype" quiz, I got the Lone Wolf. Shocker. But sometimes I'm surprised by my result. For "Which Disney Prince Is Your One True Love," I got Aladdin. Huh? I would've preferred Flynn Rider, but the quiz didn't seem to get that from my answers.

"Here's another one," my roommate Monique said, staring at her giant cell phone that is almost as big as a computer screen. "Which Jane Austen Heroine Are You?"

Ooh, yes! I sat up on my bed in anticipation, but Monique didn't notice. She was focused on the screen, her zebra-print fingernails click-clicking away.

I waited. Monique was lying backwards on her bed, her feet propped up on the headboard. The clock radio on the end table played a pop version of "O, Holy Night." She stopped tapping and scrunched her lips. "Who's Elizabeth Bennet?"

I sighed. Of *course,* she got Elizabeth Bennet. I'd known Monique a little over a month, but I already knew she was the kind of girl who gets everything. People probably just look at her and say, "Your wish is my command."

"Haven't you ever read *Pride and Prejudice*?"

She shook her head. "This Elizabeth sounds like a rock star though."

A rock star. Yeah, just like Monique with her nails and her winged eyeliner and her hair that was always bouncy and not flat on top like mine. It still surprised me that she didn't have one of the leads in our show.

"What's the link?" I asked, itching to do the quiz. I wanted to get Elizabeth Bennet too.

Monique tossed me her phone, and I typed the link into my old Android then started the quiz. I could rig it based on what answers I gave—I know Jane Austen well enough—but I wanted to get Elizabeth Bennet honestly, not by manipulating my answers.

I finished the quiz and bit my lip while it tabulated my answers, my heart rushing in my throat or my ears or somewhere else it didn't belong.

A picture popped up. A picture of Billie Piper. Blonde and curly haired and sullen looking.

"Fanny Price?" I wailed.

"Who's Fanny Price?"

I didn't answer. I read the results below the picture, describing me as quiet, shy, an outsider, spiritual, and I apparently hate exercise. All of which translated into, BORING. I groaned.

Monique threw a pillow at me. She was constantly throwing things around, leaving her clothes on the floor and her makeup spread all over the bathroom counter. If it weren't for me, our hotel room would look like a natural disaster film. "Is she a villain or something?"

"No." She wasn't a villain. She wasn't anything interesting at all. Fanny Price was a pushover. She was weak and didn't stand up for herself, and *Mansfield Park* has always been my least favorite Austen novel/movie.

Monique snatched my phone from my hand before I could stop her. She read my result. "This sounds like you."

I groaned again. "Thanks a lot."

"Oh, come on, Blair. It says you're loyal and kind. That's true."

Was it just me, or did Monique sound unsure? I had to admit that in one way I was like Fanny—shy—and I hadn't really opened up to Monique in the month we'd been sharing a room at the Lakeview Inn, rehearsing for the show together. She had gabbed on about the boyfriend she left behind in Vancouver and her best friend Molly who texted about five million times a day and her parents who decided to go to Hawaii over the Christmas holidays instead of coming to see her perform. I knew that she got mani/pedis every two weeks, her favorite lipstick was a drugstore brand, and she never had regular periods. The only thing Monique probably knew about me was my name: Blair McTavish. I wasn't what you'd call open.

Monique looked at the clock on the table between our beds and turned the radio off. "Lunch break is over. We better get back to rehearsal."

I gave Billie Piper one last look and then clicked off the quiz. Fanny Price. I was not Fanny Price. Would Fanny Price pursue a stage career? Would Fanny Price leave her mom and her little sister at Christmas time to travel to some nowhere Canadian town in the middle of the mountains for a job that barely paid pennies? Doubtful.

We both shared parents with addictions. And shyness. But that was it. There were no other similarities between Fanny Price and me. None.

I would make sure of it.

QUIZ: What Famous Man Is Your Soulmate?
RESULT: Jake Gyllenhaal

THERE'S SOMETHING KIND OF OBVIOUS ABOUT PERFORMING *HOLIDAY INN* at an actual inn. The Lakeview Inn puts on Christmas plays every year, running the two weeks before Christmas with the last show on Christmas Eve. They've done *White Christmas*, *A Christmas Carol*, and *Scrooged*. It was just my luck that the year I found out about it was the year they were putting on a musical with only two female leads. Not that I'd ever had a lead. It was always chorus for me, or Girl Number Three, or if I was lucky, I might get a line or two that no one would remember.

I walked down the hallway beside Monique, my gym bag bumping against my thigh. Monique kept her dance shoes, water bottles, and power bars in a giant, pink leather tote that probably cost more than a year's rent for my mom's two-bedroom apartment. Monique burst with stage presence onstage and off, but she didn't seem to mind being in the chorus with me. She gets noticed, she told me with a wink. I didn't know what that meant, but as long as she wasn't kicking me over with her character shoes, I was good.

Some of the other chorus members joined us in the elevator. They were chatting up a storm, and Monique jumped right in as if she'd been part of their conversation from the beginning. I squished myself against the back of the elevator and tried not to get stepped on.

The elevator dinged, going down floor by floor. The cast and crew had the entire fourth floor. The hotel manager liked to keep us away from the patrons. It was vintage snobbery—the lower class performers kept separate from the upper crust guests. Or maybe it was the raucous after-parties we had every night, despite the fact that we rehearsed all day and then performed every night with matinees on the weekends. Not that I went to these parties. Monique did, and she'd invited me, but by the end of the night, I was too exhausted to be around people or even stand. Besides, I never knew what to say and ended up standing around with no one to talk to while everyone had fun all around me.

Ugh, I *was* like Fanny Price.

No, no I wasn't. I wouldn't be. I could be Elizabeth Bennet. Or Marianne Dashwood. Or even Emma Woodhouse but without the snobbery.

The elevator doors slid open, and we filed out. I was last, and I barely made it through before the doors started to slide closed. Worried that I'd get squished by hundreds of pounds of steel, I tripped in my haste. The door caught my bag. I yanked at it as the doors slid open. I stumbled backwards.

"You okay?" Another set of elevator doors had opened, and two guys exited. My face heated. Of *course,* someone witnessed my gracelessness. And of *course,* it was Colt Harris and Marty Graham, the two male leads in the show.

Colt Harris peered at me. He was the one who'd asked me if I was okay, and I hadn't answered him yet. I forgot how to say yes, so I nodded.

He smiled so Hollywood that I wanted to either run away or swoon. Luckily, Marty snapped me out of it.

"I think the door ripped your bag," he said, fingering the worn material.

I pushed it behind me. "No biggie." It wasn't ripped from the elevator door; it was just that old.

A corner of Marty's mouth tilted. Before he could reply, Colt stepped in front of him. "Blair, let me look. Maybe something got damaged. We wouldn't want that, now would we?"

Colt's attention was embarrassing. Frankly, I was surprised he even knew my name. I was just a chorus girl after all. But he was always smiling at me, stopping to talk to me backstage, and stretching with me and always with Marty in tow. I suspected they both liked Monique, but she wasn't with me now.

"It's all right, really."

Colt shrugged. "Shall we?" It was so *1920s* that I almost expected him to hold out his hand and waltz me down the hall. But he wasn't the dancer of the two. With his deep melting voice, he had landed Jim Hardy, Bing Crosby's part from the movie. Marty was playing Ted Hanover, a.k.a. Fred Astaire, although it seemed to me like the casting director made a mistake. If anything, Colt was the smooth-talking, girl-swapping Ted, and Marty was the quieter, simpler Jim. I guessed their dancing and singing mattered more though.

I headed down the hall to the auditorium with Colt and Marty on either side. The hotel room doors were decorated with Christmas wreaths for the season, and the auditorium was lit with twinkling lights.

People stared when we walked in. Some of the other girls glared at me—girls who no doubt wanted to get into Colt's pleated Jim Hardy pants. Monique smiled and waved me over.

We were working on "I Can't Tell a Lie." My partner was a guy named Guy but pronounced the French way. He had sweaty hands and perfect feet. He never missed a step. I did because my hands were always slipping out of his. Today, he gave me correction with his heavy Québécois accent, talking over the choreographer so I couldn't understand either of them. When I tuned out Guy, I nailed the steps and really got into character as we performed full out.

"Great dancing," Colt said during break. He didn't dance during the number, just pretended to play the piano and mess up the music for Marty and the girl playing Linda.

"Thanks." I rubbed the back of my neck and then wiped the sweat off on my yoga pants. Really attractive. Monique sidled up to me.

"Hey, Colt."

"Hi, Monique." He gave her his Hollywood smile, and she flashed one back.

"You coming to Guy's tonight?"

Colt looked at me. "Maybe. If Blair can convince me."

I looked down. Why did he insist on flirting with me? It was embarrassing, and it made me uncomfortable.

Monique threw her arm around my shoulder. "Oh, she'll be there."

Colt hadn't taken his eyes off me. "Then I wouldn't miss it."

I doubted Colt had missed one of the after-parties yet while I'd never gone. Still, I could feel my knees going weak. I hated that Colt's pretty face had that effect on me. I didn't even like him. He crossed the stage to Marty. He looked back at us, making it obvious that we were their topic of conversation.

"That guy wants you bad," Monique said. "You have to come tonight."

And though I didn't have anything to do, there was something about Colt that... He weirded me out. Maybe it was the fact that I doubted he wanted me "bad" like Monique said. It wasn't like I thought I was *un-wantable* or anything, but I was pretty sure he hadn't said no to those girls who hung off him, and I wasn't into man whores. Monique thought it was because I was playing "hard to get," though I'd assured her, I wasn't playing anything. I just didn't know how to act around someone like Colt.

What I did know was that I needed to go to that party. I was trying to be Elizabeth, not Fanny, after all. Fanny would stay at home and pine after her cousin (gross). Elizabeth would go and have fun, be witty, and impress men with her "fine eyes."

"Okay, I'll go." I knew that Monique would never let me get out of it now. It was my first step into becoming Elizabeth, not Fanny.

QUIZ: What Greek Goddess Are You?
RESULT: Hestia, Goddess of Hearth and Home

THE AFTER-PARTY WAS EXACTLY AS I THOUGHT IT WOULD BE. THERE I WAS, sitting alone on the couch in the corner of Guy's room while people got drunk and laughed and had fun without knowing I existed. A couple was on the couch next to me, sloppily making out. I sipped my wine, pretending I had finer tastes, and stared off into space.

A cheer went up, and I focused on the door. Colt had arrived, extra-fashionably late. Girls swarmed him as he scanned the room. His eyes landed on me, and he made a beeline for my couch. I glanced around for Marty, but he wasn't with Colt.

Colt squeezed himself between the couple—who never took a breath when the couch sunk from his weight—and me.

"Hey, Blair."

"Hi." I stared at my half-empty wine glass.

"Having fun?"

Did it look like I was having fun? "Sure."

He paused. I watched the dark red liquid tremble in my glass. He leaned into me. "This isn't really your kind of thing, is it?"

Ya think? "No, not really."

"I thought so." I could hear a smile in his voice. "You're different, Blair. Special. I could tell from the first moment I saw you."

I looked up to see whether he was joking, but he just smiled at me all innocent and handsome-like. He still wore faint traces of eyeliner from tonight's show. It only enhanced his blue eyes. But he likely knew that and left some on intentionally.

Colt brushed a strand of hair off my cheek. "You're beautiful, Blair."

My eyes narrowed. "Are you drunk?"

He tilted his head back and laughed. "Of course not!" He put his lips near my ear. "Don't you know that you're the girl I came to see?"

Across the room, the two female leads were talking, their skinny hips bumping into each other. They both turned and looked at me. Or at Colt. Or us. The girl playing Linda smiled a knowing smile, but I wasn't sure what she knew. All I knew was that, whatever it was, I didn't know it.

The room was full of laughter and noise. The girl on the other side of Colt had begun to moan. Annoying rap music blared from the radio, someone shrieked, and Colt's hand on my leg—when did that get there?—was heavy.

I couldn't do this. I didn't know whether Elizabeth Bennet would either.

"Sorry, Colt, I—" I didn't finish my sentence. As I stood, I sloshed wine onto my sweater.

I shoved the glass into someone's hand and left.

"Blair! Hey, Blair. Wait—"

Colt was calling me, but I didn't want to be there anymore, not even with someone as handsome and Hollywood as he was.

The party had spilled out into the hall, and I dodged and stumbled around people, probably looking like a drunk who was about to puke when really I was only lame Fanny Price who didn't know how to have fun. I pressed the button for the elevator, but it was too slow, so I took the stairs. As soon as I stepped outside, the cold slapped me in the face.

Shivering, I looked out into the night. I was wearing a cardigan and jeans but no jacket. At least I had boots on, although their brown leather weren't doing much to keep out the cold. I leaned against the brick of the inn and peered across town. The Lakeview Inn topped a hill, the front parking lot sprinkled with snow-covered cars and a winding road down the hill to Lakeview proper. It was a small town of cabins and miniature homes, wide lawns lacking fences, and deer wandering the streets. No joke. When I first rode in on the bus, I saw three—one burrowing his nose in the snow, another sauntering across someone's lawn, and a third at the side of the road watching us as if it was waiting to cross. They hadn't even been afraid of the big lumbering bus and its smoky noise.

Lakeview—sleepy like a ghost town. A ghost town with Christmas lights dotting the landscape and lit-up wreaths on every single power-line post. I swore I could hear "Silver Bells" playing faintly somewhere. The light on the snow was blushy pink, and it reminded me of a Thomas Kinkade painting of a cottage in a winter scene. All that was missing was—

Yep, there it was. Snow, falling like tiny bird feathers, landing on my nose and my hair, and dotting my black cardigan with fluff.

A tear rolled down my cheek, and I rubbed it away before it froze there. Christmas had never been like this for me. It was never snowy, cheery, or twinkling. It was never idyllic. It had always been a mess. It was how I felt at the party. It was the brown slush when the snow melts. It was cold without the hot chocolate or a person to keep you warm.

I heard a cough, and I turned.

"You okay?"

At first, I thought it was Colt—that he'd followed me out here. But the voice stepped into the faint lamplight, revealing Marty Graham.

Marty had longish dark hair that fell into his face when he danced, but it was still slicked back from tonight's show. He was only a couple inches taller than I was, and there was something wonky about his nose. That didn't stop the girls from fawning over him. It was his lead status. Every show was the same; the leads got all the attention, onstage and off.

"I saw you run out of there."

I nodded. Swallowed. He leaned next to me against the wall, and we both stared out at the town nestled below us like a baby in a crib.

For a while, we didn't talk, and I relaxed. Between Marty and Colt, Marty had always been the quiet one. It was much easier with him though.

I didn't feel the need to impress him, to come up with witty and intelligent conversation.

I was still shivering, and I hunched in on myself to keep warm.

"Do you want to go in?" Marty asked.

"No." I really didn't. I liked being out here. It was as if I could pretend I was someone else, someone who had Christmases in a place like this with Santa and presents and figgy pudding or whatever normal people eat that isn't leftover KFC or week-old Chinese food.

Marty's hands were on me, and I flinched before I realized he was draping his coat over my shoulders.

"Won't you be cold?" I asked.

He zipped his hoodie to his neck and gave me his slanted smile.

"Thanks." I slid my arms into his coat and zipped it to the top. I pulled the neck over my nose. Marty's coat smelled good, like warm boy and pine trees.

"I'm used to the cold."

"Where are you from?" I asked, realizing that I knew very few facts about Marty. I felt like I knew what kind of guy he was, but I didn't know anything about him.

"A town just a couple of hours from here."

I wondered if that's how he got a lead. Maybe he knew someone. But that wouldn't have even mattered because I'd seen him dance. And I'd heard him sing. He was good. More than good. He deserved his part.

"What about you?"

I hesitated. "Detroit."

"Never been."

I stared at the Christmas painting that was Lakeview. "I've lived there all my life, but it's not home." Nowhere was. I didn't know why I told Marty that.

"Can I ask you something?" he said after a few minutes of silence. I nodded. "Was Colt...?"

I waited for him to finish, but he said nothing else. He shook his head.

"Are you two close?" I pulled my face out of the coat.

"We're roommates," he said as if that explained everything. It sort of did. It was like Monique and me. We usually hung out together. Friends by default. Colt and Marty were always together too. Maybe Marty was Colt's wingman.

I snuggled deeper into his coat. It felt like a hug. "Did you know him before?"

"Nah." He kicked some snow with his boot.

I felt like I was supposed to say something nice about Colt. They were friends and all. "He's very... talented." I flushed.

Marty straightened from the wall and then slouched back against it. "Yeah." One of his feet started tapping. He looked me square in the face. "You like him?"

I wanted to laugh. Or run away. Was that why Marty came out here? To ask me if I liked Colt like we were in the third grade. Wingman, definitely.

"He's nice." To me. To everyone. I didn't know. He was charming and attentive.

He weirded me out, but I doubted I should say any of that to Marty.

"He weirds me out." Shoot. I said it.

Marty burst out laughing.

"What?" I asked. My face was probably the color of Santa's suit by now. "Don't tell him I said that."

Marty's laughter died, but he was still grinning. "I won't." He swirled the snow with his boot, making a spiral. "Hey, you wanna build a snowman?"

I stared blankly at him. "Are you being for real?"

He picked up some snow and tossed it over his head. It dusted his shoulders like dandruff. "Sure. Unless you want to go back to the party."

I shook my head. Building a snowman sounded ten times better than that. "I've never done it before."

His eyes widened. "No way."

I shrugged, trying to cover my embarrassment. "Way."

Marty grabbed my hand before I could react and pulled me down the hill. My boots had no grip, and I started to slide. I let out a shriek as my feet forgot where they were supposed to be, and I landed on my butt. Marty came down with me, and we were both laughing and dusted with snow.

Marty's eyes were on me, and his cheeks and lips were pink; pieces of his hair had fallen across his forehead.

"Come on," he said. He got to his feet and then held out his hand for me. "We've got a snowman to build."

QUIZ: What Is the Color of Your Aura?
RESULT: White

"WHERE DID YOU DISAPPEAR TO LAST NIGHT?" MONIQUE ASKED THE NEXT morning after I'd gotten out of the shower.

I pulled on my yoga pants and a tank top and twisted my wet hair into a high bun.

"Were you off with Colt?" She raised her eyebrows up and down.

"No." I was building a snowman with Marty, getting cold and wet, but having more fun than I ever had in my life. Marty was surprisingly good at snowman building, and we ended up shaping ours into a pretty accurate rendition of Darth Vader. Then we talked, and I told him about my mom and my sister and my whole messed-up home life—things I didn't usually talk about with other people. And he listened. He cared.

But I didn't want to tell Monique any of that. It felt sacred. Like if I said it out loud, it wouldn't be real anymore.

Monique peered into my face. "You're totally lying," she said with a grin.

I turned away from her, and that was when I saw it—my face blushing and glowing like I had indeed run off with some guy last night.

"I'm not. I swear. I didn't hang out with Colt."

She gave an exaggerated shrug. "Okay. If you say so." She tied the string on her sweater, which emphasized her tiny waist. "But it would be totally cool if you did, you know. I don't know what's holding you back. The guy likes you. You should go for it."

Her bag was near my feet so I picked it up and handed it to her. "I...no. I don't think so."

Why would I want to hang out with a guy who made me uncomfortable and awkward, who made me feel less like myself? Just because he was movie-star handsome? I didn't think so. If only Monique had been talking about someone else, someone with a wonky nose and slanted smile.

She was quiet while I went through my gym bag, checking to make sure my character and tap shoes were both in there, my water bottle, Chapstick, a granola bar, and a book—for down time. The director made us rehearse the entire show every day to make sure "we didn't lose it" between performances. He was a total Nazi, but it had made the show spectacular. Practice made perfect after all.

"Ready?" I asked Monique, who was twirling her ponytail around one finger while staring off into space. She nodded, and we headed out.

QUIZ: What's inside Your Head?
RESULT: Disgust

THERE WAS A BANQUET HALL IN THE INN WHERE THEY FED THE CAST AND crew dinner every night. It was buffet style, almost like a school cafeteria but with better choices. Like the rest of the hotel, it was decorated with shiny, Christmasy things, and the speakers played an ongoing soundtrack of Christmas carols. Right then, Madonna was serenading us with "Santa Baby." I ate most of my dinners in there because it was free, but a lot of the cast didn't stick around, instead trying out different restaurants in Lakeview.

Today the tables seemed to be almost full, the line-up for the pizza bar ridiculously long. Monique was in that line, impatiently tapping her foot along to Madonna. For someone in such great shape, you would never know she loved her pizza huge, loaded and the greasier the better.

I buttered a roll and offered it to Marty. His mouth was full, so he grinned a thank you. He was sitting next to me at the round table, his chair scooted close. We had arrived early and didn't have to wait in line for our food. I slurped some chicken noodle soup, the liquid warming me from my throat to my belly. Or maybe that was Marty's smile.

"You really should watch it," he said once he'd swallowed his bite of fettuccine Alfredo. "I wish I brought my DVDs. We could've started from season one."

"I don't think *Hannibal* is my kind of thing." I'd never been into scary movies. My mom's favorite movie was *Sleeping with the Enemy,* and I couldn't watch that without getting nightmares. So a show based off a killer cannibal? Doubtful.

"It's really good," he said, biting into a piece of steak. "Trust me; you'll love it."

"He says as blood drips down his chin."

He blushed, and it was pretty adorable. "What can I say? I like my meat fresh."

I shuddered. "That's disgusting."

Marty draped an arm across the back of my chair. "Hey, you want to—"

I didn't hear the rest of that question because Colt dropped into Monique's empty chair on my other side and bellowed, "Blair! Babe!" People turned to look, including Monique.

I reluctantly turned away from Marty. "Hi, Colt." I busied myself with buttering another roll. Marty went back to his barely dead animal.

"So, you and me after the show tonight," Colt said. "I've got something special planned."

Marty grunted beside me, but I didn't look at him. My cheeks were hot, and I stared at my plate. I didn't know what to say. No other girl in this room probably would have hesitated. Colt was handsome and talented, and he really seemed into me. Elizabeth Bennet would probably go for it. She would take a chance.

Then again, even though Darcy was the catch of the town, she didn't fall for that. She told him where to go and how to get there. If I was going to be more like Elizabeth, I needed to speak up.

"I can't," I mumbled, so quiet even *I* barely heard myself.

He rubbed the back of my neck with one hand. "I even decorated," he said as if he hadn't heard me. "Christmas lights, a tree, the works! It's romantic. You have to come and see."

I glanced at Marty, and he was staring at Colt through narrowed eyes.

"I can't," I said, this time louder.

Colt's hand moved from my neck to my ear. He swept his finger down the tender skin. "There might even be mistletoe."

It was as if I'd gone invisible, except that he was staring at me and touching me, so maybe he'd gone deaf. Or maybe he was just not used to hearing the word "no."

I moved my head, shrugging away from his touch. "I said, I can't."

Words from *Pride and Prejudice* ran through my head. I wanted to tell Colt that he was the last man in the world whom I could ever date.

"Colt—" Marty began, but Colt didn't let him finish.

"Another night then." He squeezed my leg.

I shook my head.

He raised his eyebrows. "You have other plans?"

I swallowed. Yes, my plans included hanging out in my room and watching *Seinfeld* reruns. Saying that out loud sounded so pathetic—so *not* Elizabeth. I wished my other plans included Marty, but he hadn't said a word, wasn't even speaking up for me right now. I had to speak up for myself.

"I've made plans for you, babe." Colt rubbed my leg with his hand. "Me and you. Shower after the show and then come straight to my room. I'll be waiting."

"No!" I pushed back from my chair so fast it fell over. "I said, no. Don't you get it? Are you that stupid? Stop acting like such a creep, and leave me alone!"

I was shouting. I was totally and completely yelling at the top of my lungs. Blood pounded in my ears, and I was sure I was as red as a Solo cup.

An awkward silence fell over the banquet hall. Everyone stared. Colt's face turned hard. But the worst was Marty. He was giving me a look that I couldn't read. I looked away.

Colt stood up. "Geez, Blair," he said loud enough for everyone to hear, "all you had to say was no. I just wanted to spend some time with you. I thought you were nice." *But I was wrong.* He didn't have to say it; we could all hear his unspoken words.

Tears welled in my eyes. Someone behind me muttered, "What a cow." Colt turned away, and a couple of girls rushed to his side, giving me dirty looks behind his back.

I grabbed my bag from the floor and ran out of there.

QUIZ: Which Magical Creature Are You?
RESULT: Unicorn

"Blair, wait!" Monique chased me down before I could make it to the elevator.

I turned, grateful to see her for someone who would share in my misery. She was scowling at me.

"What is your problem, Blair?" she demanded. "Seriously, you didn't have to be so rude to Colt."

My heart sank. "I didn't... He wouldn't listen... I—"

I didn't know what came over me. I had never yelled like that in my entire life—not at my little sister who never listens even when I try to protect her, not at my mom who disappears for days on a bender, not at the bullies who used to torment me for wearing the same jeans every day for a month. But Colt tipped me over the edge, and I couldn't take it anymore.

Monique crossed her arms. "He's one of the nicest guys here. I really thought you were playing hard to get, but if you actually didn't like him, you just had to say so."

I scrubbed at my eyes. "I did."

She moved closer. "I've gone on and on about how great you are, even though you're a loner. People think you're a snob, you know? But I defended you. And then you do this."

I looked at my shoes. "I'm sorry."

"Whatever." She was quiet for a moment, but even though I didn't look up, I knew she hadn't walked away. "I guess if you really don't like him, you won't care if I do."

My head snapped up. "No."

Her eyes narrowed. "You *do* like him?"

"No." I shook my head. "No, I mean, don't go for him. He's not what everyone thinks he is."

She scoffed.

"Really. Monique. He's fake. What he says... And he's a player. He's probably been with at least half the girls here."

She tapped her long fingernails on her arms. "You lost your chance, Blair. It's my turn now."

I watched her walk away, my heart sinking. My only friend here and now she was angry with me. Marty too. But worse, Monique didn't believe me about Colt, and she was going to get hurt. And there was nothing I could do to stop it.

QUIZ: Which Time Period Do You Belong In?
RESULT: The Victorian Era

MONIQUE WOULDN'T TALK TO ME. COLT WOULDN'T EVEN LOOK AT ME. Marty was avoiding me.

If only the cast took the same approach. Most of the guys didn't care, but the girls were talking behind my back, loud enough that I'd hear. The girl who played Linda confronted me, asking me why I had been such a jerk, and I had no answer. My tap shoes disappeared, and it took me forever to find them in the dumpster, covered in mustard. During performance that night, someone tripped me during "Song of Freedom." Someone else pulled on my dress during the final bows, and I fell over in front of the entire audience.

I felt horrible. My insides were a twisting mess of garbage. It wasn't so much for yelling at Colt—he hadn't listened to me, and I didn't regret saying no—I knew I was right about him. But I did feel bad for losing my temper. Embarrassed that everyone witnessed it. I hated to be noticed, but this was ten times worse because I had brought it upon myself. It killed me that everyone thought so badly of me. I couldn't even try to catch Marty's gaze when he passed me backstage. I was too ashamed. I worried that I was turning into my mom—hard and rough—when I'd been fighting it my whole life.

Monique didn't return to our room after the show. I crawled into bed, glad to be alone but also worried for her. What if she was with Colt? Maybe I was wrong after all, and he was really a good guy, as charming on the inside as he was on the outside. I was happy to be wrong if it meant Monique could be happy.

I didn't know when I fell asleep, but I knew when I woke up—when Monique came back. She moved quietly around the room without turning on a light. I glanced at the clock; it was almost 1:00 a.m.

I needed to apologize to Monique, explain… She really had been a good friend to me ever since we got here, never asking for a thing in return and not caring when I didn't go to parties with her or share my deepest darkest secrets like she did. I turned on the lamp between our beds.

Monique froze. She looked at me. Her face was red, her mascara running.

I scrambled from the bed. "What's wrong?"

She turned away from me. I stopped, hovering a few inches behind her. "You were right."

My shoulders slumped. I didn't want to be right. "What happened?"

She sat on the edge of her bed. "Things were great. We were hanging out in his room, having fun. You should see the Christmas decorations he set up. They're gorgeous!" She sighed.

So he really had decorated. It hadn't been for me though.

"Then all of a sudden, he's rushing me out. He kept looking at the clock and trying to get me to leave, saying he needed to get some rest because he's a lead and all." She snorted. "I thought it was weird, so I made up excuses to stay."

I edged closer, sitting on the bed next to her.

"Another girl came to the door."

She didn't have to say anything else. I put my arm over her shoulder, and she leaned into me. "I'm sorry."

"I was so mad. But deep down, I knew. I knew even before you said it. I've been with his type over and over again. They say just the right things, they make you feel so special, and then…"

"And then."

"I'm sorry for earlier."

"Me too."

She stared at me. "What are you sorry for?"

"For yelling at Colt, embarrassing him in front of everyone."

Her eyebrows rose. "Are you kidding me? He deserved it."

"I could've handled it better."

What Monique didn't realize was that it wasn't about him; it was about me. Yes, Colt hadn't listened, and yes, he was a jerk, and yes, he probably deserved a good tongue-lashing. But I didn't want to be the person who gave it to him. I didn't want to be mean and classless. I didn't want to go hard. I had seen so many people like that in my life, and I wouldn't be the same.

Monique rose from the bed, throwing off her shirt and pulling on a tank. "We need to do something to get back at him."

I climbed back into my own bed. "Nah, we're better than that. He'll get it back sometime. Karma, right?"

She pursed her lips. "Are you sure? 'Cuz I already have a few ideas in mind."

I nodded. "I'm sure." I wouldn't be that person.

QUIZ: Which Song Was Actually Written about You?
RESULT: "You're Beautiful" by James Blunt

KARMA REALLY IS WHAT THEY SAY IT IS. COLT GOT WHAT HE DESERVED, but it didn't come from Monique or me. No one knew who put something in his foundation or how they knew it would cause hives to break out, not only on his face but over his entire body. The understudy had to take his place for our last two shows on Christmas Eve.

Marty found me after the matinee performance, reforming our Darth Vader head that had gone askew from all the snow that had fallen over the last few days.

He stopped nearby, but didn't come any closer. His hands were in his pockets, and his shoulders were hunched near his ears, probably to keep them warm. Or maybe he had something unpleasant to say.

"It wasn't me," I said, before he could. "I didn't do anything to Colt."

One corner of his mouth slanted up. "I know."

I blinked. "You do?"

He came closer until the tips of his boots were touching the tips of mine. "You wouldn't do something like that. You're not that kind of girl."

Warm tingles spread through my entire body, despite the cold bite in the air. I wasn't that kind of girl, and Marty saw it.

Better yet, I saw it too.

I wasn't bold like Elizabeth. I didn't speak my mind, and I regretted when I did. I wasn't exceptionally witty or bursting with life. But I was not boring. And neither is Fanny Price.

I was more like her than I knew, and that wasn't a bad thing. Fanny knows what's right and what's wrong, who's good, and who's good for her, and she sticks to her guns without losing who she is in the process. She never lowers herself, and I didn't have to either.

For once, I was proud to be Fanny.

"I hope I'm never that kind of girl."

His hands moved from his pockets, and he cupped my face. "I've always been a sucker for a good girl."

My lips spread in a smile. "I thought you were angry with me."

"No way!"

"Way."

"I was just surprised." He let go, turning to our Darth snowman. "I haven't known Colt that long, but I've never seen anyone talk to him like that before."

I blushed.

He turned back to me. "I should have stepped in during dinner that night—stopped him. He was being a real jerk, and I didn't say anything. I'm embarrassed that I did nothing. Like, what kind of man am I? I'm sorry."

I smiled again. I was done with all the apologies, all the embarrassment. I might've been fine with being Fanny, but I could also be Elizabeth sometimes too. Marty was the kind of guy worth being bold for.

I wrapped my arms around his neck and drew his lips to mine. He kissed me as if he'd been waiting to all this time. Maybe he was.

Something wet hit my cheeks, and I pulled away. It was snowing, white flakes falling in Marty's dark hair and on his eyelashes and dusting my cheeks with cold.

"Are you going back to Detroit right away?"

My bus ticket was for tonight after the last show. But truthfully, I didn't want to spend Christmas Eve and Christmas morning on a bus, heading to a place that had never felt like home.

I looked down at my boots and shrugged.

He coughed. "Because if you're not…"

I met his gaze. His cheeks were red from the cold, or maybe he was embarrassed. "Then…?"

"There's always an extra place around the Graham Christmas tree."

I brushed a strand of hair off his forehead. "Do you mean it?"

He took my hand and planted a kiss on my palm. "I wish for it."

I threw my arms around his neck and buried my face in his coat. I started to cry and laugh at the same time.

"Is that a yes?"

"Yes," I said into his chest.

Marty's arms tightened around my waist. We held onto each other as snow fell down around us like a curtain, shielding us from the world, or maybe welcoming us into it.

"Merry Christmas Eve," he whispered into my hair.

And for the first time ever, it was. A merry Christmas Eve.

. . . .

MELANIE STANFORD reads too much, plays music too loud, is sometimes dancing, and always daydreaming. She would also like her very own TARDIS, but only to travel to the past. She lives outside Calgary, Alberta, Canada with her husband, four kids, and ridiculous amounts of snow. Her first novel, *SWAY*, is coming December 29, 2015. You can find her at melaniestanfordbooks.com, on Twitter @MelMStanford, and on Facebook @MelanieStanfordauthor.

"She was without any power, because she was without any desire of command over herself." —Jane Austen, *Sense and Sensibility*

"Hope smiles from the threshold of the year to come, whispering, 'It will be happier.'" —Alfred Lord Tennyson

A Man Whom I Can Really Love

By Natalie Richards

Day 0

The Middleton Christmas party was in full swing. Half of Devonshire was attending, all in their best finery—the most awful collection of Christmas jumpers one could ever wish to un-see, drinking thick, homemade eggnog that had been liberally spiked by no less than five people over the course of the evening. Marianne took one sip and nearly gagged. Nobody was quite drunk enough to start singing Christmas carols, but from the way Cousin Mary was eyeing the piano, it was only a matter of time.

Aunt Jane was telling stories to the little ones by the fire. A comfortable, middle-aged woman with bright eyes and a warm smile, she was a great favorite amongst the children. Having no little ones of her own, she loved to dote on all that came into her vicinity. Marianne's little sister, Maggie, was lurking in the doorway and pretending not to listen. At fifteen, she believed herself far too old for such "childish tales," but could not resist their lure despite her best efforts.

Nora's husky laugh caught Marianne's attention, and she smiled; it was a sound she had not heard in far too long. Nora had been melancholy of late, and it was all Ward's fault. Marianne was glad he was not here tonight, for then she would be compelled to murder him, and that would be the end of the party. Despite Nora's insistence that she and Ward were simply friends, Marianne knew that her sister was in love with the idiot. Instead of seeing what was right in front of his face, Ward had chosen to date Lucy Steele of the large chest and manipulative brain, inadvertently breaking Nora's heart in the process. Ah, well, Nora's practical nature would soon help her overcome her feelings. It frustrated Marianne that her sister was so cold when it came to matters of the heart. When she heard of Ward's involvement with Lucy, Nora had gone dead white for a moment but then quickly recovered, saying, "I hope she makes him happy." Not a word had been spoken on the subject since. How could she not scream and rage? How could she feel so little? Marianne did not understand her.

A painfully staccato piano rendition of "God Rest Ye, Merry Gentlemen" assaulted Marianne's ears, distracting her from her thoughts. She winced as several tipsy voices joined the fray, further mangling the carol. It was just as well that Christmas only happened once a year; her musical sensibilities would not survive any more. She glanced at the crowd of guests surrounding the poor, abused piano and frowned when she realized John was nowhere to be seen. Her boyfriend had a lovely, melodic voice and a greater tolerance for bad music, so she expected him to be one of the first to join in.

"Mum, have you seen John?"

Clara Dashwood smiled somewhat blearily at her middle daughter. "Oh, I think he tottered off down the hall, dear. Some colleague of his from London showed up looking for him. A work emergency, I would imagine. She looked rather upset about something." She gave a vague wave of her hand.

"I'll go see what's up, then." Marianne gently bussed her mother's cheek and set off in search of her man.

John Willoughby was the cleverest, most passionate, most sophisticated man Marianne had ever met. He was also the handsomest, but that, of course, was not the reason she was in love with him. She wasn't *that* shallow. Though…it certainly didn't hurt. John worked at a prestigious law firm in

London and was on the fast track to become a junior partner in a few years despite his youth. He was planning on a career in politics one day. Marianne thought he would make a wonderful member of parliament.

As she made her way down the corridor, she heard raised voices from the study. Drawing closer, she was able to make out a woman's strident tones and John's placating ones.

"You told me that you were visiting your sick aunt, but instead, I find you here! What on earth are you doing at such a provincial, vulgar gathering? God, the noise! And there are children everywhere!"

"How did you even find me here?" John was sounding a little irritated now.

"I asked your aunt, of course. She said that you have hardly spent any time with her this past week. And she is scarcely ill; it is simply a trifling cold. What are you doing rusticating in the country when you could be in London with me?"

"My dear, I will be returning to London directly now that Aunt Louisa is on the mend. As for tonight, I was bored out of my mind and wanted to get out of the house."

Marianne was beginning to dislike John's tone as well as his choice of words. *"My dear," indeed!* It was time to make an entrance. Using more force than necessary, she shoved open the door to meet a pair of startled faces.

She smiled sweetly. "Hello, John. So this is where you got to. Who's your friend?"

She ran her eyes over the woman who was standing just a tiny bit too close to her boyfriend. She was beautiful if your taste ran to icy, elegant blondes. She wore a simple black dress that ended just above the knee and probably cost £20 a stitch. Her feet were clad in black leather boots with towering heels and pointed toes. A diamond the size of Marianne's thumbnail glittered on her left ring finger.

John went curiously pale. "Ah, this is Sophia Grey. Sophia, Marianne Dashwood."

Marianne smiled, showing lots of teeth. "Lovely to meet you." She stuck out her hand.

Sophia, with an equally insincere smile, took it. "Always a pleasure to meet any friend of John's." With that greeting aside, she dismissed Marianne entirely. "So, shall we go now? It is getting late, and there is much to discuss."

John cast a nervous glance between the two women. "Ah…"

Marianne sighed. It was a very pretty sigh with a touch of pout, and she knew it. "Must you go so early, John? The firm ought not to be making you work in the middle of the night during the holidays." There was no way she was going to allow this woman—who clearly had seduction on her mind—to leave with *her* boyfriend, colleague or no. John might not know what she was up to, but Marianne had no doubt.

Sophia laughed, a low, mocking sound. "My dear Miss Dashwood, I fear you have misunderstood the situation. I haven't come to discuss work but rather some last-minute wedding details. John and I are to be married after New Year's." She hooked her arm through his, smiling up at him. "Isn't that right, John?"

Marianne felt a chill through her bones, freezing everything in between and frosting over what should be warm and beating.

"John?" Her voice was barely above a whisper, so quiet that she could hardly hear it over the sudden ringing in her ears.

He *smiled*. It was an awful, grimacing twist of the lips but a smile just the same. A smile aimed at *her*. "That's right, love." He turned to Marianne, that horrible smile failing to reach his eyes. "Would you care to wish us joy?"

Marianne stared at him, this creature who had stolen her heart and shattered it. How could he do this to her? He loved her; she knew he did, didn't she? Every moment she spent in his company had been happier than the last. He thought the same things as she, felt the same, spoke the same. They were two halves of the same whole, right? She had spun dreams of their future together, a future full of passion and adventure. Was any of it real, or had every word and touch between them been a lie?

John and Sophia were both looking at her expectantly, waiting for her to smile and step aside as if everything was all right, but nothing was all right.

"No."

With that one word, she spun on her heel and stormed out, leaving them gaping behind her.

Marianne's hands shook as she shoved her arms into her worn woolen coat, cursing as her fingers caught on a hole in the sleeve. Grabbing her purse, she dug frantically for her keys, not pausing to wipe away the tears streaming down her face.

"Marianne, why are you leaving so early?"

Marianne turned to see her older sister frowning at her. "I cannot stay here." She bent to tug on her shoes, but stopped at the feel of Nora's hand on her shoulder.

"Mari, what's the matter? You're crying."

She was tempted to take her sister's comfort, to lean into her embrace and weep, but she couldn't risk John and that woman seeing her. Still, she couldn't stop the words from escaping. "John is getting married."

"John? *Your* John? I don't understand."

"His fiancée came here looking for him. They're getting married next month." She still couldn't really believe it, not even after he had admitted it to her face.

Nora gasped. "It can't be. There must be some mistake."

"No mistake. I have to go. I cannot stay here with them."

"Marianne, you can't drive like this. Let me get Maggie and Mum, and we will take you home." Her hand became restraining, so Marianne shook it off.

"No, you stay. I can't wait." Straightening, she shoved open the door, letting a flurry of snow in. Good. The weather matched the temperature of her heart.

"Marianne, you're too upset. Let me at least get Brandon to follow you…" Marianne didn't hear the rest of her words as she stepped out into the storm, slamming the door behind her.

She made it halfway to her flat before calming down enough to realize how utterly foolish she was. The snow was coming down thick and fast, making it difficult to see more than a meter in front of her car, and she was driving far too fast for such conditions. She realized this too late as she turned a corner and her tires spun out on black ice, sending her tired old Mini out of control. She had one brief moment of absolute terror before she hit something and flipped. Glass shattered, and her head slammed first one way then another. Her last conscious thought was that it was too cold.

BRANDON DELAFORD KNEW SOMETHING WAS WRONG THE INSTANT NORA Dashwood stepped into the room. Her face was pinched, and she was worrying her necklace, a nervous habit that gave away her feelings every time. Her gaze darted around the room, landing first on her little sister, who was completely engrossed by a story, and then her mother, who was swaying unsteadily as she hummed along to a drunken rendition of "The Holly and the Ivy." Her shoulders slumped slightly, and then her eyes met his. *Damn.* His quiet evening of hiding in the corner was coming to an end.

He stood, wincing at the sharp stab of pain in his leg. Retrieving his cane, he limped to join Nora.

"Is something the matter?"

Instead of replying immediately, she grasped his elbow and led him out into the corridor before asking, "Brandon, could you do me a huge favor?"

"Of course. What is it?" The words were out of his mouth before he could stop them. He did not really want to do anything tonight other than go home as early as could be politely managed to where a bottle of whiskey waited, but it was impossible to say "no" to the Dashwood ladies. They were among his favorite people.

"It is Marianne. She was very upset when she left, and now she isn't answering her mobile. Do you think you could swing by her flat and make certain she is well? I would go, but it is going to take awhile to collect Mum and Maggie."

Brandon's weariness vanished. "What upset her?" He shouldn't be worried; a great many things upset Marianne Dashwood: abandoned puppies, Parliament, rap music, etc. The woman had strong opinions on just about everything. She could laugh or cry at the drop of a hat.

"John's fiancée decided to crash the party. The fiancée he never told anyone he had."

"Bloody hell." He had never liked John Willoughby, had always thought that Marianne was too good for him, but he'd never thought the man was a complete idiot. If he were ever so lucky as to find Marianne in love with *him*, he would grab on to her and never let go.

God, *Marianne*. Sweet, sensitive Marianne who cried over dead butterflies and danced in rain showers had just had her heart ripped out and stomped on. "When did she leave?"

"Thirty minutes ago. She should be home by now, even in this weather." Nora bit her lip, casting a nervous glance out the window. Brandon followed her eyes.

"Damn. It's nearly a blizzard out there. She took her rattletrap Mini out in this?"

Nora nodded in affirmation.

"All right. I'll ring you as soon as I reach her place." Brandon was already headed for the door.

The road from the Middleton's to the small town of Barton was narrow and curvy, lined with sheep fields and deep ditches and currently covered with several centimeters of snow. It wasn't the snow that concerned Brandon as much as what lay beneath it, however. Tonight was the first time temperatures had slipped below freezing, and it had rained every day for the past week. The road's surface would be icy as hell.

He turned a corner and slammed on the brakes at the horrifying sight before him. His car skidded half a meter to the side and came to a shuddering stop. Any further and he would have gone over, but he neither noticed nor cared. A battered, fire-engine red Mini Cooper rested upside-down in the ditch, a light dusting of snow capping its upended tires. *Marianne.*

Brandon was out of his car in a second, slipping and sliding in his haste. "Marianne! Mari, can you hear me?" He yanked open her door. "Oh, God."

Marianne hung from her seat, her long curls brushing against the jagged remains of the windshield. Brandon couldn't see her face, couldn't see whether she was awake or unconscious or…No. "Marianne? Please, say something, baby." Not caring that he was kneeling on glass, he moved in as close as he could, reaching to gently push away her hair. She was so pale, her white skin a painful contrast to the bright red blood slowly dripping down her forehead. "Please, Mari, open those beautiful eyes." He was pleading now, but she stayed frighteningly still. Never taking his eyes off her face, he reached into his pocket and pulled out his mobile, dialing 999. "Hello? I need an ambulance…"

Day 1

IT WAS WARM AND DARK AND THICK, LIKE SWIMMING IN HONEY WHILE wrapped in a black velvet curtain. Only, no matter how hard Marianne swam or pushed against the curtain, she could not find the surface. She tried shouting for help, but no sound emerged. With effort, she forced herself to calm, to drift weightless in the dark as she attempted to figure out what was happening. After a time, she began to hear voices filtering through the curtain. At first, they were soft and muffled, but gradually they became clearer.

"…for the most part minor. Fractured radius and ulna in her right arm, bruised ribs, and minor lacerations from the broken glass. What concerns me the most are the head injuries. The worst is the contusion on the right side of her head. It caused significant swelling and a severe concussion. The other injury, a smaller bump on the back, is less serious but may have added to Miss Dashwood's concussion."

Is he talking about me? Oh God, the accident. Marianne remembered the crash, the cold. She shuddered as panic overtook her. *Am I paralyzed? Will I be trapped in the dark forever?* She did not know how long she spent fighting the curtain, but when she finally calmed again, everything was quiet. She didn't know how much time had passed, but she suspected it had been hours. *Did they leave me alone?* All she could hear was a steady beeping of machines: her heart, she realized, as it kept time with the beating in her chest. After a few moments, she heard a door open and close then footsteps approaching.

"How could you do something so stupid, Mari?" Nora's voice was harsh, angrier than Marianne had ever heard it before. "Did you think you were a tragic heroine like in one of your stories? I think part of you did when you made your 'grand exit.' I told you it wasn't safe, and a part of you thought 'he'll be sorry if I get hurt or die. He'll weep over my pale body and declare his undying love.' Is that what you thought?"

No! Marianne protested, even knowing that Nora couldn't hear her. Even as she said it, though, she wondered whether it was true. A similar thought *had* crossed her mind, perhaps causing her to drive a little more recklessly than usual. She sighed; her sister knew her well. *I'm sorry.*

Almost as if she could hear her, Nora spoke again. "You didn't think of how it would be for *us*, though, for Mum and me and Maggie, seeing you like this. When Brandon called… We thought you were going to die." A sob hitched her breath.

I am so sorry. Marianne wished that she could reach out and hold her or at least see her face. *Wait, "when Brandon called"? What had Brandon to do with this?*

"The doctors say you are in a coma and they cannot tell how badly you are hurt until you wake up. You *must* wake up, Marianne. *You must.* You know Mum and I will drive each other mad without you, and Maggie needs someone to giggle over boys with, and you know I don't giggle well. Your piano will be sad and dusty without you to play it, and…" As her words trailed off, Marianne could tell she was crying. "I need you to wake up."

I will, Marianne silently vowed.

"Ah God, I'm sorry. I should not have said all that. It's just…I love you, Marianne, and John Willoughby is not a man worth dying for."

If Marianne thought too much about John, she would lose it, so she pushed him out of her head. Her broken heart would have to wait.

Day 2

PEOPLE CAME AND WENT: DOCTORS, FAMILY, FRIENDS, COWORKERS, AND neighbors. Mum, Nora, and Maggie stayed most of the day. Trying to listen to so many voices was exhausting, so Marianne allowed herself to drift between bouts of fighting to wake up. Time seemed to pass differently while she drifted, dreamlike. She was so tired; it would be easy to drown.

No. I will not give up. I will not sink.

BRANDON SCRAPED HIS HAND OVER TWO DAYS' GROWTH OF BEARD. HE couldn't close his eyes without seeing Marianne. He saw her in her car, her body as limp as a doll's. He saw her being loaded into the ambulance with a collar around her neck and a mask covering her beautiful face. He wanted to kill John Willoughby. None of this would have happened if not for him.

Come on, Mari. Wake up. She'd come through the surgery, and the docs had stitched her poor skin back together where she'd been cut by the glass. One hundred fifty stitches in her soft skin. It hurt just to think about it.

"Brandon, you should go home. Get some sleep." Nora squeezed his shoulder. "You've done enough. I will call as soon as I have any news."

Brandon wanted to stay with every fiber of his being, but it was not his place. Marianne did not belong to him no matter how much he might wish otherwise. "As soon as you have news. I don't care what time of night, all right?"

Nora agreed, and after a final glance at the door separating him from Marianne, he left.

Day 3

TEARS FELL THROUGH THE CURTAIN, WET AND WARM UPON HER FACE. *I can feel that.* Marianne stilled, listening. *Who's there?*

"Hello, Mari. The doctors say that hearing familiar voices might help you wake up, so I brought you a book." Maggie sounded so young, so scared. "It's one of your favorites." There was a soft choking sound, a sob half-stifled. "You keep telling me I have to read it, so here it goes. 'There was no possibility of taking a walk that day. We had been wandering…'" At first her voice was hesitating and broken, making Marianne wish she could hold her, but gradually it strengthened. It became an anchor that Marianne clung to.

Day 4

GRADUALLY, MARIANNE LEARNED TO TREAD WATER. IT BECAME EASIER TO focus on her surroundings though it still took some effort. She wondered whether this was what a blind person with bad hearing felt like. It was difficult to tell how much time passed, but she knew when it was night because of the silence—seemingly endless hours of silence that made her curse hospital visiting hours. The arrival of her first visitor in the morning would have made her cry in relief if she had been physically capable of it—at least, until she realized whom her first visitor was.

"I know you would rather someone else be here." Colonel Brandon Delaford had a lovely, deep voice, but it was not the one she wished to hear. "Nora would have come, but her arsehole boss would not allow her to take any more time off. She will come in the evening. Your mum and Maggie will be by later, as well. They've decided you are not to be left alone."

Marianne gave a surprised laugh that, of course, did not escape her stubbornly unmoving lips. She did not think Brandon was capable of such language; in the time she had known him, she had never heard him use a harsher word than 'drat.' Perhaps he wasn't as dry a stick as she had thought. It was sweet of him to come after all.

"You've got them all terrified, you know, so you had better wake up soon." His tone was the same as if he was speaking of the weather rather than her life and her family's happiness.

That was Brandon in a nutshell: practical and unemotional. It was no wonder he and Nora were such good friends. He wanted her to wake up because, if she did not, his orderly world would be disrupted. She sighed; that was unfair. She did not actually know the man very well.

"Maggie told me she has been reading *Jane Eyre* to you. I do not think I have any books that you would care for, but I got the impression from your family that it is the sound of voices, not the words, that are beneficial, so I brought a mystery I picked up the other day."

God, Marianne despised mysteries. They were so contrived and formulaic with no depth or substance. If she had to listen to one, she would have to wake up quickly indeed or risk going mad. Brandon, of course, did not hear her protestations and began to read.

Brandon looked away as the doctor examined his scarred, crooked leg. His mind wandered back to the morning and how Marianne had looked. Her wounds were already starting to heal, the swelling was down, and the bruises were turning green. And yet still she slept. The doctors said that it was just a matter of waiting. Her brain needed time to heal. There was no way to know whether or when she would open her eyes.

"Colonel Delaford." The doctor's impatience said that it had not been the first time he said his name.

"Yes?"

"It looks like your previous surgeries have healed with no complications. The swelling in your hip has gone down to the point where we can now safely remove the final remaining piece of shrapnel. You were scheduled to have it removed last week but you canceled. Would you care to reschedule?"

"Not yet."

"Sir, you need this surgery. The longer you wait, the more permanent the damage could be. You may end up using that cane for the rest of your life. Or worse."

Brandon glared at him.

"Look, we had a cancellation, so I can get you in the day after Christmas. That way you can enjoy the holiday with your family. Just don't eat anything after 4:00 p.m."

Day 9

The days passed thusly: Brandon visiting her in the mornings, Mum and Maggie in the afternoons, and Nora in the evenings. Jane Eyre's romance came to a conclusion and Tess of the D'Urbervilles' began. Maggie was a vivid reader, often driving Marianne to sighs or tears. Not that Maggie ever noticed.

Nora would tell her about her day at work, describing her conversations and naming each person she met. Ward's name was often among them. Given that they both worked at the same shop, this was no great surprise, but there was something in her voice when she spoke of him that Marianne had never noticed before. She wondered whether her sister felt more deeply than she had previously suspected.

Mum's visits were the hardest. It was okay when she came with Maggie; she would sit and listen to the story, sometimes clicking away with her knitting, making occasional comments. When she came alone though, she just took Marianne's hands and cried as if she was already mourning.

Strangely, Marianne came to anticipate Brandon's visits the most. He was a slow reader, but there was something very comforting about his voice. Against her will, she found herself drawn into his mystery novel. When the villain was finally revealed and hauled away in bracelets, she would have cheered if she could. Perhaps mysteries were not so bad.

It was still early when Brandon finished the novel. Marianne expected him to leave, and she was startled when he took her hand. *What are you doing?*

"It is Christmas Eve, Mari."

Has it really been so long? And since when do you call me 'Mari'?

"I got you a gift. I meant to give it to you at the party, but... Your family will be here all day tomorrow, so I won't be here. I hope you like it when... when you wake up." Gentle hands lifted her head and she found herself resting against a warm, male chest, her ear pressed to his beating heart.

What are you doing? She figured it out a moment later when she felt a leather thong slip around her neck. He was putting a necklace on her as if she were a child...or a lover.

"I got it in Africa during my last deployment. It's an *adinkra* symbol. An Asante man showed them to me and explained their different meanings. This one is called *odo nnyew fie kwan*, which means 'love never loses its way home.' It saw me home, and I hope it will do the same for you." Lips caressed her forehead in the softest kiss she had ever felt as he eased her back against the pillows. "Wake up soon, Marianne Dashwood. The world is a darker place without you."

Marianne was stunned. For the first time, she was glad she could not speak because she could not think of a word to say. Her first thought, when rational thought finally returned, was to wonder what it might feel like if Brandon were to kiss her properly.

"Hello, Marianne."

All thoughts of Brandon's unexpected romantic side vanished at the sound of John's voice.

"This is all my fault." His voice was choked, even a little slurred. "I did this to you." Hands clutched her fingers too hard. "I'm so sorry, so very, very sorry." Big, wet tears landed on her palm as he kissed her hand over and over. "I know you probably cannot hear me"—*You'd be surprised*—"but I have to explain."

Marianne's heart leapt. It had all been a terrible misunderstanding. He wasn't engaged; it was a trauma-induced nightmare—something, *anything*.

"I do not love Sophia. I love *you*."

Marianne could have wept. These were exactly the words she wanted to hear—the words she had been secretly yearning to hear every time a new voice engaged her in one-sided conversation.

"But I have to marry her."

What?

"Her father is a senior partner at my firm. Marriage to her gives me everything I ever wanted."

Everything except for love—except for me.

"I never meant to become so involved with you. It was selfish of me, but I swear, my intentions were honorable. I thought we could only be friends."

Then why did you ever touch me—ever kiss me? Marianne felt as if her heart was breaking again before it even had a chance to heal. *If your intentions were honorable, why did you not tell me about your fiancée before I fell in love with you—before you said you loved me?*

"Then I fell in love with you, and I thought that I could give her up, but…I have debts. Big ones. I don't have a choice, Marianne! I swear; if there was any other way, I would take it!"

You bastard. Marianne wept silently, invisibly.

"I'm sorry, I'm so sorry." He sobbed the words over and over again until they lost all meaning. If they ever had any to begin with.

"What the bloody hell are you doing here?" Brandon's voice was a deep roar of barely leashed fury. "You need to leave now. How did you get in here? The nurses were told to keep you out."

"I slipped past them. I just… I had to see her." His sobs turned into less-than-dignified hiccups.

Disgust colored Brandon's tone. "You're completely pissed, aren't you? It's not even noon!"

"I had to see her. I had"—*hiccup*—"had to see her. Had to say I was sorry."

"Well you have. Now, get out."

There was a brief scuffling sound that gave Marianne the impression that Brandon was forcibly removing John from the room.

"I am sorry about that, Marianne." The anger was gone, leaving only weariness behind. "If your mum hadn't rung saying she was going to be late, I wouldn't have even realized he was here. It seems that I do not want you left alone any more than your family does, so here I am."

I do not like being alone.

Brandon sat and spoke of ordinary nothings: his childhood, his time in the army. He had served in both Sierra Leone and, more recently, Kenya, helping train the local military to disarm mines. Listening to his voice slowly calmed Marianne until her mind lay nearly as quietly as her body. With this quiet came a sense of clarity.

She was not as broken as she thought she was. Her heart hurt, but it was not the horrible, slicing pain of before. It was more of an ache now. Hearing John explain himself was awful, knowing now that he had loved her but had thrown that love away. However, it also made it clear he was not the man she thought he was. Perhaps she had judged poorly, or he had hidden it well. All his poetry, his roses, his talk of romance—it was all empty because, in his heart, he cared about himself more than any other.

Day 10

CHRISTMAS WAS A SURPRISINGLY HAPPY AFFAIR. HER FAMILY GATHERED around, full of holiday cheer that rang true to Marianne's sensitive ears though occasionally tainted with melancholy. They never left her side for the whole day, instead choosing to bring a proper Christmas dinner with them, filling the room with the aroma of lamb, gravy, plum pudding, and savory herbs. For the first time since the crash, Marianne felt a pang of hunger.

Lovely as it was to have her family around, it niggled at the back of her mind that something was missing. That evening, as Nora, Maggie, and Mum each took turns kissing her goodbye, she realized the *something* was actually a *someone*: Brandon Delaford. Her day did not seem quite complete without his visit.

BRANDON SAT ALONE, WATCHING THE SNOWFLAKES FALL OUTSIDE HIS window. The Dashwoods had invited him to their improvised feast at the hospital, but he didn't dare go and then try to explain why he couldn't eat anything. They would all fuss and worry, and he didn't want Marianne to hear it, not when he didn't know how much she understood. He simply told Nora he would be away for a few days. She was surprised, but didn't ask too many questions. He liked that about Nora.

"I'll be back soon, Marianne," he said into the silence. "It would be nice if you could wake up before I return so you'll be there waiting for me. Consider it a Christmas wish."

Day 11

MARIANNE FELT A FLASH OF REGRET WHEN HER FIRST VISITOR OF THE DAY was Nora rather than Brandon. She shrugged it off; perhaps he was coming in the afternoon today.

"Oh, Mari, you will not believe the news!" Nora paced back and forth, her steps agitated. "Lucy has thrown Ward over for his best friend, Robert, and the two of them are getting a flat in London together. How could she do something so cruel?"

Because she has the emotional capacity of a peahen?

"How could she betray someone so kind, so honorable as Ward? Plus, he is far better looking than Robert. His nose is too big, and his eyes are too close together."

Marianne could not stop laughing. This was a side of her sister she had never seen before and probably never would have if Nora knew that she could actually hear her. While her face betrayed no signs of mirth, her consciousness was chortling.

"And Robert belches. I have never heard Ward belch, have you?"

Marianne lost it.

Nora continued on in this vein for several minutes, compounding Lucy's idiocy, Robert's shortcomings, and Ward's godlike characteristics. Finally, she wound down and sighed. "I've been ranting for a good half hour, haven't I?"

Yes, Marianne replied, still giggling.

"I never do that. I never let my feelings get the better of me." She sounded forlorn.

You should do it more often. Marianne considered that her sister's constant insistence on logic and rationality in all things had always struck her as decidedly peculiar. After all, what was the point in living if you didn't *live*? Now, however, upon seeing her sister so undone, she began to wonder whether Nora had ever truly been as cold as she appeared.

"Perhaps I should do that more often."

Marianne froze, her mirth vanishing in a moment. *Did you hear me?*

"Sometimes I wish I was more like you and Mum. You seem so fearless and willing to express your feelings. I've always been stuck as the quiet, reliable one. I'm the oldest, after all. It's my job to keep you all safe." She sighed. "I'm not even very good at that, though, am I?"

Oh, Nora. This was not your fault. I was stupid and dramatic like a child. Right now, I wish I were more like you.

Nora squeezed her hand tightly but said nothing, leaving Marianne to wonder whether her sister was perhaps catching a hint of her thoughts.

Day 12

MORNINGS WERE VERY DULL WITHOUT BRANDON DELAFORD AND HIS mystery novels. Marianne was determined to give him a stern talking-to when he showed up tomorrow. He had *better* show up tomorrow.

Day 13

MARIANNE HAD AN UNEXPECTED GUEST THAT MORNING. INSTEAD OF Brandon, it was Ward Ferrars, moronic heartbreaker extraordinaire.

"Hullo, Marianne."

She imagined him wringing his hands and looking everywhere but her face. That was probably unfair and inaccurate, but she liked the image.

"I have come to ask for your blessing."

If Marianne's jaw could have dropped all the way to her ankles, it would have. *My WHAT?*

"I want to ask your sister out. I've wanted to for awhile, actually, but… Well, you know about Lucy."

Yes, what about Lucy? She dumps you and you decide you need a replacement two days later?

"What you don't know is that things have been difficult between Lucy and me for a long time now. I wanted to leave her, but every time I even hinted at it, she started to cry. She said I had made her promises, you see, and it was true. I loved her once, and I thought we would be together forever. I don't break my promises, Marianne." Her imagination plus a soft rustle of cloth added up to a helpless shrug.

Marianne decided that he was honorable in a thick-as-a-post sort of way. She wasn't sure whether she wanted her sister with someone so dense though. *You do realize Lucy was manipulating you, right?* She thought the answer to that question was likely "no."

"I just wanted you to know that I do care about Nora, and I will do my best not to hurt her."

What a lukewarm declaration. Perhaps he and Nora were perfect for each other. Her sense of fairness reasserted itself. If she had been wrong about the depths of Nora's feelings, perhaps she was wrong about Ward as well. If this coma had taught her anything, it was that she did not know the people close to her as well as she had thought. *Very well, you may ask her out. It had better be a lovely evening with flowers and wine and everything though, or you shall hear about it when I wake up. Oh, and chocolates. Nora loves chocolates.*

He seemed to take her silence as an adequate response and, after a few more assurances of his intentions, departed.

Brandon did not show up.

Day 14

SHE WAS GOING TO KILL HIM JUST AS SOON AS SHE GOT OUT OF BED. SHE thought for a moment that she managed to make her toe twitch; murder was a great motivator.

Day 15

MARIANNE WAS FUMING QUIETLY TO HERSELF WHEN SHE BECAME AWARE of a loud, thunking noise preceding a presence in the room—a strong, warm presence that smelled of sage, coffee, and soap. She sighed with relief. *Where on earth have you been?*

"I am sorry I have not visited in so long." He sounded a little haggard. There were a few more loud thunks and Marianne puzzled over the sound. It was only when she heard an awkward scrape and a hiss of breath being let out slowly as Brandon sat down that she figured it out. He was using crutches. *What happened?* She cursed the fact that she was unable to open her eyes and see for herself that he was well.

"I suppose I ought to have told you, but if you do truly hear what we say, I did not want you to fret. I had to have another surgery on my hip. It's been in the books for a while now, but I was putting it off until I knew whether you were going to get better. I would have put it off longer, but the docs told me that the longer I waited, the worse it would get."

Why did you have to have surgery? Marianne realized that she did not even know how his hip was originally damaged, much less what might be wrong with it now. She decided to ask him about it as soon as she could get her tongue to work.

"There were a couple of little problems, but nothing too serious. Just enough to keep me in the hospital for a couple of nights while they 'observed.' I'm able to move about a bit now though. The docs do not really want me using the crutches yet, but I won't tell if you don't."

What "little problems"? Her fingers itched to reach out and grab his hand, to reassure herself that he was truly well.

"Mari?" Excitement brightened his voice. "Did you just move your hand?" His hand was shaking when he grasped her wrist, holding it so the tips of her fingers rested on his racing pulse. "Can you do that again? Please, love, give me something." He called for a nurse and told her what he thought he saw, never letting go of Marianne's hand.

She tried to do it again, to clasp his wrist as he did hers, but it was to no avail. Still, she felt a new sense of hope.

After the nurse had declared everything normal and gone, Brandon leaned in close and whispered in Marianne's ear. "Soon, love, I am going to kiss you properly." He kissed each of her knuckles before thunking his way out of the room, leaving Marianne to consider whether or not she approved of his kisses or calling her "love."

IN THE WAITING ROOM, BRANDON SAT DOWN HEAVILY IN A PEA GREEN chair that had lost most of its stuffing. His heart was beating so fast he could hardly breathe. She moved! He knew she did. The nurse said that he probably imagined it, but he knew he hadn't. *Come on, baby, you can do it. Wake up!*

Day 16
BRANDON MUST HAVE TOLD HER FAMILY WHAT HAPPENED; THEY HOVERED over her every minute of the day afterwards. She could practically feel their eyes boring holes into her face and hands. Marianne could have told them it was no use; she was trying harder than ever before, and nothing was

happening. For the first time, she was looking forward to the end of visiting hours. Anything to stop them staring at her.

When it finally came time for them to go, however, she felt an inexplicable pang of sadness as if this was the last time she would see them in a long time. They each kissed her, wished her a happy New Year, and filed out. Once they were gone, she was shocked to feel a single, impossible tear slide down her cheek. *What is wrong with me? I wanted them to go.*

The silence pressed on her, suffocating her. There was an itching that started in her bones and spread outward over her skin. She couldn't tell whether she was waking up or dying.

Thunk, *thunk.* Thunk, *thunk.*

Her breath caught at the sound. She had thought that he wasn't coming today, and while she didn't blame him this time, she had been disappointed. *Hello, Brandon.*

"Hullo, Marianne." He spoke softly. "I know visiting hours are over, but I slipped past the nurses. Security here really is rubbish. What kind of hospital lets a drunk sneak in one day and a cripple the next?" He sighed. "You've been asleep too long, Mari."

Not for much longer. Marianne wasn't sure how she knew this, but she did. She would not be trapped in limbo much longer—neither awake nor asleep. *At least I won't be alone.*

"It is almost the New Year. That would be a good time to wake up, wouldn't it? It would be quite dramatic. Everyone would talk about it for ages. You would like that, wouldn't you?" He sounded desperate now, his fingers digging into her hands. "Wake up! Please." His voice dropped so she could scarcely hear it. "Wake up."

She tried, harder than she had ever tried before. *I'm sorry.*

He sat back in his chair, his hand relaxing its grip but not releasing hers. "Do you remember the first time we met?"

No. How could she not remember the day she met one of the most important persons in her life? And when did Brandon become one of the most important persons in her life?

"It was two years ago today. We were at the Middleton's New Year's party. You know how Thom and Sarah love to party. I'd been back from Afghanistan for five months. I was sitting in the corner, my back to the wall and eyes on the door because I was still such a messed up, paranoid bastard then.

Anyway, I was sitting there, slowly losing my mind because there were so many people and so much noise, when you walked in the door. Suddenly, everything went quiet. You were wearing a green velvet dress straight out of the forties and a string of pearls. You looked like you had stepped out of a silent film. I stared at you all night, and you never noticed. You were everybody's friend, the center of attention wherever you went. I wanted to talk to you, but what interest could a girl like you have in a broken, old soldier like me? There you were, twenty-one and carefree as a daisy. I was thirty-four and felt far older."

Thirty-four isn't old. Even as she protested, Marianne felt a surge of shame. She had called Brandon old before: old, dull, and unromantic. How wrong she had been on all accounts.

"I was deployed twice to Afghanistan, where I saw too much pain and death. Kenya was supposed to be easy in comparison. It would have been if not for one, tiny error. Do you remember the Asante man I told you about? The one who showed me *adinkra* symbols? Komi is only half Asante. His father was Kenyan. He joined the military when he was fifteen, only four years earlier. I was training him and his dog to detect and disarm landmines. When villagers found a mine about ten clicks from the base, I thought he was finally ready to face live explosives. He was doing a great job, but the thing had a defective trigger. I realized it was about to blow up in his face and jumped on him. Woke up a week later with shrapnel in my hip, side, and leg and that necklace tied to my hospital bed. They said I called your name when they brought me in, and he thought it would bring me back to you. It did, but not the way I wanted. I was crippled. Still am. You love to dance, and I'll never manage more than a slow waltz. Even so…I cannot help but dream of you."

I wonder sometimes whether I am dreaming all of this: you, my family, every-thing. I hope not. I hope it is real. I hope that I wake up and remember every moment, every word.

"You must wake up, Marianne Dashwood. I do not care if you love me back; I do not care if you heard every word I said to you or none of them. I only care that you wake." His hands caressed her face, cupping her cheeks, his work-roughened thumbs gently scraping her skin. He kissed her forehead.

"Why don't you ever kiss me properly?" Marianne complained, her voice rough and scratchy.

Brandon jerked back, startled to see blue eyes squinting blearily up at him. "Because a gentleman does not kiss a lady without permission."

"Well, you have it. Now hurry up and kiss me. It *is* traditional to ring in the New—" Marianne could not complete her sentence before his mouth was on hers. This was no chaste fare-thee-well press of lips and skin. This was fire and champagne and cannon fire. Wait! The booms of cannon fire were real, echoing in the distance, heralding the beginning of the New Year. Brandon was right; this would be a marvelous story to tell one day.

Marianne became aware of a hundred aches and pains that the honey-velvet sea had kept her from feeling, but she didn't care. She welcomed them because they meant that she was awake and alive and in the arms of a man she could really love.

Day 365

The Middleton Christmas party was in full swing. Half of Devonshire was attending, all in their best Christmas finery. Marianne looked ruefully down at her own festive, reindeer-pocked jumper, drinking thick, homemade eggnog that had been spiked by no less than—

"Brandon Christopher Delaford, what do you think you are doing?"

Brandon stuck his hands behind his back and straightened, smiling at her as if butter wouldn't melt in his mouth. "Nothing, love."

"Really." She moved in close, putting her hands on his shoulders, tilting her neck to look up at him through her lashes. It was a very becoming pose, and she knew it. "Now, why don't I believe that?"

"I'm sure I have no idea." Just as she knew he would, he swooped in for a kiss. She melted into him, savoring every second—even as her hands slipped lower until she snatched away the brandy he was hiding.

"You ought to be ashamed of yourself," she informed him. "The eggnog is already practically toxic, and my little sister is well on her way to becoming completely besotted."

Brandon grinned at her. "I am not going to spike it, I promise."

Marianne raised an eyebrow.

"You are."

"Me? I think not."

"Yes. You, Marianne Rose Dashwood soon-to-be Delaford, are going to pour *that* whole bottle of brandy into *that* bowl of eggnog." He pointed first at the brandy and then at the bowl to emphasize the seriousness of his intentions.

That "whole bottle of brandy" had barely an ounce of liquor in it, but it was the principle of the thing. "Make me," she said with a dazzling smile then turned and ran.

Brandon stared after his fiancée as she dashed, giggling like a madwoman, through the crowd of revelers. He saw Nora roll her eyes at her little sister then turn to laugh at something Ward said. Someone struck up some Yank Christmas song on the piano that Brandon had never heard before. No one seemed to know the words, but that didn't stop them from singing along. Clara's trembling soprano particularly stood out. Maggie was sitting by the fire, her face flushed with happiness and a touch of particularly powerful eggnog. From the other end of the room, Marianne blew him a kiss over her shoulder and cast a *very* obvious glance upward at the mistletoe hanging over her head.

She hadn't told him she loved him for months after she woke up from the coma that brought her to him and almost took her away; she had wanted to be sure it was real, to know that it was forever, and not just a dream invented by her bruised mind. He understood; she did not trust herself after what happened with John. He did not mind waiting; he had enjoyed their courtship. Not a single moment was wasted if it was spent winning her. Now, not a day passed that she didn't speak the words.

"I love you," he whispered in her ear.

"Then kiss me. Properly."

* *

NATALIE RICHARDS is a writer, blogger, and singer. She started her book review blog, Songs & Stories, in late 2010 after falling in love with Jane Austen fanfiction. Her writing can also be found on Figment, the Darcy & Lizzy Forum, TeenInk Magazine, and the *Sun-Kissed: Effusions of Summer* anthology. She resides with her family in the Oregon countryside and currently works as a waitress.

"The key to a woman's heart is an unexpected gift at
an unexpected time." —Finding Forrester

The Unexpected Gift

by Erin Lopez

The door to Doyle's Millinery swung closed behind Fitzwilliam Darcy, and with it, the howl of the snowy wind softened. The shop was unusually quiet and lacked patrons—not surprising since it was almost evening and most families had already left for the country. Still, he had expected to see a few shoppers about this close to Christmas. There was still plenty of time to buy gifts and then leave Town before the week was up.

Darcy eyed the store. Ribbons and fabric hung from one wall while another was lined with drawers for buttons, bobbles, and who knows what else. A table of patterns sat close to one of the walls with just enough room to squeeze behind it and open a drawer. Shelves of accessories were also placed about so as not to obstruct door opening or fabric viewing. Everything was exactly as he remembered it, except there were no Doyles.

He pulled out his pocket watch. It was later than he realized but not too late for them to be closed, surely.

"Mr. Darcy!" Mrs. Doyle said, a bit out of breath, after coming around the corner. "We were just about to close for the night, sir."

"This won't take long." He reached back into his jacket to replace the watch and grab a piece of paper.

"I hope you had not planned to present a new dress to Miss Darcy this

90

Christmas. You may, of course, look over the patterns and fabrics, and I will have the girls start, but I fear it won't be ready until the New Year."

"No, I am not here to buy a new dress for Georgiana. She needs some hair ribbons." Darcy handed the paper to Mrs. Doyle. "Here—she has written the width, color, and length."

"Very good, sir." Mrs. Doyle pulled the spectacles off her head to inspect the note. "Mmm. This is quite popular this season. I do believe Miss Darcy bought this color the last time she was here. Unfortunately, I sold the last of it this afternoon. We have some in similar shades if you would like to inspect them."

Darcy grimaced as this was supposed to be a quick errand. "I would rather not without Georgiana here."

"Very well." She refolded the note. "There is a chance we have some in the back. I told Mr. Doyle to place an order for this particular color last week, and the shipment arrived only an hour ago. I cannot promise it is in there, but if you do not mind waiting, we might be in luck."

Darcy looked out the window. Dusk was fully settled now, and he needed to be home to prepare for a family dinner at the Matlock's townhome. However, Georgiana told him she wanted the ribbon for tonight. She so rarely asked for anything, especially after last summer. He might instruct Mrs. Doyle to set some aside for her to fetch later. Georgiana would not fuss. She never fussed, even when George Wickham—well, it was best not to ponder on that. He turned back to Mrs. Doyle. "I will wait."

"Very good, sir." She bobbed a curtsy, and then she was gone around the corner, calling out for her husband's assistance.

Darcy walked around the store, wandering between the shelves and cases and not really looking at anything as his gifts for Georgiana were already wrapped and packed for the journey to Pemberley. Besides, he could not imagine one thing more she needed or desired.

He was making his way around a display when a small sparkle caught his eye. There, at the very edge of the shelf, was a small bundle of decorative hairpins, each one adorned with white roses and jewels lining the ends.

A sudden vision of a dark-haired woman came to his mind, her hair swept up and refined. Except he knew that, once down, it would be an unruly, beautiful tumble of curls. After all, there was always that one curl at the nape of her neck that never could be contained. How many times had he longed to reach out for it only to feel its silkiness between his fingers?

He straightened his back and pulled at the edge of his coat. It had been weeks since he had seen her—almost a month now. Whatever infatuation he still held for her must be swept away. There had always been pretty faces, fine eyes, witty smiles, and dark-haired temptresses over the years, and each had been dismissed once he determined they were not worthy. None lingered or showed themselves during the oddest of moments, so why must her face and form still plague him?

He picked up the pins and ran his fingers along the delicate craftsmanship. She was the one woman he could not have. Was it any wonder he still thought of her? It is a truth universal that men desire most what is unattainable. Her inferior connections and lack of fortune made the match impossible. It did not matter that his pulse quickened whenever he looked at her or he wondered about her in his moments alone or took such great pleasure in being in her presence. None of that mattered because he simply could not pursue her.

Yet...her fine eyes, impertinent smile, and light, pleasing form continued to creep into the edges of his consciousness time and again. Now it was her hair, or rather the memory of it, that brought him back.

It was her hair after all that first caught his attention at Netherfield. The exertion of walking three miles the day after a rainstorm made her pull off her bonnet, and thus, her hair was windblown and half-wild by the time he saw her. That made it all the easier to imagine those dark locks in a more intimate manner. Her dress and petticoat were spattered with mud, but he had not noticed. His heart had been too full—and how he had longed to follow her to her sister's room! It was the first true fantasy he had of her, one that would not escape his mind until she returned to Longbourn.

"Mr. Darcy, sir." Mrs. Doyle's voice brought him back, and he made his way to the front of the store. "Terribly sorry it took so long. However, I did manage to find it." She pulled the ribbon from its spindle and held it out for him to inspect. "Unfortunately," she said, "it is not the same dye lot as the one your sister bought last week, so the color will not match exactly. Would you still like to purchase it?"

"Yes." Darcy's voice sounded gruffer than usual, and he pushed the ribbon into Mrs. Doyle's hand. "If you will wrap it up for me?"

"Of course, sir." Mrs. Doyle then busied herself with the cutting and wrapping while Darcy looked about, doing his best to put the dark-haired woman out of his mind.

DESPITE THE SNOW, DARCY'S CARRIAGE MADE GOOD TIME, AND SOON HE was home. After a brief inquiry of Georgiana's whereabouts, he set off for the music room.

Notes were heard in the hall before he arrived at the door, and Darcy smiled when he recognized the lively piece Georgiana was attempting on the pianoforte. The last few months, her music choices had turned melancholy, but recently she seemed determined to learn merrier tunes. It was a comforting change. Perhaps, given a few more months, she may return to her old self with any remnants of that debacle in Ramsgate completely behind her.

He opened the door softly so as not to disturb her. However, as soon as she saw his face, she smiled and rose to greet him. "I had begun to worry about you." She flung her arms around him and the scent of lilacs flooded the air. "Are we still for Uncle James's tonight? It is beginning to look frightful out there!"

"It is not so bad, but we may leave early if it worsens. Our relations would be distraught if they did not see us before we left for Pemberley. Aunt Isabelle has been hinting for weeks now that she has a surprise for you, and I dare not bring her wrath upon me over a few snowflakes."

Georgiana giggled. "She could never be angry at you. No one could. You are much too kind and thoughtful."

Darcy grinned. Only his sister would think so. "Speaking of dinner tonight," he said as he pulled out the wrapped ribbons from his pocket, "Mrs. Doyle had to search the storeroom for these—a sure sign the color will be popular this season."

"Oh, thank you, Fitzwilliam!" Georgiana threw her arms around him again. In many ways, she was still a young girl, no matter how grown she appeared. "I know it's a small request and what goes in my hair does not matter to you, but they match my dress so perfectly for tonight, and I ran out when I finished my bonnet. They just—oh!"

"What is it?" Darcy asked and peered over her shoulder. The package was completely unwrapped as well as the ribbons, but still he could not see what was in her hand. "Is it the wrong color? I handed your instructions to Mrs. Doyle directly."

"No, no. It is not that. I—I believe you meant to have these wrapped separately. I am sorry. I happened upon my Christmas present early." She turned and held her hand out to him. Color crept into his face when he saw the same hairpins that caught his attention at the shop.

"No matter," he said and smiled to hide his embarrassment. "You will have other surprises next week. Tell me, do you like them?"

"Oh!" Georgiana looked at them again and shifted her weight from one foot to the next. "Well…yes. They are…nice."

"Nice? Only nice?"

"I mean, they are lovely. Thank you, Fitzwilliam." She smiled but he could detect the disappointment in her eyes.

"If you do not like them, Georgiana, I will not be offended."

"It is just…that they do not seem to suit me. That is all. I mean, they are beautiful, but since I am not yet out for another year, they are a bit too bold…for now. But I am certain by next Christmas I shall feel differently."

Darcy plucked one from her hand and twirled it around between his thumb and finger. She was right. The coloring and style did not match Georgiana's fair features or even her personality. Even by next year when she could wear bolder colors, these pins would not suit her. He put the pin back. "The truth is"—he rubbed his hand over the back of his neck—"these pins were not meant for you. I did not intend to buy them and handed them to Mrs. Doyle by mistake."

Georgiana pressed her lips together. "Oh," she said and then looked up at him through her lashes, "May I ask for whom these are intended?"

"Pardon?"

"You said you did not pick these for me. Then who?"

Darcy moved to examine the fireplace mantle.

"Well, you could not have bought them for Aunt Isabelle since I helped you select gloves for her. Did— Are they for Cousin Anne?"

"It does not matter. As I said, I bought them by mistake. I shall return them tomorrow."

"No, they certainly are not for Anne." Darcy turned towards her and watched as she examined the pins. "Aunt Catherine would never allow her to wear anything so beautiful."

"Now they are beautiful? Just moments ago they were simply 'nice.'"

"But they *are* beautiful. You do have a good taste. The one for whom you intended these probably fits them perfectly. I would imagine she has dark hair."

Darcy struggled to keep his face steady. "And how would you guess that?"

"Because the gems clash with my hair. I am correct, am I not? Do I know her?"

"No, you do not. I—" Darcy saw the hint of smile on Georgiana's face. "You are being impertinent, Georgiana. Give them back to me."

Georgiana put her hands behind her back. "Have you known her long? Does she play and sing? I take it that she has beautiful hair. Will you introduce me to her?"

"Georgiana." Darcy walked to her and held out his hand. "The pins, please."

"Not until you answer my questions." She giggled and stepped away from him.

"Yes, she has lovely hair. Now hand them over."

She shook her head. "I have one more question. Answer truthfully and I shall give them back."

"Fine."

"Do you love her?"

Darcy froze. *Love her?* "I…" He shook his head and sighed. "A connection between us is impossible."

"Oh, I…I see." Georgiana brought her hands back to her front. "When is she to be married, or has it happened already?"

"No, it is nothing like that." At Georgiana's questioning look, he knew he must continue. "When last I saw her she was very much unattached. Our connection—? It is a *peculiar* connection."

"But…how? You must love her a great deal if you unwittingly bought her a present!"

"I will likely never see her again, so it does not signify."

"But…" Georgiana looked at the pins again. "Do you miss her?"

Darcy nodded. "At times. Her conversations in particular were quite… diverting."

"You must have spent a great deal of time in her company."

"Nothing remarkable. Although, she did stay three days at Netherfield when her sister was taken ill. And now, I have answered enough of your questions. Give me back the pins so I may have them returned."

Georgiana's head snapped up. "But you cannot! Whether you meant to or not, you bought these with her in mind. You must find a way to give them to her."

"Impossible!"

"But you were thinking of her! Does that not signify…something?" Georgiana seemed close to tears, and she wrapped her fingers around the pins and held them close to her heart.

A pain in Darcy's chest erupted. Georgiana had gone through so much these last six months. He assumed this outburst must have more to do with *her* heartache than his own. He sighed. "Just because a man thinks about a lady does not mean he can or should act upon it. Love is not the only concern in these matters. There are others that must be weighed."

"Like…like money and status." She was looking at the ground now while tears ran down her cheeks. "Is that all men think about? Is there no true love in this world that is not tainted?"

Darcy walked to her and drew her into an embrace. "Love takes many different forms and paths, Georgiana. Our parents, for example, made a practical match, but later, anyone who saw them together knew how much they loved one another."

"Do you not wish for that, Fitzwilliam? To find love like theirs?"

"Yes, very much so, but the practical reasons must be considered. I have a duty to you—to Pemberley—to make a good choice in a wife. Love cannot be the only factor in such a decision."

"But what of your happiness? Do you not have a right to choose someone who would make you happy regardless of money or family?" She pushed against him with the fist that held the pins. "Is she so unsuitable that her role as mistress over everything you hold dear would ruin you forever?"

Darcy looked down at her fist as it started to uncurl, and he saw the little white flowers on the pins. Elizabeth Bennet was intelligent, and she would ably fulfill any role he needed. She was a treasure hidden away, but how could he explain that to the rest of his family and friends? Society would never understand and would look on her with scorn. Could he willingly subject her to such scrutiny?

"These pins," he finally said after finding his voice again, "would be better off returned."

Georgiana pulled them close to her and nodded. "Allow me to return them. I still have some shopping of my own. It will be no trouble, and I know you have much to do before we leave."

He kissed the top of her head. "Thank you, dearest." He gave her one last hug. "We had better go up and ready ourselves for dinner. We are already late."

"That will be all, Claire," said Georgiana. She watched her maid in the mirror as she curtsied and left for the dressing room. It was still early since the snowstorm did, in fact, prevent them from staying longer at the Matlock's.

Georgiana sat down on her bed and opened her book. Instead of reading, she stared at the pins on her dresser.

How had she not suspected her brother was in love? It would explain his odd behavior of late! It was a subtle change—one that even went unnoticed by their closest cousin Richard Fitzwilliam. She had attributed his curious manner to disappointment in her. How could he not be? She had been such a fool last summer.

She counted the weeks back. Yes, it was definitely upon his return from Netherfield that she noticed his restlessness and strange mien. Now she knew his heart had been touched by some lady. He had not said a word, but there was no need. His face was one she wore in her heart.

She would never tell her brother this, but she still harbored affection for Wickham—not the all-encompassing love she felt for him during the summer. No, that passion was gone, but the pain she felt when she still thought of him or heard his name meant he was not entirely forgotten. All those months ago, she was sure Wickham loved her and could not believe he had left without a word. She had only stopped looking for his letters or expecting him with each knock on the door. She knew he was forever gone, but love is rarely rational.

Georgiana closed her book and started pacing. She did not understand Fitzwilliam's reluctance in seeking out his ladylove. Was this mystery woman so far beneath him that a match really was not possible? She doubted that. Her brother would never fall in love with a servant or farmer's daughter. He was too honorable for that. Besides, if this woman spent any time as a guest at Netherfield then—

She stopped. Of course, Fitzwilliam's letters! Georgiana reached under her bed for the small trunk that kept all her letters. She flipped open the lid and rummaged through her correspondence. Fitzwilliam had mentioned something about two sisters staying at Netherfield, had he not? She was sure he had, and if she could find those letters, then she might even discover this mysterious woman's name and origins. Perhaps it was not completely hopeless.

She found the stack neatly wrapped in ribbon, and soon the ribbon was off and she was opening them one by one until she finally discovered what she was searching for. There, in her brother's own neat script, she saw a name and moved closer to the candle to read the letter.

We have had the most unusual addition to our party today. Last night Bingley, Hurst, and I dined with the officers quartered in Meryton, the nearby village. Miss Bingley took this opportunity to invite a neighbor, a Miss Bennet of Longbourn, to dine with her and Mrs. Hurst. Miss Bennet arrived on horseback, and after being caught in a rainstorm, naturally became ill. The doctor declared her too sick to move, and now she is recovering in one of Netherfield's guest rooms.

This morning her sister arrived to care for her. Having walked the three muddy miles between the estates, you can imagine Miss Bingley and Mrs. Hurst's disgust at her appearance.

Georgiana finished the rest of the letter, which did not mention the sisters again. She set it aside and picked up another letter marked a few days later. She scanned the first half as it seemed Miss Bingley had dictated many passages to Darcy as he wrote. Finally, she caught a name. *Miss Elizabeth.* She ran her finger over the name and then started reading.

Miss Bennet and her sister Miss Elizabeth have come down from their rooms to join us this evening. They have been here but a few days, and they mostly remain in Miss Bennet's room, but already Miss Bingley tires of them. I believe I am partly to blame. I teased Miss Bingley that Miss Elizabeth's fine eyes were brightened by the exercise during her long walk to Netherfield. Since then, Miss Bingley has been almost uncivil to Miss E as I suspect she thinks I am taking too much notice of her guest. I confess that I might see why Miss Bingley may think so. Whenever I am in Miss E's company, we tend to discuss many topics; however, we hardly agree. Miss E does not acknowledge Miss Bingley's incivility, nor does she seem affected by my opinions.

And that was all. Georgiana flipped through the remaining letters but did not find another mention of Miss Elizabeth. After this, his letters became shorter. Perhaps he was hiding something or there was more to this Miss Elizabeth Bennet than he was letting on? How very unlike her brother.

She must be the one who has captured Fitzwilliam's heart. Georgiana doubted even Bingley could have had *two* women fall ill at his home during a two-month period! No, this was certainly the woman.

Georgiana picked up the pins from her dresser and held them in her hand. There was more to this story; she knew it. How could Fitzwilliam not pursue this Elizabeth Bennet? He said himself that she was not attached to another. He implied that she was of low birth, but she just read that the Bennet sisters belonged to an estate. She is a gentleman's daughter, and Fitzwilliam is a gentlemen; so far they are equals.

Perhaps Elizabeth did not love him. Georgiana huffed. *Impossible!* He was a good, kind, fair, and generous man. Any woman he loved would never be in want of anything and would certainly be spoiled as much as he coddled his own sister. Whatever separated them was more complicated than rank and fortune—perhaps an argument between them that was not reconciled before he left.

She sat in the chair. Had he not written that they disagreed often? A strange way to fall in love, to be sure, but he always remarked how disingenuous the ladies of the *ton* were. He must love her for her honesty as well as her beauty. No wonder he missed her so, and it was even possible that Miss Elizabeth missed him as well. No argument should come between two people in love!

Georgiana found a clean sheet of paper. She quickly inked her pen and was about to put it to her paper when she stopped. Should she really meddle so? The pen twirled between her fingers until she blew out a breath and decided. She may have failed in love, but she refused to let her brother do the same.

Christmas at Longbourn was a merry affair. Even Elizabeth's father seemed to enjoy himself.

With five sisters exchanging gifts between themselves, plus the Gardiners visiting Longbourn, the gift table had overflowed with its heavy burden. Now paper and string were everywhere, as well as the din of the festivities.

"I wish we had invited the officers," said Lydia. "Then we could have Mary play while we danced!"

Mary scrunched her face together. "You know I take little pleasure in it."

"Oh, nobody would ask you anyway."

"Not true. I might not be as pretty as you, but Mr. Lucas is home from school, and we get on quite well. If he liked to dance, he would ask me."

"Ugh, you can have him. I would not dance with him if he were the last man in Meryton. He has that thing on his face."

"I believe that's called a nose, Lydia," Mr. Bennet said, and there was a round of laughter from everyone except Mrs. Bennet and Mary.

"You should not talk so, Mr. Bennet," Mrs. Bennet said and turned towards Mary. "Would he really ask you to dance? Perhaps we should visit Lucas Lodge tomorrow. Kitty's blue dress would look becoming on you. We might have to work quickly before he returns to school."

"But that's my new dress!" Kitty said, "Mary would not look well in it, I'm sure. Why can't she wear one of her own? She has plenty to look ill in!"

"Kitty, that is most unkind. And on Christmas!" said Jane. "Mary, I think you would look very well in blue."

Mary opened her mouth to speak, but she was silenced by Lydia. "Mama, I thought you said all the presents had been opened."

"They have."

"But, look here, there is one more." Lydia held it high above her head. "And it is addressed to Lizzy."

"That is not fair," Kitty said. "Why should Lizzy get one more present than all of us?"

"Who is it from, Lydia?" Elizabeth asked.

Lydia turned it over in her hand. "It does not say. All it says is 'Miss Elizabeth Bennet, Longbourn, Hertfordshire' and 'Do not open till Christmas.'"

"It arrived in the post yesterday," Mr. Bennet replied, and a smile curled at his lips, "with no return address. I hope you are not keeping any secret beaux hidden from us, Lizzy."

Elizabeth shook her head. "The only man I have is Charlie, and he pulls the carriage!"

"Maybe it is from a secret love?" Lydia said and then laughed. "Maybe it is Wickham!"

"Lydia!" Jane said.

"It is probably from a friend." Elizabeth put out her hand. "Give it here and let me see."

"Mama," Kitty said, "Why should Lizzy have a secret love? I should have one just as well as she."

"Yes, dear, I agree. I am sure if we were allowed to go to London with Jane, I could get secret loves for all my daughters. But your father is not to be moved."

"I think"—Mr. Bennet stood up and walked over to Lydia to fetch the small package—"Lizzy should open it before we decide whether she does have a secret love." Mr. Bennet held out the present for Elizabeth. "Unless"—he pulled it just out of her reach—"you would like some privacy, Lizzy, to open it in the other room."

"You know I prefer to disappoint you all and open it here instead."

Lydia turned to Kitty. "Let's see if she blushes when it is unwrapped!"

Elizabeth took the package and observed it at arm's length. "My, what fine handwriting! Very elegant and precise. I do not recognize it at all, do you, Jane?"

"No, I do not." Jane leaned closer. "Is that a London postmark?"

"Why, it is!" Elizabeth set it down on her lap and looked at the Gardiners. "There, the mystery is solved. It is from my aunt and uncle. Perhaps as an extra gift for taking my Jane away until spring."

Mr. Gardiner shook his head. "Not at all, Lizzy, we have already given each of you gift and—"

"It's from Town!" Mrs. Bennet stood up, snatching the present from Elizabeth to see for herself. "Why, it must be from Bingley! Oh, dearest Jane, I knew he had not forgotten you!"

"But it is for Lizzy, Mama!"

"A mistake. It must be a mistake. We know the Bingleys are in Town this time of year. It must be from him. I know it is!"

Jane shook her head. "I do not think so. It is not Caroline's writing."

"And why would the Bingleys send me a present and not Jane?" Elizabeth said and took it back from her mother.

"Will you open it, Lizzy?" Lydia said, "I believe it is from Wickham. I know it is. He probably had the shopkeeper write the direction to disguise the truth."

Elizabeth shook her head. "You will all be sorely disappointed. Really, Lydia, your imagination is very rapid."

She broke the seal. Inside was another wrapped item, but this time tied with a neat, beautiful ribbon. She touched the ribbon between her fingers. Just like the paper and handwriting, it was very fine. With one small tug, the knot came undone, and using more flare than usual, she pulled it completely free and unfolded the paper.

"Oh, how beautiful," Jane whispered. "They go with your coloring exactly, Lizzy."

"Let me see!" Lydia and Kitty said at the same time.

"Is it from Bingley?" Mrs. Bennet said, "It must be from Bingley!"

"Go on, dear," Mr. Bennet said. "We are all anxious to see what your beau has given you."

Elizabeth took one of the hairpins and held it high. A wave of admiration swept through the room.

"You will let me borrow them, won't you Lizzy?" Kitty asked.

"Yes, after I borrow them first!" Lydia replied.

"Mama! Tell Lydia that's not fair. I asked first!"

"I believe," Elizabeth said as she placed the pin back with the rest, "they are much too fine and elegant for every day. There might not ever be such an occasion grand enough."

"Oh, what nonsense!" Mrs. Bennet said, "No occasion? No occasion indeed! When Jane marries Bingley there will be enough occasions for everyone to borrow them."

"Was there a note, Lizzy?" Jane asked and moved closer.

Elizabeth set the pins aside until she found a small, folded piece of paper beneath them. She kept it low on her lap as she read it silently. It was not at all what she expected, and she read it again.

"Well, Lizzy?" Mrs. Bennet said, "Is there a note?"

Elizabeth folded it again and slid it back under the pins. "Yes," she said and smiled at Jane. "It was from Caroline after all. She said that she saw the pins and thought Jane and I would like to share them."

"Well, at least that is something. Of course, Bingley would make it look like it was given to both of you. He is very proper, after all."

"Yes, that is exactly it."

Lydia sighed. "Well, it would have been much more exciting if Lizzy had a secret love. Come, Mary, play for us so Kitty and I can dance!"

While Mary and Lydia argued, Elizabeth put the pins in the new book from her father and discreetly motioned for Jane to follow her. Together they slipped out of the room and up the stairs to their shared bedroom.

"The present was not from Caroline, was it?" Jane asked when the door was securely shut behind them.

Elizabeth shook her head. "I'm sorry I lied, but I could not think of what else to say."

"What did the note say? Are they really from Bingley?"

"Here, read it for yourself." Elizabeth slipped the note out of the book and handed it to her sister.

"'Dearest Elizabeth,'" she read and looked up at her. "Who is this from?"

"Keep reading!"

Dearest Elizabeth,

I feel your absence with each passing day. Please know I have not gone more than a moment without thinking of you and our last moments together. If the last words we spoke to each other were amiss, I regret ever letting them pass between us. You must know the depths of my feelings, and I hope this present will amend any hurt you may still harbor from my carelessness.

Yours affectionately.

"Oh my, who is this?" Jane asked.

"I have no idea, but now you see why I lied? Can you imagine if Papa saw this? Or worse, Mama?"

"Indeed. And you have no idea who this is?"

"None."

"Do you think—could it possibly be—Bingley? He—"

Elizabeth pulled Jane into her embrace. "No! Never. I will not believe for one moment it's from him. Besides, the note said we argued, and Bingley is much too amiable to argue with anyone."

"But who else could it be from?"

"Clearly someone I have quarreled with recently. But who could that be?" Chuckling, she said, "I have not quarreled with anyone this past month, I am sure."

"Unless it was Mama over Mr. Collins."

"Well, we can certainly rule out them! Mama clearly did not send them, and as for Mr. Collins… Well, if they were from him, I would feel sorry for Charlotte." Elizabeth took the note from Jane and studied it once more. "If it did not have my name on it, then I would have assumed it came to me by mistake."

"Perhaps it did. Perhaps it is for another Elizabeth, and she is waiting to hear from her betrothed."

"But it is addressed here to Longbourn. There is not another Elizabeth Bennet in these parts, as you well know, or I would deliver this instantly to her!"

A knock on the door interrupted them, and Elizabeth quickly put the note behind her back.

Mrs. Hill pushed open the door. "Sorry to disturb you, miss, but your mother is asking for you."

"We will come at once. Thank you." Jane smiled, stood, and waited for Hill to close the door again before turning to Elizabeth. "We should tell Papa. He would know what to do."

"No." Elizabeth walked to her bed and crouched low to pull out a small, wooden box where she kept her private journal. "No good can come from such a note. I think it best if we make no mention of it for now."

"And if others come? What then?"

"Then we will tell Papa. Until then"—Elizabeth stood and walked to her sister so she could grab her hand—"until then, please keep this between us. It may all come to naught."

Jane still did not appear as certain as her sister, but she nodded.

"Come," Elizabeth said, "before Mama searches us out herself." The two sisters left the room and headed back downstairs, letting the pins and the note rest peacefully under the bed. She could not imagine who of her acquaintance would send her such an elegant gift or write such a mysterious note. Perhaps in the spring, when she visited Charlotte and met the illustrious patron, Lady Catherine de Bourgh, she would find an occasion to wear such fine hairpins.

* * *

ERIN LOPEZ is a reader, writer, wife and mother—although not in any particular order. While she reads and writes in a variety of genres, she has a special place in her heart for Jane Austen and *Pride and Prejudice* fan fiction. She grew up in the San Francisco Bay Area where she met and married her own "Mr. Darcy," and they lived in Colorado and Arizona for a time. During their stay in Arizona, they brought two delightful daughters into the world and adopted a small, fuzzy dog. They have since returned to the Bay Area.

"If a young girl does not find adventure at home, then she must look for it abroad." —Jane Austen, *Northanger Abbey*

North for the New Year

By Sophia Rose

S alon Mystique!
Surely, a place with the words "salon" and "mystique" in the business name was vastly superior to Connie's Hair and Nails back home. It certainly cost more, but Archer Sparks insisted that Aunt Nancy and Cate receive the whole treatment at the premiere day spa. Cate was not opposed to the idea of a "pamper me" day since she looked on this trip to Tahoe with her uncle and aunt for New Year's as her big chance. Big chance for what specifically, she was not sure. Romance? Adventure? Either or both would be nice.

To go with her new sense of adventure, a new look was definitely in order. She gathered her courage and told Suzanne, the hair stylist, and Tam Tran, who did her nails, to work their magic.

Maybe it was too much magic.

Cate shifted nervously as she studied the young woman with the new bangs and blonde highlights streaking natural light-brown hair peering back at her from the mirror. Her shoulder-length hair had never had so much life and body to it.

Are my eyes more shiny and my cheeks sharper? She scrutinized her appearance for changes.

This wasn't about learning to like or respect herself. She liked herself just fine. Cate was no dazzling beauty. She was pretty—wholesome *and* pretty. And apparently not very interesting. For a young woman wanting an adventure, that just wouldn't do.

It had been months, but Cate still smarted—not from Trent breaking up with her but from Trent's parting explanation.

"You're nice and all, but…"

When she asked her friend Lisa what Trent could possibly mean, Lisa said, "Oh, come on, Cate, you know you can be a downer the way you hold so tightly to your V card and go on and on about stuff nobody cares about. And take a look in the mirror. You've got 'peaches 'n' cream, all-American girl' down pat."

Belinda had been kinder, but Cate heard the faint praise in her sister's words. "Guys like Trent can't appreciate a girl like you. He wants fast and easy, and you're, um, not."

"Cate! Are you ready yet?" Aunt Nancy poked her head around the corner. "Oh, don't you look good, dear!"

Cate could tell her aunt had no clue who she was dressed as for the New Year's Eve costume ball at the Sierra View Resort. "Let me just check on your uncle, and we'll be ready to go."

I wanted something different, and now I've got it. Besides everyone will look over-the-top. Something must and will throw a hero in my way, Cate said to herself as she adjusted the strap on the "ghost–reading" instrument at her side and made a final check in the mirror. Her costume might be confusing for those not in the know. Pilfering her dad's fly fisherman vest and a pair of old khaki pants and, from her brother's closet, worn out combat boots that he once wore when he thought they were cool, she had carefully put together her costume.

"Cate!" Uncle Archer's booming voice was outside her hotel room door. "Let's get this circus on the road."

Cate slipped her wallet, hotel key, and cell phone into her pockets then raced to leave the room.

She flung open the door and stopped short. "Hey, don't you look—"

Uncle Archer grimaced and rolled his eyes. He was a big, beefy man stuffed into baseball pants, a jersey, and a cap that was too small. He wore *golf* cleats but close enough. He was a good-natured man and content to humor his wife even if he looked silly doing it.

"He looks great, right?" Aunt Nancy danced around in her Jane Austen ensemble.

"Sure, Aunt Nancy! You did a good job. So who are you, Uncle Archer?"

"Can't you tell?" Aunt Nancy beamed. "He's Babe Ruth!"

Uncle Archer's jersey was white, yellow, and red, and it said Parker City Dusters. It was his old jersey from the annual softball tournament back home, but he hadn't played in years.

"Ah, yeah—took me a minute."

"Well, let's go, Nance!" Uncle Archer gently grabbed an arm from each of them and walked them out of their cozy lodge to the hired car. Smiling, he said, "I'm the lucky guy who gets to escort two beauties to the ball. I like what you had done to your hair, Caty. And, sweetheart, you are as lovely as ever."

He seemed happy to accept their thank-yous, but Cate could tell he needed no details of their day at the spa—the knowledge of their enjoyment was enough—although Aunt Nancy would likely share all anyway.

Cate pretended to swoon when her aunt and uncle kissed affectionately before he opened the door for them. Maybe it was further proof that she was boring, but Cate wanted a guy like Uncle Archer or her dad: kind, funny, a bit old-fashioned, and a true gentleman.

Looking around the huge ballroom full of costumed people, Cate understood why Uncle Archer had to be persuaded to attend. The resort ballroom was vividly alive with noise, movement, and color. She didn't know a soul except her aunt and uncle. Growing up in a small farm town and attending the local community college where everybody knew everybody, she wasn't used to being around so many strangers. It was a whole world of difference to this festive scene of winter vacationers set to ring in the New Year.

"And this is my niece, Catherine."

Trust Aunt Nancy. She had made a new acquaintance already. Cate turned to see a group of people in fantastic costumes standing with Uncle Archer and Aunt Nancy. Cate gaped at a better version of her costume, right down to the authentic electromagnetic reader dangling off the pretty girl's belt.

The girl shrieked. "Dirk Challenger from *Ghosts Hunters across America*! I'm Bella Stone."

"Cool! I was hoping it wasn't too lame and someone would get it. I don't expect to win the costume contest, but look at you!"

The two girls immediately launched into an animated discussion talking over each other in their excitement.

"Where did you find this?"

"I love this belt."

"But is this a real EMF meter?"

"Did you see the *America's Hottest Stars* list and Dirk Challenger was number one?"

"Oh yeah."

"You gotta see this." Bella pulled out her phone.

Cate nearly drooled with envy when Bella flashed a picture of Bella and the real Dirk at a bookstore signing.

After a time, Cate remembered the others. Her aunt was laughing at their fangirling.

"This lovely Cleopatra is Monique, Bella's mother, and the race car driver is Andrew, Bella's brother."

"Formula One, not stock car like some redneck. And it's Drew," said Andrew—correction, Drew—with a slight smile. "If you'll excuse me, I'm in the process of buying a limited edition Yamaha Viper. Only way to get around here in style." Drew clamped his cell phone to his ear and proceeded to ignore their party.

"Don't mind my Drew," said Monique. "Isn't that cute—you and Bels both chose the same character for your costume? Ghosts scare me to death, but Bels loves it. She and her friends explore old, abandoned buildings in the city looking for ghosts."

"Isn't that dangerous?" asked Aunt Nancy. "Don't street people live there, and aren't the buildings unstable?"

Bella said politely, "Of course, but we go in a large group. We have pepper spray, and Carter, my boyfriend, checks things out ahead of us."

Monique launched into a speech. "Carter Ainsley is the most popular guy at Bella's university. His father is the CEO of a bank. He is so good to her. They hate to be apart. Show the Sparks the little present he gave you so you would think of him while you are here."

Bella pulled a gold chain out of her shirt, and a heart crusted with diamonds caught the light.

"Wow!" Cate blurted, making Bella smile.

"He's a cutie. Hang on a sec!" Bella snapped a selfie. She held it up for inspection. "Not bad—I caught my good side." She giggled and flipped her long, shiny black hair. "Not that I have a bad side. Everyone says I have a stunning profile—oh, and a great body. They are so sweet to say so. I can't very well deny it because that would be lying, and I detest liars. You wouldn't believe all the people I know who lie to look good and are such fakes. I can tell you're not a fake. You're real, like me." Bella's fingers flew over the screen. "There, that ought to remind Carter to miss me." She turned to look about. "Come on! Let's check out all the costumes. Maybe there's a ghost here for us to hunt."

Uncle Archer waved her off with a smile, and the two older ladies, deep in conversation, barely noticed them leave.

Bella talked a mile a minute about ghost hunting, her two best friends, Fabian and Trish, her boyfriend, living in San Francisco, her favorite designers, her make-up tricks, and her preference to be called Bels. Cate was amazed to be accepted in this girl's sphere and took the compliment to her new hairstyle like the highest accolade coming from a sophisticated girl like Bella.

"So, where are you from, Cate?" Bella took a deep breath.

"Parker City."

"Where's that?"

"Down near Fresno."

Bella wrinkled her nose in thought. "Is that near L.A.?"

"No, not really. Fresno is quite a bit north of L.A., and Parker City is to the east of that."

"A real hickville? I've never lived outside the city. I was born in San Francisco, then we lived in Seattle with Husband Number Four, and then we came back with Husband Number Five. Drew and I are from Husband Number Two. My mom was worried that I would ruin her figure, but my dad was a plastic surgeon."

"That's um—"

"So what about you? Any brothers and sisters? How many dads or moms do you have?"

Cate felt overwhelmed by this amazing conversation about multiple dads and moms spoken of so cavalierly.

"I have six brothers and a sister. I'm the second oldest," Cate said, apologetically. "Only one dad, one mom, I'm afraid."

"Really? Like *The Brady Bunch*?"

Cate ignored this because she hated the quips people made about the size of her family and changed the subject.

"Uncle Archer and Aunt Nancy are sending my parents on a cruise for their twenty-fifth anniversary. Since Dad and Mom are both teachers, they are waiting until June and not going on their actual anniversary."

"Sounds like your uncle and aunt are loaded! They paid for this holiday here in Tahoe, right? Did I see a key for the Lakeside Lodge? That's pretty exclusive. And that diamond your aunt wears is quite a rock. Bet it's Tiffany's."

Cate was embarrassed to talk about her relations' finances even though wealth seemed to be excessively important to Bella.

"My uncle got the family farm and ranch supply store. He opened a few more stores that did well and now is semi-retired. His doctor says he has to relax more. They don't have their own kids, so they dote on us. My older brother, Jimmy, went with them on a trip last year, so this year is my turn."

"Oh, I see." Bella nodded and gave her a wink. "Lucky you!"

Cate wondered at the calculating expression she saw on Bella's face but quickly forgot about it when she tugged them off to the side.

"What?"

Bella whispered, "It's the Tylers."

"And?"

"They're from San Francisco too. Elly and I went to school together, but trust me—we weren't friends. As if." Bella sniffed. "Her dad's a judge, and she has two older brothers. Everyone says that the judge killed his wife but got away with it because he's a judge. Doesn't he look cruel? They're a bunch of snobs because the family has been rich since the Gold Rush days and they're too good to associate with the rest of us. Oh crap, they see me, and they're coming this way. Smile and pretend to be nice!"

Cate was spun around on Bella's arm as she watched Bella paste a big toothy smile on her face.

"Hi, Elly! Look at you dressed so cute as a—well I don't know, but so sweet."

The other girl was taller than Cate, slender with strawberry-blonde hair and big blue eyes. She was dressed in a white lacy blouse, pink poodle skirt with black crinoline petticoats, a black scarf tied at her neck, and her hair in a ponytail. The black and white saddle shoes and lace-trimmed anklets completed Elly's fun costume.

"Are you Sandra Dee?" Cate exclaimed.

The girl fidgeted with the tips of her scarf but glanced over with a little smile. "Nobody specific. Just the fifties. And you're a jungle explorer?"

Bella snorted, but Cate was kinder. "No, I'm a ghost hunter. So is Bella. I'm Cate Sparks, by the way, and you're Elly?"

"Yes, and this is my brother, Chris." She pointed toward the two men behind them conversing in a different group. "That's my father, Rafael Tyler, and my oldest brother, Justin."

Chris was dressed all in black like Zorro in a billowing silk shirt, tight pants tucked into high boots, a swirling cape fastened around his neck, and a gaucho hat with an eye mask. He swept off his hat exposing wavy reddish-blond locks as he executed an exaggerated bow. "Enchanted, Cate. Bella. Elly saw a familiar face, and I insisted that she come over and introduce me to her former high school friends. So, have you encountered any ghosts partying down?"

Cate was mesmerized by Chris Tyler's blue eyes and mischievous smile. She was only distracted when Bella deserted her for Justin, the older brother. Justin and their dad were tall, broad-shouldered, dark-haired men while Chris and his sister were slender with lighter hair and fair skin. Chris even had a few freckles that Cate thought were adorable.

"Um—no, no ghosts!" she said belatedly, making Chris laugh. "Oh, and I didn't go to school with Elly. Bella and I just met here. I came with my uncle and aunt."

They all turned to look out over the other partygoers.

"So what is the best costume you've seen?" Chris asked as he scanned the room. "Who's our competition?"

Cate looked about and then pointed at Elly's authentic looking outfit. "I think you have nothing to worry about. I like Elly's costume best. Just like in the old movies. That's cool how the skirt fluffs out and rustles when you move, Elly." Then she glanced over Chris's finery. "Yours too. I love the Zorro look. So dashing!"

Chris pretended to preen, and Elly poked him.

"Stop it!" Elly turned to Cate. "You're giving him a big head. Chris put together our costumes. We spent a day in Reno going in and out of shops to find all the stuff. Chris was part of drama club in college. He's got our mother's talent..."

Her voice trailed off and Chris leaped into the gap. "And her looks, as did you, but I can't take full credit. You decided what you wanted to be."

Cate looked up from their group, and her jaw dropped when she noticed Bella wrapped tightly around Justin on the dance floor with his big hand planted firmly on her butt.

Did Bella just give Justin tongue with that kiss?

Cate wondered what Justin's siblings thought of this, but maybe they didn't realize what was going on behind them.

Chris gestured toward the other end of the room.

"Care to check out the buffet, or would you like to dance?"

"I can't dance, but I would like to try some of the delicious food I noticed earlier."

"Can't dance or just being modest about the fact that you really can and will show us all up after a few token protests?"

Cate laughed. "Trust me; I'm not displaying false modesty. I will stomp all over your feet in these clodhoppers."

Chris eyed her borrowed boots. "I'll take you at your word. No offense. Are you an aspiring drill instructor, perhaps?"

"No." Giggling, she said, "These are my brother's boots. He went through a short phase of wanting to be Rambo. He's moved past it—fortunately."

Cate couldn't understand why Bella thought these people were snobby. Maybe she was right about the judge and Justin—who didn't bother with costumes and didn't come over to be introduced with Elly and Chris—but the younger Tylers were nice enough. Chris was fun and liked to tease while Elly seemed the quiet sort.

"So what do you want to be when you grow up?" Chris asked as he scooped some shrimp onto his plate.

She laughed. "An early childhood teacher. I love little children. I earn my Early Childhood Certificate in May, and then I can find a teaching spot. I also want to continue on and get a four-year degree."

"But that's just your day job."

"Huh?"

"Well, aren't you planning to hunt ghosts at night?" Chris pointed at her outfit.

She and Elly laughed.

"Oh yes, of course, we have so many haunted places near Parker City," she said, her voice laced with sarcasm. "What do you do? Are you a student?"

Elly jumped in. "Chris finished his post-grad and is in family counseling right now. He loves children too." Chris narrowed his eyes at his sister, but she continued without interruption. "He's very good with helping people who have mental illnesses. He has a practice in Reno. He keeps an apartment there, but like a dutiful, kind brother, he stays half the time at the cabin with me so I'm not lonely."

"Ah shucks, Elly! Spare me the blushes. And Elly is a flutist with the local philharmonic in Carson City and a music major at the University of Nevada."

"That's amazing that you play in an orchestra," said Cate. "Wait! I thought you were from San Francisco?"

"We are. We wintered in San Francisco and summered in Tahoe for years. Then we just lived in the city. However, Chris doesn't like the city, so he moved up here when he finished school. When I finished high school, I moved here too. Our father and Justin live in the city. Justin is an attorney with a firm downtown."

"Ah, gotcha!" Cate nodded.

She noticed the glances between the siblings. There was an undercurrent of tension that Cate couldn't figure out. She remembered Bella's speculation about their mother being murdered, and her curiosity was roused.

"And your mom? What about her?"

Elly paled and looked down.

Interesting. Maybe there was some truth to the rumor.

It was Chris who responded. "She preferred living up here. So, dessert?"

The Tylers were engaging, and the time flew. Unlike earlier with Bella, she didn't feel inferior because they grew up differently, and she didn't feel the need to defend her background. Both asked about her six brothers, sister, parents, and life in her small town. They didn't seem bored by her mundane stories. The Tylers had done some traveling all over the world. She learned that Chris and Elly were much younger than Justin and that Chris dabbled in community theater. He liked to act but only comedic roles, and Elly lived for her classical music. They loved to read and share books back and forth.

"If I had to guess, I'd say Cate loves novels too, and as we know, the person who has not the pleasure in a novel must be intolerably stupid," said Chris smirking. "Have you read *The Girl on the Train* by Paula Hawkins?"

"Not yet."

"Really! What about *The Martian?*"

"Uh-uh." Cate was finding herself embarrassed that she hadn't read much beyond what was required for school.

"Shocking!" Chris made big eyes and sucked in his breath dramatically while Elly giggled. "Let me guess. You prefer romance."

Cate thought of the Jasie Whitmore hot romantic suspense novel back in her room and blushed.

Elly shoved her brother in the arm, stopping the inquisition. "Oh, ignore him. He does speak such nonsense. What if she does prefer romances? I like them too. And so do you. Don't think I didn't see you sneaking my latest Angelique Renoir."

Not long before the costume judges mounted the dais, Chris dragged Elly onto the dance floor to jump around to "Twist and Shout." When the winners were announced, Elly placed third, and she was awarded a Touramino's Restaurant gift card and ribbon.

"Let's do lunch before you leave for home, Cate. Touramino's makes the best soup and sandwiches. We can go this week while Chris is off work so he can come too."

"But I wouldn't want you to use your gift card on me."

"Oh no, I want you to come." Elly smiled.

Cate didn't protest further when Chris said, "We would both love you to come."

Cate looked around for Bella and spotted her at the bar with Justin. Bella had since removed her outer shirt to reveal a low-cut, tight cami. The diamond heart around Bella's neck caught Cate's attention and reminded her that Bella claimed to be seeing someone else, but she let Justin Tyler grind against her on the dance floor earlier, and now they were sharing drinks.

Maybe she didn't want to offend him by turning him down. Maybe these things didn't mean as much to people like Bella and Justin.

"...Three. Two. One!" the revelers cheered. "Happy New Year!" Confetti and balloons rained down, and Judge Tyler took Elly to dance to "Auld Lang Syne." Elly smiled up at her father, and Cate thought his expression was too somber for a New Year's moment.

Was he thinking of his wife when he saw Elly?

As they shuffled through the balloons, Cate's excitement increased when Chris's arm encircled her waist, pulling her snugly against him.

"I thought you said that you would stomp on my feet if we danced. Here

I was braced for some dodge-and-weave maneuvers. It's as I suspected. You were just being modest."

Cate forgot about the crowd around them as she looked into Chris's grinning face.

"No, truly, it's common knowledge back home that I step all over the feet of any guy who asks me to dance. Tonight is different. I think it must be you, Chris. You're a good lead to follow."

She meant every word. Chris's teasing eyes warmed and stirred the butterflies in her stomach. Being with Trent had never felt like this.

Chris led them out to the hotel patio looking toward the lake. It was crisp and cold, but it felt refreshing after the stuffiness of the ballroom. He looked up at the starry night sky, breathed deeply of Tahoe's clean air, and then looked at her.

"You should know that you're utterly irresistible when you stare at me like I'm the most devastatingly handsome man in the ballroom and give me such compliments on my dancing."

"Ha, ha. But I was speaking the truth…and besides you complimented me first by saying I was a good dancer." Smirking, she said, "And you're not devastatingly handsome. That's Justin. You are, however, very charming."

Chris broke into a laugh.

He darted a glance around and whispered, "It's tradition to kiss at New Year's, you know?"

Grinning, he then leaned towards her slowly.

"Glad you're not one to buck tradition." Cate rose up on her toes to meet his lips.

Chris's kiss was soft and tentative, lingering a moment before pulling back. They swayed to the music drifting out to the terrace. Cate had been kissed before, but this was the first time she understood how a girl could go all weak in the knees. Fireworks lit up the night along the shore of the lake, matching the ones going off inside her. Chris wrapped an arm around her waist, pulling her closer to him, and cupped her cheek in his other hand. His eyes closed as he kissed her again. She brushed her hand up his silk-clad back. He smiled against her lips as his eyes opened. After the kiss ended, she put her head on his shoulder, enjoying the feel of his arms around her. When the music stopped, Chris slowly moved away, and she reluctantly stepped back too. He kissed the tip of her nose and led her back inside.

"Oh, there you are, dear!" Aunt Nancy rushed towards the couple. "Uncle Archer is tired and wants to get back."

Aunt Nancy was in a hurry, but then she noticed the good-looking young man at Cate's side.

"This is Chris Tyler, Aunt Nancy. Chris, this is my aunt, Nancy Sparks."

"Nice to meet you, Chris."

Chris shook hands politely. "Yes, I've heard all about you. You're Cate's favorite aunt."

"I'm her *only* aunt, but I'll take the spirit of the compliment as it was intended. What about you, Chris? How long are you here?"

"I'm from the area, actually. My family gathered at the family cabin for the holidays, but I live in Reno where my partners and I have a family counseling clinic. Barring emergencies, we're closed for the rest of the week."

"Fantastic—we're here for the rest of the week too. We're going on a sleigh ride tomorrow. Would you and your family like to join us? My Archie isn't going, and we reserved one of the larger sleighs that will hold a group. The driver picks us up at our hotel, and it's about a two-hour ride."

"Chris is here with his family, Aunt Nancy. He's probably busy with them."

Chris surprised her when he said, "A sleigh ride sounds fun. I don't have any plans. My sister would probably like to go. My father and brother have other commitments. We'll meet you. What hotel?"

"Lakeside Lodge on Lakeview Drive."

At that moment, Elly bustled up with the judge. "Happy New Year! Cate, I want you to meet my father, Judge Rafael Tyler. Dad, this is our new friend, Cate Sparks."

"Happy New Year, Judge Tyler."

"Happy New Year, Cate. And this lovely lady is…?" Distinguished and in his prime, the judge smiled at Aunt Nancy.

Aunt Nancy actually giggled as Cate shook hands and introduced her aunt. "My aunt, Nancy Sparks."

The two shook hands, and Nancy explained about the sleigh outing to Elly and then spoke to Judge Tyler.

"I understand you have other plans, Judge?"

Cate was amused by the judge's relieved expression before he masked it behind a polite smile.

"Yes, Mrs. Sparks. I'm meeting a friend for lunch. Perhaps we can get together for dinner later this week—Friday? We have a cabin on the south end of the lake not far from here. It will give us a chance for both families to know each other better, particularly the young people."

"That would be delightful!"

"Splendid! Christopher can give you directions and the time. If you will excuse me?"

"Of course! Goodnight, Judge Tyler!"

Uncle Archer ambled towards them, stifling a yawn. "Ready, Freddies?"

"Yes, dear! You should meet Cate's friends before we go. Archie, this is Chris and Elly Tyler. They're going on the sleigh ride with us. We're also invited to dinner on Friday."

"Sorry." Uncle apologized as he yawned again. "I'm not one for late nights. Nice to meet you both."

Chris good-naturedly admitted, "I'm a morning person, myself. Come on, Elly! We'll let these folks get to their beds. See you tomorrow at two!"

Cate was disappointed as the group broke up. She had wanted one more kiss from Chris, but that seemed unlikely in a crowd. He surprised her when he turned back to peck her on the cheek, and he winked before leaving with his sister.

CATE RIFLED THROUGH EVERYTHING IN HER LUGGAGE BEFORE SETTLING on her sister's jeans, her mom's boots, the soft, jade-green sweater she received for Christmas from her parents, and the new pine-green ski coat from her aunt and uncle. She hoped it made her hazel eyes look green like her favorite book heroine, Jasie Whitmore.

She had just pulled a green and white striped knit hat on and swiped gloss across her lips when her uncle knocked on her door. "Catydid! Your guests are here. Your aunt just texted me from the lobby that you need to hurry."

"Okay, thanks!" She burst out of the room and asked, "How do I look?"

Uncle Archer looked like a lumberjack in his faded jeans and flannel shirt. His flushed cheeks indicated he had only just returned from a walk. "Cute as a button. Knock 'em dead, honey! I'm going to take a nap, so keep your aunt from texting me every five minutes. I could kill your brother for teaching her how to do that. She's gotten so bad that she'll text me from the kitchen when I'm just sitting in the den." She kissed his cheek, and he said, "Go have fun!"

Aunt Nancy, Elly and Chris were sorting lap blankets and seating arrangements while the driver held the reins. An older couple that Aunt Nancy met the night before were already seated.

"Sorry! I'm here."

"Oh, good! I'm going to sit up front with Harris and Linda. You three get the back." Aunt Nancy pushed her toward Chris and Elly, clearly eager to be off.

Chris helped Elly in and then Cate. He unfolded a blanket and wrapped his arm around Cate's shoulders. As he leaned across her to tuck the blanket under her knees, their eyes met, and he asked quietly, "All bundled up?" The pompom on Cate's knit hat bounced with an enthusiastic nod.

When all were settled, Chris announced to the driver, "We're all in!" The leather of the horses' harness creaked, and the bells jangled after the snap of the driver's whip in the air got his team moving.

The sound of the sleigh runners over the snow, the continuous rhythm of the bells, and the muted fall of horses' hooves filled the air. She breathed in the clean scent of pine and expelled a deep breath of satisfaction.

"I love it!"

"Me too!" Elly declared. "I haven't been sleigh riding since I was a little girl. My mother liked to go too. The view just doesn't get old."

Cate's interest quickened at the mention of the mysterious Mrs. Tyler, but she was distracted by the view of the vivid blue lake and pristine snow against the green pines covering the mountains rising around Tahoe.

"Isn't this one of the trails you use for cross-country, Chris?" Elly asked. "Chris can go many miles without getting tired. He competes in The Great Ski Race each year for the Tahoe Nordic Search and Rescue Team charity."

Chris turned from looking out over the view, laughed, and shook his head in amusement.

"Don't look at me like that, Cate. I'm lucky that I can finish. I do it for fun—and to support the charity of course."

"When is it? Is it while I'm here?" She remembered how impressed she had been by the endurance and strength of the competitors from the cross-country event at the last Olympics.

"It's the first week of March."

"Oh, that's a bummer! I would love to see you race."

"It's not the sort of race where you can see all the action. It takes hours to finish the course, and there's nothing between the start and finish except wilderness."

"Still, it would be fun to send you off at the start. Do you do that, Elly?"

Elly nodded. "It's hard to find a place to park, so I drop Chris off in Tahoe City then meet him at the finish in Truckee. Maybe you could come and stay with me for the race."

"That would be fantastic. My brothers and sister would be envious."

"Any of them would be welcome," Elly generously offered. "The cabin has plenty of room for guests. Mrs. Cole won't mind as long as I give her notice."

"Mrs. Cole?"

"Mrs. Cole is our housekeeper and cook. She stays all year round since I'm there. And Chris is there a lot too. Dad and Justin come up for holidays or long weekends once in a while. She was a friend of my mother's, and she's been like a mother to us."

"Mrs. Cole is excited to have guests for dinner on Friday. She is already planning the menu," Chris said.

"Oh, I hope it's not too much having three extras."

"She doesn't mind. She likes to cook for a group. She rarely has the chance anymore. Justin won't be there. He has to get back to San Francisco for a case."

"Look! See the frozen waterfall!"

Cate looked where Chris was pointing and gasped. "That's amazing! It's like one of the gorgeous nature pictures on my mom's Klassen's Insurance calendar. It glows pure white. My aunt and uncle took a cruise to Alaska and saw the glaciers, which were actually a bluey tint because they picked up the color of the water around them—not white like this." She suddenly stopped, realizing she was babbling. "And you didn't need the play-by-play."

She looked up to see Chris's reaction. He was staring at her, amused but not uninterested. In her limited experience, guys never looked at her like this, and she liked how Chris made her feel interesting. It made her nervous…in a good way.

Cate noticed Aunt Nancy snapping pictures, and then her fingers darted over her phone screen.

"Oops!" she said, laughing, "I was supposed to tell my aunt not to text my uncle. He's trying to take a nap, but I have a feeling that he just got sent a picture of that frozen waterfall and several more. My brother Darren created a monster when he showed her how to text. Maybe the texts will all store and not get sent since there isn't much signal out here...or Uncle Archer will kill me."

The Tylers laughed.

For the rest of the trip, they made a game of it and called out whenever Aunt Nancy was taking a picture and texting.

As the sleigh looped back toward the lodge, Chris explained, "Along with the counseling practice, I want to work specifically with the treatment of depression and anxiety, which is the focus of my doctorate. I hope to finish that this year."

Preoccupied with his subject, he slipped his hand into hers, and she warmed to her toes at the touch.

Cate enjoyed how Chris glowed with enthusiasm as he talked about the work that was important to him. She felt the same way about teaching.

Elly spoke with pride. "Chris is brilliant. His clients aren't just study subjects or cases to him. He's helped some troubled teens who were on the brink of suicide and one college guy who attempted suicide. I wish..." She stopped and shook her head before looking down at her fisted hands in her lap.

Chris reached across and squeezed his sister's hand.

For the remainder of the sleigh ride, they sat in silence, listening to the sleigh bells and admiring the snow-covered views. And yet, Cate was uncomfortable not knowing what occurred to change the atmosphere of their merry outing. Her instinct told her that the loss of their mother was the cause.

Was it the tragedy that Bella mentioned? Did the murder happen here at the family cabin?

The dinner invitation for Friday night had now taken on new significance. She needed to call Bella when they got back. *What if this is my big opportunity to discover a real ghost? Wouldn't Bella be impressed?*

Chris's voice broke the silence, and her thoughts were interrupted. "Tomorrow, Elly and I are going cross-country skiing on a trail for beginners. You said you might like to learn. The equipment can be rented at the trailhead. Are you interested?"

"Really? I'd love to go. We were just going to some big golf store my uncle wants to check out. I don't care for golf and would rather go with you guys."

Cate was thrilled to learn to ski, but mostly, she wanted to spend more time with Chris.

THE NEXT MORNING, CATE STARED WITH ENTHUSIASM AT THE ARRAY OF items Bella had spread across her hotel room bed.

"I've got the whole kit that the ghost hunters on the show use: the electromagnetic field meter to track electromagnetic energy and ghostly communication, full spectrum camcorder with tripod and infrared light that will attach, footstep tracker, temp tracker, electronic voice phenomenon wristband recorder, spirit box, and Mel meter, which combines the EMF meter and temp trackers. Most of it has an eight-hour battery life." Gesturing to the pile, Bella asked, "So where are you going to look for ghosts?"

Cate didn't want Bella to know the truth: that she was hoping to use the recording equipment to trap a killer and not just a ghost.

"Oh, there's a castle on the other end of the lake that we're touring, and I thought to give it a try."

Bella looked interested until Cate mentioned the castle.

"Are you talking about the Viking Castle? I don't think anything has ever happened there. It's not really old like castles in Europe. It's a replica. But hey, knock yourself out."

Cate breathed with relief as Bella piled all the stuff back in the kit bag.

Bella stopped and turned in thought. "I didn't know it was open for the winter."

It wasn't.

"Oh, it's a special holiday tea thing for seniors. My uncle and aunt are looking forward to sitting down for some history lecture. You're welcome to come."

Horrified at the prospect of hanging out with old people for a history lecture, Bella shook her head emphatically. "No! Just...no! You really need to get out and experience some of the local scene. Drew and I are going skiing and then clubbing tonight. He's got his new snowmobile. I told him that you'd love a ride on it. He's coming by today."

"I do want to go out with you guys, but I don't know how to ski, and I'm not old enough for a club. I'll have to postpone the snowmobile ride for another day. I'm meeting the Tylers."

"The Tylers? No way! But wait a minute—which Tylers?"

"Chris and Elly are taking me cross-country skiing today."

"Bo-ring"

"They're not boring. I think they're a blast."

Bella silently handed over the bag.

Outside the hotel, Cate bumped into Drew. He was wiping down a new snowmobile.

"Hey! I thought you were never coming. What, were you comparing lipstick? Get on!" Drew gestured at the seat as he swung his leg over and started it up.

It was loud and she had to shout. "Rain check, okay? I'm meeting the Tylers."

"Who?"

"Chris and Elly Tyler!"

He gestured behind him. "They left without you. I saw them heading up to Big Heavenly Sky to hit the slopes."

"What?"

"Yeah, the redheads, right? Judge Tyler's kids?"

"Yes."

"Yeah, they went skiing with their dad, so you might as well get on."

Cate couldn't believe Chris and Elly would do that. She pulled out her phone and checked the confirmation text Elly sent that morning. There were no new texts.

"I can't believe it."

"People can be pretty self-absorbed. Now plant your butt and let's go, Candy."

"Cate."

"What?"

"My name is Cate."

"Oh, yeah. So get on. I'll take it easy since it's your first time."

"I still can't believe it. Maybe they had to run an errand and will be back in time to meet me."

"Nah, I don't think so."

Cate put her borrowed kit in the rental car then climbed onto Drew's snowmobile, taking the helmet he held out. Contrary to his promise, he revved it then drove like a crazy guy. They flew along the path. He seemed vastly amused by her shrieks as she clutched him for dear life.

Cate opened her eyes as they neared a group lined up near a ski rental shack. Her mouth opened as she recognized the two people waiting.

"Drew, stop! They're there! They're waiting for me. Drew! The Tylers!"

Drew honked at Chris and Elly before gunning the snowmobile. The

Tylers watched her fly by, screaming and pounding on Drew's back while he laughed his fool head off. Then Chris turned away before she was out of sight.

"You tricked me! They didn't ditch me, but now they think I ditched them! Take me back now!"

Still laughing, he ignored her. They were going way too fast for her to even consider bailing.

That night before dinner, Cate called Elly several times, but it went straight to voice mail.

Cate was sick with guilt.

After a night of restless sleep and private recriminations for ever believing Drew and not going with her own instinct, she sighed with relief when Elly walked into the lobby. Cate sat in one of the many chairs, attempting to read an entertainment magazine, feeling miserable.

"Elly, over here!"

Elly looked cute in a powder-blue ski jacket over black leggings tucked into black boots. Cate looked closely for signs that Elly was mad at her. Elly flicked a quick glance at Cate and fidgeted with the zipper on her jacket. She didn't look angry, but she wasn't quite comfortable either.

"Hi, Cate! I was hoping to catch you. I saw your aunt when I was coming out of the bookstore, and she said you were here. What happened to you yesterday?"

"Ugh, I feel terrible. I imagine you and Chris are mad at me for ditching you. I called and called and texted."

"I lost my phone and just found it this morning under the seat in Chris's Jeep. It needs to be charged. I would never ignore your calls on purpose." Elly looked down and fiddled with her zipper. "I did wonder why you didn't come. We thought that was you we saw with Bella's older brother. Lots of girls think he's cute and—"

"He's a jerk. He lied and kidnapped me. I can't stand him. No, I wanted to be with you guys." Elly's eyes were huge. "Okay, he didn't *kidnap* me. He told me that he saw you guys go off skiing with your dad, and so I thought it was okay to take a snowmobile ride. He frightened the life out of me with his driving, and then I saw you and Chris at the ski rental, and I begged him to stop, but he wouldn't. He laughed when I realized he tricked me."

"Some guys can be so immature." Elly hugged her. "Did you want to walk down and get that lunch at Touramino's with me? I'm on my own. I was going to have lunch and listen to my audiobook, but I'd much rather have you for company."

"Why are you alone? Isn't Chris with you?"

"He had to go handle an emergency, but he'll be back tonight. He was disappointed to miss you yesterday, but I told him there must have been some misunderstanding."

And Chris's reaction to seeing her with Drew was exactly what had made her lose sleep. Not that she wanted someone to be in crisis, but knowing that this was the reason he wasn't with Elly was a relief.

The girls picked up their lunch from the counter and settled at a table by the window. Cate spooned some soup, blew on it, and made an appreciative noise when the flavors hit her tongue. Elly smirked and wiped her lips after a bite from her sandwich. "Good, right?"

"This split pea and ham is better than my mom's," Cate whispered.

Elly nodded. "I've tried most of what's on the menu. I come here often on the afternoons I don't have orchestra practice."

They ate quietly, and Elly told her what it was like to be a music major and listened intently as Cate described her lab class working with a kindergarten teacher who was something of a martinet. Elly was a tranquil person who didn't need to fill the silence. Cate wondered whether she had music running through her head the way she gently tapped on the table at times. Cate was used to boisterous siblings at home and energetic preschoolers at work, so this calm conversation with gentle Elly was a nice change.

Elly pointed out a cute toddler near their table who was fumbling with his soupspoon. The boy grinned at his mom and nodded when she leaned in to whisper in his ear.

Cate chuckled, but when she looked back, Elly was dabbing a tear.

"I'm sorry. Sometimes little things remind me of my mother."

"Hey, it's all right. I can't imagine not having my mother or what it is like for you to lose your mom. If it's not too private or painful, what was she like?"

"She was a stage actress when she was younger. Beautiful. She had an artistic temperament—you know, the tears and tantrums stuff, but she could also be generous and kind. My father fell in love at first sight. She was in a traveling theater company, which was how dad saw her in San Francisco. She left the profession when they married, but she never lost interest.

"My father can be stern, but my mother balanced him. For years, it was just Justin, and he had mother all to himself, especially since my father was putting in long hours at the family firm and then when he got appointed to the bench.

"Years after, Chris and I came along. Justin was twelve and Chris was four when I was born. My mother had trouble with me and never recovered her health. She did best when it was quiet and calm. My father had the cabin remodeled and brought one of her old acting friends on as housekeeper.

"Mother spent time with us each morning. Chris and Justin were at school most of the day, and I was with her when she wasn't resting. My childhood was spent being quiet around the house, and I could never have friends over that would disturb her.

"Nobody realized how sick she was...then she was gone." Elly's voice drifted away, and Cate watched her gather herself after a few moments. "The cabin was shut up, and we moved to San Francisco."

Elly glanced around and took a deep breath. "I make a terrible eating companion."

"No, you don't. Thank you for sharing such a personal story. So your mom was sick. How very sad."

"Y-yes. She was sick." Elly stared at her plate. "I've never told anyone about my mother."

"Maybe it even felt better for you to talk about her."

"Actually, it did. Thanks, Cate. You are becoming a good friend. I hope we can carry on our friendship after you go back home."

"I'd love to keep in touch."

Alvin and the Chipmunks sang the "Witch Doctor" song in Elly's purse. Elly snorted at Cate's startled expression.

"Speaking of keeping in touch." She answered her phone as she paid with her gift card for lunch. "Hiya! Cate and I are just finishing lunch." She mouthed that Chris was on the line. "Oh? We haven't done that in ages." Elly's eyes rolled to her. "I don't know her plans. I will check."

She pulled the phone from her ear. "Chris wants to know if you'd like to go for a gondola ride up the mountain and see the town and the lake at night. He said he'll treat us to dinner at the restaurant up top."

"That sounds good, but you guys don't have to include me if this is brother and sister time."

Elly laughed at her and nodded at something Chris was saying.

"Chris agrees with me. You're being silly. We see each other all the time."

She put her hand over the speaker. "He's not angry with you about yesterday if you are worried."

Cate breathed a relieved sigh. "What time should I be ready?"

"Chris says six. We'll pick you up so there is no hijacking on snowmobiles this time."

"Elly!" Cate laughed and was happy to see the sad girl from earlier had departed.

AUNT NANCY LOANED CATE HER SAPPHIRE PENDANT NECKLACE AND EARrings, and swept her hair up in a twist for the special occasion. When a smiling Chris arrived to pick her up, dressed in dark slacks and a sweater, Cate was relieved she decided to wear black pants and not the jeans with her V-neck cashmere sweater. Cate was fairly certain that Aunt Nancy was snapping pictures from the lodge window when Chris arrived. That's when she noticed that Elly was missing.

"My sister is claiming a headache and told me that we should go on without her."

"Oh, no! I don't get headaches, but my dad gets pretty bad ones. I hope she can get relief soon."

Chris held the door to his Jeep open and smiled with a twinkle in his eye. "I suspect that she is probably quite recovered by now."

"Ha! The little matchmaker. Are you okay with that?"

Chris chuckled softly. "I'm actually grateful to my sister for her cleverness. I wanted to take you on a date earlier this week and was really p-o'ed that day we were supposed to go cross-country skiing. I let seeing you with Drew Stone get to me. Glad there was no interference so we could be together tonight."

"Chris, I am so sorry. I'm the one at fault for being gullible and believing Drew that you and Elly would go off and stand me up. My instinct was that neither of you would do that, but I was insecure enough to let Drew trick me. Again, I apologize to you for that."

"Don't take it all on yourself. You only met us a few days before, so how could you possibly know what we are like. Let's just forget about it and move on. Pretend we went skiing, had a lovely time, and I got up enough nerve to ask you out for tonight."

"All right. I would have said yes if you're wondering."

His charming smile made her feel dizzy. He briefly squeezed her hand before pulling into a huge parking area.

As they waited for the gondola to go up and come back, Cate made an effort not to betray her high emotions. Never had she felt such eagerness for a dinner date. Cate delighted in watching the night skiing but mostly relished the feel of Chris sitting beside her with his arm draped over her shoulder.

Cate gasped in surprise when the gondola lights went off as they moved up the mountain. The lake was nearly black, and lights were scattered along the shoreline and up into the mountains. Cars moved on the state route below, and the base resort area became smaller.

"Look over there!" Chris gestured at the skiers below with the arm that circled her.

"We're so high up. Oh, wow! I really could never do that. I'm always amazed when we watch alpine skiing in the Olympics. Do you ski downhill, too, or just across country?"

"I ski downhill. Justin and my father are really good skiers though. They'll tackle any run. They've skied all over: Colorado, British Columbia, the Alps."

"What about, Elly?"

"She can ski too." He waited a few heartbeats. "On the bunny slope."

"Be nice!"

"Hey, you asked. Elly's a hiker in summer, and she likes cross-country if we stay on the gentler trails around the town."

"I like to mountain bike and walk. Sometime I do want to try cross-country skiing...again!"

Through dinner, they exchanged stories of childhood. Chris was fascinated by her family stories, particularly the big deal they made about birthdays or the weekly family nights.

"Didn't you ever have birthday parties? Or watch movies together?"

Quietly, he said, "No, we never did, or at least none I can remember. You're lucky, Cate."

When they finished dinner, they shared a decadent chocolate lava cake for dessert. They playfully dueled with spoons for the last scrape of fudge. Chris signed the check and moved around to help her into her coat.

Cate didn't want the evening to end.

"Would you like to go out on the observation deck?"

"I'd love to." She eagerly took his hand as he led them away from the gondola and around to the side of the restaurant where they were now in semi-shadow below the lights of the restaurant above and behind. Chris turned them toward the view and stepped up beside her. The air was cold, and she shivered, so Chris put his arms around her and warmed her against his body. Her eyes moved from the view out from the deck and lifted to the man who stood with the wind at his back, keeping her warm. She stared at his lips, remembering their New Year's kiss. Chris took this as the invitation it was and bent his head to kiss her. He was not tentative this time. Cate's breath quickened when his cold hands moved under her coat to explore her curves. She broke the kiss and nuzzled along his neck even as he kissed across her jaw and toward her ear. The scent of his cologne intoxicated her, and she reveled in the feeling of his arms around her. A trill of laughter broke through and reminded them they weren't alone.

Chris rested his forehead against hers and he smiled as he caught his breath.

"I let that get out of hand. I meant only to kiss you. I'm sorry to paw you in public like that."

"You weren't alone in that, so don't apologize," she said, looking away.

"What is it?"

"I go home in three days. I have a pretty demanding school schedule. I—" She bit her lip to help hold herself together. "I don't want it to be over before we barely got started, but I don't see how we can be more than long-distance friends."

"I have thought about that. I know Elly invited you to spend a weekend with us in March. You get breaks from school. I get vacation time. We could try if you want."

"But what if you meet someone here?"

"Then I will be honest—just like you will be honest if you meet someone there."

"I won't. I've already met everyone there. I like you."

He smiled and then kissed her nose.

"I like you too. I've also met most of the local female population."

"Surely not all of Reno!" she said, laughing.

"Well, no, but I'm sure you haven't encountered all the men in Parker City either."

"You do recall that I'm from a little Podunk town where there isn't a large population? I have met all the men." And they both laughed.

His blue eyes studied her, and frown lines formed as his lips tightened. "Cate, I will always be honest with you, and I want the same in return. I don't know where things will go, and I'll make no false promises, but I really do like you, and I want to get to know you better."

He waited for her response.

"Thank you, Chris. I needed to hear the words."

Chris nodded and then pulled her close for a hug and a gentle kiss.

"It's getting cold and late, so I had better get you back before Uncle Archer breaks out his shotgun and comes after me."

"He's not like that, but my mom can be, and Aunt Nancy is probably texting her all sorts of things."

"Even worse! I don't want to get on the parental units' bad side before I even meet them."

Chris told her that he wouldn't see her until the next night for the dinner at his family cabin. Cate was curious to see it. After all she had learned from Elly, and even more from Chris tonight, she wanted to see them in their home environment. Distant thoughts of her plans to investigate were no longer important. In fact, it seemed like a frivolous and childish pursuit next to Chris's desire to help people and their families who suffered from serious mental health issues. His enthusiasm for his field had energized a new desire in her to learn more from him and to be a better teacher when she had her own classroom.

UNCLE ARCHER GROWLED. "YOU SAID RIGHT, NANCE, SO I TURNED RIGHT. This is a dead end at a private gate and not the right one."

"Yes, of course. I meant right after this one. Don't worry, Archie. We left in plenty of time. Cate, you have the wine, I hope? I forgot."

"After all that time at the wine shop and watching you guys sampling, I wasn't going to leave the wine behind."

"I couldn't tell the difference after a while," admitted Uncle Archer. "That fellow kept asking me to smell the cork, and I couldn't figure out what I was supposed to be smelling."

"Oh, here it is!" Aunt Nancy heralded, pointing toward a well-lit gate.

At the top of the curved driveway, they all stared at what awaited them.

"That's a cabin?" her uncle expressed for all of them. "It's bigger than my house and the pole barn put together."

"Elly and Chris said the judge had it remodeled when his wife moved up here permanently."

Remodeled was one thing, but this was almost as big as their hotel lodge! They all pulled their eyes back in and clicked their jaws shut in time to be greeted by the judge and Elly.

"Good evening! I see that you found us," the judge said amiably.

They were led inside, and Elly took their coats. She nearly dropped Cate's bag. "Goodness, that's heavy!"

"Sorry, I never clean the thing out," she said as she held up the wine. "We brought a thank you gift for having us to dinner."

The judge inspected the bottles and looked pleased.

"Excellent label! We'll open a bottle with the fish course. An acquaintance of mine goes ice fishing on one of the smaller lakes, so we have fresh trout."

Uncle Archer shook hands and responded, "I haven't ice fished before, but I have always thought it would be quite an experience. My brother, my nephews, and I go out to the river and the lake a few times each summer."

Judge Tyler was attentive and took Aunt Nancy's arm, complimenting her on her pretty Navy blue cocktail dress and asking about her week. Uncle Archer followed, staring at all the artwork on the walls.

Cate hugged Elly and said, "Your house is…nice."

This *cabin* wasn't dark and dingy in the corners. It was full of warmth, light, and all the modern conveniences. Every item in sight was of the best quality, tasteful, and *not* kitschy—and definitely not a creepy place crawling with ghosts.

"Thank you. It can seem big and empty when it's just me and Mrs. Cole, but it's been nice these last two weeks to have my father, Justin, and Chris here. We just took down the Christmas decorations this week, and now all the rooms seem drab."

"No, your rooms have tasteful, colorful furniture and accents."

"My mother liked lots of color," Elly whispered as they sat down in the living room. "Chris is running late, but he'll be here soon. Dad likes meals exactly on time, so Chris will make sure he doesn't hold things up."

"Hello!" called out a familiar voice from the hall. "Sorry I'm late, everyone. There was an accident between here and Reno. Quite the snarl, but at least nobody was taken away by ambulance."

"You should have anticipated the possibility, Christopher. You knew we were entertaining important guests." The judge frowned at Chris.

Chris responded pleasantly, "Yes, I should have."

A woman Cate presumed was Mrs. Cole knocked at the open door to the living room. "Dinner is ready." She didn't wait but went back down the hall.

"Thank you." The judge stood up. "Mrs. Sparks, I do believe that you will appreciate Mrs. Cole's culinary talent though your own cook is probably more qualified."

"My cook?" Aunt Nancy looked confused. "I love cooking, so I do all my own. I'm happy to try Mrs. Cole's cooking. I'm sure it is delicious."

"Ah, yes, many women like to cook for a hobby."

"*Hobby?*" Aunt Nancy mouthed at Uncle Archer, and he shrugged.

Halfway through dinner, Cate was sure the judge had the wrong impression about her family's wealth, especially after he talked of raising support for his campaign toward the next retention election for California Supreme Court. When the judge mentioned encountering Monique and Drew Stone at the resort and their boasting of an acquaintance with Mr. Sparks, the owner of the largest hardware store chain in the Central Valley, the misunderstanding was clear.

Cate wondered how they would handle this bit of awkwardness, but she wasn't kept in suspense for long.

Uncle Archer was a straight shooter and said, "Judge Tyler, I think there has been a mistake. I don't own the largest hardware store chain in the Central Valley. I own a few farm and ranch supply stores in our region of the valley. I'm sorry you were given the wrong impression. While we have a little money put by and we do support local political candidates that we feel will represent us well, we don't usually donate beyond that."

Judge Tyler didn't leap up and run them out of his house, but the rest of the meal passed without any effort to be a good host. In fact, he didn't say much at all and soon excused himself to his study.

Blushing, Elly handled her father's change in attitude with grace and invited the Sparks to join them for dessert in the family room.

"We have a treat for Cate," Chris announced. "She told me when we went out last night that she had never had fondue. Anyone up for a game of cards?"

They moved to the family room where Mrs. Cole set up chocolate and cheese fondue pots by the fire.

"Have you kids ever played Nertz?" asked Uncle Archer.

Chris and Elly claimed they had never heard of the game. Cracking his knuckles, Uncle Archer chuckled and said, "Well, let us teach you."

"Now son, you pull that card back. I called Nertz already." Uncle Archer pointed at Chris who grumbled. Aunt Nancy snickered.

"If Elly hadn't blocked my view of the table, I'd have seen that move sooner," Chris groused with a good-natured grin at his sister.

Elly stuck her tongue out before sticking a chocolate dipped strawberry in her mouth.

After several hands, Uncle Archie declared, "I hate to break this good time up, kids, but it is past my bedtime." Yawning as he stretched, he said, "I'll get the car warmed up. Tell Mrs. Cole thank you for dinner."

Suddenly, Elly remembered that she had promised Aunt Nancy clippings from her mother's plants in the sunroom at the back, and the two women left suspiciously.

Chris retrieved Cate's coat from the closet and tugged on her bag where it hung on a side hook.

Cate watched in what seemed like slow motion as the bag upended.

Chris scrambled to right it, but it was too late as the contents started tumbling out.

"I'm sorry, Cate. I hope nothing is broken," he said as he knelt down to gather items.

She saw his confusion when he came across the ghost-reading instruments. Then he saw the label and laughed.

"You carry ghost-hunting equipment in your purse?"

He finished stuffing it all back in before standing with a crooked smile of amusement.

"What, do you always keep it charged and ready in case you encounter a haunted house? Were you expecting this house to be haunted?"

He was laughing until he saw her face change at his last words. She blushed furiously and snatched her bag to quickly zip it closed.

She had never seen such a severe expression on Chris's face as she did then, and she cringed.

"You heard some rumor about my mother, right? What? You were going to set up your equipment here in our home and maybe contact her ghost? How insensitive can you get? I can't believe this."

"Chris! It's not like that. Not now. I got that stuff from Bella at the beginning of the week before I knew—before I knew you and Elly. I knew it was stupid and held onto it in my bag until I caught up with Bella to return it. I wasn't planning to use it here. Chris, please. You need to believe me."

He was looking off to the side, and his fingers tapped at his leg. Glancing at her, he said, "Come with me."

She left her things by the door and followed him up the stairs with the beautifully carved wooden banister. He pushed open a door on the second floor and turned on the lights. Waving her past, he closed the door and waited while she looked around. By day, there would be a splendid view from the large windows looking out toward the lake.

They were in a lovely bedroom suite. It was feminine, and there was a faint flowery scent in the air even though the room was cold and dusty from being shut up. Then Cate noticed that things were left out on the vanity, the dresser, and the night stands. A pair of slippers peeped out from under the coverlet. A book was face down on a table by a chair. Pictures, some signed, of a woman in various costumes with other actors covered one wall around a large painted portrait of the same beautiful woman.

This was the room of his mother, Celeste Tyler.

Cate turned toward Chris who was staring at a spot by the fireplace. There was a red Persian rug and a chair with a throw blanket slid off to the floor.

"She died right there. That's where I found her when I ran up to tell her that I got the lead in the school play. She was faced away from me, and her body was cold. My father came in after me to tell me to be quieter and calm down so I didn't disturb her if she was resting. As if anything would disturb her ever again."

Chris wiped his hand down his face.

"She was clinically depressed and suffered from severe anxiety. It came on gradually until she had panic attacks whenever she had to leave the house or there was noise, or people expressed strong emotions around her. She had meds, and she was taught coping mechanisms. My mother didn't like to be different, so when she started to feel better, she would go off the meds. We all tried to be careful around her, but we were young and didn't fully understand. Justin was an angry, rebellious teen. I was an excitable boy who shared her artistic spirit. And Elly—Elly was a little girl who sometimes forgot and would get caught up in her play."

Cate could barely breathe as she watched Chris slouch against the door, still staring at the chair where Celeste Tyler died.

"She had an attack the night before, and Father blamed us all. He said he was moving us back to the city and getting a nanny for Elly and me. He carried her up to her room, and the next day she overdosed. She left a note saying she was sorry for being so weak and sorry for the life we were all forced to live because of her. She said that she was setting us free. My father mourned her deeply. He has never gotten over her death. None of us have, but we try to work through the grief and self-blame we experience. People talk and speculate about her death, so we aren't allowed to let the past go."

Cate wanted to take Chris into her arms and comfort him as she might a small child. She started toward him but drew back when she saw his glower.

"Do you think we have a ghost here? Do you sense her? Maybe she's here trying to communicate with us now! Or maybe you want to call in a forensics team to check for foul play? Is my father your sinister villain just because he's austere and focused?"

Chris blinked and then opened the door with only one word for her. "Go."

Cate fled.

She heard a sob through the now closed door and raced away knowing this was her idiotic fault. She had intruded on this family's private pain. The guilt of deliberately looking for clues about Chris's mother and her possible murder hit her hard. She hadn't gone so far as hunting for a ghost, but she had speculated about their family tragedy. Shame and remorse filled her for the pain she inflicted.

Chris and Elly had come to be so important in her life, and it was all over now.

"Cate? Are you all right?" Elly and Aunt Nancy were standing in the hall when she ran down the stairs.

"Um, no, not really. I need to go. Thank you for everything, Elly." Cate walked out of the house with tears flowing.

On the ride back, Aunt Nancy wiped away Cate's tears and insisted Cate tell her what was the matter.

"Aunt Nancy, I really messed up, and I hurt Chris. He must hate me."

"Chris doesn't seem the type. Now tell me what happened."

And so, she started from the beginning.

"But I changed my mind and was planning to return Bella's equipment. I went to her hotel twice, and she wasn't there. I didn't feel comfortable leaving it at the desk since it's worth several hundred dollars.

"We went to the wine shop and walked around getting souvenirs for the family at the other shops. Remember we got back late and had to hurry to change for dinner? I didn't think to empty the bag. It all spilled out, and Chris was sharp enough to figure out why I had the equipment in the bag."

Aunt Nancy handed her a tissue.

Cate told her about Chris taking her to his mother's room and revealing the truth.

"I'm sorry, honey. I surely am. For you. For the Tylers. I think Chris was taken by surprise. Give him time. He'll forgive you."

"We're only here for two more days. We leave on Sunday."

"Yes, and it may take him more time. You need to understand that and respect his space."

A hot bubble bath, a bag of chocolate, and a hundred pages of *Harry Potter and the Deathly Hallows* made her feel marginally better.

She had mentally created a new list of New Year's resolutions. Her heart was bruised, and her mind worried whether Chris would get over her foolishness.

Cate deleted all the *Ghost Hunters across America* episodes from her laptop, took the GHAA theme music ringtone off her phone, deleted the GHAA app, rolled up her New Year's Eve costume, and put it in the garbage.

Then later, she removed the costume from the garbage and put it back in her suitcase after remembering that those were her dad's clothes and fishing vest that he would definitely want back.

Cate was surprised when Elly arrived smiling the next morning. "Are you feeling better?"

"Yes, I am. Thanks. I'm sorry I ran out on you last night. You must think I was behaving oddly."

"No, actually, I was scared that maybe it was something in the food. Chris didn't feel well either and told me he had to go home. He was supposed to stay the weekend. I popped in to see if you were free and wanted to hang out with me today."

"Chris might not want us to get together."

"Oh no, why would you think that? I texted him this morning to check on him and said I was going to visit you." Elly smiled. "Did you have any particular plans for today?"

Other than spending her last day with Chris on a long date? That plan went up in smoke last night.

"Not really. My uncle and aunt want to go up in the gondola and visit the restaurant after I told them how wonderful it was."

"Mmm, yes, so would you like to go with me and listen to our orchestra practice this afternoon?"

"That sounds neat. I'd love to do that."

Elly's orchestra practice wasn't especially interesting, but she perked up whenever Elly mentioned Chris.

"Chris comes to all my opening nights and always asks for an encore. He's so loyal and attentive." Smiling at Cate, she said, "He's going to make some lucky girl very happy."

Unless it was her, she didn't want to hear about Chris making any girls happy.

On the way back, Cate remembered Bella's ghost-hunting kit.

"Elly, do you have enough time for me to drop something off for Bella?"

"Oh sure! Which hotel?"

"Hotel Tahoe."

Elly navigated the weekend traffic easily and slipped into the drop-off area at the front.

"Isn't that Bella with her mom? She looks upset."

Bella's clothes were wrinkled as if she had slept in them, her hair was messy, and her make-up was running with her tears. She looked outraged as Monique tried to calm her.

"I do wish you hadn't posted those pictures of you and Justin Tyler skiing and clubbing together, Bels. However, I'm sure you can convince Carter that he misunderstood and can get him back once we get home." Monique rubbed her daughter's back.

Cate jumped out with the kit bag. "Bella!"

Bella turned, recognized her, and dramatically flung herself into Cate's arms. "He used me and then threw me out. He's a beast—a cold, unfeeling beast. A user! I hate him."

"What are you talking about?" Cate examined Bella. "Who? Are you hurt? Should you call the police?"

"Ha! I really should do that. I would love to see Justin Tyler's face when the police bang on his door, but that's not likely. His dad's a judge, and everyone knows the rich, snobby Tylers. They can victimize innocents all they want and get away with it."

Cate had forgotten about Elly in all the excitement. All at once, Elly appeared at her elbow. "You take that back, Bella Stone. My brother didn't attack you. It was the other way around. You were all over him at the New Year's Eve ball, and I saw you glomming on to him just yesterday. Justin is always honest with his women. He never promises anything. If he threw you out, it's because you were clingy and wouldn't take a hint." Elly stepped closer to Bella and hissed, "In fact, my friend works at the day spa of this hotel, and she overheard you planning a big summer wedding and speculating about what Justin is worth in dollars. You've had it in for our family since the first time Justin overlooked you. Everyone back in San Francisco has known for years that it's a case of sour grapes."

Elly returned to her car, and Cate spoke quickly to Bella, "Um, here's your ghost-hunting kit. Thanks for the loan."

Leaving Bella speechless, Cate joined her friend in the car.

They were silent nearly all the way back to Lakeside Lodge.

Then Elly started giggling. "I have wanted to tell her off for years. She and her friends were so mean back in high school. I was intimidated by them then. I was still having a hard time after my mother's death, and they were especially cruel to new girls. They suddenly changed when Justin came to pick me up from class. Then they were back to being mean after Justin made it clear that he didn't date jail bait."

"Ugh, I can't believe I thought she was nice. I'm just making mistakes and errors in judgment right and left."

"Bella can be very nice and friendly to those with whom she makes an effort. You both share a love for ghost hunting."

"Well, that's lost its appeal, so now we have nothing in common. And now I know where she was all those times she wasn't at her hotel or answering my texts."

Elly giggled. "Justin sure can pick them. I really hope that one of these days he'll stop playing around and settle down with a nice woman. He puts up walls that make him emotionally unavailable. He was a decent guy before my mother died, and I know that guy is still in there somewhere. I want *both* my brothers to find nice women."

Cate heard the hint behind Elly's words. If Elly only knew, she'd be protecting her brother from the likes of Cate. Chris would eventually tell Elly, and Cate's error in judgment would lose her Elly too.

"Yeah, I know what you mean. I want my brothers and sister to find good people too." After a moment she said, "I want you and your brothers to be happy, Elly. You and Chris are special to me now. I'm sorry if my presence dredged up sad memories. I didn't mean to hurt anyone."

Elly looked confused, but nodded and hugged her before Cate got out at the front of her lodge.

TWO DAYS LATER, CATE WAS HOME, AND LIFE RESUMED AS IF SHE HAD NEVER left. Her mom was happy she was back. Her sister pushed her pile of fashion magazines and clothes off Cate's bed as her way of welcoming her home. Her brothers seemed excited for all of five minutes. Her dad kissed her cheek and checked to make sure his missing fishing vest and favorite pair of trousers had returned intact. And her cat sat with his back toward her, giving her the silent treatment for going away.

She texted Elly and told her that she was home safe. Elly responded with a sad face and "miss you," but then she heard nothing more as she settled in to routine.

Nearly a week later on Saturday afternoon, she was up in her room holding her phone and debating a call to Elly.

"Cate! There's someone here to see you," her mom called up the stairs. Her brothers all echoed this down the hall so that mom's announcement was repeated loudly at least three times. They had done this stunt for years to embarrass her. The routine was no longer embarrassing but part of the family fun.

"Coming, Mom!" she shouted back, and her brothers picked it up, echoing her words.

Her sister was still embarrassed by it. "Shut up! You sound like dweebs." And they all echoed *her*.

Cate raced down the stairs. She was shocked to see who was standing in the small foyer.

"What are you doing here?" she blurted.

"Catherine Marie! Manners!" snapped her mother.

Cate barely heard her. She looked at Chris, and she was struck dumb by his quirky smile and sparkling mischief-filled eyes.

Is he here to tell my parents how stupidly I behaved?

She looked over at her dad watching college basketball as he graded papers. He didn't look more than mildly interested in Chris. Mom was more concerned that Cate show proper manners toward a guest. This would not be their reaction if Chris had told about the ghost equipment debacle.

"Um, hi! Would you like to come through to the kitchen?"

"Sure."

Mom cleared her throat and stared pointedly at Chris.

"Oh! Mom, this is Chris Tyler. We met him up at Tahoe. Chris, this is my mom and dad, Clint and Patty Sparks."

"Yes, we've met. He introduced himself at the door. Don't you plan to take his coat?"

Cate blushed.

She watched Chris struggle not to laugh.

"Let me take your coat, please."

He removed his coat and scarf, and she hung them in the closet. Spotting the pile of shoes by the door, Chris kicked off his loafers and added them to the pile. He smiled and followed her back to the kitchen. He looked about curiously as they passed to the back of the house.

"Jake, Matt, this is Chris Tyler. Chris, these are my brothers."

Her brothers were engrossed in their Wii game and gave Chris a "hey" without looking away from their game.

"So, what can I get you?"

She pointed toward the coffee pot, the kettle on the stove, and the refrigerator. Mom's kitchen was stuck in the 70's, but it was tidy.

"Water's fine. Please." Chris took a swallow of water from the bottle and set it down to stare at her. She played with the saltshaker, waiting for an explanation of his all-day travel to her house. Finally, he drew a deep breath. "I'm sorry for what I said to you. You did not deserve that. I let my emotions about my mother get away from me. Anger is an easier feeling than pain. I felt worse when I was no longer angry. I was cruel to you. Please forgive me."

She gulped back the urge to cry. "Of course! Chris, I felt so awful for my stupid idea. I'm glad you understand. I really did forget it was there in my purse."

He moved around the island that she put between them earlier and opened his arms. She hugged him fiercely. He leaned and snagged a few napkins from the holder to give her as she blubbered into his sweater.

"Elly told me about what happened with Bella and the interesting conversation you girls had in the car about wanting your brothers and sister to find others to make them happy. Elly then told me exactly who she thought would make me happy."

"Um, well, I haven't actually worked on a list like that for my siblings. I figure I have a few years before it's necessary." Cate looked shyly into his handsome face. "Who did Elly pick? Anyone I know?"

He leaned back against the high breakfast bar counter and pulled her to stand close to him. He tapped her on the nose.

"You. Normally, I frown on my kid sister matchmaking, but I happen to agree with her choice." His lips grew into a wide smile. "You're warm, caring, honest, and utterly adorable."

"And not boring?"

"Definitely not boring."

His laughing blue eyes darkened. "I'd like to keep seeing you, Cate. I know long-distance relationships are not easy, but I would like to try."

The quiet kitchen was invaded as three of her brothers and her sister trailed her mom, all with opinions on dinner. Her mom ignored it all as she went to the drawer by the phone mounted to the wall. She pulled out her coupon folder and leafed through.

"We're getting subs from Sub Giant. Cate, is Chris staying? What kind do you kids want? Kyle, go ask your dad what he wants on his sub."

Cate raised an inquiring brow at Chris as he processed the Sparks' family dinner frenzy.

"Still want to give dating a try?"

Chris looked about at the organized chaos and beamed. "Absolutely! What are the choices, Mrs. Sparks?"

"Call me, Patty. Meat, cheese, veggies, bread choices—Sub Giant has it all."

CHRIS SAT DOWN ON THE FLOOR AT THE COFFEE TABLE WITH CATE AND two of her brothers while the rest piled on the furniture for family movie night.

Dad put the movie in, and Mom turned off the lights. Chris chuckled and planted a kiss on her forehead when the title appeared.

"*Beetlejuice?*" Jake said aloud. "This is going to be silly, isn't it?"

"Maybe it will be about scary ghosts," Matt said hopefully when the couple's car ran off the road.

"If it is, we can send Cate with her ghost-hunting skills after them," Belinda teased from across the room.

"I've given up on that now," she announced to the room.

"Since when? You've had the hots for that Dirk dude for three years now." Darren was skeptical.

"Since last week. Now hush up and watch the movie."

"I'll bet she threw Dirk over when she met Chris," Jake loudly whispered.

Chris burst out laughing and hugged her affectionately. "Did you throw him over for me?"

"You are so much better than a guy in a jungle explorer costume crawling around moldy, old mansions."

"I should say so."

"Shhh!" chorused the room.

Chris's hand tightened in hers, and she was relieved that he overlooked her foolish notions and thought her "utterly adorable." Sitting on her family room floor and eating sandwiches with her family and this dreamy man while watching a cheesy movie wouldn't be perfect to many—I leave that to others to decide—but to Cate? She had done well, and this was perfect happiness. Going north for the New Year was only the beginning of her romantic adventure.

* * *

SOPHIA ROSE, a northern Californian transplant to the Great Lakes region of the U.S., is a quiet yet curious gal who dabbles in cooking, snooping about old places, gardening, and is encouraged in her writing pursuits by an incredible man and loving family. Writing has been a compelling need of Sophia's since childhood, and being a published author is a dream come true.

"O Christmas tree, O Christmas tree, You can please me very much!
How often has not at Christmastime, A tree like you given me such joy!
O Christmas tree, O Christmas tree, You can please me very much!"
—"O Christmas Tree" ("O Tannebaum")
traditional German Christmas song

Winter's Awakening

. . . .

by Anngela Schroeder

Fitzwilliam Darcy swirled the warm liquid in his cup before pouring in a spot of cream and a spoonful of sugar as he looked around the coffeehouse in Lambton. Since the arrival of his good friend Charles Bingley and his sister, Darcy's estate was not as appealing as it had once been, and he felt the need to escape his guests that morning. *Home is no longer my own*, he thought with no little resentment. *If only Miss Bingley had gone with the Hursts to Scarborough for the holidays.* He grimaced as he tried to push the morning's machinations of Caroline Bingley from his mind. *Bellowing at Mrs. Reynolds to demand Cook properly prepare my egg! Is that how she imagines the mistress of an estate behaves?* A shudder raced down his spine at the image of Caroline Bingley in his bedchamber, and he cringed, sloshing some of his tea over the edge of his cup and onto the table.

Waving away the owner's daughter, he reached for his own handkerchief to wipe up the spill and barely perceived two new customers entering the shop. The women made their way to an empty table beyond his sight.

"It is so exciting to be traveling through the North Country. And to think we may see snow before we return home. Does not that idea please you?"

"Yes, of course it does. Nothing would bring me more joy."

"Then why does your smile say otherwise, dear sister? We are far from home in the wilds of Derbyshire. Will you not tell me what occurred when you went to visit Miss Bingley last week?"

The name "Bingley" caught Darcy's attention, and he tilted his head in the direction of the table behind him.

"I am afraid if I do, I will not be able to quell my tears. Miss Bingley assured me that her brother knew I was in town and was not interested in seeing me. He was too busy pursuing his upcoming courtship with Miss Darcy to renew any acquaintance with me."

At this, Darcy's body grew rigid, and he stifled a gasp. *It cannot be! Miss Elizabeth? Here in Lambton. Not five miles from Pemberley?*

"So, I can only conclude that Mr. Bingley did not feel for me what I felt for him." The conversation lulled before she said, "I only hope there is another man that I can love as I did him, or I fear I shall never be happy."

Darcy's throat constricted. *Did Miss Bennet truly love Bingley and not just his fortune?*

"I only wish, Lizzy, that I could understand why Miss Bingley feigned friendship with me. She seemed as dear a heart as any would be yet so cold and uncivil when we met in London. Mama believes she was acting on behalf of Mr. Darcy."

"Mr. Darcy? What would Mr. Darcy have to do with this?"

Darcy leaned back further. "Well, he is Mr. Bingley's closest friend. Mama believes that he influenced him to quit Netherfield to marry Miss Darcy."

Elizabeth harrumphed. "I do not believe Mr. Darcy capable of such deceit. I believe that, although we are beneath his society, he must see that we are above the Bingleys. The Bennets have resided at Longbourn for generations. In regard to the interference of his friend, I believe that was all Miss Bingley's doing."

Darcy knew it was most ungentlemanly to listen to the private conversations of ladies; regardless, he was gratified to hear Elizabeth defend his character. It was with a heavy heart that he realized her faith was misplaced. *I did separate my friend from her sister. I believed the mother to be mercenary and the daughter to follow her mother's demands.* "Obviously, I was mistaken," he mumbled to himself.

He continued to covertly listen as the Bennet sisters' conversation progressed. "Lizzy, it sounds as if your feelings towards Mr. Darcy have changed. Would you say you have a tender regard for him?"

Elizabeth's laugh shocked Darcy to the core. "A tender regard? For a man who finds me tolerable but not handsome enough to tempt him? No, I can guarantee my feelings towards Mr. Darcy have not changed."

"Sister, keep your voice down. This village is only five miles from his estate."

"You are right, Jane," she whispered. "Do you think he treats the villagers of Lambton with any less disdain than he did the people of Meryton? His manners were not those of a gentleman, and I would hardly excuse his actions towards Wickham. Withholding his promised living so that Mr. Darcy could continue to make the poor man suffer out of jealousy?"

There was a moment of silence as Darcy winced at Elizabeth's accusations.

"NO, MY FEELINGS FOR MR. DARCY HAVE NOT CHANGED. I FEEL HE IS THE last man in the world I could ever be prevailed upon to marry." With that, Elizabeth took another sip of her chocolate and settled into her thoughts, unaware of the gamut of emotions she had infused in the soul of the man she could not see, quickly walking through the kitchen and out the back door.

Not fifteen minutes later, an impressive carriage with a distinguished crest pulled up in front of the establishment. Elizabeth arched an eyebrow at Jane as they saw the door of the vehicle open, but could not see its inhabitants. They did not have to wait long as Miss Caroline Bingley walked in wearing a look of disdain they remembered well. Jane's gasp was stifled enough that the woman did not hear, but the young girl walking in behind her did. She hesitantly gave Jane a tentative smile, and walked up to the shopkeeper as Miss Bingley began barking demands.

"Has Mr. Darcy of Pemberley been here? His sister is attempting to locate him, and we do not have time to lose." Her superior attitude was not mirrored by her young companion.

"What Miss Bingley means to say, Mr. Smith, is that my brother left for the village earlier this afternoon, and before we went back to Pemberley we thought we would check to see whether he stopped by his favorite shop for your special blend of tea."

"Yes, Miss Darcy," the man said, turning from the older of the two women and softening his expression. "He was here until about a quarter of an hour ago, sitting at that table. He left in all haste. Said he did not like to leave his horse tied for so long after a ride."

Elizabeth and Jane blanched at the revelation that Mr. Darcy had been sitting in such close proximity to them. They were almost unable to regain their composure as Miss Darcy turned and said, "Oh, look. He was here. He left the handkerchief I embroidered for his birthday. It appears," she said giggling, "that he spilled some of his tea too." She sighed, picked up the article, and turned to glance at the Bennets.

It was at that moment Miss Bingley gasped as she recognized the two women before sputtering, "Miss Bennet! Miss Eliza! Whatever are you doing here in Lambton?"

"Miss Bingley." The ladies nodded, and Elizabeth smiled in amusement as Miss Bingley regained her equanimity. "We are here as guests of our Aunt and Uncle Gardiner from London. They have business here, and we accompanied them from town for a holiday."

"We never could have imagined we would have the pleasure of seeing you here," replied Jane gaining courage. "Pray, are all your family well? Mr. and Mrs. Hurst? And Mr. Bingley?"

"Yes, yes," she said in a strained voice. "They are all well. Charles and I are here for Christmastide as guests of the Darcys." With that, she seemed to remember the young woman standing at her side.

You cannot escape the introduction now. Elizabeth noted the young lady was slightly taller than herself with golden ringlets framing her large blue eyes. She looked to be about Lydia's age but carried herself with much more decorum. Elizabeth smiled to herself, prepared to witness manners just as detestable as Mr. Darcy's were. However, she was surprised by the reticence of the young girl.

"Miss Georgiana Darcy of Pemberley, may I introduce you to Miss Jane Bennet and Miss Elizabeth Bennet of Longbourn? Acquaintances we made in Hertfordshire."

"Miss Elizabeth Bennet?" the young girl asked.

"Yes."

"Of Longbourn?"

"Yes," Elizabeth repeated as all three women looked intently at Miss Darcy.

"I beg your pardon. It is just that you know my brother, Fitzwilliam Darcy of Pemberley."

"Yes, we are acquainted, Miss Darcy," Elizabeth said with a little trepidation. She could not comprehend the expression on Miss Darcy's face. The next question startled not only the Bennet sisters but Miss Bingley as well.

"Might I request, that is if you are not already engaged, the pleasure of your party's company tomorrow evening for dinner? We will send the carriage for you—"

"Pardon?" Elizabeth interrupted.

"Oh, I am sorry, Miss Elizabeth. I just..." Miss Darcy's face fell, and her eyes dropped to her feet.

"Miss Darcy, please," Jane said. "You have only surprised us. Allow me to accept on behalf of our family. We would be delighted to join you tomorrow evening."

"Excellent. My brother will be most pleased. Shall we send the carriage for you?"

"No, thank you, Miss Darcy," Elizabeth replied, regaining her ability to speak. "My uncle keeps a carriage. We would be most delighted with a visit to Pemberley."

"Lovely. Well, until tomorrow then. Come, Miss Bingley," she called and walked out the door. Elizabeth could hardly keep her countenance as a stunned Miss Bingley almost forgot to take her leave of the two women with whom, only a week ago, she surely thought she would be done forever.

She heard me! She heard me call her tolerable but not handsome enough to tempt me. Darcy rode his horse hard through Pemberley Woods trying to shake the emotions coursing through him. He was learning to deal with frustration, but it was the anger he was trying to abate. "How dare Wickham poison her with lies! How could she believe him?" *According to her own words, old man, you are not a gentleman. You were rude and disrespectful to the people of her village.* "I freely admit," he said to his horse, "that I did not want to be in the company of anyone when we first arrived at Netherfield, let alone strangers." *My feelings were too raw. That was only shortly after Ramsgate, and I did not feel comfortable leaving Georgiana again.* "True, but no one in my company, including Bingley, knew that was the reason for my behavior," he said again aloud. *All they saw was my rejection of all ladies at the assembly—except for the women in my own party—and my attempt to ignore the older woman next to me for above a half hour.* "In that light, Miss

Elizabeth's charges have merit." *However, for her to have heard me say she was not handsome enough to tempt me? That is the furthest thing from the truth.*

He sighed and slowed his horse to a walk, rested his head on the mane of Ulysses, closed his eyes, and whispered so that his words would not be used against him by wood nymphs or humans. "She tempts me every second of every day. In my dreams, when I am looking at my ledgers, when Georgiana is playing the pianoforte for me. She is a constant thought and temptation." He choked back a sigh. "There is nothing to be done. She made her sentiments towards me quite clear, and even if she had not, I cannot offer for her. Yes, as she said"—he nodded—"she is the daughter of a country squire, and though her family has been established at Longbourn for generations, she has no connections, no dowry, no standing in society. It is for the best that I heard her scathing sketch of my character so that I may now attempt to force Elizabeth Bennet from my heart." *I must conquer this!* And with that, he dug his heels into the side of Ulysses and bade him run on.

"OH, JANE," ELIZABETH CRIED, BARELY ABLE TO CONTROL HER AGONY UNTIL arriving at their private sitting room at The Inn at Lambton. "Do you think he heard me?"

"I most assuredly believe he did." Jane removed her bonnet and gloves and handed them to the maid. "I warned you, Lizzy." Jane smiled. "You, my dear sister, will now have to make amends. Decrying the man in his own town? What will you do?"

"I do not know. What will I do? I must see him tomorrow night for dinner. In his own home!"

"Yes, you must. And I will see Mr. Bingley." The tone in her voice made Elizabeth reconsider Jane's plight. "Do you think, Lizzy," she asked as she sat down and looked at her hands, "that Caroline Bingley was telling the truth? You saw Miss Darcy today. She is quite lovely."

"Yes, she is. However, I do not believe Mr. Bingley would fall in love with a child and attempt to pursue her when she is not even out in society. Furthermore, I do not believe Mr. Darcy would allow such a thing to occur before his sister was presented at court. So"—she sat down in the chair next to Jane—"I believe tomorrow will be the day Miss Bingley prayed would never come."

"You did what? You invited the Miss Bennets to dine with us to-morrow evening?" Darcy caught himself and had to regain his hold on the situation as Georgiana looked to be on the verge of tears and Caroline Bingley on the verge of triumph. He took a deep breath. "Georgie, I apologize for speaking so sharply. We can discuss this after dinner."

"I agree, Mr. Darcy. Those Bennet girls are nothing but mercenary, following you and my brother all the way to Derbyshire to try and force an entanglement—"

"Caroline!"

"I thank you for your opinion, Miss Bingley," Darcy said. "I never noticed any mercenary tendencies in either of the women. If you please, I would rather not discuss this at the dinner table."

"I agree on both issues," Bingley said heatedly.

Miss Bingley rolled her eyes at her brother, sending a knowing smile in Darcy's direction. "Of course, Mr. Darcy. We must protect the sensibilities of one as innocent as our dear Georgiana. If you would like, I will dispatch a letter to The Inn at Lambton cancelling our plans for tomorrow evening. You should not have to worry about such trivial responsibilities. Those are for a woman to perform, not such a busy master of the house."

Georgiana's eyes widened at the presumption, and Darcy had to school his features not to give the woman a set down.

"I thank you, Miss Bingley. I will continue to write my own correspondence until I am to take a wife. In situations such as this, Georgiana would write the letter. However"—he glanced at his sister who was pushing the food around on her plate silently—"I believe the re-establishment of the acquaintance can only be a good thing, and I am pleased my sister made the effort. We shall have a stimulating night tomorrow, eh, Bingley?"

"You look lovely, Jane. Do not worry. Mr. Bingley will be charmed."

The following evening, Jane and Elizabeth were seated across from the Gardiners in the carriage en route to Pemberley. Jane's continual fussing with her gown did not go unnoticed by anyone in the party, and her aunt quickly added, "Jane, you are a sweet girl. I am unfamiliar with Mr. Bingley, but if he is anything like Lizzy has said, he will be an amiable gentleman even if his affections are not truly engaged."

At this, Jane sighed, and her sister leaned over and took her hand. "It is better to be prepared, dear Jane, although I do not believe our aunt knows the breadth of possibilities she might witness tonight. I dare say, if Mr. Bingley is uncertain of his affections, seeing you this evening will change his defect rapidly."

"Do you truly believe that, Lizzy?" Jane asked quietly.

"I do. And I also believe that is the reason Miss Bingley seemed so put upon when we saw her yesterday."

"And what of Miss Darcy?" asked her aunt. "It was mentioned that she is quite reserved."

Elizabeth paused for a moment and then said, "Well, Aunt, I have been told of her imperiousness and disdain for others, but I must admit that I noticed none of that yesterday. She seemed kind and attentive if not a little shy." Elizabeth smiled slightly thinking of Caroline Bingley. "I am actually quite surprised that Mr. Wickham would have described her as such, considering he was such an intimate acquaintance of the family."

Both girls turned at once at the loud gasp from their aunt. "Did you say Mr. Wickham? A Mr. George Wickham of Pemberley?"

"Yes, Aunt. We met him in Meryton when the militia was quartered there." Jane raised a quizzical brow at Elizabeth before turning back to her aunt. "Do you know him?"

"I cannot say I would ever allow that young man to travel in my company. Although I know that, throughout his youth, his circles were more elevated than he deserved, he and I have never crossed paths. For that I am grateful."

"Aunt, I know not of what you accuse Mr. Wickham, but I do believe he was treated most unfairly by Mr. Darcy. Mr. Wickham stated—"

"—that Mr. Darcy's father promised him a living, and upon the elder Mr. Darcy's death, the younger Mr. Darcy refused to honor that promise?"

Both Jane and Elizabeth's eyes widened in astonishment. "Why, yes. How did you know?"

Mrs. Gardiner only smirked and turned to look out the window while the other carriage occupants glanced back and forth between themselves. "Girls"—Mrs. Gardiner quietly stared out into the darkness—"promise me you will forget whatever that man told you. I assure you they were all lies."

"Of course, Aunt. If that is your wish," Elizabeth said. *What could my aunt mean by this revelation? I have never found anything but charm and ease in Mr. Wickham's countenance and pride and conceit in Mr. Darcy's. I trust my aunt most assuredly but am afraid she has allegiances to the owners of Pemberley after growing up in a village that owed much of its existence to that great house.*

"Girls, what I am about to tell you must remain faithfully within the walls of this carriage."

"Madeline, do you think this is wise?" her uncle asked, fidgeting with the buttons on his jacket.

"Edward, I must be able to protect your family as I was unable to protect my own." After a moment of contemplation, she began. "It was several years ago, but I wonder whether you remember my brother's child, Cecily? She made your acquaintance one year around Michaelmas. You were very young."

"Yes, I remember her. She was several years older than Jane."

"We both thought her very beautiful and charming. She allowed us to wear her bonnets and use her parasol on our walk to the park."

"Yes, Jane, she did."

Elizabeth continued. "And, if I remember, she is living in America with her husband. They have lived there for several years, is that not so?"

At this point, Mrs. Gardiner looked longingly out the window. "No, Lizzy, it is not so. That is the story our family created to protect her memory." Mr. Gardiner reached over and took his wife's hand. Nodding with determination, she said, "For years, my uncle was a tenant of the elder Mr. Darcy, and after my brother's death five years ago, Cecily moved to live with his family. It was there she became acquainted with the young Mr. Wickham.

"His reputation amongst the townspeople was dissolute, and when my uncle Turner discovered her affections towards the young man, she was forbidden to see him. Wickham had convinced her that he would be getting a substantial inheritance from the Darcy estate with the death of the elder Mr. Darcy, and they would marry." She paused and began rubbing her temples with her fingers. "For whatever the reason, he did not receive the inheritance, and he immediately cried foul, maligning the young Mr. Darcy to whoever would listen. It was put about that the young Mr. Darcy had offered him the living and, when refused, granted him a substantial payout instead."

Overcome by emotion, her aunt could not continue the story.

This tale sounds similar to Mr. Wickham's, but how can I be sure my aunt has not been mislead?

Mr. Gardiner clasped his wife's hand and took up where she left off.

"Girls, what I am going to tell you is not for the ears of delicate young ladies. However, your aunt feels incumbent to protect you. Cecily was with child." The sisters blushed, but their uncle continued. "Being a naïve young girl, she did not understand the complexities of men and did not realize her plight until halfway through her time. She confided in a younger cousin that, when she informed Wickham, he…he denied the baby. She threatened to go to the young Mr. Darcy and tell him what had occurred and what he had promised her. He…well he…"

"My family believes he beat her," Mrs. Gardiner said quietly. "He beat her so badly that she never woke. My uncle found her in the woods and carried her to his house. His youngest daughter said Cecily left to meet her husband, and she was not to tell her father until they returned from Scotland. The babe arrived the next morning but did not survive. They had no proof to support their belief in Wickham's guilt, but he had an alibi. I will not sully your sensibilities, but suffice it to say, we know he lied. My uncle and his family left for America within a fortnight to escape the shame.

"The young Mr. Darcy learned too late of Wickham's actions and sends money every Christmas to try and make amends. He is a good man, no matter what others would lead you to believe."

A thick silence hung in the carriage, daring either sister to speak. Finally, Jane began to cry. "Oh, Aunt. How horrible for your family. I am so sorry we ever believed Mr. Wickham."

"Now, now, Jane. I did not tell you these things to distress you, only to warn you of what kind of people reside in the world. There are many who will impose themselves upon your sweet and tender hearts. Do not be fooled by idle compliments with little substance. Men of merit will offer you more than pretty words." She quickly shook her head as if clearing thoughts from her mind. "Now, my dear, stop crying, for it will not do for Mr. Bingley to see your eyes red and swollen."

"Yes, Aunt." She took a handkerchief out of her reticule and dabbed at her eyes.

"Tonight"—Mr. Gardiner looked across to each of his nieces and winked, attempting to dispel the somber mood—"we will enjoy the delights of Pemberley and show both Jane, and you Lizzy, to your best advantages."

Elizabeth, too, was anxious about this discovery of her favorite's guilt. *That could not be right. Mr. Wickham could not be such a scoundrel, could he? Was I truly so deceived by him?* However, knowing and loving her aunt and uncle, she realized there was only one answer to the question. *Yes, and what a fool I have been! It would appear Mr. Darcy possessed all the goodness while Wickham merely the appearance of it. How can I go to Mr. Darcy's house, partake of his hospitality, and converse with his sister, all the while knowing I helped spread the untruths through Hertfordshire about his character?*

Elizabeth was not used to being wrong, nor was she used to being ashamed. However, she knew the sensation would not pass quickly enough as the carriage rolled on. "Uncle, in the letter I received from Kitty this morning, she stated that Wickham has been showing a distinct interest in Lydia. Her high spirits would not generally worry me except that she has been invited to spend the holidays with Mrs. Forster along with a select group of officers." She shook her head. "You know Lydia and her propensity for silliness. I worry now that her foolish behavior may ruin us all."

Jane nodded. "In a letter I received from Lydia, she informed me that Mr. Wickham was just the sort of man she could see herself marrying, and if he offered for her, she would accept him immediately."

"This is most grievous indeed," Mr. Gardiner said, wiping his brow. The carriage reverted to silence, as the party was lost in thought.

After several minutes, Elizabeth, not generally of low spirits, asked, "Do you think the house will soon come into view? These woods are so extensive, I worry that dinner will be served before we arrive."

"Patience, Lizzy." Her uncle chuckled with relief to see the cloud of gloom, which had earlier descended, lift.

Giggling, Jane said, "Uncle, I think you ask too much of her."

"You are quite the tease tonight, dear sister, but I am in possession of other wonderful qualities."

"Such as...?"

"Such as the ability to judge people's character. And that, Jane, is how I know you should not be nervous about Mr. Bingley this evening." At Jane's hopeful look, Elizabeth continued. "Your gown is lovely, the maid did a wonderful job with your hair, and it has only been three weeks since he last gazed upon you. I believe tonight will be a triumph."

Elizabeth smiled brightly before turning to face the window. *A triumph for you, dear Jane, but with this new revelation, I can only feel the shame of my actions.*

OF ALL THE DAYS TO BE CALLED AWAY TO MANAGE A DISPUTE BETWEEN TENANTS, Darcy thought as he rode towards Pemberley. He had been anticipating Elizabeth's arrival since the moment Georgiana informed him of her invitation. *Now, I am not even at Pemberley to welcome her. What a marvelous impression I continue to make.*

"And what of it, Fitzwilliam?" he replied to himself out loud. "You know how she feels about you. You are most likely the last man in the world she would ever be prevailed upon to marry!" A thought niggled at his conscience that he tried desperately to repress but to no avail. *I must concede: my manners in Hertfordshire were unbecoming a gentleman.*

At that moment, Fitzwilliam Darcy dug his heels into Ulysses and pushed harder through the well-known trails of Pemberley's woods.

"MISS DARCY, THE MASTER HAS ARRIVED HOME AND WILL BE DOWN SHORTLY. He said he will meet you here in the music room before dinner."

"Thank you, Weston." Georgiana gently nodded as the butler exited the room. They had been sitting in the music room above three-quarters of an hour with Georgiana delaying dinner until her brother's arrival. She enjoyed the Miss Bennets, as well as their aunt and uncle. Further, Georgiana was grateful to learn Miss Elizabeth's uncle was in trade, assuring the lack of conversation with Miss Bingley, who was seated on the opposite side of the room.

FOR ELIZABETH'S PART, SHE HAD FOUND MISS DARCY CHARMING. THEY had spoken of the countryside, dances, art, and books. However, it was not until Elizabeth asked about music that Miss Darcy become animated.

"I must say my favorite composer is Beethoven. His Sonata 23 for Piano is my favorite."

"Is it?"

With feeling, Miss Darcy replied, "It is so full of life and love. I am consumed when I play it." Her enthusiasm immediately ceased. She looked across at her companion, Mrs. Annesley, who nodded kindly and smiled before she attempted to continue with the conversation in a more subdued fashion.

Miss Bingley sniffed from across the room. "I have told her, if she must like a German composer, to at least allow her affections to lean towards Handel. He took on citizenship and pledged allegiance to the monarchy.

Beethoven remained a German." Miss Bingley shook her head in dismay as Miss Darcy lowered her gaze and fidgeted with her hands.

"I understand you play and sing very well, Miss Darcy," Elizabeth attempted to set the young girl at ease.

"I do play, but not very well," she demurred.

"Might we hear from you this evening?" Jane asked as Mr. Bingley stood to get her refreshment.

"I thank you, but I am not sure I am up to the task. Miss Bingley's skills are far superior to mine, and I have not played much in company."

"Come, dear Georgiana, play for us," Miss Bingley intoned in her nasally voice. "None of your false modesty this evening. I am certain neither the Miss Bennets nor the Gardiners will have heard anything so superior."

The fear in her eyes was evident as she looked from Miss Bingley to Elizabeth and back. "Miss Bingley, I bow to your superior playing skills instead."

"No, no, my dear. I insist. Charles, do you not wish to hear dear Georgiana's talents on the pianoforte?"

"Yes, of course," Mr. Bingley said, handing the glass of punch to Jane. "As long it is what she wishes."

Sensing more shyness than false modesty, Elizabeth moved in to help the young girl. "Miss Darcy, if it would help, I could sing while you play."

Her eyes shone with gratitude. "Would you, Miss Elizabeth?"

"I would, but I ask you to not test my range," Elizabeth whispered with mischief in her voice. "I have not had the training of a proper master in years and am afraid I will embarrass myself greatly in front of your company this evening."

"Although, I do not believe your opinion for a moment, I will allow you to pick the song."

They walked to the pianoforte together, flipping through the music until they found one upon which they both agreed. Then, Miss Darcy began to play.

AS FITZWILLIAM DARCY CAME DOWN THE STAIRS, HE HEARD THE PIANO. Recognizing the cadence of his sister's playing, he was surprised that she would willingly perform for their guests. *What would possess her to...?* And then he heard her and knew. He walked towards the open door, and positioned himself where he might observe her unnoticed.

Drink to me only with thine eyes,
And I will pledge with mine;
Or leave a kiss within the cup,
And I'll not ask for wine.
The thirst that from the soul doth rise,
Doth crave a drink divine;
But might I of Jove's nectar sup,
I would not change for thine…

There she sang, utterly affected by the music. True, the women of the ton had greater social status and financial entitlements to attract suitors, but Elizabeth Bennet had something they did not: a love of life that captivated him and made one of the most sought after men in England a shell of a man in her presence.

The song came to an end, and true enjoyment was expressed by all the guests, save one. Georgiana looked up from the piano, and a large grin spread across her face.

"Wills!" She bounded off the piano bench and towards him. At once, she seemed to remember herself and slowly walked towards him holding out her hands. "Brother, I am so glad you are home. Cook has held dinner as I would not start without you."

"Oh, Poppet. You did not have to wait, but I am grateful you did. Cook has made my favorite tonight, and I was alarmed that Bingley might devour it all," he teased, smiling at his friend. There was an awkward pause as he cleared his throat.

"Excuse me." He bowed to his guests. "Miss Bennet, Miss Elizabeth, welcome to Pemberley. I trust you are enjoying your stay in Lambton."

"Why, yes, we are, Mr. Darcy. Thank you," said Miss Bennet.

"Would you do me the honor of introducing me to your friends?"

"Of course. Mr. Darcy, this is my aunt and uncle, Mr. and Mrs. Edward Gardiner."

"A pleasure, sir."

"The pleasure is mine," Darcy replied, bowing. "You are welcome to Pemberley. I apologize for not being here to greet you but hope you will find Cook's offerings will make up for it."

Mr. Gardiner smiled. "I assure you, Mr. Darcy, we are grateful to be in your company this evening and have been entertained well by your charming sister."

"Thank you, sir." Darcy turned to Miss Bennet. "I hope you are well. And your family?"

"Yes, Mr. Darcy, they are quite well. Thank you."

Stealing a glimpse at Bingley, he asked, "And I trust you have found the company satisfactory?"

She blushed. "Why, yes, Mr. Darcy. I thank you."

Stepping toward Elizabeth, he smiled. "What a pleasure to find you in Lambton! Are you enjoying your trip?"

"Yes, sir, we are. My aunt grew up in Lambton and has spoken often of the surrounding natural beauty. We hope to see some of it while we are here."

"You grew up here, ma'am?" Darcy asked, turning to Mrs. Gardiner.

"Yes, sir. My father, Mr. Turner, owned the bookshop when I was a child before he inherited a small manor from a distant relation."

"Turner?" Darcy asked. "Once we had a Mr. James Turner as a tenant."

Mrs. Gardiner looked directly into his eyes. "Yes, sir. James Turner was my uncle. The family now resides in America."

Darcy bowed to her. "It is an honor to have you in my home, ma'am."

"Whatever can Mr. Darcy mean?" Caroline Bingley hissed behind her fan to her brother who stood at her side. "Does he not realize that she is a nobody whose husband is in trade? From Cheapside?"

"Caroline"—Charles gripped his sister's elbow and leaned in to whisper to her—"you forget yourself. You are not the mistress of either Pemberley or Darcy. Hold your tongue!"

"Charles, don't be ridiculous!"

Miss Bingley had not been as discreet as she believed, and Bingley's red face matched those of others in the room. Darcy was hot with anger as he attempted to ignore the brazen insolence of his best friend's sister.

Miss Bingley glided across the room and clasped his arm. "Come, Mr. Darcy. Shall we go in to dinner?"

It took everything within his power to civilly acknowledge her and allow his tone to maintain a calmness he did not feel. "Yes, thank you, Miss Bingley." He removed her hand—"Georgiana?"—and placed his sister's gloved one upon his arm. As Miss Bingley eagerly reached for his other one, he turned and extended it in the opposite direction. "Miss Elizabeth. Shall we?"

ELIZABETH WAS TOO STUNNED TO DISAGREE. SHE GENTLY CLASPED HIS ARM, and a frisson like lightning shot through her. He must have felt it as well because his eyes, which had angrily glared at Caroline Bingley only a moment before, turned to her as dark pools.

Lowering her gaze, she answered Miss Darcy's idle chatter and was shocked again a moment later when Mr. Darcy led her to the head of the table and released her to the seat to his left. Following the Gardiners and Miss Annesley, Miss Bingley frowned when she found she was to be escorted to dinner by her brother along with Jane.

"AND HOW LONG WILL YOUR STAY IN LAMBTON BE, MRS. GARDINER?"

"Our plans are not fixed, but we hope to be home with our children for Christmas. We only await word from the solicitor before we leave. It could be tomorrow or as late as next week. We are uncertain."

"Of course. And may I ask about Mr. Turner? I have not had a tenant who farmed the land as well since his departure. I hope he has met with success."

"He has, sir, I thank you for asking."

"Please give him my regards when next you write to him. He is much missed." He nodded, and a look was shared between Mr. Darcy and Mrs. Gardiner. Elizabeth was puzzled by this complete stranger seated beside her. He was charming, attentive to her relations, an excellent conversationalist, and truthfully, much more handsome than she remembered.

"Wills," Miss Darcy said quietly, "We almost forgot the tree. May we go tomorrow and find one?"

"Georgie, you know it might be too early…but if you have your heart set on it—"

"I do, Wills. Oh, I do. Might we ask the Miss Bennets to join us?" she asked expectantly, looking across at Elizabeth.

"Of course. Miss Elizabeth, might we entice you and your sister, as well as your aunt and uncle, to join us in a feral family tradition?"

Elizabeth raised her eyebrows and grinned. "'Feral,' sir? Whatever do you mean?"

Mr. Bingley laughed. "I completely forgot. It's time to hunt for the tree, is it not?"

"Miss Elizabeth, I will tell you a Darcy family secret, which my aunt Catherine to this day still holds against my father's lineage." He winked at his sister, who began to giggle. "When my great-grandfather Darcy came of age, he took a tour of the continent in the early seventeen hundreds. There he met a beautiful German girl whom he greatly admired and was determined to marry. She was from moderately noble birth—her father had what we would now call a small estate—and was respectable, but my great-grandfather knew she was not what his parents had envisioned for him. But he could not live without her, so with no notice to his relations, he married the girl and brought her home as his bride. Because he was the first-born son and heir to Pemberley, his parents were irate. Her maiden name was Bachmeier, which means farmer by the brook. You can imagine their dismay at such a common name. However, there was nothing to be done as he had announced it in the papers in London before his return, and the banns had been read. So, to compensate for their disappointment, his parents referred to her as the former Lady Brookston.

"The young girl was beautiful and charming but only spoke tolerable English. It was a love match, you see? And they made their home here at Pemberley and hardly stirred beyond other than when their own children needed to be exposed to London society."

A scornful sniff by Miss Bingley seemed unnoticed by all but Elizabeth as she raised a delicate brow. "Mr. Darcy," Caroline said, simpering, "I do not understand your pride in the German culture. True, one should be proud of one's relations, but position amongst the highest in this nation is by far superior to their past from a minor country."

"Miss Bingley, it is not merely pride in my ancestry but in my ancestors. My great-grandfather did not allow his position in society to dictate his choices. And since his time, all Darcy men have chosen to marry for love." At that, he glanced at Elizabeth before continuing his story.

"Odelia Bachmeier brought many German customs to Pemberley. Along with a delightful strudel recipe, which Cook has made especially for this evening, she also started our family tradition to choose and cut a tree for Christmastide."

"You mean you cut down a tree?" Miss Bennet asked slightly perplexed. "What do you do with it?"

Miss Darcy clapped her hands. "It goes in the ballroom, and we decorate it with ribbons, apples, nuts, candles, and my favorite—"

"Gingerbread!" she and Mr. Darcy said together.

"My cousin once told me of this tradition." Mrs. Gardiner smiled, lifting her glass to her lips. "And how the night before Christmas you would hold a ball for the tenants. It was his family's favorite time of year."

"The Christmas ball," Miss Darcy cried. "Oh, Wills. Might we have one again? Is there time?"

He paused. "If you wish. I presume Mrs. Reynolds and Cook would be able to prepare something, but not until next week."

"Oh yes, Brother! And I could make the kissing boughs."

Mr. Darcy attempted to contain the smile forcing its way across his face before it was dashed from his countenance.

"Mr. Darcy, I am astonished that you would lower yourself to frolic with the servants and tenants."

There was a collective gasp, but before Mr. Darcy could respond, Mr. Bingley declared, "Caroline, I believe you are unwell."

She turned to him with furrowed brows. "No, Charles, I am quite well, thank you."

"You misunderstand me, Caroline. I believe it is time for you to retire. I am afraid you have a headache."

"Charles, I—"

"I will brook no opposition, Caroline. Your health is of the utmost import. I will be up to speak with you after dinner."

Her mouth dropped open as she looked from Mr. Bingley to Mr. Darcy then around the table at the other guests. Only Mr. Bingley and Mr. Darcy were looking at her, one's anger more obviously masked than the other's.

"Yes. Now that you mention it, I do feel a headache coming on. I believe it might be the company." Mr. Darcy's intake of breath alerted her to her own slight. "Forgive my words. They were not meant to offend. I was expecting a quiet holiday and was not prepared to be in company with so many unexpected visitors."

Mr. Darcy moved to stand when Elizabeth countered, "Not at all, Miss Bingley. It is lucky, then, that you are not the mistress of such a grand estate, as I presume she would be prepared at all times for unexpected events."

Mr. Darcy raised his glass to his lips and swallowed a drink while Elizabeth watched his attempt to hide a smile.

"Yes, well, good night." Miss Bingley huffed, stood up, and dropped her napkin on the table. "Charles, do not bother coming up. My headache has increased, and I am straight for bed. I will speak to you in the morning." She escaped the room with a flourish of feathers and rustling silk.

The silence in the room was interrupted when Mr. Darcy spoke to Mr. Gardiner. "Sir, would your business in town permit you and your party to stay at Pemberley as our guests for the celebration? If you need further inducements, I have a pond stocked with inhabitants who have been ignored for far too long."

Mr. Gardiner's eyes lit up but for only a moment before he shook his head. "Perhaps. I am grateful for the invitation, sir, but as Mrs. Gardiner said earlier, our plans are unfixed because of my business."

Miss Darcy cleared her throat. "Mrs. Gardiner, might the Miss Bennets stay?" Mr. Darcy turned to her in surprise as she pushed forward with her cause. "We will be traveling to town ourselves in three weeks time for the New Year and would be happy to convey them. Mrs. Annesley, my companion, will be here with us, and there is plenty of room at Pemberley..." Her shyness returned as she lowered her eyes then peeked up at Elizabeth's aunt.

Her aunt seemed to look to Elizabeth for any type of confirmation and then looked at Jane, who only smiled demurely. She then looked to her husband who nodded his approval.

"Mr. Darcy, I believe we can safely leave them under your protection, especially with Mrs. Annesley in residence."

"Of course. Your nieces will hardly have time to be alone as my sister is quite taken with them." The room erupted into gentle laughter as Miss Darcy blushed. "If everyone is finished"—he stood beside his chair— "let us forgo the separation and adjourn to the music room."

"It was kind of Miss Darcy to invite us to look for your tree, sir."

"Not at all. Purely selfish intentions on her part. She takes great pleasure in your company. Combing the woods of Pemberley with you only makes her task more enjoyable."

"And yet, I am not combing the woods with her, sir. It is you who must keep me company," she teased with a playful grin. "Your sister subjected you to a day of monotony. How will you ever recover?"

Darcy looked ahead to the rest of their party—where Georgiana was merrily teaching Jane and Bingley the refrain of an old German traditional song—and then grinned at Elizabeth. "I am not sure, madam. But, I am of a strong constitution, so I will endure."

"Why, Mr. Darcy," Elizabeth quipped. "I realize I am 'not handsome enough to tempt you,' but have a care for my vanity." She raised her chin in mock defiance as he reached up and caught her arm. At his touch, she froze before he released her.

"Miss Elizabeth." He lowered his eyes before raising them to meet hers, and allowed a smile to tug at the corner of his mouth. "Once again, your defect is to willfully misunderstand me. Pray, believe me when I say that I was sorely misguided to stifle Bingley's interference with my foul mood the night of the Meryton assembly," he whispered. "My words were spoken before realizing how truly wrong I was. You are..." He swallowed, uncertain whether he should continue. *Just say it, man. Here is your chance!* "Miss Elizabeth, it has been many months since I have considered you one of the handsomest women of my acquaintance."

She gasped and seemed at a loss of how to respond. He took her hand and placed it on his arm before continuing on the path.

Noticing her heightened color, he quietly said, "I fear I have surprised you with my confession. Did you have no knowledge of my regard?"

"No, sir." She shook her head gently, her brown curls bouncing. "I believed you to despise me."

"I assure you Miss Elizabeth, despising you is the furthest thing from my mind."

They fell into silence again. After a moment, he interrupted her thoughts. "Might I ask how you feel about this disclosure?"

Gathering her thoughts, she gazed up at him. "Sir, I know not. You remember I have long attempted to make out your character..."

"Yes. And still you have little success?"

She hesitated before answering. "The master of Pemberley I have met is much altered from the guest at Netherfield I had known. My mind is a muddle."

A thoughtful look crossed his countenance before he responded. "I assure you, Miss Elizabeth, the man is as he always was, only more content in his surroundings."

They continued to walk, all the while breathing in the scent of the pine and crisp frosted air of Pemberley's woods. The crunching of pine needles and light chatter from the group ahead could not distract them from their own solitary thoughts. Eventually, they crossed a small stone bridge over a stream and moved past a number of large boulders.

"I learned to swim in this stream." Darcy broke the silence. "I was eight years old, and my mother forbade it."

"Why?" Elizabeth asked, placing her other hand on his arm. He seemed to glow at the warmth of her touch.

"I had a brother who was two years my senior. Henry was the heir and was everything lively and good. He was so like my mother with a fair complexion and a laugh that filled all who knew him with joy." He chuckled. "I favor my father: dark hair and reserved in company. While visiting my aunt and uncle's estate in Matlock when I was six and Henry eight, we had snuck away from our governess to sail boats on the little pond. His sailed to the middle and stopped. Being the more adventurous of us, he jumped in and, while swimming to retrieve it, called back that he was going to touch the bottom." Here Darcy paused and looked off into the distance. "When he did not come up, I ran for my father, but it was too late. His foot had become entangled in an old tree root, and he drowned. From that point on, my mother forbade me from going near water. Neither she nor my father ever got over the loss of Henry."

"Oh, your poor dear mother." Elizabeth squeezed his arm. "But, Mr. Darcy, surely you don't blame yourself. That cannot be true."

The silence sat between them before he continued. "Miss Elizabeth, the ghosts of my past do not haunt me as much as they used to. I admit, I am often on guard for every situation for fear an unseemly event will occur that I could have prevented."

"But, you were a child."

"Yes, but had I known how to swim…" He frowned. "So, although determined to obey my mother, I was resolved to prepare for any occurrence. Wickham and I would come down here and practice swimming almost daily that spring."

"Wickham?" she gasped stopping mid-stride.

"Yes, Miss Elizabeth. I am aware you are friends with the man."

"Merely acquaintances, I assure you."

"Well, whatever the case, he and I grew up like brothers, taunting each other to run faster, jump higher, ride harder. When Henry was lost, he became my childhood playmate, and my family allowed it, hoping that I would grow up with a confidante for my future. He loved Pemberley almost as much as I did, and he knows every inch of this forest. But we have since had a falling out and have severed ties." His last sentence was filled with venom as he unknowingly looked ahead at Georgiana.

After a moment more of silence, Elizabeth said, "Mr. Darcy, I am afraid that I owe you a sincere apology."

He turned to her with raised eyebrows. "I cannot imagine why."

She took a deep breath and bit her lip before slowly beginning to speak. "When Mr. Wickham was presented into the neighborhood, he began to disparage your name and fabricated events that I now understand could not have occurred. However, as my vanity had been injured at the assembly, I was inclined to believe him. I apologize."

"Miss Elizabeth, you are not the first to be taken in by his arts." He looked again pensively at Georgiana then continued. "He has ruined, or nearly ruined, many respectable young ladies with false truths and flattery. I am only grateful you were able to discern his true character before your name was added to the list. I would not have forgiven myself."

She blushed for the second time in as many minutes and kept her gaze averted. "I thank you, sir, but do not deserve your kindness." She began to slide her hand from his arm until he reached up and covered it with his own.

"Let us agree that we have misjudged each other and vow to begin anew."

"Agreed," she replied softly.

They were interrupted by a shout from an exuberant Georgiana not far ahead. "Wills, I found it. The perfect tree! Come here!"

He grinned at Elizabeth and squeezed her hand. "I am coming, Poppet. Let us see what you have found." They stopped before a giant twenty-foot fir tree with far-reaching boughs. "Georgie, I believe you have done it again. This looks more perfect than last year's and might well touch the ceiling of the ballroom."

"It is perfect!" They were all admiring the tree as Darcy called out to the Pemberley woodsman to bring him an ax. The ladies of Longbourn exchanged looks as Darcy removed his greatcoat, jacket, vest, and cravat—remaining in his shirtsleeves.

"It is the long-standing tradition for Darcy men to chop down the tree themselves," Georgiana explained.

"Of course," Elizabeth said breathlessly, seeming not to know where to look.

"Not at all." Miss Bennet shook her head and bit her lip to control the unabashed grin seeming to spread across her face.

"Only once a year does Darcy have to do such strenuous activity." Bingley rubbed his hands together and laughed. "Believe it or not, I think he revels in it."

Darcy bowed to the ladies, quickly brought the ax up, and began chopping at the tree.

Elizabeth was unable to remove her gaze from Mr. Darcy's form. Other than her father's tenants tending their fields, she had never watched the work of a man—and certainly never a gentleman! She admired Mr. Darcy's arms as solid as the steel on the end of the ax blade. His sweat had dampened the fine lawn of his shirt and caused it to stick to his skin, defining his shoulders. *He is magnificent.* She tried valiantly not to stare but could not stop herself. *After his next swing, you must look away,* she would tell herself again and again, but to no avail. Finally, his swing powerfully knocked the tree over, and he turned to smile, his dimples winking at her. *He caught me!* She felt the heat rise to her cheeks at his penetrating gaze. The black pools of his eyes, which she once believed were examples of disgust, bore through her, and she realized they were far from it. Her heart raced, and she looked down quickly. However, her eyes settled on his chest, which was more splendid than his back, and she let out a gasp. Attempting to control the unladylike thoughts, she chirped, "It is a shame Miss Bingley could not come today."

"Yes. Pity." Mr. Darcy expelled a deep breath, handed the ax to a young woodsman, and picked up his coat from a nearby stump.

"Her business in the village must have been of some import." Miss Darcy picked up her book and reticule while the two women followed her example and stood to begin walking back to the manse. "She has never missed the opportunity to come with us and hunt for our Christmas tree. She always seems to enjoy the activity."

I can understand why! Elizabeth flushed and closed her eyes, shaking her head quickly to remove the vision of Mr. Darcy in his shirtsleeves. *It is something I would not miss either if I could help it.* She was surprised at her bold thoughts and attempted to dismiss them before they were conveyed across her face.

"Are you well, Miss Elizabeth?" he asked softly, his voice caressing her name as it rolled from his lips. He had silently fallen in step beside her, causing her to start.

"Yes, sir. I am quite well, thank you." Her voice broke before regaining control. She could not look at him, for all she could see in her mind was Mr. Darcy, informally dressed, participating in the savagely masculine act of moments before. Her pace increased as she quickly caught up to Miss Darcy and linked arms with her. *Indeed! Caroline Bingley must have had something of import to take her away from Pemberley this morning.*

"And you say you are acquainted with the full estate of Pemberley, is that correct?"

"Yes, Miss Bingley, I am. However, I am uncertain as to why you need my assistance. You have yet to explain my mission to me." The dimly lit room in the public house was fairly empty at this time of day, and yet the man still looked over his shoulder.

"Mr. Wickham, I would think that a man in your financial position would not question the services needed since I will pay you more than a year's worth of wages in the militia."

"I am not questioning you, Caroline." She gasped at the familiarity as he continued. "I only need to plan my escape. If Darcy catches me anywhere near his estate or his sister, he will hang me himself."

"Well, that is not my concern. It was fortuitous that my maid heard of your arrival in the village."

"Yes, fortune is smiling on me," he said as they bowed their heads together to discuss their plan.

After half an hour, he leaned back in his chair, shaking his head while a smirk played across his lips. "You have thought of everything, have you not, Caroline?"

Getting up to leave, she grinned, sliding him an envelope filled with money. "Just be certain you meet with success, Mr. Wickham, or else, my plan for you will be much more grievous!"

The morning was crisp, the sun peaking over the far off cliffs of Dovedale, when Elizabeth slipped out of the house while the other occupants slumbered. She had not slept well, every dream filled with either the regimentally clad, villainous Mr. Wickham or the shirtsleeve-attired, untamed Mr. Darcy in Pemberley Woods. She blushed at the vision of Mr. Darcy that had paraded itself through her mind every time her eyes closed. *Lizzy, this will not do.* She marveled at her rapid change in perception of both men.

She wandered aimlessly towards yesterday's worn path, stepping over logs and brambles and allowing her feet to guide her to her destination. It had been almost an hour since leaving Pemberley, and she only hoped the solitude of the old stone bridge would allow her to clear her thoughts. Sighing, she rested against it and shook her head.

"What a mess I have created for myself," she said aloud to the birds twittering above her. Her heart was beginning to have inklings towards the master of Pemberley, and although it was evident he admired her, he could not—nor would he—ever offer for her. "I am merely a poor gentleman's daughter with no dowry and three very silly sisters," she said to a bird perched above her. "Who would take me?"

However, I do not believe Mr. Darcy would trifle with my feelings. Did he not declare yesterday that he had thought me one of the most handsome ladies of his acquaintance? "One of the most handsome, Lizzy. Not the most. One of the most..." The water babbled in the creek below as it lazily flowed and led her in the opposite direction of the manor. *I will walk just a bit further. It will not do to worry Mrs. Reynolds or Miss Georgiana, or even Mr. Darcy.*

She walked until she reached a stump to rest. Opening her reticule, she took out an apple and some lemon biscuits she had procured from the kitchen. As she finished her treats, she softly began to sing a Scottish folk song:

But Black is the color of my true love's hair.
His face is like some rosy fair,
The prettiest face and the neatest hands,
I love the ground whereon he stands.
I love my love and well he knows,
I love the ground whereon he goes...

She looked across from where she sat and realized it was the same spot they had stopped the day before to cut down the tree. In her mind's eye, she could see Mr. Darcy powerfully swinging the ax. She blushed at the memory of his shirt clinging to his body and let out a soft giggle before she was interrupted by a male voice.

"I do hope you were singing that for me, Miss Elizabeth. I do appreciate your admiration of my hands and hair."

She started. There was Mr. Wickham standing across from her, and she immediately clutched at her reticule.

"Mr. Wickham. What are you doing here?"

"I have come to visit some old friends in the neighborhood since I am no longer in His Majesty's service." The smile he directed at her caused the gooseflesh on her arms to rise. "I found a much more lucrative and *pleasurable* inducement here at Pemberley."

"Mr. Wickham, I know not of what you speak, but I wish you luck in your new employ. Excuse me; I must be getting back to the house." She rose to leave, but he stepped in front of her.

"No, Miss Elizabeth. You will go nowhere unless I say so. You are my means to the life I deserve."

"I do not understand, sir. My father has little money if kidnapping is your design."

"You mistake me, madam. I will collect my bit from another; then I will force Darcy to pay me to keep it quiet."

She gasped at his words and stepped back. "Who? I do not understand what you are intending? I have done nothing that Mr. Darcy would need to keep quiet."

"I see your fear, girl. Is it the attention of Darcy that surprises you or that there are gentlemen like me in the world who would take advantage of such things?"

Her ire rose at his base implications. "I know what you are, sir. And you are no gentleman! I am aware of your history with Cecily Turner and how you harmed her, killing her and her unborn child."

"Yes, well, that was unfortunate." His indifferent tone angered her as he continued. "She was a sweet girl but had become too attached to me. Then, to go to Darcy? I could not have that!" He shrugged. "At any rate, she is with God now, and I am sure she is an angel."

"What do you know of angels, sir?" Elizabeth shot back. "You, who leave your trail of deceit and lies wherever you go!"

"Those are strong words, Miss Bennet. But deceit and lies do not always give me what I need. You know"—he paused looking at her innocently—"you can blame Darcy for what will happen to you today. Had he not stopped me from eloping with Georgiana in June, you would be quietly embroidering screens in Hertfordshire while I lived the life I deserved amongst London society."

Her mouth fell open. "You were to elope with Miss Darcy? But she is only a child and has not even come out into society."

"Yes, and she has an abominable allegiance to her brother, which I soon discovered upon his untimely arrival in Ramsgate. But, I can still get my revenge and get the money I desire through you." She stepped back again, and as his voice lowered, she noticed the knife he carried at his side. "But I believe we might enjoy ourselves today, as you and I were always good friends." Elizabeth gasped, finally realizing his intent. "Yes. You will be ruined today, Elizabeth. You will become one of those women cast out by her family unless Darcy pays me to be quiet. And even then, he will not have you. You will be tainted, and you will both be miserable, and his misery will be my joy."

His last statement made her shudder. "You are truly an evil man."

"If you think that. 'The end excuses any evil.'"

"Quoting Sophocles will not help you, sir. I insist, on your honor, that you allow me to return to the house at once. And I will speak of this to no one."

He scoffed. "My honor? My honor? Madam, I have no honor left. It was stripped from me by Darcy. Now, come." He roughly grabbed her arm and dragged her further down the path. As her piercing shrieks carried through the trees, he laughed. "You can scream all you want, Elizabeth. We are easily two miles from the house, so no one will hear you. However, the clouds in the sky concern me, and I fear we must find shelter before it snows."

They walked for another quarter of an hour before arriving at a small cave, where he threw her to the ground. "Now," he said, untying his cravat, and removing his coat, "Shall we begin?"

As she crawled backwards towards the rear of the cave, her hand grasped a large, jagged stone. She took a deep breath and waited for him to come nearer. "That's a good girl." He snickered. "Why fight what will happen anyway?"

As he put his hands on either side of her head and drew her mouth to his, she swung her hand up and slammed the rock into his temple knocking him down.

"You chit!" he screamed, falling into the wall. "How dare you!" She scrambled up and rushed towards the entrance as he lumbered after her, his long strides overtaking her at the mouth of the cave. Seizing her arm and pulling her against him, he sneered, "It is good to see you have some spirit in you, Elizabeth. It will give me a better story to torture Darcy with." He grabbed her face and forcefully brought her lips to his, viciously kissing her. She tried to pull away from him, but his grasp was too strong.

A moment later, he stepped back, and scoffed. "That, Elizabeth, is only the beginning."

Trembling, she bowed her head in submission before raising her eyes to meet his.

Mr. Wickham's grin spread as he once again grabbed her face. Before his lips could meet hers for the second time, Elizabeth raised her knee, assaulting him between the legs and causing him to fall to the ground.

As she turned to flee, he seized her ankle, pulling her down. "Oh, you will get it now. There will be no mercy!" His pained breaths came short and quick as he battled against her pummeling fists, finally pinning them above her head. "And now, I will have you," he sneered, grabbing at her pelisse and tearing the fabric from her shoulders. Her exposed skin only seemed to make him more insistent, and he laughed at her pleas while pulling at her petticoat. His intentions were interrupted when the sound of hooves echoed down the path.

"Elizabeth! Miss Elizabeth, answer me! Where are you?" Mr. Darcy rounded the corner and, seeing Mr. Wickham, alighted from his horse and tackled his childhood friend. His fist flew and caught Wickham in the jaw, knocking him unconscious. Mr. Darcy rushed to her and knelt beside her curled, motionless form. "Are you hurt, Elizabeth? Answer me, my love. Did he harm you?"

Brushing her hair from her temples, he saw her peering blankly straight ahead. Finally, she whispered, "I am fine, sir. Shall we return to the house?" Attempting to stand, she righted herself for only a moment before her knees buckled and she collapsed into his arms. The gravity of the situation hit her all at once, causing her to sob uncontrollably. He gently stroked her back and cooed softly into her ear.

At that moment, Mr. Bingley and a young man in Darcy livery charged around the bend on horseback before pulling up their reins. "Miss Elizabeth! Darcy! Is all well?" He jumped from his horse, looked about, and discovered Mr. Wickham sprawled on the ground. Darcy quickly directed Bingley and the servant to bind Wickham's hands and put him on Darcy's horse, Ulysses.

By now, Elizabeth's tears had ceased, and she was resting her head against Darcy's chest, breathing in his scent of leather and sandalwood.

He looked up at his friend. "Bingley, send back help. She cannot possibly return on foot. And send for the magistrate!"

"Of, course. At once. And I will inform the ladies that Miss Elizabeth has been found safe." And with that, he mounted his steed, and the two men and their prisoner left.

Mr. Darcy took off his great coat and wrapped it around her. She only stiffened for a moment before relaxing into him as he gently stroked her back and held her head to his chest.

Tears trickled down her cheek as he gently tilted her chin up and smoothed her hair.

"How did you find me, sir?"

A storm quickly spread across his features as he looked above her. "Mrs. Reynolds found me and commented that she was concerned you had been out longer than she anticipated. While checking the grounds, one of the gardeners said they saw you walk into the woods down the same path we had taken yesterday. My concern did not grow, however, until one of the stable hands said he saw a man who looked like Wickham at the pub last night." He shook his head and attempted to soften his features, looking into her eyes. "But what could Wickham mean by this—harming you? You are not a loose woman but a respectable acquaintance. I know him to be base but now see he only acts on his animalistic desires." Darcy's mind was wandering in numerous directions. "What would bring him back to Pemberley? Surely, he must know that, if caught on Pemberley's land, I would hand him to the magistrate for trespassing."

Elizabeth lowered her gaze before replying. "He alluded to a conspirator in the crime—the crime of compromising me so that he could fully seek his revenge on you."

"On me?" Mr. Darcy replied, stepping back and looking at her while still holding her shoulders. "How could he—"

"I am only relieved that you rescued me," she interrupted. She straightened her shoulders, causing Mr. Darcy's hands to fall at his sides as she brushed off her skirts. Attempting to hide the quiver in her voice, she continued. "Now, I thank you, sir. But we should return to the house. My sister and I will pack our bags, and if you would be so kind as to return us to The Inn at Lambton, we will leave before dinner so as not to cause a scene in front of the servants or Miss Georgiana."

"Miss Elizabeth, I—"

"No, sir. It will not do. I am ruined, and your sister shall not be around one such as me. She is too innocent—too good."

"Yes, she is," he said quietly, stepping towards her. "And, yes, you are ruined. But can your reputation not be saved by marrying the man who ruined you?"

Elizabeth drew back in shock. "You would have me marry him? He who is so vile and corrupt? Is that the life you would hope for me?" Tears of pain and anger began to stream down her cheeks again.

"Miss Bennet, according to society, it must be so. He who has ruined you must make you an offer to save your reputation."

She was sickened. *How can he suggest I marry Mr. Wickham?* And yet her sisters would be ruined if she did not; Jane could never make a match with Mr. Bingley. Sobbing, she cried, "I cannot. I cannot."

"I realize that, my dearest Elizabeth. But, as you stand here with my arms wrapped around you, you are compromised, my love."

"What?" She lifted her head from his chest with wide eyes. "What do you mean?"

"All I saw was Wickham attempting to bring you harm." He shrugged. "However, I have succeeded. We are alone in these woods, and I am taking liberties by stroking your back"—he moved his hands slowly up and down her spine—"by touching your skin"—he grazed her cheeks with his fingers—"and kissing your lips." He slowly leaned down to meet her mouth, and she only hesitated a moment before surrendering to the feel of his lips on hers.

Her fears erased, she reluctantly drew away at the sound of approaching horses. "I see your point, sir."

He brought her hand up and kissed her open palm. "Come along, Mrs. Darcy. We have much to prepare."

"How so?" she asked reveling in her future title.

"We must turn the Christmas ball into our engagement ball. That is, if you will have me?"

She arched her eyebrow and cocked her head to the side. "If you promise me one thing, sir?"

"Anything, my little wife." He brought her hands to his lips and kissed her fingers.

There was a quick intake of breath before she replied. "Promise me that, next year, we will have two trees at Christmas."

"As you wish, my dear, but why two?"

"One which we can discover with a party of friends, and the other," she began shyly, lowering her eyes, before finally looking up at him through her thick lashes, and reaching up to lay her hand on his chest. "The other, my husband and I will find on our own."

Happy was the day two young maidens from Hertfordshire married the men they loved—both considered to be prodigiously good matches for a poor gentleman's daughters. The two couples waited only long enough for the banns to be read and the Bennets to arrive from Longbourn before the vows were said.

Joy abounded throughout the little party and that of their acquaintances. Georgiana was introduced to, and besotted with, a young man from a neighboring estate who had been at Cambridge for a few years. The following year, after her coming out ball, he petitioned Darcy for her hand.

The Gardiners, with their children, often split time visiting their favorite nieces at both Pemberley and Netherfield. With Darcy's connections and Mr. Gardiner's excellent business sense, they have increased business for Gardiner Imports three-fold.

To keep the honor and reputation of Miss Elizabeth Bennet intact, Wickham was tried for trespassing on Pemberley. With his debts owed, as well as the angry mob of fathers and brothers of young ladies across the county, he was given a one-way passage to Australia.

And what of Caroline Bingley? During his questioning by the magistrate, Wickham spilled the truth of her involvement. In order not to injure his future bride, Bingley did what any honorable betrothed would do—he married his sister off to an obscure lord from the Isle of Wight and settled her with only half her dowry.

And finally, our beloved couple: Darcy and Elizabeth grew in love and numbers, increasing their family by three sons and one daughter. The children romped through Pemberley Woods like their mother but also followed social strictures like their father, content in the joy of learning wherever their imaginations and feet would take them. But every year on the first day of winter, Darcy and Elizabeth would wake up early in the morning, put on their warmest attire, and disappear into the woods with only an ax and the promise to return by the end of the day. When asked by the children why they could not come, the answer was always the same:

"Tomorrow we will go find our family's Christmas tree. But today"—he turned to wink at his wife—"today is just for your mother."

* *

ANNGELA SCHROEDER lives in California with her husband of fifteen years and her three rambunctious sons. She has a degree in English with a concentration on British Literature and a Master of Education. She has a slight obsession with Jane Austen and all things British. She enjoys traveling, baking, and making her family's world a magical place. She has published two other novels, *The Quest for Camelot*—book one in the Daughter of the Roundtable Series, and *Affections and Wishes*, a Jane Austen-inspired, modern-day romance. Follow her on Facebook at Anngela Schroeder-Author, on the Web at Anngela-Schroeder.blogspot. com, and on Twitter @schros2000.

"Find something you're passionate about and keep tremendously interested in it." —Julia Child

Delivery Boy

by Suzan Lauder

The keys disappeared before her eyes.

"Crud." She dropped to her knees and shoved her free hand into the deep snow beside the doorway. "Double crud-crud."

It wasn't enough that she had to take the bus because her ratty, old car couldn't handle a fresh snow. Or that, in spite of the fact she was a half-hour late, the restaurant was dark. They should be opening any minute now! Where were Kate and Lyddie? And Elvis...? Elvis should have been in the kitchen heating up the ovens and grill ages ago. What if customers were at the front door? Like Mr. Williams, for example. He was a carryover from Giorgio's days, who might now be waiting in the cold while she demonstrated her abilities as klutz of the year at the service entrance.

The snow fell into the hole her hand made, so she couldn't see where she was foraging. Her exasperated huff of breath threw a blast of condensed air into her line of vision. Times like this warranted a growl! She adjusted the box of groceries to balance on one hip while she tore off her mitt, buried her bare hand in the snowbank, and felt around some more.

A car pulled up and parked on the street. Its lights helped her see the area.

The keys! She shot up to unlock the screen door. Of course, the cheap thing was frozen!

The sky, pink with the city lights on low clouds, was addressed in her frustration. "Of all the… I can't believe… Why the *mfff* does this always happen to me?" She muffled the curse. Who knows why? She wasn't afraid to swear. Could be because of the guy who had climbed out of the car on the street a moment ago.

"Can I help you?"

She jumped. He was way closer than she anticipated. Her lips pressed together as her head whipped around to assess whether to freak out over a stranger sneaking up on her or to be glad for an offer of assistance. Too bad the information to help her deliberate was nonexistent. She shoved her frozen hand into her pocket and hitched the box higher on her hip.

He was tall and bundled up. *Trust a snowstorm to make everyone cover their entire bodies and faces as if they were in the Mexican military police.* The tips of his lashes already had a light layer of frost, but they were thick and dark at the base, almost as if they had eyeliner. He could be one of Giorgio's Italian cronies. That was all she could make out from his sheepskin-lined distressed leather coat with the collar up and a scarf tied around it, a heavy, dark turtleneck pulled over his lower face, and a watchman's cap tugged low on his head.

The car at the curb was a Jeep. He didn't have to take the bus.

"Uh, the door is frozen."

"Hold on a minute. I have some lock deicer."

His boots squeaked on the hardpack under the fresh snow, which meant it was freakin' cold for a cloudy night! She stomped her feet in reflex.

"Those are good boots," he said as he approached.

"Huh?" He pointed to her hot pink Sorrels. "Oh, yeah."

She stepped back to let him pass by—but not fast enough—and he brushed against her. In her northern down parka, she jutted out into the path in a certain area. To her relief, he didn't seem to notice.

He sprayed and fiddled with the latch. It was a pretty cheap screen door—aluminum. His body bent over it was bound to create more warmth than the piddly bottle of deicer. *Wow, he's got some pretty broad shoulders.*

"Keys?"

"Huh? Oh, yeah." She fished them out of her pocket. The icy metal stung her bare hand.

The latch worked, and the door swept aside a path of snow as he opened it. He continued, and once he'd unlocked the heavy oak door behind it, he held out his arm for her to enter.

"Thanks." She elbowed the light switch and glanced back. He'd followed her into the building. Was this creepy? Impossible to say right now. She eyed him. He was scrunched in on himself a bit. He may be cold, or embarrassed—hard to tell. Even with his shoulders folded forward and his hands in his pockets, he was still a big guy with long, lean legs below his coat. "Can I help you?"

He tugged down the layers over his face to reveal a light, scruffy beard. "Are you Elizabeth Bennet?"

"Yes."

"I'm Billy. Francine sent me. I'm supposed to start today."

"She never mentioned anything."

"Sorry." He motioned towards the door. "I can come back tomorrow, if you like."

She'd informed Francine Thomas, her former boss at Gardiner-Thomas Design, that she'd had trouble replacing Denny, who helped in the back and drove deliveries for the restaurant. Francine was involved with charities that found jobs for people on welfare; this must be some work-benefit thing. She'd better not have sent some dirtbag ex-con!

He seemed okay—a little shy and nervous, that was all. "No, it's okay. I have plenty for you to do. First, put this stuff away." She handed him the box and led him into the kitchen. "Cans on the shelves to match what's there, but put the new ones behind. Fresh in the upright cooler. Once you're done, you can start to clean the floors. Everything you need is in that closet. You have to pull the equipment and shelving and stuff out and do a super-good cleaning behind it. Elvis should be here soon. He can help with the heavy lifting, but don't bug him once he starts cooking. That should keep you organized until it's time for deliveries."

"Deliveries?"

"Yeah. Good thing you have a Jeep."

His mouth hung open slightly around some pretty well-formed lips, but he looked a bit stupid all the same. The mustache was heavier than the rest of the beard, and it reminded her of Saddam Hussein.

"You knew you'd drive your own vehicle, right?"

He shook his head.

"Giorgio used to have a car for deliveries, but it crapped out before I inherited. These days, delivery boys bring their own car."

He continued to appear baffled. She'd better quit saying "delivery boy." He was no boy.

"We pay mileage on top of your wage. You share the tips you get at the door with Elvis, and you get a portion of the restaurant tips for what you do to help out between deliveries."

Voices came from the restaurant. She'd check on them after she was done with the new guy.

His brow was furrowed. Did he not understand, or did he expect something else?

Paperwork! "You need to fill out some paperwork, but it's going to be busy tonight because of the snow. How about I dig it out for tomorrow, and you fill it out before you start your shift?"

"Yeah, sure."

"Excuse me." She walked past the ovens and grill into the bar area.

The sight of the restaurant still made her proud after several months. She'd redecorated it from top to bottom, the location of the big antique wooden bar the sole reminder of its former setup. The renovation was the last design job she'd ever do now she had her diploma from Le Cordon Bleu and had inherited the restaurant from Giorgio Vicano.

The dated Italian pizza place with its pretentious alcoves, chipped plaster statues, fake columns, ostentatious chandeliers, and plastic pond had given way to a cozy, rustic space. The menu retained the secret recipes but enhanced them with some traditional Italian flavors and high-quality ingredients, not just those Americanized toppings Giorgio had moved towards over the years.

Three regular customers stood inside the front door: Mr. Williams, an elderly man who had dinner at the restaurant every night since she could remember; Collin Hunsford, a creepy, know-it-all barfly, now the husband of Elizabeth's college friend, Sharla; and Jana, a former bartender.

Elizabeth exchanged pleasantries with Mr. Williams and offered him his usual house wine. Jana had gone behind the bar, unlocked the cooler, and handed an open beer to Collin, who plopped down beside Mr. Williams at the bar and sucked back a large drink. Elizabeth's eyes narrowed at Jana as she poured a small carafe for the older gentleman.

"How did you get in? Do you still have keys?"

"You changed the locks, remember?" Jana replied. "Lyddie's outside having a smoke. She let us in."

That lazy waitress was supposed to have opened already! Elizabeth must have shown her frustration on her face because Jana shrugged and rolled her eyes before she proceeded to pull chairs off the tables.

"You're not joining her?" Elizabeth asked Collin as she helped Jana.

"Trying to cut back. Besides, I don't smoke pot."

Elizabeth groaned. "She's smoking a joint before shift?"

"Just a couple of hoots. She always does," replied Jana. "She's still a great waitress."

It was true; she wasn't lazy at all. Lyddie hustled her ample butt, had a mind like a steel trap for orders and the preferences of regular customers, smiled and joked with everyone, and flirted her way into generous tips, yet she came off as a dumb blonde. Elizabeth had always known that pot was part of the culture of the musicians, and some late-night restaurant staff joined them.

The phone rang, and Jana answered. "Alimento dell'Amore![1] How can I help you?"

"Do you know anything about Francine sending me a delivery boy?" Elizabeth asked Collin.

"Nope. But she's got some big shot coming in to be a celebrity chef with you."

"What?" She noticed Billy standing at the door to the kitchen.

"Some corporate guy won a contest. He's supposed to be here all week."

"Aw, crap, that's *this* week? Now I have to endure some chef wannabe underfoot in my kitchen giving me tips he read in *Gourmet* magazine!" Her face dropped into her hands. "Kill me now!"

A male voice cleared his throat.

"Oh, Billy! Sorry, do you need something?"

"Beer company was just here. I signed for the delivery. I hope that's okay."

"Oh, yeah, sure! Thanks!" Good initiative for minimum wage labor. He'd taken off his coat and the watchman's cap, revealing a lean, trim body and a head of thick, curly hair, mussed from the cap. Hmm, he was pretty hot. If she was into beards, she'd be interested.

1 Food of Love

"Band is unloading, too. Should I help them?"

"Only if they ask. As a rule, no one touches their stuff but them."

"Okay. When does Elvis arrive?" He grinned. "Sorry, that just sounds funny. You know, the band's here, and we're expecting Elvis any minute."

Ka-thunk. That's what happened in her chest at his smile. *Holy mother of…he's gorgeous!*

"He's the Croatian cook," offered Collin.

"Croatian? I suppose Elvis is some Americanization of a name with no vowels?"

"Nah, his parents were mad about Elvis Presley."

Elizabeth's chest was still tight. "I'll text him to see what's up, okay?" Some unexplained lilt in her voice made her sound like a goofy schoolgirl.

Billy nodded. "If there's anything I can do to help, let me know."

Don't say that. I don't want my mind to go there. "Don't worry, with this weather, no one wants to drive. It won't be long until we have deliveries, and you won't have time for anything else."

"Okay, boss."

"Everyone here calls me Lizzy."

He smiled and nodded. *He has to quit doing that, or I'll never get anything done around here!*

"You got orders like crazy. I keep having to put people on hold," said Jana.

Elizabeth pulled out her cell phone and punched in a text to Elvis. "R u ok?"

Several customers entered and seated themselves near the stage. Jana brought them menus and returned to make their drinks.

"Thanks, hon."

"No problem. It's what I'm good at."

"Yeah, but you got your degree while you worked here because you wanted more. Now you don't have to schlep cocktails."

"It's fun when I don't have to!"

"Kate will be here if the band's here. Oli's Angels are playing, and her partner's the bass player."

"I'll cover until Lyddie comes in."

"Okay. I'd better turn on the ovens and grill." Elizabeth tied her hair in a messy bun. "I could be on my own in there tonight."

"On a Friday—with a band and a snowstorm," said Jana. "How are you going to manage?"

She shrugged. "Bust my butt, pretty much. No different than when I was in chef school. Or the storm could get worse and everyone stays home—and we go home early."

Lyddie came in, giggling and flirting with the saxophone player.

"Is Kate coming with Marie?" Elizabeth asked.

The sax player said, "Yeah, she texted me that they got stuck, but they're on their way."

Lyddie added, "I'll just leave the 'Seat Yourself' sign out until she gets here."

Elizabeth's phone beeped. "Bus stuck on street. I walk. 1 hour"

"No!" She frantically texted a reply to Elvis to get indoors; it was too cold to walk. He could wait for another bus or go home if he was close.

Beep. "Close 2 home. No need me?" His Croatian accent came through, even while texting.

She typed her response. "I can manage. Not many customers"

Beep. "Ok. If u say so. Take it easy"

"Thanks"

She sighed before she spoke to Jana. "No Elvis tonight. I better get into that kitchen." She waved to Kate and Marie, who had arrived with a group of customers. Being near a residential neighborhood, she expected a good crowd of walk-ins, even with the weather, because Oli's Angels was a popular band.

"How about I take the phone for a while until Chuck gets here?" asked Jana, referring to her new carpenter/model boyfriend.

"Thanks, hon! I appreciate it."

Billy was putting away the mop and pail when she entered the kitchen. She lit the flames for the major cooking equipment.

"What am I going to do for specials?" she asked herself as she surveyed the fresh meats and fish in the cooler.

"What are you good at?" It was Billy. *Why does he always have to stand so close?*

If she avoided his gaze, she could remain collected while she planned her menu. "Lots of things, but I'm on my own, so it has to be simple. There's not much *mise-en-place*,[2] so I'll prep as I cook."

"I can cut up a few things if you want."

"Yeah, cut your hand off."

---

2 A cooking term that literally means "putting in place." This can have a wide definition of any preparation work done ahead of time in a kitchen or restaurant, but typically refers to small containers of prepared ingredients on hand for the chef.

"I, um, took a cooking course or two. I wanted to be a chef, but I couldn't finish."

"Really?" She pulled a cap off a hook on the wall and put it on.

"Yeah." His eyes were on her hair as she tucked it into the cap. "You know, your long hair is pretty, but you're cute in the cap."

She shouldn't have glanced at him. He could tell her anything, and she'd believe him. How could she be crushing on a bearded delivery boy? "Thanks."

"No problemo, boss."

"Lizzy."

He nodded. "Just let me know what you need, and I'll help, okay? That's what I'm here for."

Thank you, floor, for holding me up. Thank you, cooler door, for something to grip. She could have melted with an offer like that. *Come on, Lizzy. Get serious. He's an employee, and pretty soon, you'll have a restaurant full of customers and a list of phone orders to get out. Start delegating, and then shoo him out the door and into his Jeep to ferry your delicious meals to impatient people in their homes.*

"Okay. Elvis got some fresh walleye. I'll grill it and serve it with a limoncello reduction. That's one. I prepped lamb legs yesterday. That's two."

"Won't it take too long? To roast the lamb?"

"It's boned and butterflied, so it's fast in the pizza oven. Now—sides."

"You had some nice rapini in your box of groceries. All it needs is to be steamed and tossed in oil with some aged cheese—do you have cambazola?"

She nodded. He was helping her with her menu? Pretty impressive. Gourmet delivery boy. "That sounds great."

Encouraged, he continued. "Maybe you could make a big pot of rice for timbales as a time saver."

She shook her head. "No, a simple winter pasta. Ground walnuts, olive oil."

"Nice! Do you do a starter with your specials?"

"Friday is antipasto, so it's just a matter of plating it."

"I can do that."

"We'll see. I used to be a designer, so the aesthetic is big in my dishes. My arrangements for the meats and cheeses are something I take pride in, and it's not just piling it on a plate."

"If you show me…"

"We'll see. Show me how you are with a knife, and maybe you can do some veggies for my pizzas."

"Yes, boss."

She rolled her eyes as she handed him some fat mushrooms and a chef's knife. He trimmed them and began to make paper-thin slices.

"No, we need them meaty for my pizzas."

He nodded, and a rapid staccato of steel on wood resulted in a pile of equal thickness slices, just as she liked.

"That's good. The bins for the *mise-en-place* are marked, and the produce is in the fridge. Make sure they're all filled. In the meantime, I'll staff the hot line. As soon as the delivery meals are ready, you're off driving."

"Okay."

"Thanks, Billy."

He smiled. Her insides flopped and clenched again, but when she smiled back, they eased.

The two worked side-by-side for about forty minutes, once in a while crossing paths so they had to do-si-do around one another. Each time brought a little laugh.

At first, not too much was said outside of the questions Billy posed about the work he had before him. He was efficient and adapted easily. He even managed to emulate her arrangement for the antipasto platter well enough that she set him to plate a few. While he arranged the antipasto, he initiated a conversation, first about the weather. She described her nightmare bus trip, garnering his laughs, teases, and sympathy.

"I'm driving you home after this. You don't need to go through that twice."

"You don't have to."

"It's no problem."

"Thanks. I'd appreciate it!" Due to the snow, none of the buses would be on schedule. She had to admit, the anticipation of an indefinite wait for a bus had her on edge, so a ride was welcome. In addition, she was relieved to no longer expect to be crammed in a standing position for an hour with all the others who didn't want to drive.

"You own this place?"

"Yep."

"How long?"

"Just over a year now. I was good friends with the former owner. I hung out here while I was in design school. At first, I got takeout or popped in here to eat and listen to music, but I started to study here so I could watch

Giorgio in the kitchen. He encouraged me when I said I wanted to go to Le Cordon Bleu to become a chef. I apprenticed at the Four Seasons and thought I'd try to move up in the hotel restaurant business, but when Giorgio was hit by a car and passed away, he left this place to me in his will."

"Wow! That's some story. I'm sorry about his accident."

"Thanks. He was a nice guy—also a frugal businessman. The place was free and clear of debt but needed an overhaul to be successful. I'd convinced him to do the odd update here and there over the years, but he was cheap. Even his menus had tape over the old prices with the new ones marked by hand on top, and his prices were low! I sold my house to finance the renovation and revamped the menu."

"You got a great review from the Mystery Dining Maven."

He reads the food reviews! Did he come to her restaurant for that reason? Probably not. A higher level staff member might seek her out, but a driver? "Caroline Bingley thinks she's a mystery, but most restaurateurs know who she is. She's demanding and infantile, and if you do exactly what she says, she might give you a decent review. She'll be in tonight as she has a crush on half the band. I knew her preferences from Giorgio's menu, so it wasn't too hard to get her favor."

"Did you...were you in a relationship with the former owner?"

She shook her head. That was heartbreaking. Giorgio had a thing for her; she had known it for years. She caught the yearning expression as he gazed at her when he thought she wasn't paying attention. Yet, he'd never acted on it, other than the odd bit of flirtation. She had believed their relationship remained a friendship of two people who loved food and music until that night at the hospital. "No. We were good friends but nothing more. He was older and had these old-school, old-country Italian values that would have never worked for me, and I wasn't wife material because I wasn't Italian. A couple of the waitresses went after him, but he'd never have a relationship with the help. They'd just turn around and screw someone in a band, anyways. Oh, sorry."

"Sometimes, that's all it is," he replied in a gruff tone.

"What do you mean?"

"Girls like that just screw."

This was a little uncomfortable, so she said nothing.

He didn't divert his attention from rolling slices of Hungarian salami as he spoke. He was flushed. "I mean, they want something from a guy. He owns a restaurant or plays in a band, and that's the sum total of the attraction, his status in her eyes. She can tell her friends she's with someone important, but she could care less about who he is inside, whether he wants a traditional wife, or any other things he values. A woman like that will dump him once someone more interesting shows up." He paused and pressed his lips into a line. "Guys do it too, most of the time for superficial things, like if the chick is hot. There needs to be more…respect, caring about the other person to some level."

The uncomfortable sense that hung in the air changed ever so slightly. An appreciation for his character emerged as he spoke of how he valued others' feelings. But guilt appeared as well. Earlier, he had made her so hot, she might have jumped his bones if he'd made a move, and he was nobody. And an employee!

"You're right," was all she said.

"Sorry, I didn't mean to get heavy on you."

"It's okay. It's nice to hear a guy talk like that." She closed the last hot pack. "Do you want something to eat before you go? There's pizza for the staff and band."

"I'm okay. I had some antipasto."

"That's good. Then you're outta here. Do you know the city well?"

He started to put on his outerwear. "Lived here all my life. But if there's a new subdivision, I've got a GPS, and the Jeep can go through anything."

She grabbed a pen and paper. "Here's my number. Text me if you have any trouble, okay?"

"Sure." Once he'd punched it into his phone, he took the pile of hot packs.

"In fact, it'll be slow going because of traffic. You know—abandoned cars and stuff. So could you text me in an hour with your status so I know and don't worry?"

"Will do, boss."

She opened the door for him, and a cruel blast of cold air hit her. "'Lizzy,' please."

He winked as he squeezed past her, but this time didn't brush against her. "I like calling you 'boss.'"

She rolled her eyes and smirked. "Fine. Text me in one hour. And drive safely."

The moment his broad back was out the door, she closed it to keep out the cold. It was undeniable, the attraction she felt for him, and she didn't like how distracted it made her. She'd have to call Francine tomorrow and ask for a different person to be assigned. She'd pay him for the week and give a good reference.

What, are you kidding me? Stupid girl. No way could she tell Francine she couldn't work with him because she had the hots for him! That would mortify her! She'd just have to suck it up and act like a professional—treat him as an employee and get over her silly crush.

"Silly crush" sounded so innocent and naïve. She knew what she wanted, nothing innocent about it. Talking this evening just made it worse. She liked him. A lot. He was sweet, funny, and sensitive. And without that scruffy beard, she was afraid he'd be devastatingly handsome.

The door opened again, and her heart leapt. The person who came in was shorter and stouter than the one who just left.

"Hey, Lizzy! I make it!"

"Elvis!"

"How you doing without me?"

"Hectic, but I survived. The new delivery guy helped out."

"Billy. Yes. I meet him outside. Nice car."

"How did you get here?"

"Neighbor has Jeep too. Not new like your friend though."

A *new* Jeep? She hadn't paid enough attention. *Interesting.*

Elvis put on a cap just like hers. "Show me what we make tonight."

Time to get back to business.

ELIZABETH STARTED WHEN SOMEONE TAPPED HER SHOULDER. AFTER THE kitchen had closed, she'd settled at the band's reserved table while they played indie tunes, a pleasant distraction from the commotion of the restaurant.

Billy's touch had jarred her back into reality, and his handsome face wasn't unwelcome. His head tilted toward the kitchen. He wanted to talk where it was quieter.

"You finished the last run?" she asked as she stepped into the kitchen.

"Yeah."

"Did it go okay?"

"Yeah. I have the tips here."

He passed them to her, and she unlocked a drawer, put them in an envelope, and locked it again. "Great. The tips get split when we close up later. Anyone who's gone home gets their portion next shift. I pay weekly on Fridays and wouldn't pay you until next week, but if you need cash, I can pay you for tonight."

"No, I'm okay. Can I do anything more?"

"Thanks, no. Kitchen's clean, and Elvis has gone home already."

"Elvis has left the building." He affected a dramatic voice, and she chuckled. "I thought I'd hang around and listen to the band until you're ready to go."

"Sure. Come on, join me." She was about to head into the bar when the phone rang. It was Jana's boyfriend, saying the tow truck had arrived, and he'd be on his way soon.

When she hung up and turned back towards Billy, he was in conversation with Lyddie. With her natural Scandinavian coloring and fresh face, Lyddie could be a caricature of a farmer's daughter, tall and blonde. She was a bit heavy, but all in the right places. She giggled and stuck out her butt and boobs when she leaned over to whisper in his ear. Billy flushed and gazed at his shoes as his hands burrowed deep into his pockets. His lashes fluttered forward, and the instant he saw Elizabeth, his eyes lit up as his head snapped to face her. The corner of his mouth lifted.

She tilted her head to the bar and set off in that direction, a little conscious of him following. As they walked, she twisted her head around. He was right behind her, eyes down. Was he checking out her butt? "Um, do you want a beer? It's on the house for surviving the first shift."

"Excuse me?" He shoved his hands into his pockets again, and his shoulders shrugged. It was as if he was trying to make himself smaller, like in the kitchen earlier.

Too noisy for him to hear. She'd have to wait until they were at the table. Once seated, she motioned for him to lean over and repeated herself. His hair tickled her nose, and he smelled good.

When she pulled back, comprehension lit his intelligent eyes. His face moved close alongside hers. "No, thanks. Driving."

Kate, a tiny waitress with long dark braids, came up to them to take their order.

"I'm having cranberry and soda, if you want one," Elizabeth said loudly.

He shifted his glance from her to Kate. "Plain club soda would be nice."

"Coming right up!" Kate headed to the next table.

Billy examined Elizabeth as though she were on stage, captured in the beam of huge, hot lights. She squirmed for a moment in her seat. *Make conversation!* Leaning forward, she asked, "Do you like the band?"

"Yeah. I've seen them before and figured I had to stop by the bar tonight."

Silence and some more staring. His scorching gaze was too intense, and she became self-conscious. She turned away and touched her hair, which she'd let down once the kitchen was closed.

His voice startled her. "It's really pretty."

"Yeah, that's what you said earlier. Um, thanks." That sense of a spotlight was closer than ever now.

The corner of his mouth lifted. "You're blushing."

Her mouth dropped as she eyed him, defensive. "I do not blush!"

"You should be used to compliments." The statement might have been smarmy if he hadn't worn a playful grin on his face.

"Oh, please!" Her hands flew to cover her face. When she split her fingers, his blush and sheepish expression elicited a laugh from her.

"Sorry, I have no idea where that came from. I'm not that guy."

She reached over and touched his hand. "I know. It was funny."

His hand turned under hers, and she panicked, snatched hers back, and dropped it in her lap. The impulsive move could have offended him, yet he said nothing, so it was hard to tell.

"One club soda!" Kate would never know what good timing she had!

"Thanks," said Billy as he reached for his wallet.

Elizabeth spoke loud enough for Kate to hear. "It's okay. On the house."

Billy pulled out a tip for Kate, whose sweet smile and thank you removed some of the tension that had hung in the air a moment before.

Once she was gone, Billy raised his glass. "Cheers." Elizabeth responded in kind. Both turned to the band and listened for a while. During the applause after a solo, he caught her eye and smiled.

Ka-thunk. His eyes were melting her again. "Um…Did it go okay tonight?"

"Yeah."

She squeezed her eyes shut for a moment, peeked at him, and responded contritely. "Sorry, I asked that before. You must think I'm a ditz."

"I, uh…" He glanced off to the side, then back, and then leaned in to speak into her ear. "No, I admire you a great deal." When he sat back

DELIVERY BOY

again, his eyes bored into hers. His intent was unmistakable; his regard was not about her clean kitchen or antipasto art or business acumen. His engrossed expression made her go blank while tiny hairs prickled on her overheated skin.

Nothing was said, but his long gaze made the statement. Her nerves made her mouth go dry, so she wet her lips, and his eyes darkened and dropped to stare at them. His own lips fell apart, distracting her dedicated focus on his eyes as her gaze fell to the curve of his mouth. He leaned forward...

The room broke out in enthusiastic applause as the music ended, and she twisted to face the band as she clapped. She castigated herself once again.

THE MAIN ROADS HAD BEEN PLOWED, BUT WHEN THE JEEP REACHED HER street, it was still full of snow with few vehicle tracks. She became lighthearted at the sight of the fresh carpet that glittered in the streetlights as if it was trying to compete with the colorful holiday displays on the homes of her neighborhood. She loved this time of year for its sparkling, hushed nights.

"You can drop me here, and I can walk the rest of the way."

"Don't worry. I'll get you to your door."

He focused on the road as his Jeep plowed through the deep snow with ease.

"So, what were you and Lyddie talking about?"

His eyes darted in her direction before returning to the street. "Um, you."

Do not ask! Keep the lid on that can of worms.

"It was all praise, and she expanded on details you failed to mention when you said you inherited. How you didn't have to sell your house to finance the renovations because Giorgio left you five rental houses, and you could have sold any of them for the cash. Instead, you sold four to employees for a dollar each, and mortgaged the fifth to pay off their student loans."

"That's what he would have wanted. Giorgio helped everyone go through school, kept their spot while they took classes, and shuffled hours to help them manage their time."

The Jeep turned into the driveway and stopped. Billy turned off the ignition and twisted in his seat to face her.

"You're avoiding the fact that you deserve the praise."

Rather than respond, she stared into her lap, but his gentle fingertips

188

lifted her chin and tugged her face towards his. The temptation to gaze into his eyes was strong, but she closed hers instead, and sure enough, the warmth of his lips pressed against hers. They moved slightly, sensuously, and his beard tickled.

The kiss was chaste enough, yet the prolonged contact said that, if she wanted more, she could have it. She pulled away and placed a firm hand on his chest to urge him back to the other side of the Jeep.

"Billy, sorry, this isn't right. I, um, I don't think you should come in to work tomorrow. I'll get Francine to make sure you have another gig right away, and if not, I'll pay you until she does."

His eyes became wide, and his mouth hung open before he spoke. "What? You're firing me?"

"I can't—"

"You're darn right, you can't. I just started today. You have to give me a chance."

"I'm sorry, but—"

Hurt laced his words. "Don't you dare dismiss me now that we've started to relate to each other so well! I'm not imagining it."

"That's not—"

The pitch of his voice rose. "After all I've gone through to connect with you. I mean, I tried not to want you, but you came back. You came back from the dead!"

That stupid newspaper article! But what does that have to do with anything? "I don't understand. What did you go through?"

He sighed. "It sounds crazy, doesn't it? I thought so too." He looked at his fingers as they flexed over the steering wheel, then back at her. "I was attracted to you the first time I saw your picture in the newspaper. You had just won that environmental design award in college for the self-sufficient village concept. I have no idea why I was so drawn to you, but the sensation was profound. So I followed your internship, your career in the newspapers—every mention, every article. You were the star, yet you chose the earthy, social services design rather than corporate offices.

"I knew it was crazy, so I went on a remote eco-tourism holiday for a few months to get away from news and social media—anything that mentioned you. I needed to distance myself from those articles. When I came back, you were dead, and I...I didn't take it well."

She had to explain, but the situation was so complicated. "It was all a huge misunderstanding. I slipped on the ice and fell, hitting my head so hard I passed out for a couple of minutes. I felt fine, but they wanted to keep me in the hospital overnight for observation.

"Giorgio showed up, distraught over my accident. He told them he was my husband so he'd be allowed to visit. I assured him I was okay, but he wouldn't calm down. It was his fault, he said. He had to protect me and ensure it never happened again—keep his eye on me. To appease him, I asked him to take my purse for safekeeping.

"After he left, he...he hooked up with a...a woman he met in the waiting room. As they were leaving, a drunk driver swerved onto the sidewalk, and they both died on the spot. Some reporter got bits of information and leaked the names of the casualties—except he overheard the E.R. staff mention that Giorgio had my purse and concluded the woman with him was Giorgio's wife. Me."

He nodded and continued. "I...I couldn't handle it—your death—and I was...away...again for a while. But Caroline Bingley's review was recent, and it had your photo, so I was frantic to discover the truth. I'd never felt such a weight lift as when I verified you were still alive.

"I saw you for real for the first time in my life at Kate Brant's opening for the photography-multimedia show on the English National Trust houses at the University Gallery. You didn't like me much." He brushed a curl from her shoulder.

She tried to remember that night. *Who did I talk to at Kate's opening?* She was uncomfortable at these things, as it was a bunch of artists and well-heeled patrons, people who spoke a different language than she did. Was he one of the waiters? Or one of the students who hung around the gallery hoping to score free food?

"Just a couple of weeks ago, we met up again. The Alzheimer's fund-raiser."

She had been one of the business owners who dressed up as Mrs. Claus.

"We had a great time that evening." His voice was warm.

"I don't remember you being there."

"I was your Santa. But you had no idea it was me. It took me a bit to realize it was you."

It had been a wonderful evening. She and her Santa Claus—pairs of them were servers and entertainers for each large corporate table—had a blast performing the roles and teased each other like an old married couple. He was so much fun—but he shouldn't have been there!

She snorted. "What lazy corporate executive conned you into taking his spot?"

He didn't answer; instead, he continued. "I had to see you again, so I asked Francine to get me a gig at your restaurant. Okay, it may have been the wrong approach, but it turns out you needed the help tonight."

Was this weird, creepy? It should be. "My regular delivery guy takes his band and goes to Texas every winter, and you show up a week later. Convenient." Derision was evident in her tone. "I think you're replaceable."

"Elizabeth, you can't turn me away. I've tried to forget you, but there's something about you... We would be good together."

"I'm your stalking victim, you mean."

"What? No, it's not like that!" His inflection showed he was incredulous.

"You read every newspaper article, go to events I attend, take the role of someone else to get close to me, arrange a job at my restaurant to be near me, and you deny you're a stalker?"

"Elizabeth, please. I know you're mad, but how did you feel earlier? Am I wrong that you're attracted to me? It was okay when I was just a guy—nobody special."

"Except to me! You manipulated and tricked me into thinking you *were* special. *We* were special! Don't you see? I had to end our work relationship so we could have a personal one! I was planning to invite you in, and...and..." Her face flamed; she'd almost admitted she'd intended to sleep with him after knowing him but a few hours.

He leaned over, his voice gentler. "Please, let's go back to that..."

"No. Effing. Way." She grabbed the door handle, flipped it open, leapt down onto the snowy walkway, and rushed to her door.

"WHERE ARE YOU, LIZZY BENNET? I HAVE A BONE TO PICK WITH YOU!"

"Back here, Francine." Elizabeth prepared herself for an overdue lecture.

Five days had passed since she'd dismissed Billy. Tomorrow was Thanksgiving, and the restaurant would be closed, but she and Elvis were busy preparing for a meal hosted by a mental health and addictions help line charity. The kitchen was already full of the aroma of sautéed onions and fresh herbs.

She was certain Billy complained to Francine. Well, she was unwilling to discuss why she told Billy not to come back, not even her initial reason.

"There you are!" The perfectly manicured and coiffed person that was her former boss appeared. "I'm buying lunch."

"Francine, it's the day before Thanksgiving! I'll make you a sandwich, and we can talk while I work."

"Elvis, you can manage without her."

The voice of Miss Bossy.

Elvis shrugged his shoulders to his ears and made that "it's not important" mouth of his forebears. "For maybe one hour, of course!"

"That settles it. Chuck and Jana are waiting at the restaurant. Let's go."

"Vegan?" Maybe they were in the wrong restaurant. Francine was a true carnivore! However, Elizabeth was proven wrong.

"I heard this place was excellent. Have you tried it?"

"A few times."

Jana waved at them from the back of the restaurant, before she disappeared around a corner. They followed her to a table out of view of most of the place.

"This is unacceptable," said Francine as she raised her hand to flag down a waiter. "I'll ask for a better table."

"Not in that fur coat, you won't," said Chuck. He was a beautiful man, and next to Jana, it was hard to believe such an attractive couple could exist.

Francine pouted, but the waiter appeared to take their drink orders, so she put on her best smile. "Proseco, please."

"I'm sorry, but we don't serve alcohol here."

Francine rolled her eyes. "One of *those* restaurants. Fine. A Pammy-Pommy please."

"We don't carry Pammy-Pommy."

"This is a vegan restaurant?"

"Yes, ma'am."

"Pammy-Pommy is healthy. Why not?"

"Pammy-Pommy is a non-sustainable product. It uses syrup from corn, which could otherwise be used as food, and the pomegranates require extensive irrigation, wasting water."

Francine huffed. "Fine. I assume you have mineral water that isn't going to kill any trees or whatever?"

The waiter affirmed it, and Francine agreed as she waved a dismissive hand. The others ordered their drinks.

Francine peered at Elizabeth, who glanced at Jana and Chuck for support. They were regarding her strangely too. "So what's this I hear that you didn't hold onto Darcy for two nights?"

She tried to figure out what Francine was getting at. "Darcy? Fitzwilliam Darcy?"

Francine nodded. "I don't know why you couldn't even grant him a sous chef job for more than one shift. Might I add, he paid a huge amount to the Mood Disorders Association Benefit to win that prize. Huge."

The silent auction! "You never said Darcy was my auction winner! How could that detail slip your mind? Wow! *The* Fitzwilliam Darcy. I'm surprised he'd want to schlep food around in my kitchen when he could choose any restaurant in the city."

Francine cocked her head and said, "Come on, honey, you're the hottest new restaurant in town. I told you, everyone who's anyone wants to be on the inside. Foodies would die for that. And Darcy bought it for a small fortune."

"Collin said someone rich was coming, but he was a no-show. Just my luck. It would be cool to have Fitzwilliam Darcy play chef at my restaurant." The richest man in the city was pretty hot, after all. Maybe she'd act normal around him on her own turf rather than a tongue-tied doofus like before.

Chuck spoke up. "Lizzy, come on. I saw him drive off with you when I was arriving!"

"What the—"

"Language!" Jana said. "Lizzy, Chuck and Darcy are old friends. Chuck went to high school at Pemberley Prep, you know."

"Yeah, I knew Chuck came from money. No surprise he knows Darcy. But it was Billy who drove me home." She turned towards Francine. "The new delivery boy you sent over."

Francine appeared confused. "I never sent a delivery driver. I haven't found one yet. It's one thing to get help from the shelters for heavy lifting work, but another to have their own vehicle."

"Well, one showed up with a brand new Jeep…" *What the—* She grasped her head with both hands. "F—"

"LANGUAGE!" As soon as it was out of her mouth, Jana clapped her hand over it. With a mortified expression, she flitted her eyes around the restaurant to determine whether anyone noticed. One pimply teen glared at her over his shoulder but went back to his sandwich.

With a roll of her eyes, Francine drawled, "For a bright girl, you have a lot of difficulty putting two and two together."

The waiter returned. "Everything okay?" They assured him all was well. "Sorry for the wait, but your drinks will be here in a sec. In the meantime, are you ready to order?"

The group agreed, and when it was Elizabeth's turn, she merely said she'd have what Jana ordered. She couldn't think about food right now. Instead, her mind strained to remember the face with thick eyelashes and a Saddam Hussein mustache over sensuous lips.

When he was gone, Elizabeth stage whispered to the others, "Billy is Fitzwilliam Darcy?"

They nodded, and Francine explained. "He arrived at the Schizophrenia Gala Saturday night in a tux with some young floozy when he was supposed to be at your place. I confronted him, and he was pretty miffed. Said you'd fired him." She leaned in as she tapped her fingernails on the table. "What did he do? Better yet, what did *you* do?"

The accusation was unfair. They had no clue what an asshat Billy was, yet they were blaming her. Asshat was the victim? Asshat, who stalked her all these years.

"He didn't say who he was. Just called himself Billy. I thought he showed up for the delivery job. He never said anything about the auction. He helped us out the one night, but I didn't need him the next."

"You what?" exclaimed Jana. "You did, too!" She spoke to the others. "She rented a pickup and drove herself! Elvis has been driving since because they can't find anyone good."

Chuck piped in. "He's Billy to his friends. Just like you're Lizzy. He'd only introduce himself as Fitzwilliam if it were business or a formal situation."

Like Kate's art show at the University Gallery. Fitzwilliam Darcy had been formal when he'd introduced himself to her, and she freaked because she couldn't believe it was him. She'd stared at the top button of his suit, noting the fabric might well be more expensive than her car.

He had said something banal to the top of her head, and her head rose in response. He had a cold, aloof facial expression. In response, she had made a general comment about the art show, trying her best to sound like a sophisticate who wasn't affected by him. *Cool as a cucumber.*

She hadn't even convinced herself though. Instead of attempting to recover, she'd escaped as soon as possible. In all likelihood, he thought she was a bitch the way she'd behaved that night.

But Mr. Santa didn't scare her off. She knew the guy was at the very least a manager at some prestigious firm, but whoever he was, he was funny, and she had the best time in a long time.

"How did you not recognize him if you know who he is?" asked Francine.

"Beard," said Jana as the waiter handed out the drinks.

Elizabeth took a sip from her fresh juice and nodded. "A nasty, scruffy beard and heavy mustache."

Chuck had an air of disbelief. "But everyone else knew who he was."

"Not me," said Jana. "Not until you told me. No one else did either. At least, no one said anything. He was dressed super casual too, not like all the photos in the press where he's all bespoke-suit formal. You can't blame Lizzy too much.

"But geez, Lizzy, you studied the guy almost as if he was your homework assignment, so I'd have thought you knew every lump and bump no matter how hairy any part of him was."

Chuck howled after he snorted his coconut milk through his nose. Francine tried in vain to stifle a snigger while Jana let out a nervous chuckle at her own double entendre.

"Sorry, badly worded. But it's true."

"He stood in a different way, as if he were shy." She was defensive. "Darcy stands up straight. He has great posture. And he's always confident and composed. Billy was kind of hunched over."

"So his eagerness wouldn't show," Francine said, laughing. At Elizabeth's raised eyebrows, she said, "Come on, hon, you're a big girl. He tried not to be obvious, but he wanted to meet you in the worst way, and spent a pile of money to do it. You know I worked on you for a while to get you to agree to this. He thinks you walk on water, and I thought it was a good chance for you two to get together."

This was going nowhere. They seemed to think his obsession was innocent, and she had to set them straight. "He's been stalking me."

That got their attention.

"He went to events I went to, paid to work in my restaurant, and pretended to be a delivery boy to get close to me. He could do anything else for his huge money at that fund-raiser but wanted to work for me! That's stalking!"

"Events? How many?" Chuck asked.

Who cares? "Two."

"Coincidence. You both go to a lot of similar events. Besides, even if he had, two is not stalking."

"Maybe he was creative in how he approached you to ask you out, and that's all. It all sounds pretty up front to me." Francine was all too sensible.

Elizabeth faced her to amplify her point. "He also kept newspaper clippings on me." *No one can argue his ethics now!*

Jana wielded the real dagger. "Like the 'Darcy Files'?"

Her damned face betrayed her, as she couldn't control the mortification that swept over it.

Jana explained to the others. "She's kept newspaper clippings of Fitzwilliam Darcy over the years. When I saw the file, she claimed she kept them because she aspired to his level of leadership in the business community. But a lot of trees were killed to create such a thick folder."

Elizabeth stared at the table because she didn't want to see their faces or divulge any more. The first article was saved for that reason, maybe even the first ten. He said wise things, made great business decisions, volunteered within the community, and supported the charities she favored.

Before long, he could say anything and she'd keep the story, better yet if it had a photo. She loved admiring those photos. Soon, every mention of him was recorded, and she found herself surfing the web for new articles.

"You were infatuated with him?" Chuck asked. "If I had any idea, I'd have hooked you up a long time ago." He glanced at Jana. "I don't know how we missed introducing you two in the first place. Darcy and I are pretty tight."

"You do a guys' night with him, hon. I've met him once," said Jana.

"Two pretty messed up people together? Not a good idea," Elizabeth mumbled.

"At least you have something in common." The sarcasm dripped from Francine's voice.

"No. No, it's not like that," Jana said to Francine. She turned to Elizabeth. "You're both pretty normal most of the time."

The statement was worthy of her eye roll in Jana's direction.

Jana put her hand over Elizabeth's and continued. "You're both excellent business people, hard workers, loyal friends, humanitarians, and more intelligent, sensitive, and empathetic than most. You were drawn to each other even though you hadn't met because you saw the real person within those clippings. You saw the pattern behind them, representing the values and ethics that matched your own. I think you'd have to search long and hard to find a better partner."

She squirmed in her chair as she glanced around but couldn't fix her gaze on anything. Dear Jana. Always so positive. And naïve.

"I don't think so. I burned my bridges with him pretty good." She raised her gaze to her friends. "Francine said he had a date Saturday. It was pretty easy for him to get over it."

"Tall and blonde?" Chuck asked. The waiter returned with their food.

"Yeah," replied Francine, her perfect eyebrows raised, "and young, or at least, she appeared that way to me."

"Sister. Back from private school in England."

"Really?" Francine was incredulous. "She was sophisticated; I saw her from a distance. I knew he had a little sister, but…wow, she's grown up!"

Chuck nodded and bit into his lentil burger.

Elizabeth couldn't think of eating now, the way her stomach was churning. *This is cray-cray.* Billy, Darcy… It was impossible to reconcile herself to the situation.

"Listen, I gotta go. It's a huge amount of work, and I shouldn't have gone and left Elvis alone. He's a great chef, but he has no interest in being anything more than a cook who takes orders."

"Are you okay?" asked Jana.

"Yeah, fine. It's just that the restaurant…well, it's a big day tomorrow."

"Sure, hon. Let's get your lunch packaged."

Francine swallowed the red cabbage and quinoa slaw she'd been chewing. "Mine too. I'll drive you back."

She shook her head. "It's okay. I'll flag down a cab. Thanks."

Jana disappeared in search of the waiter. Silence reigned at the table as the others ate their meals.

All at once, panic hit Elizabeth. She stood and put on her coat. "I guess I still need you to find me a delivery boy." She almost walked into Jana as she rushed towards the door. The lunch package was passed as part of a half-hug before she escaped.

The cab ride allowed her to calm the overwhelmed sensations that had caused her to flee. She breathed deep into her belly and brushed away automatic thoughts of Fitzwilliam Darcy and Billy the delivery boy. Calm took longer than expected.

9 a.m. Thanksgiving morning.

Beep. She checked her phone. It was Elvis. "Lizzy it wet down here. Broken pipe"

Please let whatever leaked be clean! "Water pipe?"

Beep. "Yes. I close water already"

Good. It was Croatian speak; he'd shut off the water. "Ok, mop it up. I'll be over right away"

Beep. "Too much for mop. Half foot"

She couldn't imagine that much water! "Ok. How are the ovens?"

Beep. "Gas. Light up top"

Good. No worry about a short circuit. "Are the trays ready?"

Beep. "Hot. Probes say so"

"I'll see if we can get it over to the hall ovens early"

She needed to keep four turkeys and four large trays of stuffing at a safe food temperature until noon when the homeless and neighborhood people began to arrive.

Sharla, who was organizing volunteers, picked up on the first ring, and Elizabeth explained the situation. No problem, Sharla lived close to the hall and had the key. She'd start the ovens right away, and they could carve the turkeys there.

She texted Elvis to tell him she was on her way.

Beep. "Wear rubber boots"

It was a wading pool. The kitchen wouldn't be too much of a problem since almost everything was raised, and Elvis had taken care to move items higher. But her beautiful new floors in the restaurant! And how long would they be shut down for the cleanup and replacement?

Her sous chef stood beside her as she surveyed the damage. "My cousin works for construction. He brings pump and extractor right away," he said.

"Oh, Elvis, you're wonderful! Thank you!"

"They take off the walls, you know. Mold."

Her heart dropped. "What?"

"Wet part of walls get cut off in case of mold. Not just floors to fix. Big fans to dry."

"Aw, crap! It'll take longer before we can reopen!"

Elvis made his "it is what it is" face. "Cousin takes care of you. No worries."

"Thanks, man."

"You are welcome. You call insurance now."

"I'll try tomorrow. No one's around on Thanksgiving."

He shook his head. "They work 24-7. Loss mitigation."

"Huh?"

"They make sure you dry right away so less cost for them."

"How do you know all this?"

"Cousin in construction. Lots of money in insurance restoration jobs."

She sighed. "Well, I'm in over my head."

"Tell you what. I phone insurance guy. We load food. I stay and wait for him."

"You're the best, Elvis."

He shrugged and made that Croatian "whatever" face.

SHARLA HAD TOLD HER TO GO THROUGH THE MAIN ENTRANCE AS THE BACK would be blocked by a large delivery truck. Sure enough, a van with a logo from an audio-visual rental company was at the rear door. The front door was unlocked, and inside, Sharla was nowhere to be seen, but the ovens were on. Half the trays were already installed when Sharla poked her head in.

"Do you need a hand?"

"Sure. I have some boxes yet."

"I have to stay while they set up the big TV, but a couple of volunteers are just standing around over there, so I'm sure they can spare one."

"A big TV?"

"Someone with deep pockets thought the people would like to watch the game together, so they're installing a big TV in the smaller auditorium. I'll send someone out."

As she went to collect her next load, she noted the table with disposable razors, combs, toothbrushes, and small bars of soap: freebies for the guests, many of whom were homeless or impoverished.

Her head was in the back of the van when help arrived. "Here. Hand that to me." The voice was gravelly.

She squinted into the sun behind him as she put a box in his arms, turned for a second one, and plopped it on top.

"They're light!"

"Lettuce," she said. "Last year, a volunteer brought a huge bowl of salad and it disappeared in a flash. It turns out lots of homeless or low-income people want healthy foods, and salad is a rare treat at soup kitchens and shelters in winter. I figured I'd bring lots so more can have it." She plopped a third on top, but it was too much, as the stack was over his head. "I thought since you were tall..."

"Yeah."

"I'll take this one."

She reached up and closed the door that had hidden her helper's face. "Billy?"

His eyes dropped to the ground and he cleared his throat. "Hi, Elizabeth."

The beard was gone, but the Saddam Hussein mustache was heavier. Her fingers twitched; they wanted to touch the smooth skin on his cheeks.

"Um, thanks for helping."

"That's okay, boss."

The old nickname comforted her.

He trudged toward the auditorium, slowing his pace so she walked alongside him. "I thought Sharla said you had food to go in the ovens."

"Those trays are already inside. Lots of stuffing. Last year, they had no stuffing..."

"...but stuffing's the best part." They said it in unison. The giggle pushed through the back of her throat and escaped, earning a grin from him.

Ka-thunk. *Oh, Fitzwilliam Darcy, you still do it for me!* Yet, she didn't feel as awkward at the moment as at other times. She wanted to impress him. "I made four trays. I hope it's enough."

"Not inside the turkeys?"

"I wanted to make more than the turkeys could hold since most of the others who bring turkeys won't make stuffing. My turkeys are cut in half lengthwise and cooked on top of the tray of stuffing to get a little essence in each batch. Elvis experimented for a while and came up with a perfect mix of butter, stock, and a trace of duck fat to make the stuffing right."

"Wow, genius!"

"He's the best!" She hesitated a moment before she asked the question that had burned in her mind since she saw him today. "So are you the TV guy? I mean, did you donate it?"

He turned his eyes away. "I guess you figured out I'm not a delivery boy."

Delivery boy. She had to quit using that phrase. He'd picked up on it, and it was so wrong for a man like him. "I had to have it pointed out to me," she replied.

When he stopped, she was still moving, so she had to spin around to discover why.

He was staring downward again. "Elizabeth, I'm sorry. I was an ass to assume you might want a relationship when you didn't even know who I was."

She scrunched her eyes together. "You forget—I wanted it too. Just…well, I have boundaries about dating staff."

He blew out a puff of air. "Well, my stupid pride ruined the evening. Shit, it ruined our friendship."

"You haven't paid attention if you think that's the case. We've gotten along fine today until we started to worry about regrets."

His head rose, but he wouldn't meet her gaze. Instead, he stared across the street. "Yeah, I got lucky there. I mean, I know you didn't care much for me. I guess you thought I felt entitled to waltz into your kitchen because I paid for the privilege." He huffed and glanced at her, then back into the distance. "Thing is, you're right. I *did* expect I could get what I wanted if I paid for the privilege. But when you didn't realize…you thought I was a delivery boy…well, it took me aback, and I didn't know how to react. You were relaxed and nice to me."

"I got some 'splainin' to do about how nice I was to you at the art show."

He faced her again. "No, I understand now. I realize your discomfort was a reaction to my attitude. No one would be sanguine when treated as if they were of less importance. I was…haughty."

His face was so introspective. Unless she came clean, he would take all the blame. "Not all the time. Santa and Mrs. Claus had fun."

"You didn't know it was me that time, either. You made me relax and enjoy myself rather than putting on a show of my own importance."

"I've thought a lot about how I'm perceived and realized I distance myself because I'm uncomfortable with strangers, yet it's rude. The worst part is I felt justified in behaving in a cold manner. Until you showed me how insufficient pretensions are to please a woman worth pleasing."

Wow. Heavy thoughts. She shivered. "How about we get the rest of this stuff inside where we can have a coffee and talk more?"

"Sounds good to me, boss."

Darcy stood taller than he had at the restaurant and moved with the grace of a man comfortable in his own skin, remarkable for such a tall, broad-shouldered man. *What a great butt.*

He turned to walk towards where she sat at one end of one of the many long tables, and he gave her a little smile.

"It's pretty hot," he said as he passed her a Styrofoam cup. "Sorry, they just had the powdered stuff."

She blew on her coffee. "I'll wait a bit."

When he was settled, she had a question. "If you found me so...interesting...from the newspaper, why didn't you ever try to meet me?"

"You were too young, for a start. It was when you won that award and internship. Even so, I interfered. I approached Ed Gardiner with a renovation project for Darcy Enterprises' head office and asked that the Longbourn Scholarship recipient be involved. But he told me you'd already chosen your project."

"That's interesting! I remember the chance to participate in a multi-story office design project. My project had challenges that intrigued me, so I stuck with it. A renovation of an after-school center in a poor area. The space was tight, and it had a feel-good aspect too.

He nodded as he tried a sip of his coffee. He made a face.

"That bad?"

"I'll live."

"It's what you get at these things: percolated coffee from those big urns." She continued. "But it turned out extra funding became available, and the project became the design of a new wing, which was great, as I could use my imagination for what would be best for the kids. An anonymous donor showed up..." *Oh, wow! Was it possible?*

His dark lashes hid his eyes, which were fixed on his coffee cup. A dark curl drooped down onto his forehead, making him adorable.

Elizabeth softened her voice. "I don't understand. Why be anonymous? You...you gave half that amount to the burn center at Netherfield Memorial Hospital, and they named it after you."

He shrugged. "I didn't want recognition. I... It was for you. As much as

I respect Gardiner-Thomas Design and believe in the programming at that center, I did it for you."

The passion in his focus on her made her break eye contact. He did that to her. It was always too much. No, that wasn't right; it wasn't enough to release the discomfort. She needed more from him than a steamy stare. "You should take pride in your philanthropy."

He shook his head. "It's not as special as it appears. My father made several fortunes before he was my age. I grew up accepting a role in giving to the community."

"Yes. The first time I paid attention to you. 'Shares in Darcy Enterprises enjoyed a jump today when Fitzwilliam Darcy officially took the reins after acting as CEO during the illness of his late father, George Darcy. The younger Darcy has already made a name for himself in his leadership of several charities. Many men of twenty-three with his fortune would leave the day-to-day business to employees and enjoy their good fortune with cars and parties, but Fitzwilliam Darcy follows in his father's footsteps as a hands-on manager who has already proven himself with several strong acquisition decisions.' I was in awe."

"You were just a kid! And you must have quite the memory."

Crap. Time to come clean. "I, uh, have six file folders and a spreadsheet."

"Huh?"

"I mean, about you. Printouts of press, clippings, brochures—so much information, I had to sort it, so I used several categories for business decisions, board memberships, major funding, as well as the functions you attended, the women's names attached…"

"Good lord. You've got my life on a spreadsheet?"

She sucked her lips into a line as her eyes flicked about the room, avoiding landing anywhere too close to him.

"Now I feel a lot better about my fascination with you. I mean, am I right? You were stalking me too?"

She studied her hands in her lap. "Not exactly. At first, it was admiration of you as a business leader and philanthropist, kind of like I wish I could be like you. My friends knew about it and teased me. At some point, I became sensitive to their judgments and quit mentioning the files. It became private."

"None of them were important. The women."

She gawked at him.

"I wanted you to know. Just society dates for functions."

"You no longer need them now the blonde is old enough to go with you."

He appeared confused until it dawned on him. "Georgie? She's my sister."

"Yeah, I know. Just teasing." They shared a smile. "You're okay with this?"

"With what?"

"My spreadsheet."

He leaned back in his chair with one arm over the seat back. "Pot, kettle. I'm relieved I'm not the only strange one in this relationship. It feels like, I don't know, karma? We both were attracted to a public persona, right?"

She conceded it was correct. He straightened up again.

"But when we met, it was different. At least, it seemed that way to me. You had no idea who I was, and you treated me differently than I'm accustomed to, and I liked it, a lot. You showed me the person, and I'm more attracted to her than the girl who won the scholarship."

"And I fired you."

"So you could get into my pants." His smug expression and cheeky tone indicated his pleasure in evoking those desires in her.

It was impossible to suppress a grin as her face became hot with embarrassment. "You're incorrigible."

He laughed. "You're not the only one who can tease!" He became serious again. "So, are we good? I mean, I'm awfully sorry we argued, and I want to start again."

"Yeah. But let's go slowly, okay? I'm enjoying this, getting to know the man behind the image, and I want to savor it—make the feeling last."

He reached across the table, his palm up. "Anything you say, boss, as long as we're together." That was all he needed to say. Her hand slid into his, where he squeezed it then held it with care. They remained that way for a few moments, regarding their joined hands, until he broke the silence.

"If we're going to get to know each other, it might be a good start if I introduce myself." He tugged his hand free as he straightened to sit tall in his chair. His hand was thrust towards her to offer a handshake. "My name is Fitzwilliam Darcy." The voice he used was low-pitched, comical, and affected, as if he was acting a role, and she was reminded of their time together as Santa and Mrs. Claus. A loud laugh popped out of her unexpectedly, and she placed her hands over her mouth in embarrassment that they might draw attention from others in the hall.

After ensuring she could speak without a large audience, she feigned a serious response. "Pleased to meet you, Mr. Darcy. I'm Elizabeth Bennet." She grasped his large hand for a firm handshake, but the sensation was strange when his hand collapsed at the same time.

"Owww!" His playful retraction of his hand made her mouth drop open.

"Mr. Darcy, you need to be taught how to shake hands! No one likes a limp handshake!"

"I look forward to the lessons!" His raised eyebrows now had her in stitches, and she collapsed on the table. When he collected both of her hands from the table and caressed them in a more romantic manner, her laughter calmed, and she tilted her head to meet his affectionate smile.

"Hey, I'm hosting a party next week, at my home," he said in a sincere tone. "Just a few friends, but it's sort of a celebration for a few of my buddies and me. Would you like to come?"

House party? "As a guest?"

His thumb rubbed over the back of her hand as if it wanted to make a point. "As my date."

Tingling sensations covered her entire body. This was a good thing. "Yeah, I would."

"Great."

It dawned on her that next week was December. "Monday, right?"

"That's right." His brow was furrowed.

"December first. Shaving party?"

His eyes lit up. "Yup! You know about Movember?"

"I do, but I didn't put two and two together until just now. You don't shave your mustache for the month of November to raise awareness for prostate cancer."

"I can hardly wait to get rid of this thing." He was animated. "You have no idea. It itches like mad! It looks like shit too, right?"

She smirked but was honest. "It makes you look like Saddam Hussein."

He groaned. "I hoped maybe Omar Sharif. At worst, Groucho Marx."

The laugh was impossible to hold back. He flushed. "Nope. Sorry," she said.

"I tried the beard because I thought it might make me look less stupid, but you're supposed to be clean shaven except for the mustache. The other guys chided me pretty hard, never mind my sister. And I thought I was the rule-follower in the family!"

"I have to say, I won't mind when it's gone. You're much handsomer without it."

"Thanks, I guess."

"But it was kind of cool the way the kiss tickled."

His face lit up, and he searched the room for a clock. "Are you staying to help?"

"Just to serve. They have their own kitchen help."

His eyes twinkled, and one side of his lips lifted. "We have an hour. Want to go find someplace to get tickled?"

Holy cow! Her toes curled all by themselves, and every inch of her skin became alert with anticipation.

Her silence must have sent a message. "Don't worry. We'll go slow," he said gently. "How about we find a hallway or closet in the building, just for a little necking?"

She laughed and squeezed his hand. The expression on his face was priceless: relief, glee, and fiery urgency. He leapt up, and they scrambled, hand in hand, to a place where they could learn things a newspaper can't tell.

Sharla and Francine were waiting, glasses of champagne in hand, as Elizabeth kissed Darcy goodbye before he joined the head table, which was packed with local celebrities. She paused to watch him walk away; his body was fabulous in a tux.

When she returned her attention to her table, Francine rolled her eyes. "You two got it bad."

Her cheeks had the heat of a light sunburn. "We do!"

"I spoke with Anne at the Mood Disorders Association today. They're thrilled that Fitzwilliam Darcy will be the honorary campaign chairman for next year's fundraising."

"He's just as thrilled. Even though he detests being the center of attention, he expects he'll enjoy working with the caller for tonight's big ole live auction. I have to agree. It sounds like fun."

"Yes, it will be. Darcy also managed to procure a few interesting packages to bid on. Like a private rooftop dinner with an English male model—guaranteed to bring in big bucks."

"Brrrr. At this time of year?"

Francine shook her head. "I'd ask Mr. Gandy to cuddle under a big blanket if I paid for the big prize! But he isn't available until June, so that's when the prize will be collected. Can you imagine waiting so long to see him?"

"Not my type. I'll pass."

Sharla piped in. "Yeah, your type is at the head table."

"Guilty."

They continued with pleasant chatter about other prizes as they ate their sumptuous meal.

"Where did they get such perfect wild leeks this time of year?" asked Sharla.

"Odds are they're super expensive," said Francine.

"Farmed in a climate-controlled barn, and you're right about the cost," replied Elizabeth. "I wish I could use these for my specials, but I think I'd have to charge far more than my customers are willing to pay."

"I'd give it a try," said Francine. "Your place has the right reputation. One super-pricey meal among the affordable ones won't be out of place. Average diners will splurge, and you may expand your clientele if you're known for that special touch."

"Good point. I think I'll sneak into the kitchen and ask Catherine for the name of her supplier."

Francine explained to Sharla. "The executive chef is Darcy's aunt."

Elizabeth rose but took another forkful of the delicious vegetables before she left her friends to chat.

When she returned, dessert was on the table, and the program had started. She squinted at Darcy, who happened to notice her at the same time. She grinned at him, and he gave the slightest nod, though his eyes were affectionate. *So serious in public, yet so animated with me!*

"I love you." She mouthed the words. When he placed his hand on his heart, no one else was in the room.

But they called his name, and he broke the gaze. He rose to applause and moved past the others at the head table to the microphone.

He spoke well, related the example of a friend with treatment-resistant depression, and cited the one-in-four statistic of patients who have difficulty finding the right regime of medication and counseling. His speech segued into the announcement of the first of the prizes for the live auction.

The bidding was lively as the professional auctioneer rattled off the amounts bid for luxury prizes including spa weekend getaways, home renovation packages, jewelry sets, and exclusive golf club memberships. Francine put in a few bids on the English model, but backed down long before the final award of the prize.

Darcy stood tall, handsome, and clean-shaven as his attention was divided between each bidder and the auctioneer. Elizabeth wasn't bidding, but she browsed the brochure as others around the room bid on items. The excitement in the air escalated with each successive bid. She set aside her brochure while the last and biggest prize, a luxury eco-tourism vacation, brought in competition in five-digit amounts.

Something was wrong with Darcy. He was less attentive to the final bidding war, his face solemn in spite of the excitement. But it was momentary as he snapped out of it and followed the action again.

She began to daydream about being in his arms after they got home when she was pulled out of her reverie. He announced that one final item had been added to the auction.

"I request your indulgence in a story," Darcy said. "A year ago, I won a prize in the silent auction at this particular event: an opportunity to work in the kitchen at Alimento dell'Amore. There, I met the most wonderful woman in the world, and she's here tonight. Can I get a spot on Elizabeth Bennet for a moment?"

Francine shouted out, "Over here!"

Elizabeth found herself blinded when all she wanted to see was Darcy.

Mercifully, the light went back on him, and amidst a field of bright dots in her vision, he continued. "I invite the audience to bid on an event that will happen in front of you this evening. In fact, you're going to bid on the most important event of my life. You see, I'm in love with this woman, and I want her to be my wife.

"So how much are you willing to pay to hold the ring while I propose to Elizabeth Bennet right now?"

Elizabeth's eyes welled up with tears, and she attempted to swallow in spite of her heart blocking her throat when Sharla leapt to her feet. "One hundred dollars!" *What the...*

"Five hundred dollars!" Francine was next with the money she'd meant to use to buy a date with Mr. Gandy.

A buzz filled her ears. *Must be the noise of the room going crazy with bids.* But one thing was all that mattered: gazing at her love as his face misted a bit before her eyes.

All of a sudden, he was walking towards her, taking both her hands in his, and going down… *Oh, lordy, he's on one knee!*

"Yes," she blurted.

His voice was soft, but she heard it over the crowd's murmur. "I haven't asked the question yet."

"Okay, fine. But I have one for you."

"What's that, boss?"

"Who gets to keep the clipping?"

* *

SUZAN LAUDER'S enjoyment of variety is evident in her dynamic career, food interests, hairstyles, and of course, her writing! No one story can predict the style or setting for the next as Lauder continues to experiment with her craft. Mad about historical research and learning new writing techniques, she's an active member at the Austenesque fan site, A Happy Assembly. Her unique Regency romance with a mystery twist, *Alias Thomas Bennet*, was published by Meryton Press in 2013.

Lauder's fascination with the Regency period inspired her creative blog series, the *Thrift Shop Regency Costume Experiment*, a project that transforms found, re-used, discount, and vintage items into quality, Regency-era outfits. The amusing and resourceful approach includes original patterns, and it has garnered support from Regency and upcycling bloggers and fussy Regency costumers.

Lauder and Mr. Suze live on beautiful Vancouver Island, BC, Canada, with two tabby cats who supervise her projects.

"Love sought is good, but giv'n unsought is better."
—William Shakespeare, *Twelfth Night*

The Food of Love

by Maureen Lee

Yorkshire, December 1812

Anne pressed her face against the glass of the frosted window, staring down at the snow-dusted steps of the entryway. Her breath left a patina of fog on the glass, and she lifted the edge of her muslin sleeve to wipe it clean. Why was there still no carriage coming down the drive? It was midday, and her cousins had said they would be at Harlow House by late morning. Admittedly, the journey from London to Harrogate was not a brief one, but they had spent the night at a carriage house in Yorkshire and should have only had a few hours journey ahead of them. Anne sighed, looking at the blanketed, white landscape before her. Perhaps they had been delayed by the weather.

She was anxious to see her cousins of course. Being the only daughter to a far elder brother, Anne craved the sisterly companionship of her uncle's daughters. Harriet and Fanny were younger but far more worldly with their stylish, London upbringing, and Anne eagerly awaited their stories of London balls and the latest fashions. But this time, it was not the arrival of Harriet and Fanny that had left her pacing the landing, hoping for a glimpse of the carriage. The previous summer, her cousins had taken in Roger de Brun, a French refugee and distant relative of her aunt Eliza.

210

She had met M. de Brun briefly when her family passed through London on their way to their summer lodgings in Bath, and she was instantly fascinated by him. His lilting accent, a mop of pitch-black curls, and his slate grey eyes—he was unlike any gentleman she had ever met. Men like M. de Brun were not to be found in Harrogate; they were all banal conversation and stifling propriety. Roger de Brun had an air of mystery and sophistication that Anne found intoxicating. She had become determined to prove herself worthy of his charms when her cousins announced M. de Brun would be accompanying them for their annual Christmas holiday.

She stared at the stack of papers she had left on the settee in the window. Anne had devised a means of ensuring she would spend a great deal of time in M. de Brun's company over the coming month. In previous years, her cousins had prepared a play for the epiphany—a festive and ribald way to occupy everyone during their visit. It was typically too cold for any outdoor activities, which was Harlow House's best feature, so the girls had taken to days of merriment in play rehearsals. It would not seem odd then that she was so eager to renew the tradition. She had simply selected a work that allowed her to pursue her aims *discreetly*.

Shakespeare's *Twelfth Night* for the twelfth night of Christmas was utter perfection! She would play the witty Viola; Harriet was well suited to the haughty Lady Olivia; and Fanny, being meeker than both Anne and Harriet, would play the smaller role of Maria. The swarthy M. de Brun was a natural fit for Duke Orsino, and so Anne would woo him as Viola does in the play. It was the ideal scheme while maintaining all bounds of lady-like propriety outside the proceedings of rehearsal.

Anne's visions of herself as Viola wrapped in Orsino's arms were dispelled as she noticed a dark smudge coming down the walk against the quiet blanket of white. Could her cousins really have encountered bad weather and sent a messenger to recount their delay? She pressed her face harder against the glass and, recognizing immediately who it was, gave a little yelp of excitement. For coming down the lane, dusted lightly with snow, was their neighbor James Turnbull. James was only a few months her senior, and they had grown up together, running wild on Harlow House's extensive grounds, playing hide and seek in the trees, and swimming in the lake. For as long as she had known him, he had been her dearest friend. He typically joined them for holidays, but she had forgotten about his arrival in the excitement of awaiting her cousins. After all, one's oldest friend could hardly be considered half as thrilling as the impending arrival of the mysterious M. de Brun.

Still, James was always a comfort to her. His good sense, steady presence, and merry eyes would be a welcome distraction. So, Anne removed herself from her post on the second floor and went down to greet him. By the time she had bounded down the staircase, Mr. Frith had opened the front door and she saw James attempting to knock the snow off his boots before stepping inside. He looked up and caught her just as she descended the final step and broke into a wide smile. She could not help but meet him with a grin of her own.

"Miss Riley! I had just asked Mr. Frith to go and find you."

She inclined her head in greeting, "I saw you through the second floor window. I was looking out for Fanny and Harriet's carriage."

Once, she might have run to him and given him a warm hug, but as she had grown older, she realized the impropriety of greeting any man in such a familiar way (or at least several scoldings from her mother had forced her). Instead, she stood in the hallway, feeling awkward and frustrated at the regulations of society. Why should she not hug a man she had known all her life, who had taught her to swim and seen her run with her hair flowing wild? James knew her better than even her own parents did, and yet she was forced to incline her head and restrain herself from embracing her dearest friend. She realized she was staring at him.

"I am so sorry. I have forgotten my manners. Will you not come into the parlor for tea?"

He moved into the parlor and seemed to look at her queerly as she threw a longing glance back at the front door that Mr. Frith was shutting quite firmly.

"Anxious for their arrival, are we?"

"Yes, they assured us they would arrive sometime this morning, and now that it is going on mid-day, I worry the weather has caused an accident."

"I am sure they are fine. You are merely excited at the prospect of seeing your cousins again. It has been half a year since you saw them in London, yes?"

"Yes, I suppose you are right. A watched pot never boils and all that. I am glad you have come. You can distract me."

"Always glad to be of assistance, Miss Riley. Though goodness knows you have had no trouble finding ways to distract yourself over the years."

"Oh! 'Miss Riley,' indeed. You must call me Anne. You always used to. I cannot abide this false sense of propriety society has imposed on us with age."

"As you wish. Speaking of distractions, what entertainment have you devised for us this year?"

"Well, it is not Christmas without a play. It is one of your favorites: Shakespeare's *Twelfth Night*. Remember that Christmas several years back when you first introduced me to Mr. Shakespeare. It was with this very play, and we sat by the fire with you reading the love poetry of Orsino so beautifully. I have never forgotten it."

James tucked a mahogany curl behind his ear as the late morning light caught his hair and gave it the golden shine Anne loved so well. He looked pleased. "Of course, I remember that night. You were the first to share my enthusiasm for Shakespeare. I am happy that you remember it so fondly. You are to be Viola, of course?"

She blushed and immediately found something extremely interesting in the pattern on the Indian rug beneath her feet. "Well, yes. But, you have always said I had the greatest flair for the poetry of Mr. Shakespeare's language. You know that Harriet and Fanny could not give it the same emotion. And besides, Harriet would complain about having to dress as a man, and Fanny would forget all her lines—"

"I was only teasing. Of course, there could be no more perfect Viola than you. And who is to be your Orsino?"

He looked at her expectantly. Anne had been dreading this moment. Of course, James would expect to play the part. He had read it so beautifully that night and many times since.

Anne blushed. "Actually, I thought M. de Brun—you remember, the French cousin of Harriet and Fanny's? I thought he would be perfect. He is our invited guest after all, and he has had such a dreadful time of things, having to leave France. I thought it might cheer him to play the lead."

James looked briefly taken aback but recovered quickly. "Of course, you are quite right. You are always so mindful of your guests. Shall I be your Sebastian then?"

"Well, yes, but I had rather hoped you might take on a dual role. You would be so delightful as Malvolio, James. Nobody can be officious quite like you."

James looked surprised but quickly covered his confusion with a smile.

"Yes. I—I do like to keep things orderly and proper. And who then shall be the Lady Olivia?"

"Oh, I think Harriet is perfect for the part; do you not agree?"

"Perfect for what part?"

Anne turned to find her cousin Harriet standing in the doorway. Mr. Frith was standing next to her, looking aghast at her interruption.

Noting the butler's obvious agitation, Harriet chuckled. "It seems I have put Frith out of sorts by not waiting to be announced." Harriet removed her muff, tossing it at Mr. Frith, and sauntered rather grandly into the parlor. "It's not as if we've never been here before." James looked on, trying to stifle his amusement at Mr. Frith's indignation, as Anne rushed to greet Harriet with a kiss on the cheek.

"Oh, it is so good to see you. We had a dreadful journey this morning. Father and Mother are sorting things with the luggage. I cannot think where Fanny and M. de Brun have gone. But what is this about a perfect part for me?"

"I thought, perhaps, we might be a bit literal this year and do *Twelfth Night*, and I thought you might play the Countess Olivia."

"Goodness, a countess. *Too* divine. Of course, it is perfect. You always know best when it comes to these things, Anne."

Before Harriet could babble on much more, Mr. Frith coughed and announced, "Miss Fanny Rochester and M. Roger de Brun."

Anne turned and locked eyes with Roger de Brun. She felt herself turn the color of a radish and looked determinedly at her feet but not before she took in M. de Brun's knowing gaze and dazzling entrance. His winter cloak was dusted with a light snow that had fallen on his shoulders in the distance from the coach to the house, and he was wearing a tricorn hat cocked dashingly atop his raven curls. His eyes, as grey as the English Channel, bore into her as they had six months ago. James spoke first. "Well, will you not join us for some tea? I expect you have had a tiresome journey and could use some refreshment."

Finding her voice, Anne exclaimed, "Oh yes, you must be in desperate need of tea," pulling both Harriet and Fanny onto the chaise lounge and leaving the gentleman to the armchairs.

Excepting her Aunt Eliza and Uncle Henry, who Anne assumed would retreat directly to their rooms, the entire party had arrived for Christmas. Anne stared longingly across the room. She would have much preferred to have M. de Brun next to her on the chaise. But she consoled herself in the knowledge she would have plenty of time to speak with him over the next month and turned to her cousins with pleasure.

The next afternoon, as Anne stepped into the parlor, she heard Harriet complaining. "Oh, it's so wretchedly cold and dreary again today. I do so hate the snow." Anne steeled herself for a difficult afternoon for she loved the Yorkshire winters, particularly at Christmas when the snow was welcomed as part of the festivities. It was but one of many points upon which she and Harriet disagreed.

Vowing not to let Harriet dampen her first rehearsal with M. de Brun, she glided into the parlor, handing out scripts she had copied herself over several sleepless nights. Harriet and James already knew what parts they were to play, but she had yet to reveal the cast to Fanny and M. de Brun.

"Fanny, you'll be Olivia's lady-in-waiting, Maria."

Fanny murmured in assent as Anne passed her a sheaf of papers. She had expected such a response as Fanny was shy in the presence of all but Anne and Harriet.

"Now, M. de Brun, as you are our special guest this Christmas, you are to have a plum role. Would you do us the honor of portraying the Duke Orsino in our trifling, holiday tradition?"

M. de Brun looked solemn and spoke in his eloquent, accented manner. "I am afraid I cannot. As you know, the French are against the titled nobility, so it would be rather poor form for me to accept, would it not?"

Anne was crestfallen and dropped the remaining papers to the floor in shock; all of her scheming for the past month had come to naught. How foolish she had been to assume that M. de Brun would assent to this ridiculous request. As she bent down to gather the pages, she looked up to find a slight smile at the corners of M. de Brun's mouth.

"I am only teasing you, Miss Riley, of course. I am happy to take part in your play. I am taking refuge in England after all, *and not just for the beautiful women.*" He whispered that last part, so only she could hear, as they both reached to gather the papers scattered at her feet. And when she looked up at him in shock at his scandalous suggestion, he merely winked at her and brushed her knuckles with his fingers as he returned the script pages to her arms. She remained in a crouched position, looking up at M. de Brun like a startled animal for a moment too long.

Recovering herself, she continued to distribute her handwritten scripts and was surprised to find James eyeing her in confusion.

James cleared his throat and said, "I suppose we should read it through first."

"I should not think that necessary."

James snapped his head to eye M. de Brun. "And why ever not? Should we not familiarize ourselves with the language before putting it to its feet?"

"Oh, but my cousins have led me to believe that you are all old hands at this Christmas play business. Why not expedite the process?"

James turned to look to Anne for support. But Anne was already looking at M. de Brun adoringly. "Yes, of course. You are quite right. I do not know why we bothered with such things in the past. Let us take our places and see where that leaves us."

M. de Brun crossed the room to take a position near Anne's side, leaning to whisper in her ear. She glanced at James then back to M. de Brun and broke into peals of laughter.

James cleared his throat uncomfortably. "M. de Brun, the play begins with your speech—if you'd be so kind?"

With a quick wink at Anne, M. de Brun strode to the center of the room and began. "If music be the food of love, play on." He placed one hand to his forehead and clutched at his chest. He heaved a melodramatic sigh. "Give me excess of it, that, surfeiting, the appetite may sicken, and so die." James exhaled, rubbing his face with his hands. Anne could feel his disdain as he glanced at her, but she reminded herself that she was only being a good hostess by giving M. de Brun the best role.

"That's splendid!" she exclaimed. "I can feel your heartsickness. Just like that."

The afternoon proceeded in much the same way: Anne showered M. de Brun's acting with praise while ignoring James's pointed looks. Harriet routinely crossed the room to stare at her reflection in the window and make remarks about how she had always thought her complexion was suitable for a countess. Fanny, with a stricken look on her face, studied her lines assiduously and had to be called upon frequently to speak on her cue.

"I do think that Sebastian's grief for his lost sister would overwhelm each moment he is on stage," said James.

M. de Brun interrupted. "Nonsense, my dear man. The beautiful Olivia has just offered herself up to him. I cannot abide that a man would not forget his grief at such a moment."

"I am surprised, after all you must have suffered in France, that you know so little of grief," James snapped.

Harriet and Fanny gasped at the hard edge in his voice, and Anne chided him. "Really, James, there's no excuse for rudeness. I quite agree with M. de Brun's assessment of this moment."

James found himself quite at a loss for words. He had spent many hours poring over the works of Shakespeare in the Harlow House library with Anne, and she had never displayed such blatant misunderstanding of the work before.

"Perhaps, it would be best if M. de Brun played both Orsino *and* Sebastian then. If you will excuse me, ladies. I have some business this afternoon that I must attend to." And with that, he strode brusquely out of the room.

Anne started to run after him, but M. de Brun caught her arm. "Let him go, Miss Riley. We might be better off to allow him his sulk."

THE NEXT MORNING WAS CHRISTMAS EVE, AND ANNE AND HER COUSINS took to decorating the house with her usual bright-eyed zeal. As the young ladies of the house decorated, M. de Brun found his height to be of use to their efforts. They hung evergreen boughs from the bannister and trimmed the fir tree. In recent years, Anne had introduced a Christmas tree to the merriment after Harriet and Fanny had related the story to her of this new tradition Queen Charlotte had introduced at Windsor. Fanny draped garland from its boughs while Anne delicately placed the small baubles she had sewn over the last year throughout its branches. Anne had also made a star for the top of the tree, much like one she had seen in a German etching, and she asked M. de Brun if he might place it atop the tree.

He met her with a dazzling smile, his grey eyes gleaming. "Of course, Miss Riley. It is my pleasure." He arranged the star with a delicate artistry so that it perched atop the tree for all to admire. They were all cooing over their handiwork when Mr. Frith entered the parlor. "Miss, I am sorry to interrupt, but Mr. Turnbull has asked if he might have a word."

Anne hesitated, casting a glance at Roger de Brun. She regretted the way she had left things with James in rehearsal the day before. Though he had been the one to storm off, she still felt guilty that it was somehow her responsibility. He had never behaved as such before. All their lives he had never been anything but warm and amiable, excepting his occasional

THE FOOD OF LOVE

scolding for her lack of refinement. She was loath to miss a moment with M. de Brun, particularly when things were going so well. The maid was laying a fire in the parlor, and the room was magical with Christmas cheer. With her needlework of the past year and M. de Brun's assistance, the house looked more festive than ever before.

As if he sensed her very thoughts, M. de Brun nudged her companionably. "Go ahead, Miss Riley. Tend to your friend. We will all be here when you get back, playing cards before the fire, I daresay."

"Very well, but do not forget we must rehearse later." In the back of her mind, she was thinking of the final embrace they had yet to practice. She hoped the scene would require many tries to perfect.

So, it was with a rather downcast air that she met James Turnbull in the hall; he was oddly holding her velvet, forest-green winter cloak.

"What have you got that for?"

"I asked Mr. Frith to have it brought down. I thought you might like to take a turn in the gardens. I know you love the snow and have not had the chance to go outside much with your present company."

Anne felt herself warm to him. She had been yearning to spend some time in the snow, but she had forgotten with the excitement of the decorating party. She heard herself feign nonchalance. "Very well, if you insist." And then, before she could stop herself, she said, "I hope you are come to apologize for your dreadful behavior yesterday."

Mr. Turnbull looked properly cowed. "As of matter of fact, that was exactly why I have come. I was hoping you might allow me to explain myself."

After she quickly replaced her silk slippers for half boots, he proffered his arm. Then Anne fastened the clasp on her cloak, and James led her out into the wintry grounds. She relished the crunch of her boots on the snowy paths and sighed at the contrasting splash of red against the snow that signified the appearance of the colorful berries that delighted her every winter. The water in the fountain was frozen, creating an accidental ice sculpture. Slowing her pace, she stopped to listen to the blanket of silence that only came with the snow. She breathed deeply, taking in the sense of peace in the gardens, and noticed that James was studying her face intently. They were returning to that sense of ease she always felt in his company. M. de Brun's arrival had flustered her so completely that she had almost forgotten how much more herself she felt in James's company.

"Anne. I must apologize for my behavior yesterday. I do not expect you to readily forgive me. I have no excuse but that of my wounded pride. M. de Brun is, of course, your guest and a stranger in this country. You were only according him the hospitality and kindness he deserved as such. You were kind and considerate as you always are, and I was unconscionably rude."

Anne ground a hole into the snow with her half boot, slightly embarrassed by James's apology. Here in the fresh air, away from M. de Brun's steely gaze, she realized she had lost her head and completely ignored what she knew to be good sense. Yet, James was willing to assume all the blame. He had called her kind, and her heart had fluttered to hear him say it. Anne credited the sudden hollow feeling in the pit of her stomach to her own shame. She looked up to meet his gaze, and she was struck by the warmth of his hazel eyes, which held a glimmer she had never noticed before.

"Of course, you are forgiven. You are too kind and full of praise when we both know I am not without my shortcomings. But, if you will only say that you will join us for Christmas Eve supper as you always do, we shall go on as if it never happened."

James looked at her queerly, as if he wished to say something more, but remained silent. He offered his arm and turned to face the house. "As you wish, Miss Riley." She paused at his sudden return to formality but was wary of destroying the fragile détente they had reached. She placed her hand through the crook in his arm, noticing the strength beneath his greatcoat. She looked up at him in surprise, but he was staring determinedly at the house. Wrapping her arm a little tighter around his, she walked on to the house with him in silence.

THAT EVENING, AFTER A FULL MEAL AND WITH THE PROMISE OF CHRISTMAS morning, the impromptu acting troupe had a jovial rehearsal. James had made everyone laugh with his exaggerated impressions of Malvolio, and he surprised them all when he pulled scraps of yellow fabric out of his waistcoat to make his very own "cross-gartered stockings." Harriet had laughed so hard, she complained James would break her stays, and Anne had needed to recline on the chaise to catch her breath. Her eyes sparkled as she surveyed the room. This was just as she intended—an entertaining diversion—and she acknowledged with pleasure that M. de Brun had not taken his eyes off her once that evening. It was hard to ignore the unrelenting pressure of his unyielding gaze—though each time she turned to meet him, he looked pointedly off in another direction as if he spotted something quite fascinating across the room.

The formal rehearsals had mostly fallen by the way side. Fanny was asleep by the fire with a book on her lap while Harriet and James argued over the merits of Sebastian and Olivia's love, continuing to rehearse in the corner near the Christmas tree. Anne was staring into the fire, determined to avoid the inevitable rushing of blood from her head and dizzy sensation she experienced each time she so much as glanced at M. de Brun. But suddenly, his hand was on her shoulder. "Miss Riley, I wondered whether you might show me the finer assets of your library."

He offered his hand, and she rose from the couch. "Oh, of course, but I am afraid you might be disappointed. We have hardly any first editions. Papa is not much of reader."

"I am certain the library must have as many delightful features as the ladies of Harlow House."

At that, Anne felt herself begin to buzz with excitement, a tingling sensation that began in her toes and shot straight up her spine. She tucked a chestnut curl behind her ear. "M. de Brun, you are too kind."

"Well, you cannot expect that a lady with your unaccountably fine eyes and warm smile would have escaped my notice."

She looked at him with a startled expression. No man had ever been so forthright with her before. She led him deeper into the library, prepared to show him one of the only treasures Harlow House could call its own: a collection of John Milton's shorter poems, scribbled by hand and presented to an ancestor of the Rileys who'd been at Cambridge with the poet.

"We do have one manuscript of some value. I am not sure if you have an interest in Milton. I find his poems a bit dry myself. I prefer novels like those of Anne Radcliffe."

"Ah, I am a fan of Miss Radcliffe myself. Her novels were a comfortable escape from the perils of my daily life when I lived in France."

It was the first time he had mentioned his country since his unfortunate joke at their first rehearsal.

"Do you miss it terribly?"

He looked wistful. "I do. Further, I do not know when, if ever, I shall be able to return. It is a difficult thing—to lose one's home."

"I cannot pretend to know how you feel. I have lived at Harlow House my entire life and have never been away for more than six months to enjoy the season in London or Bath. If I was told I might never return, I do not know what I should do."

"You would go on, as we all must." And when Anne looked up to offer him a word of comfort, she noticed he had tears in his eyes. She reached up to gently brush away the tears, and he clasped her hand to his cheek, kissing her palm and caressing it as he held it to his face.

"You are so warm and so alive, Miss Riley. So full of poetry and light. You captivated me from the very first."

"But it has been the same for me. I have thought of none but you since our brief encounter last summer at Aunt Eliza's."

He took Anne into an embrace, pulling them further into the shadowy corners where they might be obscured by more bookcases. She continued to caress his cheek as he rested his head atop hers. She knew for certain that this was most improper, but at that moment, she did not care. Suddenly, she heard him chuckle.

"What is it?"

"Look up, Miss Riley."

Anne craned her head to discover that she and M. de Brun were standing under a sprig of mistletoe.

She giggled. "Oh, my father always hangs it here at Christmas. It is his little joke—a tryst in the library. Of course, he never expects anyone to actually find themselves under it."

"What a shame. I think we should see that his efforts aren't for naught." And with that, he pulled her tight to him and kissed her with a force that matched the power of his gaze. Her knees crumbled under her, and she only remained upright by the strength of his embrace. Still, she was reminded of James's strong arms... What an odd thought to have while she was kissing another man, but she dismissed it as quickly as it came.

She had never been kissed before, much less by a man as handsome as M. de Brun. Shaken to her core, she felt quite unable to stand on her own. Still, she sought to return his kiss, circling her arms around his neck and looking deeply into his eyes as they broke apart. They were no longer the grey of the stormy English Channel but a darker, richer color—the sky at dusk lightened by the twinkle of a few stars. Her head swam with the same dizzying effect she had experienced only once before when she had taken a spill while riding. She felt at once the immensity of their actions and jumped when she heard James calling after her.

He kissed her silently on the cheek, putting a finger to his lips to quiet her, and they broke apart as she answered back. "We'll be right there, Mr. Turnbull. I was showing M. de Brun our Milton."

ANNE WOKE WITH A START. SHE HAD BEEN HAVING A SIMULTANEOUSLY frustrating and lovely dream. She was dancing at her wedding, a vision in ivory silk. Well-wishers surrounded her, and she felt encircled by a strong pair of arms as she danced. But she could not make out her husband's face.

She lay in bed assuring herself that it could only have been M. de Brun. She had gone to bed as if in a waking dream, excusing herself early after James had nearly discovered them in the library. She fell asleep with her hands dreamily pressing at her lips, as she sought to return sensation to them. She thought, perhaps, they might be bruised. The force of his affection had not shocked her. It was the same unrelenting pressure she felt every time he looked at her.

She sat up with a start. It was Christmas morning, her favorite day of the year. How could she have forgotten? She bounded out of bed, hurriedly wrapping a dressing gown around her shift. Pressing her ear to the door adjacent to her room, she determined that Fanny and Harriet were sound asleep. All the better—she had not missed her Christmas tradition. She was not normally an early riser, but on Christmas morning, she preferred to be the first out of bed to have a moment to take in the stillness and enchantment of the holiday all on her own. She did not call the maid to dress her; all the guests were asleep and she would only be downstairs for a moment.

Quietly closing the door behind her, she crept down the stairs. The morning was quiet and still as a fresh blanket of snow had fallen overnight, muffling the trills of birds and the dawn proceedings of the servants. She tiptoed into the parlor and hurried to the tree, looking up at it in awe, fingering its needles, and bringing the evergreen scent to her nose.

"I thought I might find you already up."

She jumped at the masculine voice, fumbling in vain to pull her dressing gown about her neck. Turning to face the figure near the mantel, she sighed in relief to find only James standing there.

"You startled me."

"I do apologize. I was hoping to catch you before the others rose, and I seemed to recall your penchant for an early morning wander on Christmas morning."

She smiled bemusedly. He knew her so well. She was struck with a heightened awareness of the impropriety of her appearance.

He coughed and looked at the ground. "And I am also sorry that I have caught you out and spoiled your solitude. I should have known. I..."

She was mortified. Everything was always so easy and friendly between them, but ever since M. de Brun's arrival, all had gone cockeyed. And now, here she was in a state of undress, unable to come up with a witty retort. He stopped his incoherent muttering and they stared at each other. For the first time in many years, she really looked at him: his careworn face, tanned and freckled from his laboring on his small estate; his warm, brown curls tinged with a golden sheen; the scar on his nose from that summer he taught her to swim; and those hazel eyes that left her feeling as warm as if she might be curled by the fire. She had never thought him uncommonly handsome before, but perhaps she had never truly looked. She was startled to find herself drawn to him, and she began to take a step towards him.

He stopped her with his voice. "I wanted to give you your Christmas present before the others woke." He held out a small box.

Careful to keep her hands taught around the neck of her dressing gown, she crossed to him to take the box and sat down in an armchair. She gasped as she unfurled the tissue—it was a necklace, a single pearl on an emerald ribbon. She would recognize it anywhere. It had been his mother's, and it featured prominently on her portrait hanging in the hall of the Turnbull home—though the pearl had always been on a black ribbon when she wore it.

"Oh, James, this is too fine a present. I cannot—"

He put a hand up to quiet her. "Of course you can. She always wanted you to have it. I have been remiss in not giving it to you sooner. But you see, I wanted the right moment, and I've changed the ribbon. I thought the emerald shade would suit your coloring better."

She was overcome, and as she lifted the necklace to tie it round her neck, her hands began to shake. Why could she not control her emotions in his presence? It was, she was certain, the renewed sense of grief she felt at this sharp reminder of his mother, a woman she had always admired.

"Allow me..." He stilled her shaking hands and gently took the necklace from her, tenderly brushing her hair to one side and tying the ribbon around her neck. She felt his hands linger at the nape of her neck, and feeling a strange tingling sensation, she faced him.

"Well, how does it look?"

He smiled at her, but it was tinged with sadness. She knew he must be remembering the sight of his mother with the same pearl tied round her neck.

"Perfect, as I knew it would. Anne, I must—"

Peals of girlish laughter filtered through the ceiling.

"Harriet and Fanny must be awake. I should go. I must dress for breakfast."

She stole to the door, but he stopped her with her foot lingering on the threshold.

"Happy Christmas, Anne."

Without turning to face him, she murmured, "Happy Christmas, James," and raced up the stairs to her room, a blooming sense of confusion overwhelming her.

THE REST OF THE DAY PASSED UNEVENTFULLY. THEY ATE FAR TOO MUCH, and M. de Brun had declared the Christmas goose "a sheer masterpiece of poultry." The day was filled with good humor, the exchange of lovely trinkets with her cousins, and the general sense of goodwill that seems to fill homes on Christmas day. Embarrassed and perplexed by the intimate nature of James's gift, she strove to avoid his gaze for the remainder of the day, but it wasn't difficult as M. de Brun was so enchanting.

He was scandalous! He brushed against her knee under the table so many times during dinner that she was certain it could not be an accident. And when they had finally rehearsed the final scene that afternoon, he had held her with such passion as he declared her "Orsino's mistress and his fancy's queen." He leaned down to kiss her as the happy couples united at the play's conclusion, but she had turned her head at the last moment, noticing James's disapproving gaze. Instead, he grazed her cheek and whispered in her ear, "You are my fancy's queen."

She blushed and felt her stomach plunge as she unwittingly placed her hand to the new necklace around her throat. James would have been aghast at such a treacly appropriation of Shakespeare's words, but to hear them come from M. de Brun thrilled her. She knew their behavior was scandalous! If her mother knew she had been carrying on this way—well, she did not dare think of what she would say. But she felt certain that M. de Brun was bound to make his intentions known soon.

Harriet and Fanny declared themselves exhausted from the day's proceedings and skipped off to bed, and Anne was left sitting between M. de Brun and James.

"M. de Brun, you must be missing your family in France this evening," James said.

Raising his eyebrows in bemusement at Anne, M. de Brun cleared his throat to respond. "Yes, certainly, Mr. Turnbull. It is painful to be apart from the ones you love any time but especially at Christmas. However, the pleasurable company of my cousins and amiable young ladies has softened the blow. But tell me, Mr. Turnbull, why are you not at home this evening?" As he said this, M. de Brun reached to refill Anne's teacup and gently lingered as he brushed against her fingers.

"I only meant—" James looked at Anne with a look of distress, seemingly pleading for her to smooth things over. She met his gaze with a firm look of admonition. He coughed and stared into the fire.

Anne waited for either of the men to apologize, but they did not, and after a few moments of silence, James mercifully declared it time he headed home and left her sitting alone once more with M. de Brun.

Hardly waiting for James to be out of the room, M. de Brun leaned across the couch and took Anne's hands in his. He pushed back the lace cuff of her sleeves and began to shower the tops of her hands and insides of her wrists with kisses.

She was both thrilled and uncertain how to respond, but then he lifted a hand to gently cup her cheek and began to speak.

"Miss Riley, you must allow me to confess. In a mere four days, you have managed to enchant me as no other woman has. I felt from the first moment I laid eyes on you that you would be my downfall—"

"Your downfall?" she whispered breathlessly.

"Yes, the woman who might finally end my merry days of bachelordom." Throughout this, he had been enfolding her into an embrace, and with a wink, he leaned down to kiss her full on the mouth. She felt a faint dizziness wash over her again as he held her firmly and leaned her back against the settee, his hands drifting lower and the kiss growing more passionate. She thought she might swoon, and she raised her hands to push him back.

"M. de Brun, you must allow me to confess that I have loved you from the very first. From the moment I saw you, I knew I could love no man but you."

She was looking directly into his eyes, and she saw them spark as he leaned down to kiss her again, more gently this time. Barely raising his face from hers, he gazed into her eyes and declared, "I love you too, Miss Riley."

A sharp cough drew her gaze to the doorway of the parlor, and Anne was horrified to see James standing there in his cloak and hat. His face held a mix of embarrassment, hurt, and fury, and she immediately pulled herself into an upright position, smoothing the locks of hair that M. de Brun had pulled loose.

James's face blanched—his brown freckles stark against his white face.

"M. de Brun, an express arrived for you as I was leaving."

"Thank you, sir," he said coolly as he smoothed his waistcoat. He then rose to stalk out of the room, snatching the letter from Mr. Turnbull's hands. James stared icily after him and then turned to face Anne.

She returned his gaze wordlessly, tears pooling in her eyes. She felt as if she had betrayed him and their years of easy friendship. No explanation or apology would excuse the scandalous nature of her behavior. What is more— he had likely interrupted what she was certain was going to be a proposal.

Through her tears, she tried to speak. "I…James, I—"

"Good night, Miss Riley." His face had turned to stone, and he turned on his heels, leaving Anne to throw herself onto the settee and sob.

AT BREAKFAST THE NEXT MORNING, M. DE BRUN SEEMED DELIBERATELY cold to her. He barely met her gaze to ask her to pass the sugar, and besides requests for food, he would only utter a "yes" or "no." Anne felt wounded, as if someone had pummeled her all evening. She was embarrassed, but he had almost proposed to her last night. How could he treat her this way?

Harriet and Fanny thankfully did not seem to notice, attacking their breakfasts with vigor. Perhaps he merely needed some time to recover, and he would return to his affectionate ways after breakfast. Anne thought that, perhaps, if they rehearsed the final love scene, his outpouring of passion would be reawakened.

"I think we should begin with the final scene after breakfast."

"There will be no play."

The clatter of the silverware and Harriet's smacking of her toast were cut off as a chilly silence pervaded the room at M. de Brun's announcement.

Anne felt the sting of tears in her eyes once again, which she had not thought possible since she was certain she had cried all her tears the night before.

Before Anne even had the chance to question M. de Brun's sudden disagreeableness, Harriet whined, "Why ever not?"

M. de Brun softened at his cousin's questioning. "I am sorry to disappoint you all, but I received some rather upsetting news yesterday evening. I must be off straightaway."

Anne looked at him for an explanation, but he pointedly avoided her gaze. He rose from the table and turned to go. Overwhelmed by the turn of events, Anne did not see his last, wistful glance at the top of her head before he forced himself to leave the room.

Barely managing to speak through her tears, she muttered, "Excuse me," and ran weeping from the dining room to her bedroom. She looked longingly out the window, placing her hand against the glass, trying to reach down to him as she saw him soon after mount his horse.

"M. de Brun!" she cried, but of course he could not hear her and began to ride away from Harlow House, his cloak fluttering behind him, a red and brown blur against the snow-covered driveway. This only served to increase her misery. Collapsing on her bed in a flood of sorrow, she wept until she fell into a fitful sleep.

A WEEK AND A HALF HAD PASSED SINCE M. DE BRUN'S ABRUPT AND MYSterious departure, and little had been done to abate Anne's sorrow. Harriet and Fanny had tried admirably to restore her spirits, offering to take on extra roles in the play so they could still present it to the family on the Epiphany; Harriet had even suggested a walk in the snow. Despite her cousins' best efforts, Anne wandered listlessly from room to room, sneaking off to the library to stand under the sprig of withered mistletoe while she wept uncontrollably.

She felt certain that M. de Brun would have left a letter or sent word explaining his departure and the possibility of his return. He had essentially proposed to her after all; how could he suddenly leave her with no word of explanation? What was more—she had not spoken to James since his mortifying discovery of her with M. de Brun. He had not come for Christmas supper, as was his custom, on the day of M. de Brun's departure. And when Fanny had gone to ask for him, hoping that his presence might cheer Anne, his manservant had explained that Mr. Turnbull had left only that morning with no word of where he was going or when he might return. When Anne had wondered aloud where he was at supper that night, Fanny had no choice but to relay the strange news of his own departure.

Anne had refused to eat for the rest of the meal, feeling resolutely that she had been abandoned by both her intended and her best friend in less than a day's time.

After a week without so much as a whisper as to either gentleman's whereabouts, Anne's spirits sank. Approaching a fortnight with no word (and the impending departure of her cousins), she had all but given up hope of ever hearing from M. de Brun again. She was shocked, then, to have her misery interrupted when Mr. Frith entered the parlor mid-afternoon and announced, "A letter for you, miss."

Harriet and Fanny exchanged anxious glances while Anne rose to take it from his hand. Hardly daring to breathe, she looked down at the letter. "Why, this is in James's hand." She cracked the wax seal, and another piece of paper fluttered to the floor.

Anne retrieved the piece of paper from the floor, noticing that it was from M. de Brun. She could not tell her cousins. They did not know, whatever they had guessed, about the assumed arrangement between her and M. de Brun. Ignoring their hungry glances, she retreated to her room to read her letters. She was desperate to read M. de Brun's note, but thought it perhaps best to start with James's correspondence.

Dearest Anne,

Her heart fluttered as she read his greeting, but she pressed forward knowing she was just anticipating M. de Brun's letter.

I am afraid I have much to explain to you and a very short time in which to do it. I am sitting at an inn waiting to see M. de Brun married this afternoon.

Married? But he was to have married her. How could this be?

I know this will come as a shock to you as you had supposed yourself engaged to M. de Brun (and he assures me his intentions were, in your case,

*entirely noble, though the impropriety he inspired in you leads me to question
the sincerity of his claims). At any rate, I will now relate my story to you as
it happened.*

*I had determined not to speak to you after seeing the way you were
carrying on with M. de Brun. I found the man intolerable and could not
fathom why he should so make you lose your head. But needing to speak
with your father about a shared border on our lands, I came to the house
and discovered that you had taken refuge in your room after the sudden and
inexplicable departure of M. de Brun.*

*While I never liked the man, I could not abide what appeared to be his
very sudden abandonment of you and determined to set out after him the
next day. I managed to trace him to an inn in a derelict corner of London.
He was, I am sorry to tell you, not alone but sleeping soundly with a rather
buxom Frenchwoman. At my insistence, he joined me outside where, after
much urging, he revealed the truth to me. This woman, Marianne, had been
his lover in France, and he had abandoned her when he sought refuge in
England. The letter that called him away from your home had told him of
Marianne's arrival in England with their child he had never known existed.
When I inquired as to whether he'd set things right with Marianne, he
seemed to insist that she was only a temporary problem and he would return
to you and his cousins in due course.*

*I could not abide his abandonment of that woman and her child. Even at
the cost of your happiness. I have spent the last week convincing him that the
only solution was to marry this poor woman as he ought to have in France.
It took all of my powers of persuasion, but he has assented, and we are off to
church this afternoon. He has insisted I include this letter of his, and I do so
against my better judgment. Know that your cousins need never know of your
indiscretion. I have advised M. de Brun to present Marianne to your aunt
and uncle as the wife he had thought dead when he escaped to our shores.*

*You need not call on me when I return. I do not expect your gratitude.
What I have done, I have done for my own conscience—whatever
that may reap.*

—James

Anne was so distraught and confused that she could not weep. M. de
Brun was to be married—and to a woman whom he had abandoned? And

they had a child? And James had saved her from this irreparable harm. She placed her hand on the pearl at her neck, steeling herself for a new wave of grief as she opened M. de Brun's letter.

Darling,

You must believe that it is only you I have loved. Marianne was an indiscretion that has become a permanent fixture in my life. I would have returned and married you. You must believe me. I will regret losing you all the days of my life.

Yours,
Roger de Brun

Anne had expected M. de Brun's letter to tear her apart, to break the remaining pieces of her wounded heart. But strangely, all she felt upon reading it was disgust. She thought on his raven curls, unsettling grey eyes, and forceful hold of her on the settee, and she shuddered. He had certainly not been the man she thought he was, and she was glad to be free of him. How could she have so completely misjudged him?

But then her eyes caught the final lines of James's letter.

You need not call on me when I return. I do not expect your gratitude. What I have done I have done for my own conscience whatever that may reap.

It was so final, and his words struck her to her soul. She clasped her pearl necklace to her and sat in stunned silence on the bed.

How could she have been so blind? It was not M. de Brun she loved. That had been merely infatuation, a girlish fantasy. Always, always, it had been James. Who else could make her laugh? Who else valued her intellect and her wit? Who else set her so at ease and made her feel wholly herself?

She must have loved him since they were children and been too blind to see it—she supposed, since that day he saved her in the lake while he was teaching her to swim.

And had he once loved her? She was certain of it. Had that been what he had been about to tell her that day in the snow and then on Christmas morning? She untied the ribbon at the nape of her neck and held the pearl in her palm. He had given her his mother's necklace and gone so far as to choose a new ribbon in her favorite color. She clutched the necklace to her heart and wept.

He might have loved her once, but he did not now—not after she had thrown herself at a scoundrel flippantly in his presence. The letter made that clear. *"You need not call on me when I return."* He never wished to see her again. She acted scandalously, and he was disgusted with her. She could see there was no way to undo the damage she had done.

She placed her head in her hands, as her body was racked with sobs. For it was too much to bear to have lost two loves and a singular friendship in the course of one afternoon.

A MONTH HAD PASSED SINCE THE DAY JAMES'S LETTER ARRIVED. ANNE HAD managed to lift her spirits slightly; the Christmas season was over, but the snow remained, and she took long walks in the cold to bolster her courage. Only when she thought on James and how much she loved him did she feel herself sink into the depths of self-pity. She had seen him from afar a few times, bringing inquiries for her father about his land and their shared border.

Her cousins, with their parents, had returned to London, where they would be greeted by M. de Brun and his wife. James, and seemingly M. de Brun, had kept their word and not revealed the truth of Marianne's situation or Anne's involvement in the affair. For that, she was grateful. The loss of James's love was cross enough to bear. She wore his mother's necklace every day as a reminder of what she had lost through her own ignorance and vanity.

It was on another chilly January afternoon, wandering the grounds of Harlow House, that she spotted him leaving her father's study. Lost in a memory of Mrs. Turnbull, James's kind and warmhearted mother, she smiled at him as he waited for his horse. Suddenly, he was coming toward her. She turned to find a tree or a sculpture behind which to hide but found herself quite exposed. They had not spoken since he had sent the letter, and she feared she might dissolve into a puddle of tears at the first sign of coolness from him.

"Miss Riley! Anne, Anne, wait!"

She had turned and was frantically looking for an escape route when he gently brushed her elbow with his hand. Knowing there was no escape, she steeled herself and turned to face whatever reprimand he might have in store. He took a step back as tears pooled in her eyes.

"I'm sorry. I—I just wanted to wish you a Happy New Year. I would have liked the greeting to be more timely, but I have not seen you since my return."

And with that, he turned to go, a slump to his shoulders.

She forced herself to call after him, "Happy New Year, Mr. Turnbull." She hoped the use of his proper name would show contrition for her indiscretions.

He stopped, squared his shoulders, and faced her. She was startled to see tears glistening in his own eyes. "Have you truly not forgiven me?"

"Forgiven you? But it was you who told me never to call on you when you returned."

"How could you think such a thing?"

Her heart leaped, but she dared not allow herself to hope.

"Your letter made it clear that your disgust at my indiscretions made it necessary for you to distance yourself from me."

James stared at her, a mystified grin spreading across his face. "You thought that? You really thought I could turn my back on you like that after our years of friendship?"

"Yes, if I had betrayed your trust so horribly."

"You really think so little of me?"

"It is not *you* that I think little of, James, but *myself*. I have been a fool—throwing myself at a man who proved to be an utter scoundrel. And doing so in your presence, when all this time it's been you who—and I did not know—I didn't know until I read your letter and thought I had lost your good favor irretrievably."

He grabbed her hands and pulled her to him. "My dear, dear Anne. You could never lose my favor." He cupped her chin and raised her face to meet his so she was staring deeply into those hazel eyes she had come to realize she loved so completely. He gently brushed the tears from her cheeks and, holding her face in his hands, smiled at her.

"I have loved you for as long as I can remember—your chestnut hair, your merry green eyes, your strong chin, your tendency to feel too deeply and love too quickly, your wit—all of it."

She broke her tears with a laugh. "I must have loved you just as long, only I did not know it yet."

He slid his arms around her, engulfing her in his strong and reassuring embrace. He smelled of firewood, old books, and soap, and she buried her face in his chest, inhaling his intoxicating smell. He clutched her to him, nestling his head against the top of hers and caressing her hair gently with one hand.

"I thought you could not love me. That I would only ever be like a brother to you. And then, when I forced M. de Brun into that sham of a marriage, I convinced myself it was for the girl's sake and yours. But it was my own damnable selfishness. I thought surely I had lost you forever—not merely as mistress of Turnbull Manor but as my confidante and friend."

"It seems we have been at cross purposes."

"Rather like Viola and the Duke Orsino, no?"

She giggled. "Shall I be your mistress and your fancy's queen?"

"And so much more. You shall be my equal, my partner, if you will have me. Anne Riley, I love you."

"Oh, James, I love you too."

"Then will you do me the honor of accepting my hand?"

She was too overcome to respond and merely nodded her head vigorously in assent. At this, he drew her even closer to him and kissed her. This was not like being kissed by M. de Brun—all sharp edges and breathless pressure. It was gentle, kind, and tentative, just like James. She responded eagerly, wrapping her hands around his neck and standing on her toes to meet his height. He swept her off her feet into his arms, twirling her in her winter cloak and never once allowing their lips to part all the while. After what had become a decidedly dreary Christmas, it seemed it would be the happiest of New Years.

. . . .

Maureen Lee is a writer, actress, director, and producer. She currently works at the USC Libraries as a program assistant and is also working towards an MA in Arts Journalism, reporting on arts, theatre, and entertainment. She has written for Turner Classic Movies, Ms. In The Biz, @ This Stage, and more. You can find her previous holiday romance story, "From Keats with Love" in the *Christmas Nookies* anthology. When not at USC, she works on theatre productions throughout Los Angeles. She is a native Angelino who hates driving and cites peacoats and scarves as her favorite clothing items. An Anglophile, she attempted to fulfill her dream of attending Hogwarts by completing her master's in British History at the University of Oxford. She is a cockeyed optimist, life-long Janeite, rom-com aficionado, classic movie buff, musical theatre geek, and general pop culture enthusiast.

"I believe in being strong when everything seems to be wrong. I believe that happy girls are the prettiest girls. I believe that tomorrow is another day, and I believe in miracles." —Audrey Hepburn

Christmas Miracle on Oyster Bay

by Denise Stout

Oyster Bay, Maryland

E ven as Lissa turned the sign from closed to open and then unlocked the door to her bookstore, The Printed Word, she felt the impending doom of a snow day. An hour before, the snow twinkled down like the crystals on her favorite mica glass glitter-encrusted Christmas star, but now the snow blanketed Main Street in a thickening layer. It was a matter of time before schools went from a delay to a closure, and the only traffic would be those sprinting to the supermarket to get the essentials of milk, bread, and toilet paper. No thoughts toward books nor the Tot's Reading Corner she had planned for today. She sighed at the loss of business.

Years ago, Lissa looked forward to the snow days, but now she really needed the money. If business didn't pick up soon, she would have to make some serious decisions about the shop, and her ability to pay next year's taxes on the old Victorian it was housed in. When Pop and Mimi left everything to her, she changed it from Pop's Newsstand to a full bookstore, adding gift items and local crafts to lure the ever-increasing tourist traffic to their small town of Oyster Bay, located on the western shore of the Chesapeake Bay in Southern Maryland. But, last year, the local university changed their bookstore to a partnership with a big box store, and it carried all the same books she carried—with a large faculty or student discount. Competition was an increasing hardship with the locals buying there now too. She recently stopped carrying newspapers and magazines, but now her future seemed more uncertain. Moms still brought the children in for story time, and book clubs still met in her sunroom conservatory, but many of her regulars had stopped coming. Even the free coffee, tea, and homemade mini muffins couldn't lure them away from the Starbucks at the university store.

Lissa looked around the shop while running her hands on the quarter-sawn oak counter Pop had made to fit with the Victorian woodwork. It was stained the same rich mahogany color of the grand, sweeping staircase and upper gallery with lots of built-in shelving and beautiful wood panels on the walls. The two parlors on either side of the enormous foyer were almost twins in size, and each led to curving turrets, which made it a prominent feature on Main Street. Only the front rooms housed the shop. The back rooms were her personal space though she tended to live more on the second floor. It was really too much house for one person. And, it was getting harder to maintain both the house and the store. In fact, Lissa had been forced to shut off the third floor to help keep expenses down. She'd had a few offers from people wanting to buy her out to make a bed and breakfast or cut it up for offices and apartments. She was fighting hard to keep this place her own. If only there could be a Christmas miracle for a windfall—any windfall. The trust from the sale of the farm was depleted by her college tuition years ago.

She sighed. *Might as well take advantage of a slow day and start decorating for Christmas.* In a week, Lissa would have her annual holiday open house, followed a week later by the town's Midnight Madness sale. In some years past, the following day became a bonus sale day by capitalizing on those in town for the weekend. They were usually big sales days, and she had ordered extra at the trade show for the sale. All the decorations on the trees were for sale except for her mica glass glitter-encrusted stars. They were family keepsakes from Germany and just about the only things she had left with memories of Pop and Mimi, her maternal grandparents who raised her from the time she was a little girl. She had grown up in this store, so days like this made the sentimentality of holding on to the past—and her livelihood—all the more daunting as she thought toward the future. She had given up a career in the city to come home and take over when her grandparents were failing. Lissa couldn't bear to lose the shop too.

As she was in the storeroom gathering boxes of Christmas decorations and items to sell, Lissa heard the tinkling of the bell on the door. Surprised, she rushed out with some of the boxes still in her hands. Her jaw dropped to see that it was handsome law professor Simon MacGregor who taught at Oyster Bay University, part of the state college system. He had a reputation for being curt, arrogant, and condescending, which had not endeared him to the residents. And, since the new university bookstore had opened, he hadn't been in The Printed Word. Despite his reputation, she couldn't afford to dismiss a customer, so she put on her friendliest smile as she greeted him.

"Hello, Dr. MacGregor. How may I help you?"

He looked up from the pictorial coffee-table books on local lore and wildlife and smiled. Well, it was more of a half-smile. He usually wore a sour look on his face, which suited his outwardly dour personality. She was surprised to note that his eyes were blue, almost the color of the bay on a bright summer's day. The lines around his eyes softened as he acknowledged her presence. He was probably close to forty if not slightly over. And he was very fit. Even wearing an overcoat, she could see his broad shoulders tapered to a narrow waist. He really was a striking guy.

"Hello, Lissa. How are you today?" He still wore the half-smile.

"I'm well. What brings you out on such a snowy day?" she asked suspiciously then smiled. She hoped her smile covered that well. No need to scare off a customer, regardless of his disposition. One couldn't be choosy in this business; money is money.

"I was hoping to enlist your help." He brushed the snowflakes through his dark hair with his long, tapered fingers. "Last year, you had an open house and had delicious hors d'oeuvres. Someone mentioned you made them yourself. I'd like to hire you to make them for a faculty holiday event I'm hosting."

Lissa dropped her packages in shock. As she bent down to pick them up, he had already grabbed them and offered her a hand up. She took the packages from him, placed them on the counter, and realized she hadn't answered him. "I'm not a caterer. I just make them for my customers for the Christmas open house and Oyster Bay's Midnight Madness sale. Happy customers spend more money on books and gifts," she said with a grin.

"Oh," he said dejectedly. "I didn't think it through. That makes sense." He stared at her intently for a moment. "Would you consider it anyway? It's not a huge party, and I'm willing to pay for your time, plus the supplies. We are entering the Christmas season: 'peace and goodwill' and all that goes with it. Jen, my receptionist said you might be in a position to help." He had a desperate look on his face.

Ah, she got it. Jen, her dearest friend, must have suggested it. *I wish she had given me a head's up.* "I could think about it. I've never done anything like that. I don't have a commercial kitchen, so that might be an issue. Can't break any health codes, especially since I don't have a food vendor license." She winked at him, suspecting he'd know the law better than anyone. "The food I have out for my customers is free, so I skirt the law on that. So far, no one's gotten sick."

"Since it's a private party not being paid by the university, I don't think there would be a problem, legally speaking. You'd be doing me a huge favor. Please?" This time there was a full smile—a real smile. It made him look younger. And quite attractive.

She didn't have a good reason to say no, and she could use the money. It might even get her a new customer or two. And those blue eyes! Like a yearning puppy. "If I agree to do this, we'll have to sit down, go over the head count, pick a menu... And, I may need you to help me do the shopping." She paused in thought before going on. "We'd have to go inland to get everything at bigger stores like Wegmans or Costco. Would that work for you?"

"Of course. That would be great." He pulled out his phone and opened it to his calendar. "How about the first Friday night in December?"

"No, that's Midnight Madness. But, the next evening, Saturday, would work. I could make most of the food at once for both events. I can't close the shop early—I need the Christmas shoppers—but I have temporary help for the season, and one of the girls could close for me. Then, I'd have time to get everything prepped for serving. Do you have any classes this morning? We could go over some things now."

She walked behind the counter, pulled out a journal she used as a date-book, and started writing some notes. She looked up to find him staring at her—not her but her hair. "Is something wrong?"

There was a frisson of energy as he reached over and touched her copper-colored, curly hair. "No, you have some glitter in your hair, and it caught the

237

light." He pulled back his hand and cleared his throat. Then in a business-like manner—perhaps his trial lawyer voice—said, "Classes are canceled. I have some time."

WITH THE PARTY PLANNING COMPLETED, HE STOOD AND APPEARED READY to leave. "Are you having the party at the university or your home?" she asked before he could exit. She thought she had heard he rented a small house in Oyster Bay while he still owned a larger townhome in Georgetown. Like many of the professors, he didn't live there full-time. It was an easy enough commute.

"I hadn't thought that through. I'm not sure the cottage can accommodate everyone invited, and the conference room for our department isn't ready." He seemed stumped. The dour look returned to his countenance. He thumped the counter a few times with his fist.

"Dr. MacGregor, I'm sure we can figure out something." She gave a pleading look at his fist. Definitely, his trial attorney background was coming out. No wonder he was such a good litigator. She wondered why he had given up trial work to become a professor. Definitely not for the money. And he obviously had money based on his clothes and house in the city.

He looked at his fist and shrugged. "Simon. Please call me Simon. I can't believe I forgot to reserve a room at the university."

"Dr. Mac—er, Simon. I have an idea. Since it might be too late to reserve a room, and it would make things easier for transporting, why not have it here?" She walked over to the French doors, opening them into the conservatory that was usually closed to the public except for book clubs. "During the Christmas season, I use this room for special holiday-themed books, holiday gifts, and crafts from local artisans. I always put a tree in the center. This room, combined with the main store, would be large enough to accommodate everyone. And since it's a private event, I can still make the food for you. What do you think?" She turned to him with a half-smile of her own.

He seemed to be weighing the options, calculating the space. "May I go in and look around?"

"Sure. I was planning to tackle the Christmas decorating early when you showed up," Lissa said with a smile. She walked into the large room attached to the shop in the converted Victorian. She wondered what he thought of one woman living in a space so large. Even in a town this small, she could sublet and make a tidy profit by renting it for offices and apartments. She always loved the tall windows, which let in lot of light on a sunny day. And at Christmas, it was the perfect room for a Christmas tree.

"Ah, that explains the glitter," he said as he followed her into the room. "Is that another room?" he asked while pointing to a door by the fireplace at the back of the room.

"Yes, it is. The fireplace isn't functional at the moment. I usually have the room shut off except for special occasions or if book clubs want a place to meet. Sometimes, I do my Tots Reading Corner in here too. We never had a piano, so it was never used as a proper conservatory when I was a child. I grew up in this house. Of course, I'm probably stating the obvious and boring you with TMI." She turned to look at him, and he appeared to be genuinely interested in her every word. "Pop had rented the room, along with this room"—she motioned for him to follow her into the other room as she continued—"as an office for a few people before. The conservatory has a separate entrance from the front door, but I keep it locked. This office room could be used for coats during the party, and it opens to the powder room behind my kitchen through another door. You could use all of this plus the two front parlors that make up the main part of the shop. Will the shop work for your party?"

"It will suit."

It was a perfunctory remark. Obviously, he was back to his brusque nature. *I need the money. Not desperate...but I need the money.* They walked back to the main room of The Printed Word. She smiled politely to him as he gathered his coat and briefcase. Funny, she never noticed he had put them on the tufted chair earlier. "I suppose you'll write up a formal contract for me to sign?"

"Normally, I would, but I think I can trust you, Lissa. Good faith contract in a small town ought to be worth something."

She nearly fainted on the spot. The dean of the Oyster Bay College of Law didn't demand a formal contract. Lissa quickly realized she had more to lose than he did, however. She held out her hand to shake his goodbye. "I guess I can trust you too, Simon." A tingle traveled up her arm when their hands met.

"My word is as good as gold."

After he walked out the door, she wondered whether he felt the energy that passed between them. Or had she only imagined it. Secretly, she'd always felt an attraction from the moment Jen introduced them—in spite of his demeanor. Jen had told her his bark was worse than his bite; perhaps Jen was right. Regardless, it was either the smartest contract she'd ever negotiated or the worst. Like everything else in her life, she wasn't sure. Betrayal would do that to a girl.

DOUBTFUL ANYONE ELSE WOULD STOP BY THAT DAY, SHE DECIDED TO decorate the trees first. Locals and tourists loved to pick the ornaments off them rather than out of baskets. She thought it helped them imagine the ornaments on their own tree. She'd even spied customers taking photos to replicate hers at home—she was known for her artfully decorated trees. Once in a while, a customer would ask whether the entire tree was for sale. This year, the answer might be yes. While fresh trees always smelled good, artificial was safer in The Printed Word with all the books and the Victorian structure.

Reaching into a box, she pulled out a large photo album. It was her "magical tome of Christmas decorating" as one of her friends had dubbed it. The scrapbook was used as a reference for the placement and bejeweling of the trees, and she *was* the Christmas decoration fairy.

The tree in the conservatory was twelve feet tall. Fortunately, it was three sections easily put together and, blessedly, pre-lit. All the bulbs seemed to be working, and the largest mica glass glitter-encrusted star went on top. She added some ribbon in a gauzy ivory to cascade down and then set up the smaller trees the same way in each of the front parlors. Each tree would have a theme of ornaments. A popular one had a beach and sea theme with pastel colors, sand dollars, starfish, shells, and other locally sourced handmade ornaments. However, the big tree was her pièce de résistance: her Victorian tree with vintage ornaments. Something for everyone—local, tourist, or related to the college.

She only needed to input the ornaments into her inventory then place the boxes corresponding to each tree before she could hang the ornaments. At the moment, it felt like an overwhelming task. Decorating the trees could wait until tomorrow, so she changed the focus to hanging the garland and wreaths. By six, she'd had enough and decided to call it a day. The lights were on timers to turn off, so she went to the kitchen to eat then upstairs to catch up on email and read before going to bed early.

The next morning, the snowfall kept everyone at home again; she was able to get the ornaments scanned into her system and ready for hanging in the afternoon. She had a week before Thanksgiving, and it would be nice to have it all done before that weekend. Black Friday was typically a slow day with everyone driving to the mall. The Saturday after was usually busy with the national trend to Buy Local and Shop Small Businesses, and she had made that her annual open house. This year, Black Friday would also be a good day to shop for food and try a few things needed for the next week's Midnight Madness and subsequent "catering" job. It would be a trial run for some new foods.

The weekend disappeared with the decorating done and the bustle of shopping picking up on Main Street. Even a couple of friends stopped by, and it was fun catching up as they gave her unofficial wish lists for their husbands or boyfriends.

BEING A SINGLE GIRL WITH NO FAMILY IN A SMALL TOWN USUALLY MEANT several invitations to Thanksgiving dinner and an inevitable attempt at matchmaking. She had several options this year but accepted Jen's invitation as she felt like part of the family there and hoped there would be no matchmaking. Jen was married to Anthony, an English professor, and they sometimes included other young professors. The conversation was never awkward when the topic of books came around.

She was surprised when she walked into Jen's home to find Simon there— and only Simon. She'd texted back and forth with Simon to confirm a time to go shopping, but she hadn't seen him since that first day. However, he acted aloof and seemed to ignore her until they found they were seated across from one another at dinner. Jen's younger daughter, Brenna, was seated next to Lissa, and her sister, Lacey, two years older, was next to Simon, both vying for attention in the conversation. She realized they had obviously been set up, but Simon was unfazed by their contrived circumstances. He barely spoke during the dinner conversation.

"Simon, are your parents in town?" Jen asked.

"No."

"Where do they live?" Lissa inquired.

"Florida."

"Simon's parents are retired, but they're very active and travel a lot," Jen offered.

"Do you see them often?"

"Not really."

"Will you see them over the holidays?"

"No, they'll be in Europe."

"Oh? Lissa spent a semester abroad in college," said Anthony.

The conversation seemed to plod on forever in this manner. He answered questions better by text.

After dinner, Lissa and Jen cleared the dishes and then joined the others in the family room. As she took her seat, Simon asked, "So, you went to college?"

"Yes, undergrad, then I started law school, but I quit to come back and help my grandparents near the end. I was working at a firm and wasn't happy, so it wasn't hard to quit. I realized law wasn't the career I thought I wanted. I took over the store and have been content ever since," she said with a smile. "I've never regretted my decision to come back to Oyster Bay."

"I had no idea."

"That I was more than a 'shop girl'?"

"I didn't mean it like that."

"Not everyone finds the career they want in college. I didn't. I'm happy with what I've chosen. I was able to be there for my grandparents when they needed me just as they were there when I needed them. They raised me from a very young age—and they weren't young themselves. They gave up a lot for me. I'd do it again."

"Did you ever want more?"

"What, a family? Children? Of course, but not everyone wants a small town life. Some relationships don't work out. But I haven't given up. Not everyone is as lucky as Jen and Anthony." Lacey and Brenna crawled on her lap. "And, I get to spoil my wonderful goddaughters. I have friends who are like family—*are* family—to me." After hugging the girls, she stood up. "Girls, Auntie Lissa is going home. I'll see you soon to hang out when your parents have their date night." She kissed the girls, Anthony, and Jen and nodded a quick goodbye to Simon.

After the awkward Thanksgiving dinner, she dreaded the idea of shopping with Simon, but it was too late to back out. When she made commitments, she honored them. They'd texted back and forth a few times, and he even offered a halfhearted apology—"in case I made you uncomfortable"— but it didn't seem to soothe her wounded ego.

It had been a sunny Wednesday afternoon, but the sun would be setting soon. They'd be traveling against rush hour traffic and should be able get all their errands done in one trip by leaving before dinner. Luckily, the food they needed to pick up should stay fresh for the weekend. She made two lists for herself: one for Midnight Madness and one for Simon's party. As she was waiting for him to pick her up, she checked the details on each list again. She also had a third list for Simon with suggestions for alcohol and local wineries. She didn't realize he was there until the bell on the door jingled. When she looked up, she saw he had flowers.

"Here. I apparently put my foot in my mouth, so I thought you'd like these."

"Thank you. They're beautiful, but it wasn't necessary. I do appreciate the thought," she said with the hint of a smile.

"Well, shall we?" He beckoned her toward his car, an Audi Q5—exactly what she thought a man of his caliber would own.

Most of the drive was in companionable silence but for the music in the background. Breaking the peace, Lissa said, "I made a list for you with alcohol suggestions. I left most of the brands up to you—I wasn't sure exactly which you'd prefer." She grinned encouragingly at him. "Even though I'm catering, I'd like you to feel comfortable making suggestions or changing anything. We still have time."

"You've done a great job with the lists. I don't want to interfere."

"It's not interfering. I'm sure you don't have a problem speaking up in a courtroom," she countered.

"Ah, but the courtroom is my domain. The kitchen is the caterer's domain."

She laughed. "At least, you didn't say it was my 'place'—as a woman."

"I wouldn't say that," he said, his voice gruff. "I just remember how my mother liked to take charge and plan a party down to the smallest detail. She was a perfectionist and didn't like anyone else involved."

"Simon, I'm not your mother," she said teasingly. "I may be a bit more casual, but it will still be lovely. I wouldn't embarrass you. I know that, as the dean, this is important to you. I just want you to know that, if there's something—anything —you want to add or delete, it's okay." She reassured him by patting his arm gently. "And while you're at it, loosen your tie and relax." She pointed to the store. "This is Costco, not circuit court or a lecture hall."

"Yes, ma'am," he said with a wide smile. He tossed his tie in the back seat before getting out and opening her door.

Later, after all the shopping, he surprised her by suggesting dinner at a Thai place. Lissa had brought coolers to transport the cold food, so she agreed. All was going well at dinner until Roland walked by.

"Lissa, Lissa Robicheaux, is that you?" He bent down and kissed her on the cheek. "How have you been? Still running Pop's Newsstand?"

"Actually, it's a full-fledged bookstore, The Printed Word. It's been a long time, Roland."

"Simon, looks like you've got my girl. How did you manage that? I heard you left the firm." Lissa saw the muscle in Simon's cheek twitch.

"Simon and I are friends. We're here enjoying a nice meal. It was good seeing you." Fortunately, Roland took the hint and left, but not without kissing her on the cheek again.

"*Roland Moore* was your boyfriend?"

"Like I said, some things don't work out." Lissa lifted her wine to her lips and took a sip. "I don't want to talk about life's mistakes when we are having such a nice dinner. Just know that, by the time I realized he was cheating on me with another guy's wife, it was time for me to go home to Oyster Bay. So I did. It hurt. A lot. I learned what kind of guy to avoid in the future." She put her glass down on the table. "Let's talk about something else."

They left the restaurant and drove home in silence. He glanced her way occasionally, she noticed, as if he wanted to say something but then appeared to reconsider it. His profile betrayed nothing of his thoughts. She studied his strong jaw and discovered a bit of grey in his thick, but short, dark hair. She'd never been so alone or close to him before, and a consciousness of the car's intimate space enveloped her. The smell of his cologne—masculine with a hint of citrus—ignited her senses.

When they pulled up to The Printed Word, Simon opened her door and helped carry all the supplies into the house. He seemed to take extra care unloading the car. She also imagined that, perhaps, he pitied her, and she hated that. Until Roland stopped by their table, they had seemed to be having a lovely outing. *Strange coincidence that they knew each other...* It would be so easy to completely fall for Simon. He was clean-cut and refined and, as she discovered through their evening's conversation, very kind—even if he was a bit of a stuffed shirt. He wasn't quite as reserved once he loosened up. He must not be too much of a Scrooge if he's throwing a Christmas party for his colleagues and friends. And he did have a taste for the finer things in life. But their worlds were too different. And she did not trust her own judgment when it came to her heart. Her whirling thoughts finally resolved that Simon would never date someone like her, a small town girl, anyway. She had to remind herself that this was a catering job. Nothing more.

"So, I'll come over early to help you set up before the guests arrive."

"Perfect. I'll take care to stay out of the way during the party. Just freshen up the food when needed," she said.

"You're welcome to be at the party as a guest too."

"I wouldn't want to confuse your guests when you're the host and I'm acting as the caterer." She smiled, hoping her smile looked more genuine than her heart felt.

"Regardless, you're not 'hired help.' You'll be there as my friend too. I don't want you hiding in the kitchen all night." Then he surprised her when he bent to place a kiss on her cheek.

She attempted to gracefully step back, but that spark of energy had warmed her through. *And where did that kiss come from?* She smoothed her copper curls and remembered her resolution of just moments before. "Yes, well, we still have a *business* arrangement, and I wouldn't want your guests to get the wrong idea about me." She walked him to the door, and as they said good night, he managed to kiss her on the cheek again.

THE NEXT NIGHT, SHE PREPARED EVERYTHING SHE COULD IN ADVANCE FOR Midnight Madness. Fortunately, Oyster Bay stores opened later that day to make up for staying open late, giving Lissa time to re-check the sweets she had baked the night before. Her mini red velvet cupcakes were always a hit; customers were always trying to get her to divulge her secret family recipe. Plus, she had black and white cheesecake brownies and homemade Christmas cookies in addition to the hot cider and friendship tea she made in the morning, and all seemed ready to go. Throughout the day, tourists, parents of college students, and the fine weather kept her part-time helpers bustling, indicating maybe even a record breaking sales day.

Out of the corner of her eye, she saw Simon walk in with a box of potted poinsettias. Lissa overheard one of the girls tell him how the shop handled deliveries. Before Lissa could say hello, he put the flowers on the counter and kissed her.

"I brought you some poinsettias for the party. I thought you might like them for tonight too," he said smiling as he hugged her. "I meant to bring them by earlier, but one of my graduate students was having a meltdown over a less than stellar grade. Not sure this one will make it through law school." He let his hand finger one of her curls before he stepped back casually.

"Ah, Simon—I don't know what's going on," she whispered. "And I can't talk now, but you and I have a business relationship—period. I have customers. This is a small town. People talk." A little embarrassed, she could feel those piercing blue eyes on her back as she walked into the conservatory to assist a customer. But one thing was certain: that kiss, ever so slight, had passion behind it. And it had lit a fire she hadn't felt in a long time. She looked over her shoulder, and he was still watching her. Lissa didn't know what to think. He was full of surprises, and she knew she was playing with fire. He was someone she could fall in love with, and she had promised herself she would never let herself be broken again.

She noticed Simon walk out of the shop, and she caught his eye as he looked back at her through the conservatory window before heading down the busy sidewalk. She sent him a text message to smooth things over:

"Thanks for the flowers. They're lovely. Please park in the alley behind the house tomorrow night. Come in the kitchen—it will be unlocked. We'll talk after the party."

LISSA WOKE AT DAWN, PREPPED WHAT FOOD SHE COULD FOR SIMON'S PARTY, and restocked the store before opening. At three, she let the girls manage the store on their own as she finalized plating more of the mini red velvet cupcakes she served the night before and adding salted caramel brownie bites, pecan tassies, and profiteroles to the menu. After heating the savories, which included her bite-sized crab cakes, mini quiches, and lavosh pinwheels, she put out a few more trays of Christmas cookies and added festive touches with candy canes and rosemary (to mimic pine twigs).

She had really outdone herself, knowing how important this was to Simon. Since he insisted she be a guest, she needed to look the part, so she donned her best "little black dress," pearls, low heels, and a simple up-do. She looked very elegant for a "caterer." A quick spritz of her favorite fragrance, Amazing Grace, and she walked down the back staircase. The kitchen doorbell rang as she was setting the hors d'oeuvres and sweets at stations in the three rooms.

"Lissa, you look breathtaking." It was almost a whisper as he placed a quick kiss on her cheek.

"You look quite *dapper*, yourself," she said archly. He wore a smart, black Armani suit with a red silk tie. When she breathed in the same cologne, her heart skipped a beat. Wiping her hands down her sides, she attempted to compose herself. "Ready?"

"I had a few last minute invites: potential donors to our endowments and a few friends from the District. Will that be a problem?" he asked sheepishly.

"Lucky for you, I made extra. And if we're desperate, I have a few leftovers from Midnight Madness in the fridge." She grinned. "And, there should be enough room to not alarm the fire marshal, depending on how many people you invited. I've got more food to put out. I can help you with the punch if you like. I set out Mimi's crystal punch bowl."

"I don't know how I can thank you enough."

"Simon, you're paying me."

"There is that, but I do appreciate all the work you're doing—the extra details, little touches. You have a way of making simple things look extraordinary."

"Simon, enough chit-chat—it's almost time to welcome your guests." She smiled as she walked back to the kitchen. "Now set up the bar. They always want a drink first."

Most of the night, she kept a low profile, refilling when things were low, picking up empty plates and glasses, and monitoring that no one was leaving intoxicated. She felt it wasn't her place to over-mingle with the guests, but Simon didn't seem to mind as he introduced her around. She even heard some of his friends speculate on whether she was Simon's girlfriend.

She was glad Jen and Anthony were there. Her friends provided a safe zone for conversation, comforting in a room full of Simon's friends and acquaintances.

When Jen said, "I'm so glad you have a boyfriend like Simon," Lissa almost dropped the stack of empty plates she was collecting from around the conservatory.

"Wh-what are you talking about? We're not a *couple*."

"That's not how Simon talks about you. I know we haven't had a lot of time for a good, girls-only talk, but things sure look that way. Look at this party. You went above and beyond a simple catering job. I think you succeeded in finding 'the way to a man's heart is through his stomach.'"

"I made sure to do a great job because he's your boss and Anthony's friend. You're reading too much into it. Plus, you know I enjoy all this, and sometimes I tend to go over-the-top using my *Southern Living* holiday books as a guide. But, how does that add up to a relationship?"

"You must know he has a bit of a crush on you. Always has."

"Jen, I don't understand. I've barely had the chance to know him. No dates, just getting together to plan the party, shopping for the food and drinks, a few calls, and texting. I met him at the little party you threw when he first came to town, and I've always spoken to him when stopping by your office, but how did that progress to him being a boyfriend?"

"I think that's all it took. Plus, he knows you from me talking about you—a lot. You and I *are* best friends. My guess is he's finally at a point in his life that, if he finds 'the one'—you—the hunt is over." She shrugged her shoulders. "You just had a birthday. Weren't you the one saying, if the right guy came along, you were ready to try love again? You two are perfect for each other. And, a little push from me hasn't seemed to hurt either one of you."

"That kiss!"

"What kiss?"

"How did I not see this coming?" Lissa muttered as she walked to the kitchen.

Jen followed her friend. "Look, I think you've been overwhelmed with the store. You've carried everything by yourself for so long. You don't have to be alone. It's time to open your eyes. There's a great guy interested in you: successful, mature, not the kind of man to toy with your heart." Jen took the plates from Lissa and continued. "I've seen him in action. He didn't follow in his father's footsteps to go into the safe side of corporate law. He was a trial lawyer, a real pit bull in the courtroom. But, he has a compassionate side too. He's taken cases pro bono and won. He chose to leave that world to take a position as dean and professor. He led the Adopt-a-Family in our office, got his students involved. He does things quietly, but he's a remarkable person. I think he's just the kind of man you've been looking for."

"I don't know what to say."

"He was really impressed at Thanksgiving. After you left, I think he had a new appreciation for you. You both left that fast life in the city to do the things you want to do. He just doesn't express his feelings. For such a self-assured man professionally, he's reserved personally. Some mistake that for arrogance. He's not. Plus, he's one of Anthony's best friends. I wouldn't pick just anyone for you."

"This is so much to take in—to consider. Reconsider." Lissa picked up a stack of paper napkins. "Well, time to mingle and check the food. Thank you." She hugged her friend before moving back into the crowd, sorting her thoughts as she checked what was left.

"LISSA, ARE YOU OKAY?" SIMON ASKED QUIETLY AS HE ENTERED THE KITCHEN.

Lissa startled then smiled. "You're a stealth the way you come in so quietly."

He returned the smile. "I think the party's about over. Guests are leaving, but some want to thank you before heading out."

"Thank me?"

"You're my friend and hostess for the evening."

Remembering what Jen had told her, she followed him out and helped him say goodbye. Then Lissa started cleaning up. Although the next day was Sunday and the store would be closed, she couldn't bear to leave the mess. Jen and Anthony offered to help, but she shooed them out. As she checked the rooms for glasses to pick up, she turned off the music. It was then that she felt Simon's eyes on her. He hadn't left. He quietly helped her gather the remains and followed her to the kitchen.

"You did a marvelous job. My colleagues and friends were impressed. My parties are usually forgettable. Thank you."

"I'm glad you're happy. I've never done anything like that. I'm relieved it all worked out. And, I doubt your parties are forgettable." She turned to point to a stack of covered trays. "There are a few leftovers for you to take home." While washing the soapy dishes, she said, "I had to laugh when I overheard a few speculating if I was your 'secret girlfriend.'"

"'Secret girlfriend?' Really? I hope it didn't offend you. You do look really beautiful tonight. Not a typical look for a caterer." He winked at her while drying a dish she handed him. "Perhaps, they were trying to figure out if you're available. Are you?"

"You think one of your friends was interested in me? Me?"

"You must know how beautiful you are."

"No. Don't say things like that." She looked away, very uncomfortable with the conversation, scrubbing a platter that was already clean.

"I wouldn't say it if I didn't mean it." He took the last plate from her, rinsed it off before drying it, and added it to the stack. "It's not in my nature to give out compliments if I don't mean them." Sighing then leaning back against the counter, he said, "Do you want to settle up the bill tonight or meet over lunch tomorrow?" He picked up the trash bags and headed to the back door.

"Simon, you don't have to take out the trash. I can get the rest of this. I have most of the bill tallied. I just need to double-check. It can wait until tomorrow. And you don't have to take me to lunch."

"Perhaps, I *want* to take you out to lunch. It would give us a chance to talk more, get to know each other better."

"Is this a business transaction, or are you asking me out on a date? Because it sounds like more than business."

"If it were a date, would it make a difference?"

She pondered for a moment. "I suppose a date would be fine. More than fine. Nice." She smiled as she turned her kitchen radio to Christmas music. As she finished putting the dishes away, Simon took the trash out and then came back into the kitchen. She was humming along to "Rockin' around the Christmas Tree" when she heard him snicker. "What's so funny? And why are you staring at me?"

He pulled her into an embrace and then started swaying to the music. "You looked like you wanted to dance," he said while spinning her. "I think you're one of those rare gems many underestimate: a smart girl who loves books, hums to Christmas music, helps a guy out when he needs to host a party, and is so radiant, I just can't resist the urge to kiss her." And he did.

Softly, tentatively... And then deeper. Insistent. It was the perfect kiss, and Lissa felt herself leaning into him, putting her arms around his neck, running her fingers in his hair. Her body tingled with a frisson of energy she had not felt in a long time, if ever. She suspected he was finding that lost part of herself. She broke the kiss—"Simon..."—though her hands were still around his neck.

"Lissa, am I moving too fast?"

"I...I...I don't know. This is so unexpected. *You* are so unexpected. I hadn't thought beyond our business relationship. I've never seen this side of you." She moved her hands to his shoulders and leaned back to look into his eyes—those piercing blue eyes. "I'm trying to reconcile the law professor with this…this passion…this passionate man before me. So gentle, so kind, so different. An amalgam I never expected."

"I'm only a man. And, yes, when I have to be, I don't back down. I win cases. I can be ruthless in the courtroom. I'm blunt. And honest. I don't let my students cut corners. That's my job. But, if you let me, I can show you that I'm more. I'm the kind of man who will treat you with respect, and care for you as you deserve if you'll give me the chance." His last words ended with another sizzling kiss.

"Um-hm."

"Was that a yes?"

"Yes."

LISSA WAS HAVING THE MOST MARVELOUS DREAM. ENTANGLED IN BED WITH a man, his arms wrapped around her, her hand splayed on his warm chest, she could feel his heart beating. Her eyes popped open. *I am in bed with a man.* She looked into those blue eyes to find him smiling at her. She whispered, "Hi."

"Good morning, beautiful," he said softly with a kiss to the top of her head.

"Good morning. I guess I wasn't dreaming after all." As she glanced at the clock, she realized she had slept longer than usual, but she felt fully sated. "Oh," she said almost as a sigh. "I must look a sight." She moved her hand from his chest to her mussed up curls.

"Definitely not dreaming. You look lovely." He stilled her hand then brought it to his mouth for a kiss.

"Simon, we should probably talk about last night. I don't usually do that. In fact, I never do that. What I meant is…I don't sleep around." Blushing, she continued. "I don't want you to get the wrong impression of me—which, of course, makes no sense after what we did."

"We didn't do anything wrong. Why? Do you regret it?"

"No. No, I don't regret it. It was wonderful and beautiful. You made me feel things I haven't felt in a while. And to be honest, that scares me."

He smiled. "Why does that scare you?"

"My future is so uncertain. I barely know you. I don't have a plan."

"I don't have a plan either, but I'd like to get to know you better. Let the future wor—"

"Oh, goodness. The quilt. *The quilt.* Mimi's quilt! I've jinxed everything."

"Jinxed? What about the quilt? It's pretty."

"In my family, each daughter is given a quilt, but she's not supposed to use it until she finds 'the one' because she's supposed to save it for her wedding night, for her one true love. It's tradition. And I've cursed it. I used it before I was supposed to." She turned away from him. "It was so pretty, just sitting in my old trunk, and the holidays made me miss Mimi—my grandma—who made it, so I put it on my bed. And last night, I forgot, and I ruined it. With you." She was practically in tears.

"Lissa, I really don't think one night with me has ruined the quilt. Or jinxed it. Or us. It's a quilt. A tangible and tactile fabric bedcovering. Yes, it's pretty. Yes, you have a family legacy passed down to you, but the legacy is still there. The quilt will not ignite in flames just because we used it."

"Of course you would be pragmatic; you're an attorney! You think logically. Reasonably. And, the quilt is a big deal. *To me.* But, it's a double wedding ring quilt. A marriage quilt. And I thumbed my nose at it. And stop trying to be so practical. It's not helping. It probably *will* catch fire now that we messed with the juju."

"The juju? You're acting like there's a voodoo curse on it."

"Hey, I was born in New Orleans. There could be a *voodoo* curse on it."

"Well, then, let's get married. Negate the curse. Then you and the quilt will be safe."

"Simon, don't make fun of me. Just because you don't believe in it, it's not funny to say that." In an attempt to cover her embarrassment for her outburst, she teased, "And rather ungallant to make a fake proposal to a crying woman." She brushed the tears away and turned her lips to his.

He put his arms around her. "I'm not making fun of you. I'm trying to point out that the quilt doesn't make a difference. You can still use it. It's not tainted." He kissed her. "And the proposal wasn't fake."

She stared at him and looked deeply into his eyes. "Why would you ask me to marry you? We barely know each other. I'm in danger of losing my shop, and if I can't pay the taxes, I might even lose my home. You don't love me. You don't really know anything about me."

"I know you're a strong, talented, and beautiful woman—unlike anyone

I've ever known. With your coppery curls and green eyes, you've enticed me like a siren since the moment I walked into your shop. If anything or anyone is casting spells, it's you. I want you as I've never wanted another woman. And I think we could be good together. We get along great, you've impressed my friends, you've made an impression on my heart, and I do care for you." He kissed a tear that escaped her eyes. "And the money? I have money. I can help you."

"I don't need you to save me, Simon. I created the mess I'm in, and it's up to me to fix things. I would never expect you or anyone to marry me to protect me. I can do this on my own—succeed or fail, it's my responsibility." She wrapped herself in the quilt. "I'm going to shower, then I'll go down and make us breakfast. Maybe we can go for a drive and talk this afternoon if you don't have papers to grade. I know this is finals week."

THE QUIET WAS ALMOST DEAFENING AS THEY ATE BREAKFAST. HE WOULD look at her as if to say something then change his mind. Lissa turned on the radio, but she couldn't stand to hear the Christmas music. "I'll Be Home for Christmas" reminded her too much of last night and yearning for something that was only a dream. They'd crossed over to a new relationship status—no regrets, just the fear of giving her heart too soon. It couldn't be real—the "love of a lifetime" already—could it? Christmas had a way of tricking oneself into believing things: Christmas magic, Christmas miracles. But Christmas love? Bah-humbug! Now who's being the Scrooge? It was easier to change the station.

"You're a great cook. I haven't had a breakfast like this in ages."

His dark hair was till damp from the shower, and he hadn't shaved. The scruff of his whiskers gave him a relaxed, unkempt, yet handsome appearance. And she wondered whether this was his look on weekends: laid-back and carefree. Seeing him across the table, she could almost imagine him as a husband...her husband, and as a father...to their children.

"Thank you. I don't often get to cook for others unless I'm at Jen's or taking care of the girls. They like to cook and bake with me. They especially love my brownies."

"Brownies, huh? Do you have any of these special brownies so I can see why the girls love them so much?"

"Brownies for breakfast? Counselor, is that *legal?*" She walked over to a glass dish and used a spatula to lift a brownie out and put it on a plate. "Here, you be the *judge*."

He ate the brownie slowly, savoring each bite. "I'd marry you just for the brownies."

She pretended to punch him in the arm. "Stop proposing or else you might find yourself stuck with a wife and a mountain of debt, and she'd be unable to afford to make brownies."

"I'd work another job."

"Okay, the joke's over. No more joking about marriage."

"I do owe you for the party. Show me the grand total so I can write you a check. I'm going to have to take a rain check on lunch. You're right. I do have a lot of papers to grade before the semester ends this week."

She pulled out her datebook and looked at her notes. "You paid for the groceries when we went shopping. All of the decorations were already in the shop, and all of the serving ware was mine, so there's not anything to charge. She took the paper and tore it in two. Consider it a gift from a friend. Merry Christmas!"

"That wasn't our agreement. I agreed to pay you for the party. That includes your time and effort, baking, serving, rental space…all of it. You know that was part of the agreement."

"I can't charge you. Not now."

"What's changed? We had an agreement: you cater the party, and I pay for your services."

"Simon, we don't have a contract in writing, remember? And, I can't charge you—not after we slept together. It just wouldn't be right."

"Lissa." It was the trial lawyer voice starting to come out. "Because we slept together, I can't *not* pay you for the party. *That* would not be right."

"Simon, like it or not, the dynamics of our relationship—whatever it may be—changed when we slept together. Stop being a litigator for a moment. Think about it. It's not right to charge you. I wouldn't feel right about it."

"You agreed to the job before all of this."

She thought for a second. And she was a smart businesswoman. She did agree to the job, and she needed the money. In the end, she could separate the personal from the business—had to. Her heart was in the game. Now it was time to put her head in too. "Okay, you win. You're right." She went to her laptop, printed out an itemized list, totaled it, and handed it to him.

He pulled out his checkbook, wrote her a check, and handed it to her. "Now that we have that out of the way"—he put the checkbook in his pocket—"we can talk about *us* and our next date."

"Next date? When was our first date?"

"I think it's safe to say the dinner at the Thai restaurant was a date. Last night's party felt like a date too. You were on my arm for a lot of the night. You seemed very at ease with my friends. And"—he looked at her tenderly—"*they* really liked you. While the rest of last night was unplanned and perhaps a bit fast, I don't regret it. I hope you don't either."

"Shouldn't we take things slowly? I do like you. A lot." *I think I love you, and it scares me.* "I don't regret last night." She blushed. "But, we did rush in like fools, jumping feet first. I want us to both be certain. I'm overwhelmed with the store. I really could lose it."

"You're still not sure? We obviously have chemistry. We both enjoyed last night. We like each other's company. Where's the problem? I don't see one."

"I've spent so much time being independent. I'm not used to someone—a man—wanting to be there for me, date me…or more… I don't want to be a burden when my life is such a mess."

"Life is messy. You don't have to go it alone. We can go slowly." He put his arms around her and held her tightly. "I don't know who hurt you the most, but you have to let down these walls you've put up. Let go of the power it has over you. Move forward. I'm here, and I want you." He tilted her head gently and began kissing her, tenderly, then deeply, urgently, until they both had to come up for air with hearts racing. "Lissa, I… I'll call you this week. Let me *woo* you." And with that, he walked out her back door into the snow. It was the first time she noticed it was snowing. Beautiful snow—like the day he showed up a few short weeks ago.

A FEW DAYS LATER, JEN BROUGHT THE GIRLS OVER SO SHE AND ANTHONY could go Christmas shopping now that the semester was over. Lissa loved her time with the girls, though it did make her yearn for children of her own. Simon had called and wanted to take her to dinner, but she begged off since she had the standing date with the girls. They had baked Christmas cookies and were watching Christmas movies when there was a knock at the kitchen door.

"Aunt Lissa, someone's at the door!" the girls shouted in unison.

"Let me get it, girls," she said as she rushed ahead of them to the door. "Dr. MacGregor, to what do we owe the pleasure?" She smiled shyly at him. "Do come in."

As he entered, he handed her a large bouquet of red roses. "I heard my favorite girls were visiting, and I thought I'd come and see what you're up to." He kissed her on the cheek and whispered, "Simon. I'm Simon. Even the girls call me Simon."

"Lacey and Brenna, *Simon* missed the fun of baking cookies. Do you think he's allowed to eat any? And perhaps he wants to watch a movie with us or play a game?"

"Yay!" The girls each grabbed cookies off the platter as Lissa put the flowers in a vase.

As soon as Simon shed his coat and draped it over a kitchen chair, they thrust the cookies at him. He was dressed casually in jeans and a sweater. Country club casual in Ralph Lauren. Always put together. She felt like a mess in her Costco green sweater and black jeans, plus a Christmas apron covered in flour and sugar.

"These are the best sugar cookies ever. You gals are great bakers."

"We used the cookie cutters and decorated them."

He took the glass of milk Lissa offered. "Nothing beats milk and cookies." He reached into her curls, plucked something out, and teasingly said, "Sugar crystals—you always have glitter in your hair." As he kissed her cheek, he murmured, "I love that sweater on you. That color brings out the fire in your hair and the brilliance of your eyes."

"Wh-what?"

"You were wearing it when I came into the store to ask about the party."

Before she could reply, the girls started jumping up and down, vying for attention. "Why don't you girls take Simon into the family room, and I'll finish cleaning up." She motioned for them to go into the other room. Apparently, he really meant it when he said he was going to *woo* her.

"Let's play a game!" Lacey exclaimed. "I know—we can play Twister." Brenna got it out of the cabinet near the television and set up the game.

Simon flicked the spinner and called out the colors and directions as Lissa finished in the kitchen. When she came in to see how the game was going, the girls suggested they take over so Lissa and Simon could play.

As the game progressed, Lissa lost her balance and fell, causing Simon to fall on top of her. When she looked into his eyes, her heart melted. He hovered over her for a second before succumbing to temptation, and he kissed her thoroughly. The sounds of giggling made them come up for air just as Jen and Anthony walked in.

"Aren't you two a little old to be playing house...er...Twister?" Jen said, laughing.

Simon helped Lissa to her feet, and he didn't let go until he and Anthony shook hands, but then he put his arm around Lissa again. "Never too old. I bet you and Anthony still play," Lissa said with a wink.

Anthony jokingly asked Simon, "What *are* your intentions with our Lissa?"

Jen gave him a look, but Simon had a quick answer. "Entirely honorable."

"Then perhaps you should marry her and take her off our hands," said Anthony.

Simon laughed. "I would if the lady would agree."

Brenna and Lacey jumped up and down with excitement. "Do we get to be flower girls?"

Jen glanced at Lissa. "Don't put your cart before the horse, girls. Aunt Lissa and Simon aren't engaged, so they're not getting married. Daddy was just teasing."

"That's right, girls. It's not time to plan a wedding. When you see a diamond on this finger"—she held up her ring finger—"then you'll know I'm engaged, and then you can start helping me plan for a wedding."

"Will that make Simon our uncle?" Lacey asked.

"Only if I marry Simon. It could be another guy who puts a ring on my finger." Lissa went into the kitchen to pack up the cookies for the girls to take home as Jen helped them get ready to go.

"Oh my gosh! What was that? You need to be careful with his heart," Jen whispered to her as she entered the kitchen.

"Jen, what about my heart? You're my best friend. Shouldn't you be worried about my heart?"

"I've been worrying about your heart for years. I would hate to see you blow a great thing with a wonderful guy because you're stuck—trapped by this house and an obligation to whatever Pop and Mimi may have instilled in you. I don't think they meant for you to put your life on hold if all this didn't work out. You're entitled to have a wonderful life. Don't let the albatross drown you when someone who cares for you is offering you a lifeline."

Jen hugged her friend. "Dreams can change, and be for the better, especially when you have someone to love and share your life with. Don't throw it away because of a well-intended promise to keep the shop running. Those deathbed promises aren't always what you think they mean. Pop and Mimi wanted you to be happy, loved, and have a family." As the others came into the kitchen, Jen kissed her on the cheek then ushered the girls out the door with Anthony in tow.

"Sweetheart, what's wrong?" Simon asked as he brushed a tear from her cheek while looking at her.

"Jen just said something. I know her heart was in the right place, but it's hard to accept."

He pulled her into his arms and just held her. "Maybe I should go too?"

"No, stay with me. Please." She leaned her head on his shoulder with her hand splayed across his heart. "I'm sorry for my comment in there. Rather than sounding funny, it was insensitive—mean-spirited—which was not my intent. I don't know why I keep saying silly things like that. I don't want to hurt you or push you away. You're so wonderful and don't deserve it." She wrapped her arms around his neck and looked deeply into his eyes. "I keep feeling like this is a dream, I'll wake up, and you'll be gone."

"Lissa, I—"

"Let me finish, please…" She ran her right hand gently across his cheek and over his jaw. "I think I felt…a little unworthy of all this. Unworthy of happiness. Unworthy of you. It's so beautiful—what we have. I don't want to lose it, risk the future with flippant remarks that self-sabotage and, worst of all, destroy the best thing I've ever had in my life. I know I sound like I'm rambling…" While running a finger across his lips, she continued. "What I'm trying, rather poorly, to say is: there's no one else I'd rather be with. I want you to stay."

"Sweetheart, I'm not going anywhere," he whispered as he leaned in for a kiss—a deep, assuring kiss to assuage any lingering fears.

LISSA WOKE UP TO THE SOUND OF THE SHOWER RUNNING. SHE THOUGHT for a second of joining Simon, but she still had a shop to run, and so far, Christmas sales were going well. She might even sell all of her Christmas items and turn a profit for the end of the year. There could still be a Christmas miracle.

"I see you left the quilt on the bed. Does that mean you've made peace with the curse, or is the jury still out?"

"You're funny. I'm going to use it to trap you into marriage." Realizing what she said, she flushed. "Don't worry, we're using protection. *I didn't mean it like that!*"

"Believe it or not, I knew what you meant the first time. But for the record, the proposal is still on the table."

She rolled her eyes at him as she went in to get her own shower. When she finished, she found a note on the kitchen table.

"Sweetheart, apologies. I couldn't stay for breakfast. I needed to get home and change before work. There are a few loose ends to tie up. Then I can spend a lot of time with you as I'm off till the end of the year for winter break. Let's get together for dinner? Love, Simon"

Love? She loved that he signed his letter with "love."

LISSA AND SIMON HAD BEEN SPENDING A LOT OF TIME TOGETHER OVER THE past week: dinners out or at home, decorating a tree they picked out together, getting to know one another better, making plans for a future. They had truly become a couple. This was going to be a wonderful Christmas. Earlier, a box had arrived with matching stockings—embroidered with their names—to hang on the mantle near "their" tree. She was looking forward to surprising him with them later. He'd brought some ornaments from his house to add to her family keepsakes. It was the happiest she'd been in years.

With most of the students now gone for break and the tourists only around on weekends, the store's business from the locals was usually feast or famine. It was a quiet day, so she decided to look over the accounts to get a better idea on how things stood. She resolved to make some serious decisions about her future. And, while sales were going steady for the season and could possibly turn a profit, it was not a sustainable profit—not enough to support herself. The past couple of years had been tight as it was; the new bookstore had definitely put a nail in the coffin. It was time to face facts: she could not go on like this. Just what were her options? If this place wasn't going to house The Printed Word, the only options were to sell the whole building or start renting out space. There were no other viable alternatives.

She pulled out the blueprints to study how the house had been divided for the bookstore. The original pocket doors would help her reconfigure the shop for renting office space. The other options were not ones she even wanted to consider. She couldn't bear to split up the house to make apartments. And she didn't have the money she would need to convert the house into a bed and breakfast. Regardless, she didn't really want to own a bed and breakfast. She was done being self-employed and scraping by. She needed a steady income. Rental office space was steady as long as it was occupied, and that could supplement income from a *real* job. She knew she could call a friend at the realty office to find out the going rate for rental space based on square footage. Perhaps Simon could help her write up a lease.

The tinkling of the bell on the door caught her ear, and she was shocked to see Roland come in. *What could he possibly be doing here?* "Roland, this is a surprise." She welcomed him politely. "How may I help you?"

"Actually, I'm here on legal business. I have something for you. Don't worry, I think it's good news. I was cleaning out Dad's office, and I came upon some correspondence that was meant for you. Dad had handled legal business for Pop, and I think it's related to that. He didn't get a chance to bring this over before he passed away." Roland's father had been a family lawyer in town. He had always hoped Roland would take over the practice, but Roland liked life in the District and the salary of a litigator. His father had passed away a few months ago, and Roland was helping get the files in order so another lawyer could buy the practice. "I figured your boyfriend wouldn't mind me dropping it by. MacGregor is my wife's former boss."

She decided to let the comment go. It was no business of Roland's what her relationship with Simon was—or wasn't.

"Let me see what you have." She took the envelope. "I'm impressed it's sealed."

"It was addressed to you—not my place to open it just because I'm cleaning out Dad's files."

She slid her finger under the seal and began to open the envelope. As she pulled out the papers, she saw a letter and legal document. The document was from New Orleans. She felt dread then. Here *was* the voodoo curse. No one had heard from anyone in her father's family—in New Orleans—since her parents died when she was young. Pop and Mimi brought her home and raised her here. She took a deep breath and read the letter from Roland's father.

Dear Lissa,

    I received this document from a firm in New Orleans. They had sent me the release form because, years ago, I was the mediator when Pop and Mimi corresponded with your relations' lawyer down there. The last of your kin has passed on. After the estate was sold to pay expenses, bills related to illness, and the back taxes on the homestead—it had to be liquidated to free the outstanding debts—the remaining monies were put in trust to be settled on your thirtieth birthday per the terms of the will and trust. As the beneficiary, you are to sign the enclosed form in the presence of a notary, then return it to the firm. At that point, the exact denomination for the trust will be revealed and released to you. It's my understanding that the value is approximately one hundred thousand dollars. They will arrange to wire the money to the account of your choosing. In addition, your paternal grandmother wanted you to have the enclosed locket.

Regards, Henry

Lissa nearly fainted. She reached into the envelope and found a smaller one. Her shaking hands opened it, and she found an ornately engraved gold Victorian-style locket on a chain with a handwritten note. Inside the locket was a small picture of a woman who looked like a doppelganger of herself. The note said simply:

We always loved you, but we felt it best for your Pop and Mimi to raise you. It's what your parents wanted. Maman Robicheaux

There were tears running down her face. She tried to brush them away, but Roland noticed.

"It was good news, right?" Roland asked earnestly.

"Yes, the best. Thank you so much for bringing this to me." She surprised herself and gave him a hug and a kiss on the cheek.

At that moment, Simon entered the store. Their eyes met. He frowned but said nothing. Instead, he immediately turned around and slammed the door behind him. "Roland, thank you so much for dropping by. I appreciate you taking the time to personally deliver it. That meant a lot. Do me a favor: lock the door behind you when you leave." She rushed out the door searching for Simon.

OUT OF BREATH AFTER CHASING HIM UP THE STREET, SHE MANAGED TO catch his arm. "Simon, stop! Please! Let me explain what you saw. Don't be angry with me. It's not what you think."

Instantly, he drew her to him in an embrace. "I'm not angry with you, sweetheart. He just grates on my nerves. I don't like him, and I don't like that he hurt you." He leaned back and cupped her face gently as he finished his apology with a kiss while wiping the tears from her face. "Please don't cry. I don't want to ever be the cause of your tears. It's just...well, I was afraid I'd slug him; it was better I left. After I walked away, I realized that wasn't fair to you. But trust me; I needed to cool off before I came back."

"I'm glad you didn't—slug him—though he may deserve it. But, this time he's doing his job as a lawyer, and it's important. I need your help. *I need you*. Now, if you have time? I just received this unexpected...I don't know what to call it...maybe, a miracle? Please come back to the house with me."

He looked into her beseeching green eyes. "A miracle, huh? It's the perfect season for one. Let's go back."

THEY WENT IN THROUGH THE KITCHEN DOOR AFTER DIGGING IN A POT where she had a key hidden. She had raced after Simon without taking her keys with her, and Roland had actually locked the store for her.

"I don't think that's really the safest place to hide a key."

"I'll have to give you a spare key for next time, I've been meaning to anyway with all the time you've been spending here. Then you won't have a reason to lecture me."

"A key, huh? Now who's moving rather fast?"

"Simon, you can be so exasperating!" She kissed him quickly. "I have good news, and I need your help—your legal expertise. Please sit. I have to get something from the shop." She returned momentarily and placed the envelope and blueprints on the table while settling down next to Simon.

"What is all this?"

"A Christmas miracle." She smiled tentatively as she pushed the blueprints to the end of the table, then she pulled out the contents of the envelope Roland had brought earlier. "I need you to look at the blueprints and help me figure out the best way to sublet the shop as offices so I can generate some income, and I need you to help me figure out if this trust, this possible miracle, is legal."

"You need me for legal help?"

"Simon, why not? My *boyfriend* is a lawyer, a law professor, and the dean of the law school! Do you need a dollar for a token retainer?" She jokingly nudged him.

"Your *boyfriend,* huh? I guess that qualifies you for a one-time pro bono document review." He smirked as he put on his reading glasses and looked over the legal paperwork. Then he examined the letters and the locket. He glanced over at the blueprints. "First, the trust appears to be legitimate. I'll call about it first thing tomorrow. The keepsake is a high quality gold piece of jewelry with a French hallmark. It's a little more valuable than a new piece, but not so much to prevent you from wearing it if you choose. Your ancestor bears a striking resemblance to you." He smiled as he handed it back to her. "As for the blueprints, there's no way I will help you sublet those rooms as offices. You now may have the money for some alterations or repairs, but I think you ought to keep the money and use it for taxes on the house and other day-to-day expenses. You have another standing offer on the table to consider—with an addendum."

She looked puzzled. "Another offer? What kind of offer? Who else knows?"

He pulled out some papers of his own from his briefcase, plus a small gift bag. "Just your boyfriend. And this is a long-term commitment: a permanent offer with fringe benefits. I think this proposal is worth your consideration."

"An offer with fringe benefits? You've piqued my interest." She gave him a sideways glance. "Did you say proposal...?"

"Ahem. As I was saying. I propose you allow your intended husband to help you restore the house back to the home it was meant to be. Your husband would be in a position to invest in your home if he sells his home in the city. In exchange, your husband would like to have a home office in one of the parlors. This would be a personal library and office for him, but you may gain entrance whenever you please." He looked at her again over the rim of his reading glasses, grinning. "In addition, your husband would like to help you fill the home with children. These papers"—handing her another document—"show that your husband is financially able to provide the investment opportunity he has offered upon the sale of his current home. He has a respectable job with a decent salary to help you maintain or exceed the lifestyle to which you are accustomed. He's in a position to help you and support you in your decision making regarding your future. But most of all, he loves you. With all his heart. And, he offers this addendum as a token of his love and proposal of marriage."

As Simon pulled the jeweler's box out of the bag, he got down on one knee. He held out his hand and took hers in his then placed a beautiful princess-cut, two-carat diamond ring on her finger. "Lissa Robicheaux, will you marry me? Marry me because I love you. I love you more than I ever thought I could love someone."

Tears streaming down her face, she took his face in her trembling hands and kissed him while whispering, "Yes. Yes. Yes. A thousand times, yes. I love you too. And I'll marry you."

It was snowing on Christmas Eve, and the lights on the tree were as dazzling as the sparkling snowflakes hitting the window outside the conservatory. The lights from boats on the bay twinkled in the distance. Lissa and Simon had managed to put together a beautiful, intimate wedding with help from Jen and Anthony and, of course, Lacey and Brenna. A couple of close friends attended, and somehow, Simon had managed to get the minister to come over between Christmas Eve services to perform the ceremony in their home. They would have just enough time for a honeymoon before Simon returned to work after winter break. Lissa was still contemplating her next job, but for now, she was content to oversee the restoration of the old Victorian. The Christmas miracle money was set to hit her account any day, and she would start closing The Printed Word after their honeymoon. Closing the store wasn't as hard as she imagined, considering a whole other life was opening up. The double wedding ring quilt was still on her bed—well, *their* bed—and she decided it couldn't be cursed since Simon was "the one," after all.

DENISE STOUT dreamed about writing from an early age, guided along the way by some special teachers who took an interest in her writing and encouraged her to pursue her words in print. She loves to write stories about strong women who strive for the best, sometimes faltering, but who always have the fortitude to pick themselves back up again while finding love along the way.

A frequent contributor to FindSubscriptionBoxes.com, she also reviews books, movies, and products. When not driving carpools, watching her boys play sports from the sidelines, or volunteering, she loves to read. And write. And watch Jane Austen adaptations. Denise lives in the Baltimore area with her husband and three sons.

"There are as many pillows of illusion as flakes in a snow-storm.
We wake from one dream into another dream."
—Ralph Waldo Emerson

The Clock Doesn't Lie

by Linda Gonschior

he clock doesn't lie.

Whoever said that never needed to replace the batteries in the scratched, tin-framed clock hanging behind the counter of the small diner in the truck stop outside Meryton.

Danielle tucked some loose strands of hair behind her ears and climbed up on the wobbly stool. One hand braced against the wall's surface, her outstretched fingers fell short of the clock's bottom edge.

"Darn it!"

She stepped down onto the floor, relieved to be on solid ground again but annoyed that the clock still stubbornly read 10:45. The second hand bounced in place, as if poised to race the minute hand at the first opportunity.

Picking up a spoon from the serving tray under the counter, Danielle prepared to do battle once again, her eye firmly fixed on the target to distract herself from the unsteady stool.

A jingling bell announced the entrance of a customer through the side door, startling Danielle before her other foot left the floor. Cheeks flushed when she saw the tall, striking young man approach the counter, and she hoped he had not seen her awkward maneuver. Danielle put on her friendliest smile, her eyes taking in his impeccably groomed appearance and tailored suit.

"Merry Christmas! What can I get you? Coffee?" She pulled a menu from the holder and held it out to him.

He glanced at the plastic covered sheet but made no move to take it. His gaze then travelled the length of her arm and along the slope of her shoulder, briefly lingering on her lips before coming to rest on her enquiring eyes.

"Just a coffee," he said then belatedly added, "Thanks."

"Sure. One coffee coming up!" Danielle was used to every kind of customer: the tired-of-being-on-the-road truck driver, the excited-to-get-home college kids, the cranky children, and the chatty old married couples. This young man did not fit into the usual categories. *Yet.*

She set the cup of coffee in front of him at the corner table where he sat staring out the window at the wildly swirling snow. He didn't move, giving her a perfect opportunity to examine his profile. It took but a moment to appreciate the strong jawline and note the firm set of his mouth and an equally well-defined nose. Danielle drew his attention away from the window to the steaming cup.

"Sugar, cream, and milk are there," she said, pointing to the containers lined up where the table's edge met the wall. "Would you like something else? Maybe a piece of pie?"

He shook his head; even that small gesture carried an air of seriousness. "No thanks." Then he returned to his vigil.

Danielle shrugged and returned to her spot behind the counter. There had been little business this cold Christmas Eve. Only the desperate-to-be-somewhere were traveling, and there were finer places to stop for a meal. That brought her curiosity to bear on the young man.

He was undeniably attractive and well dressed. Better than well dressed, his clothing screamed wealth. What brought him to Dan's Diner at the Meryton truck stop in a blizzard on the night before Christmas?

Her imagination took flight.

He's heir to a big family fortune but had a falling out with Daddy over his wild lifestyle. Daddy said, "Grow up or get out." So he got out. Now he's regretting the decision and trying to figure out how to get back into Daddy's good graces.

Having solved that mystery, Danielle returned to her tasks. The floor needed to be swept, the counter wiped, and that clock needed new batteries.

She tackled the first two and hoped the diner would be empty soon so she could get to the third.

Typically, she swept when no one was present since inevitably she wound up humming, if not singing. This time was no exception in spite of the young man's presence. Danielle suddenly caught him watching her, and she blushed furiously. She was thankful that at least she'd been humming a Christmas song.

"Do you have far to go?" she asked in an attempt to distract herself from the feelings of embarrassment.

He didn't reply right away. When he finally spoke, Danielle had forgotten the question.

"Another hundred miles."

Her eyes widened in surprise. "Tonight?"

"No, not tonight." He gestured toward the clock. "Too far to cover now."

Danielle looked over her shoulder and scowled at the clock, still stuck at 10:45. "That's not right."

He apparently misunderstood. "I tried to leave earlier but, you know, work." He shrugged. "Then the snow."

She was too familiar with working on holidays but was surprised all the same. *The rich boy? Working?* Then she chuckled to herself, remembering that it was her imagination that had given him an idle life. Now she would have to rethink the story behind him.

"You mentioned pie earlier. What, um, kind have you got?" He was studying her with soft, grey eyes.

"Apple, pumpkin, lemon meringue, cherry, and coconut cream." She stopped just short of adding, *"Don't have the coconut. It's frozen and horrible."*

"Any of them homemade?"

Danielle's smile came readily. "The pumpkin was made fresh today, just for the holiday."

He nodded and, for the first time, smiled. "That's what I'll have. Pumpkin pie, please."

"Yes, sir. Won't be a moment." Her own smile persisted all the way to the kitchen.

HIS EYES FOLLOWED THE GENTLE SWAY OF HER HIPS AS SHE WALKED AWAY, and when she was out of sight, he turned his attention to the diner itself.

There was nothing special about it although he conceded that the inside was bright and clean, more so than he would have expected of a roadside truck stop. The sign outside proclaimed the establishment to be Dan's Diner, and he briefly wondered how Dan had the nerve to leave a pretty, young woman to work alone on Christmas Eve.

He glanced at the clock again. He couldn't believe how late it was—until his attention was caught by the quivering second hand—and prompted him to compare the time on his phone.

"Well, it's not so late after all." He frowned at the clock, wondering whether he dared take it down and fix it.

IN THE KITCHEN, DANIELLE WAS REVISING HER PREVIOUS OPINION OF HER customer. *Okay, so he's a rich guy with responsibilities. Works far from his family. Trying to get home to Mom and Dad's place for Christmas, but he's not going to make it. He'll stay at a fine hotel tonight and arrive home tomorrow in time for the big family meal. Nobody makes a better holiday dinner than the fancy cook working in the fancy kitchen with every expensive appliance money can buy.*

With a slice of her pumpkin pie on the plate, Danielle added a dollop of whipped cream. She was quite proud of her baking skills.

When she returned to the table, he was speaking softly into his cell phone. Danielle set down the plate and a fork then quickly retreated. The clock was calling her name.

The dilemma remained: how to get the clock down from its perch without, in short, looking like a complete fool. Not for the first time did she regret storing the stepladder in the outside shed. The last time she had used it, there were still flowers in the planters on the window ledges. Danielle narrowed her eyes and made a face at the clock. Its second hand teasingly waved back and forth. *That's enough! You are not going to defeat me this time!*

A quick glance over her shoulder confirmed that her customer was occupied on his phone. Danielle focused on her unsteady perch, determinedly gripping the long-handled spoon that would ensure success. Carefully climbing onto the stool, she sought that feeling of balance before extending her arm toward the bottom of the clock's frame. The spoon was *just* long enough to slip behind the tin; a deft twist to the side would pop it off the nail.

The stool suddenly shifted under her feet, and Danielle felt herself falling away from the wall. There was a split second to curse the clock—and hope she wouldn't break her neck—before the expected impact. Surprisingly, there was no pain.

Danielle's eyes opened to find herself firmly in the man's arms. In the next moment, his grip relaxed slightly, allowing her feet to touch the tiles.

"Are you okay? You aren't hurt?"

Danielle breathed again as she shook her head. "I'm fine, I think. Thank you." Her legs gave way when she tried to stand.

His grip immediately tightened, drawing their bodies closer. His voice was quiet, his mouth close to her ear. "Relax and breathe deeply."

In another moment or two Danielle's heart stopped racing and she was steady enough to stand on her own. "Thank you again," she said, taking a step back. "I should have known better than to use a stool."

"I'm just glad you weren't hurt." His eyes looked away briefly then met hers once more. "And that I was able to catch you."

Danielle giggled nervously. "So am I!"

He bent down to retrieve the wooden spoon she had dropped and handed it to her. "Would you like me to get the clock down for you?"

Before she could say a word, another jangle of the bells brought a rush of wind and snow through the open door.

"Dani?" called a man's voice. He was bundled up in a heavy parka with a toque covering his head and face. As he stomped the snow from his boots, Danielle took advantage of his distraction to push the loose strands of hair back from her face and smooth her blouse. She noted Mr. Handsome quietly slip back to his table by the window.

"Ah, there you are! Mighty cold out there, Dani. Could you fill my thermos for me? It's going to be a long night."

"Sure thing, Jim." She took the container from his gloved hand. "What are the roads like?" she asked while watching the hot coffee pour into the thermos and hoping her hand wasn't trembling as much as her insides.

"Terrible!" Sweeping one hand toward the windows while pushing the toque to his forehead with the other, he said, "Nobody in his right mind would be out there, except the plow drivers of course."

"Of course!"

"Say, you wouldn't happen to have any of your pie left, would you?" Jim grinned at Danielle's nod. "I'll have some of that too."

Danielle laughed, plunked his thermos on the counter, and tightened the lid. "I'll be right back with the pie." She stole a glance toward the table by the window, pleased to see a smile directed at her. Acknowledging him with a shy smile of her own, Danielle continued to the kitchen door, not realizing until a moment later than she was holding her breath. Jim's voice rolled through the diner as she disappeared from sight.

"Better make it to go, Dani! Gotta get back out there!"

ACROSS THE ROOM, A PAIR OF CURIOUS EYES WAS NOW TURNED ON JIM. THE plow driver seemed to be *very* familiar with the young waitress, and again the man behind that gaze wondered why she was working alone on such a night. Maybe things were different in small towns. Maybe a pleasant, attractive young woman didn't need to worry about over-eager men trying to impress her to the point of harassment or shady characters looking for a quiet place to cause trouble and steal a few dollars. Then again, perhaps the plow driver didn't simply happen to drop in. He could be more than a regular customer on a stormy evening.

One thing was certain. If she had been completely alone ten minutes earlier… He refused to complete that thought. It was enough that she was unhurt.

And she smiled at me.

An insistent buzzing turned his attention back to his phone, but it didn't dispel the picture of her in his mind.

DANIELLE'S THOUGHTS WERE RAPID WHILE DISHING OUT THE SLICE OF PIE to-go for Jim. *Mr. Handsome isn't going to get very far when he leaves here. Not much point in even trying, from what Jim said. Maybe I'll suggest he stay at the bed and breakfast in town. Not what he's used to, I'm sure, but beats getting stuck in a ditch and freezing to death.* A shiver ran through her with that last thought. Securing the lid on the pie's container, she returned to the counter.

"Here you go, Jim."

The plow driver took the container from her hand and gave her a ten-dollar bill. "Thanks Dani. Take my advice, sweetie. Close up and head home. The highway's shut down already. Brian and I are just keeping up with the main roads in and out of town."

"Thanks for the warning. It's been quiet tonight, I admit." Danielle nodded toward the tables. "One customer to see to, then I'll go home."

Jim looked over to where the young man sat, noticing him for the first time. "Hey, buddy! That your car in the parking lot? You won't get anywhere in that tonight. I can drop you off at Silver Valley B & B if you want."

"Thanks, but no. I'll figure out something."

"Suit yourself." Jim turned back to Danielle and said quietly, "He won't be figuring out much, I'm sure. Don't stay here all night just because of him, Dani."

"Don't worry. I was going to suggest Silver Valley too. He'd be crazy to try and drive out of here."

Jim pulled the toque down over his face, gathered up his thermos, and called over his shoulder, "If you're here when I come by again, the offer still stands." Then he headed out into the storm.

Danielle crossed to Mr. Handsome's table and picked up the empty plate. "He wasn't kidding, you know. This snow isn't going to let up until morning."

He met her gaze, considering her words. "How are you getting home, then?"

Danielle grinned. "I have a snowmobile. Faster than a four-by-four could get me home from here!"

His eyebrows rose, reflecting obvious surprise at her explanation. "You're serious?" A smile spread across his face. "About the snow, I mean?"

Danielle had been prepared to give him an earful, thinking he didn't believe she was able to handle a snow machine, but his last comment stopped her. "You have to take the snow seriously. Too many people don't and get hurt, or worse." She studied him closely: the manicured fingers and hands that showed no signs of calluses, the finely tailored suit that emphasized a well-toned body underneath, and an air of self-assurance in spite of his obvious naiveté regarding the snow. Shaking her head, Danielle spoke plainly. "You really are a city boy, aren't you? Jim won't be back here for at least a few hours. He'll expect me to be gone. Unless you want to become a statistic, I suggest you let me take you to the B & B. I don't know what you're driving, but if Jim says it's not going to make it through this, you'd best pay attention."

"I got the message loud and clear. It was stupid of me to turn down his offer." He peered up at her, a faint smile on his lips, but said nothing more.

Danielle broke the momentary silence. "I just need to close out the till and make sure everything is turned off in the kitchen." His phone buzzed with an incoming text message. Danielle noticed the name of the sender was feminine. "I'll be right back, and then we can leave."

"Wait," he called out. "What do I owe you for the coffee and pie?" He reached into his pocket, pulling out a handful of bills, then offered her a twenty. "Here, keep it. I have the feeling I'll owe you for more than that." His phone buzzed again.

Danielle headed for the kitchen as he attended to his messages. The routine of closing up allowed her mind to wander again. *Mr. Handsome has a girlfriend or a fiancée. Or a wife. Of course he has! Even if he were the Wild, Spoiled Rich Boy, he'd still have someone to worry over him. He's stuck in a snowstorm on Christmas Eve in a middle-of-nowhere town where nobody comes close to equaling his monetary worth. Why else would he toss me a twenty for a cup of coffee and a slice of pie? Girl, just do what needs to be done and go home.*

Before turning off the kitchen lights, she took a last look around the room then locked the back door. She rang in the price of his coffee and pie and dropped the twenty in the tray, setting the change aside in a separate section. Danielle finished balancing the till and locked the drawer. The diner would be closed until after Christmas Day, or until the roads were clear. There was no sense in opening if nobody could leave home.

A quick glance at Mr. Handsome confirmed he had put away his phone as he gathered up the few items he'd brought in with him.

"Do you need anything from your car?" She looked at his polished shoes. "Boots, maybe? A warm jacket?"

He shook his head.

"Phone charger?"

He grinned. "In my pocket."

Lord, he's cute. "You are going to be cold." Danielle looked him over then frowned. "Wait a minute." She walked to the far corner of the diner where a small door led to a storage closet. She handed him a fleece shirt and a helmet. "I always keep a spare helmet here in case one of my sisters wants a ride home. This shirt was left behind by somebody months ago. It's not much, but it's big, so it should fit over that fancy suit of yours." For a moment, she thought he would refuse to take them, but he hesitated only a moment before he held out his hands.

The shirt *was* big, and Danielle seemed hard-pressed not to laugh at the sight of his finely tailored trousers accented by the blue plaid fleece, the shoulders of which were at least three inches too wide for his frame in spite of the suit jacket underneath.

"It will definitely keep you warm for the short trip," she said encouragingly, watching as his fingers picked at one cuff. "I'll bring the snowmobile around to the door. Then I can finish locking up, and we can leave." Danielle was out the front door and into the dark, snowy night before he could say a word.

"I must look like an idiot," he mumbled. There were no mirrors, so he pulled out his phone again and set the camera so he could see himself. "Oh, yeah. Idiot, first class. Anna will love this." He pressed the button to take a picture, wondering whether he would find it as amusing in the morning. Examining the photo, he then pulled at the shirt in an effort to reduce the lumps.

It was a hopeless task.

DANIELLE TRUDGED THROUGH THE DRIFTS THAT HUGGED THE SIDES OF the building. Her ride was parked under a small lean-to behind the diner, a snow-covered lump the only sign it was there. She pulled the tarp free, sending most of the snow flying. What remained was easily brushed off. Coaxing the engine to start, she was rewarded with the rhythmic chug before pushing in the choke to speed it up to a steady purr.

The light from the door spilled out across the snow as Danielle brought the machine to a stop and left it idling to go back inside. Just as she flicked off the remaining interior lights, the face of that clock, still poised at 10:45, taunted her. It would be waiting for her return. One lone bulb in the back hallway sent a thin beam, which barely illuminated their way out. Then she turned off the big sign out front, leaving the colored Christmas lights merrily twinkling in the windows. The only light that remained was from her snowmobile. Ushering him out ahead of her, Danielle locked the door then turned to mount the machine. She waited for her passenger to get on, but a quick glance to the right showed Mr. Handsome was awkwardly standing there. She didn't know whether to laugh or sigh.

"Have you ever been on one of these?" she shouted over the noise of the engine. He shook his head. Danielle gestured to the space on the seat behind her. "Get on the back, wrap your arms around my waist, and hold on tight!"

He quickly followed her directions, not wanting to spend any more time in the cold than was necessary. She felt his arms slide around her cautiously. Danielle hoped she wouldn't lose him in a snowbank on the first turn. As they lurched forward when she engaged the throttle, his arms squeezed her ribcage, and his upper body toppled backward before managing to fight gravity.

It was barely a ten-minute ride to the Silver Valley B & B, but the challenge of fresh, unbroken snow and deep drifts set Danielle's pulse racing with every twist and turn. It was exhilarating to see the powder fly and feel her passenger's firm body pressed close into her back, his strong arms wrapped securely around her waist.

ALL TOO SOON, THEY ARRIVED AT THE FRONT OF THE B & B, AND DANIELLE parked just beyond the steps leading up to the veranda. As soon as they stopped, her passenger disentangled himself and slid off the back. Danielle felt the cold air rush across her back, and something like disappointment crossed her mind. She swung her leg over the seat and left the snowmobile running. "It's less trouble than starting it again." Then she led him up the steps to the front door, keenly aware of how close he was. Without knocking, she stepped inside and waved him to follow. Removing her helmet, Danielle called out, "Mrs. Renfrew?"

Standing beside her, Mr. Handsome also slipped the helmet from his head and promptly tried to redirect his hair to its former perfection. He looked around the new surroundings until his gaze came to rest on a plump, grey-haired woman wearing an apron, who appeared from a door near the end of the main hallway. Her face lit up with a smile.

"Dani Whitman! Merry Christmas to you, my dear! What brings you to my house at this hour tonight, it being Christmas Eve and all?"

"Merry Christmas, Mrs. Renfrew. This gentleman is stranded here because of the snow. Do you have room for him to stay the night?"

"Well, of course I do!" she said cheerfully. "Any friend of yours is welcome in my house, Mr... er..."

Danielle suddenly realized she had not once asked him his name. *What was I thinking?* She was at a loss for words as her cheeks began to burn with embarrassment.

The young man stepped forward, offering an outstretched hand and sparing her further awkwardness. "Chris. Chris Meisner."

Mrs. Renfrew took his hand in both of hers. "Very nice to meet you, Mr. Meisner. Like I said, any friend of Dani's is welcome. Now, where shall I put you? Oh, the Alabaster Room, I think."

Without releasing his hand, she headed for the staircase, pulling him along.

Danielle watched them disappear at the top of the landing but could still hear the older woman chattering away, never pausing long enough for her guest to reply. She felt very much alone in the empty hallway. In a few moments, Mrs. Renfrew returned and spoke to Danielle as if she had never left.

"Are you on your way home now, Dani? It was so kind of you to look after that nice young man. How unfortunate to be stranded in a strange place on Christmas Eve! I hadn't realized you didn't know him until he mentioned it upstairs, but he's all settled in now. Are all of your sisters home for the holidays?"

Accustomed to Mrs. Renfrew's rambling manner of conversing, Danielle replied without thinking. "Yes, we are all home this year." *What did he say about me? Is he coming back down? Should I just leave now?*

"Your mother must be so happy! I wish my children lived closer, but there you are. Not everyone can be so fortunate. Well, your friend is settled in. Oh, I said that already. Oh! He's not your friend! I forgot, but I must say, he *is* a nice young man." Her expression changed, eyes opening wide with alarm. "The pies! Excuse me, Dani!" She abruptly turned and bustled down the hall, disappearing through the same door from which she had earlier emerged.

Danielle shook her head, still berating herself for not asking his name. Gathering up her helmet, she glanced at the staircase and realized that Chris had returned. He looked exactly the same as when he'd first walked into the diner: perfectly attired and not a hair out of place.

No, not exactly the same, she thought. There was a relaxed air about him and the suggestion of a smile about his mouth.

He held out the plaid fleece and her spare helmet. "Thanks for finding me a place to stay…and for the ride here." For the first time, he truly smiled—a warm, friendly expression that was reflected in his eyes.

Danielle felt an elation tinged with regret as she accepted the helmet. "You'd best hang onto that," she said, indicating the shirt. "You will probably need it when you get your car tomorrow."

Both instinctively glanced at the window. The snow continued to fall heavily.

"Thanks. I'm sure I'll need it even if I don't get my car."

"Yeah." Danielle straightened her shoulders and tried unsuccessfully to fix her gaze anywhere but on his soft, grey eyes. "You may be stuck here for a while." That thought was not difficult to accept. The next was less pleasant.

"I'm sure your girlfriend will be worried if she's expecting you tomorrow."

His eyebrows rose. "Girlfriend?"

"The...um...one you were texting in the diner."

A grin hovered on his lips as he tilted his head to one side. "That was my sister," he said, stepping a bit closer to Danielle.

"Oh..." She could almost feel the heat of her embarrassment again and hoped it didn't show in her cheeks. "I just presumed...silly me...but really, it's none of my business."

He chuckled—a low, throaty sound that did not travel far in the open hallway. "I have to say that I presumed the same about you and that plow driver who offered me a lift."

"Jim?" Danielle laughed, her embarrassment momentarily forgotten. "His wife certainly wouldn't like that."

"Just to put your mind at ease, I have informed my sister that I'm stopping here tonight. There is no one else interested in my whereabouts."

Danielle wasn't sure which part of his statement was intended to comfort her, but she felt an odd lurch of her insides all the same. As he continued to smile, his gaze holding hers, she stumbled over her next words. "Well, my Mom and Dad will be expecting me home."

His smile faded. "Oh."

"I mean, that's where I live. That's why they are expecting me. And my sisters." She bit her lip to stop the babbling. "I don't have...anyone else...either."

They both laughed at the awkwardness of the moment.

Eventually, his gaze was again drawn to the window. "I'm seriously beginning to doubt if I'll even find my car in the morning, let alone be able to drive it anywhere!"

"That is a distinct possibility. How about I come by to take you back to the diner? Your car will need to be uncovered before Jim plows the parking lot; otherwise, you'll never get it out. The snow will be piled up around it."

"I'd like that." Chris chuckled. "Not the part about my car being buried, but I *would* like to see you again. I know it's Christmas, so you might be too busy to—" He fell silent when she raised a finger to his mouth.

"I wouldn't have offered if I was too busy. Besides, I'd hate to see you ruin your nice shoes if you walk all the way to the diner in the snow."

They grinned at one another, the rest of the world momentarily forgotten. Warm air rose from the radiator grill beside them while a chilly draft from under the front door blew sharply across the floor. The smell of cinnamon and apples filled the hallway, but Danielle discerned something in addition: a subtle, spicy scent that could only be a man's cologne. Without realizing it, she inhaled appreciatively and blushed to see Chris studying her intently when her eyes came back into focus.

"That baking does smell delicious," he said quietly, as if not wishing to be overheard.

"The baking..." Danielle repeated absently. "Oh, yes...the baking...does smell delicious." Then she noticed that he was staring at something overhead. She looked up and giggled.

Mistletoe dangled above them.

"You must be wanting to get home. Your family will be worried."

Danielle found herself nodding. "My parents won't be expecting me for a while yet, but I am eager to see my sisters. Two of them have been away at college, so our visits have been few and far between." *What's gotten into me? I'm rambling on like a schoolgirl with a crush on the star of the football team.* Parking the helmets on a nearby chair, she adjusted her scarf and zipped her jacket up as high as it would go. Then she handed the spare helmet back to Chris. "You'll need this tomorrow." She reached for her own, preparing to slip it on, when Chris's fingers came to rest on her hand.

"Thank you."

Danielle wasn't sure whether he had spoken the words or she had only read them in his eyes. There was one thing she was sure of: she had no objection as he brought his face closer to hers.

A soft chime sounded, only once.

Chris turned his head to see a small, ornate clock set on a shelf near the stairway.

Danielle followed his gaze. *10:45?* "Is every clock broken?"

"No, it's working perfectly."

The time no longer mattered when Chris's lips brushed hers in a brief, sweet caress.

"Merry Christmas," he whispered. "And thank you for rescuing me."

All she could manage was, "You're welcome." Anything else she wanted to say would have sounded silly. There was nothing to do now but leave. Her hand fiddled with the strap on the helmet. "I'll see you in the morning then."

"I'LL BE HERE." HIS FINGERS TRAILED ALONG THE BACK OF HER HAND AS HE prepared to let her go. "Waiting for you."

A teasing glint in her eyes brought a smile to his lips. "I'll bring you some boots too," she said, pulling the door open and stepping out into the cold.

Chris stood in the open doorway, watching Danielle put on her helmet and trudge through the snow to her machine. "Drive carefully!" he shouted over the engine and the sound of the wind.

Danielle touched one hand to her helmet in a salute then revved the snowmobile into motion. Chris shivered in the cold but didn't move until she had disappeared into the swirling snow and darkness.

It was Christmas Eve. He felt like a kid all over again, looking forward to seeing the delights that Christmas morning would bring.

. . . .

LINDA GONSCHIOR has entertained the art of writing since elementary school but never allowed it to come to fruition until *Pride and Prejudice* lured her deeper into the exploration of Jane Austen's characters, relationships, and "what-ifs." Seventeen years after writing *Reflections* as a short story, its publication as a full-length novel as well as the subsequent *A Tarnished Image* has opened up a new world with new friends and shared obsessions for all things Austen.

Living on a large acreage in rural Niagara, Linda shares her home with her husband, son, cat, dog, and dust bunnies.

"If your dog doesn't like someone, you probably shouldn't either."
—Unknown

*"To find someone who will love you for no reason,
and to shower that person with reasons, that is
the ultimate happiness."* —Robert Brault

A Perfect Choice

by Lory Lilian

November 16, 1811

Elizabeth rambled through the gardens of Netherfield, enjoying the peace and solitude of a few silent moments. It was a cold mid-November day, and a gentle breeze brought the scent of winter.

She had been a guest in Mr. Bingley's house for several days—caring for her beloved sister who had fallen ill while dining with Mr. Bingley's sisters—and her worry for Jane was as strong as her distress after each interaction with the other residents of the manor.

She liked Miss Bingley and Mrs. Hurst far less than her elder and kinder sister did as she had the chance to witness their true natures behind the polite smiles and civility. She could easily feel their disdain, which grew unbearable when her mother and younger sisters visited the day before. Mr. Darcy displayed haughtiness with his dark stare and obvious contempt! How could such a cold man be the friend of a warm person like Mr. Bingley?

Not that Mr. Darcy did not have a reason for his contempt. She cringed, remembering how her mother openly argued with Mr. Darcy about the advantages of the country and the disadvantages of Town; even the amiable Mr. Bingley struggled to keep his countenance. She easily imagined the cruel discussions that must have followed that visit once she escaped to Jane's room. Poor, dearest Jane—if only Mr. Bingley would be wise enough to see her worthiness beyond all the other unpleasantness of their family.

Caught in her thoughts, Elizabeth stumbled on a fallen tree branch. Bending to toss it off the walking path, a movement in the hedge caught her attention. Mr. Darcy's impressive black dog shot out of the hedges, and a cry escaped her. With no handler in sight, Elizabeth shivered, wondering whether she was in danger.

When the dog barked and wagged his tail, she relaxed. "What is it?" The dog barked again then lay on his belly, his eyes on the branch in her hands.

"You want to play?" She smiled, waving the branch and waiting until she had his full attention before throwing. The dog immediately ran after it, retrieved it, dropped it at her feet, and then sat.

"You are such a smart, beautiful boy." For the first time in days, she felt lighthearted, laughing and playing with the dog. Abruptly, the dog abandoned the branch, took a few steps back, and then sat again heralding the sudden presence of Mr. Darcy. She blushed, recognizing the same astonished—and certainly disapproving—glare from the day she first appeared at Netherfield, windblown and muddy after walking three miles to see Jane.

"Mr. Darcy..." she said, hiding her dirty gloves along with her embarrassment.

"Miss Elizabeth...forgive my intrusion. I heard Blackie barking and I was...I apologize if he disturbed you. He is not usually friendly with strangers, but he is not dangerous either."

"Oh, he did not disturb me...and I can see he is not dangerous. We have become quite good friends, as you can see."

"I am glad to hear that. Although I am a little surprised—"

"That he was bored? Or that he wished to play? Or that I understand the feeling? Or perhaps that your dog liked me enough to seek my company?"

She looked at him archly and expected him to remark upon her impertinence; instead, a smile—which he obviously struggled to conceal—twisted his lips.

"That he came to play with you. He is rather restrained with strangers, as I said. Though I am not surprised that he sought your company. May I dare ask why you presumed that?"

"Come sir, let us not dissemble. We have never been friends. I understand I am not as accomplished—nor as handsome—as the young ladies of your acquaintance. And I am certainly not accustomed—nor partial—to gentlemen with little amiability and even fewer faults. I also know that you are displeased with my—and Jane's—presence here. Rest assured; we will depart as soon as possible. Now if you would excuse me, I need to return to the house."

As she returned to the house at a quick pace, she found her answer did not give her the satisfaction she expected. She heard steps and knew he—and his dog— were following her. She smiled when she felt the dog's touch on her hand but startled when Darcy's gentle but decided grip on her arm stopped her.

"Miss Elizabeth, please forgive my brashness. I do not want to detain you, but I cannot deny my astonishment at your words, and I cannot waste the chance of offering you my explanations."

"That is wholly unnecessary, sir. I apologize if my words were offensive; we both know that my behavior is often far from what it should be."

"Please... May I ask the favor of a few more minutes? Perhaps we could walk together toward the house. Even if you do not consider me a friend, I hope you would enjoy Blackie's company enough to bear mine too."

"Very well, we could speak a little longer—at least until Miss Bingley espies you."

The shadow of a smile flashed across his face. "Miss Elizabeth, let me assure you that I have no intention of deceiving you in any way. It is true that your presence here is a disturbance from the usual schedule, but it is by no means unpleasant, except for Miss Bennet's distressing illness. And even if I might not show it as openly as Blackie, I enjoy your company. In truth, I look forward to our conversations as I have rarely enjoyed such interactions more."

Elizabeth looked to his face to gauge whether he was trifling with her. However, his stern countenance proved that he spoke the truth.

"I can easily see your disbelief, Miss Elizabeth, and it makes me wonder at my manners to have created such a poor impression. I thank you for the chance of refining it. Please do not believe that your loyalty toward your sister is not admired. We all hope for Miss Bennet to recover soon, but your presence here will be missed."

"I confess, I never suspected that you might enjoy our conversations. I was rather tempted to believe otherwise."

"Why is that?"

"Why? For countless reasons... If you remember, just two days ago, we spent half an hour in the library without your saying a single word!"

"I see...Indeed this is a very eloquent example. I confess that I am rather uneasy in conversing at times, especially with someone I have known only briefly."

She laughed. "If you consider someone you have met a month ago as *briefly known* and find them hard to address, I fear that a new acquaintance has not the smallest chance of hearing a word from you. I could call this a surprising fault in a gentleman known as being without faults."

Another small smile appeared.

"I have never pretended to be faultless. And I admit I do not possess the easiness that other gentlemen have in engaging in lively banter."

"I must wonder why a man with an excellent education and remarkable intelligence finds it difficult. Unless he has no interest in doing so..."

"I admit this to be also true. But it is not the case in your situation, Miss Elizabeth—quite the contrary."

She glanced at him with puzzlement.

"It is rather strange that my dog is responsible for this chance meeting."

She laughed, suddenly feeling more at ease in his presence. "I would not put the entire liability on Blackie—but he did have his share of assistance."

Hearing his name, the dog moved closer and touched his head to her hand.

Elizabeth patted his head. "He seems a well-trained dog."

"Thank you. I keep him under good regulation. He is very young—not two years yet—and he is larger and stronger than he realizes. A Great Dane must learn his power over others as well as obedience and discipline. For me to let him run unrestricted, I must be able to trust him completely."

"It seems difficult for you to put your trust in those around you." She gasped. "Forgive me, sir, I should not have said that."

"Do not apologize, please. Yes, I believe you must be right. I have been forced to rely on no one but myself for many years now."

Elizabeth's puzzlement grew at this strange confession. She had no time to reply as Darcy continued.

"I believe Blackie misses my sister Georgiana. He spent much time with her when he was a puppy, and she spoiled him."

"How lovely. Miss Darcy must be a kind, sweet young lady. I imagine she misses you both too. Have you been long separated?"

He hesitated, and she noticed his brow furrow.

"She prefers to live with me in our London family home or at Pemberley. We have not seen one another since August. She has decided to spend a month with my uncle's family at their estate. But we do write to each other regularly."

"I believe I would have found it difficult not to see Jane for so long. I hope we will always remain close to each other, even after she is married."

"I see. Do you expect Miss Bennet to marry soon?"

"Not that I know of. But it is not impossible; Jane is not only exceptionally beautiful but the kindest, gentlest, and most generous person that I have ever known. She always sees the good in people and always thinks of others before herself. Any man should be proud and grateful to have her as his wife."

He said nothing more but turned his eyes forward while they walked in silence to the house.

ELIZABETH SPENT MOST OF THE AFTERNOON IN JANE'S ROOM, PAYING LITTLE attention to the discussion with her sister as she pondered her meeting with Mr. Darcy.

Later that evening, she took extra care in her preparations for dinner.

As Jane was much improved, both were joyful to join the dinner party. Except for a slight pallor, Miss Bennet looked as beautiful as ever.

Elizabeth discerned Miss Bingley and Mrs. Hurst's false concern, exclaiming delight at seeing Jane and expressing several times how *sad* they would be after Jane returned to Longbourn the very next day.

Elizabeth was tempted to proclaim, "*Do not worry. We do not want to stay a day longer either.*" She checked herself as she met Mr. Darcy's amused eyes and that slight smile as if he was able to guess her thoughts.

Mr. Bingley's solicitude and Mr. Darcy's warm civility toward Jane could not be denied nor could Elizabeth's notice of the Bingley sisters' disapproving looks.

After dinner, there was no separation of the sexes, and the entire party moved together to the drawing room. Mr. Bingley attentively seated Jane near the fire, charming her in quiet conversation to which Miss Bennet responded with a sweet and becoming blush.

Mr. Hurst found a comfortable chair in which to enjoy his drink while Miss Bingley and Mrs. Hurst attempted to engage Mr. Darcy. The gentleman politely declined and turned his attention to writing a new letter.

Elizabeth smiled and chose a book from several placed on a small table, pleased and amused with the development of the evening.

Unexpectedly, Blackie appeared at his master's side, wagging his tail upon discovering Elizabeth. She put down the book and patted his head. Laughing, she accepted the dog's raised paw. Only then did she observe the ladies of the house looking at her with disdain and Mr. Darcy staring at her. She felt the heat of her cheeks as they burned in embarrassment.

"Miss Eliza, as a friend, let me advise you not to play with such a large dog while in company. I do not remember seeing any of our acquaintances make such a spectacle."

Both Elizabeth and Jane blushed at such open censure. And yet, Elizabeth's amusement overcame other feelings.

"I thank you, Miss Bingley, for instructing me on such courtesies with delicacy. I shall consider it for future occasions," she said, turning her full attention to Blackie.

"I will also mention your recommendation in my letter to Georgiana, Miss Bingley." All eyes turned to Mr. Darcy. "She too enjoys playing with Blackie, and I must warn her about the impropriety of her gesture." Elizabeth's cheeks burned again, and her own smile widened.

Miss Bingley dissembled. "Oh, I did not mean to…it is just that—I really do not think you should trouble Georgiana with such things. As I said, I have rarely met such an accomplished young lady…"

"Do you not intend to warn my sister *too* in regards to proper deportment with the dog?"

Miss Bingley's panic increased.

"Indeed, sir, it was not a criticism, only a friendly warning for Miss Eliza. I am sure Georgiana would never…"

Darcy raised his eyebrows to Miss Bingley as if to encourage her to go on. But Elizabeth took pity on her and attempted to end the debate.

"I appreciate your friendly warning; still, I shall take the liberty to play with Blackie. After all, it is likely that we will not meet again after tomorrow. I shall miss him."

"And I am sure he will miss you too. He misses Georgiana and seemed to find comfort in your company. He might even associate you with my sister. Now I doubt he will have anyone to recompense for your absence." Elizabeth's puzzled gaze locked with his.

"Oh, I doubt anyone, including the dog, would confuse Miss Eliza with dear Georgiana. There is absolutely no resemblance in features, hair, height, posture, tone of voice—no resemblance at all," Miss Bingley said with an obvious effort to remain calm.

"Perhaps not," Mr. Darcy replied. "But dogs, unlike some humans, detect an affectionate nature, kindness, and a gentle manner, which I would say are quite similar traits in Georgiana and Miss Elizabeth."

"Shall we have some music?" Mrs. Hurst hastily opened the pianoforte and started to play. Elizabeth's astonishment and subsequent racing heart allowed her little comfort the entire evening, and not even Blackie's playfulness compensated for the shivers Mr. Darcy's scrutiny incited.

Later, before they settled into their beds, Jane said, "But Lizzy, Mr. Darcy was very kind—did you notice? He asked me how I felt several times. And in truth, he appeared uncommonly friendly with you!"

"He was different from his usual self, I admit."

"And he did, in his way, protect you from Caroline. Not that you needed it, but his resolution was obvious. He seems to admire you, Lizzy."

"Oh, do not be ridiculous." She laughed to conceal her embarrassment. "Dearest Jane, since you claim Mr. Darcy protected me from Caroline, would it be possible to admit that she tried to attack me? Is it possible that you finally see her offensive behavior?"

"I did notice that Caroline is not very kind to you. And the friendlier Mr. Darcy seemed, the less congenial Caroline became. I am not a fool, Lizzy dearest. And I am not oblivious to your attempt to avoid speaking of Mr. Darcy's friendliness to you, either."

"Jane, let us sleep now. Tomorrow we will finally return home."

THE NEXT DAY, ELIZABETH TOOK LEAVE OF THE WHOLE NETHERFIELD PARTY in a lively spirit. And yet when Mr. Darcy bowed over her hand, she could feel her cheeks warm.

Mrs. Bennet wondered at their return without much cordiality and was sure Jane would have caught cold again. Their father immediately teased them about spending so many days in a house with two gentlemen, one of whom smiled too much and the other not at all.

The younger sisters, Kitty and Lydia, were wild to share information of a different sort. Much had been done and much had been said in the regiment since the previous Wednesday: several of the officers had dined with their uncle, some new officers had joined the regiment, and "Colonel Forster is to be married!"

More than once, Elizabeth found herself oblivious to the conversation around her. Her father found great amusement in having to repeat some questions twice, and Jane even worried that she might have fallen ill too.

Elizabeth assured her she was perfectly well. However, she kept remembering conversations with Mr. Darcy, his expressions, his gaze—the significance of which she was suddenly uncertain—and more than anything, the way he seem to side with her during the previous night's exchange with Miss Bingley.

Briefly, she wondered whether perhaps his invitation to dance a few days ago might not have been in jest. Surely, she could not allow herself to presume that Mr. Darcy's politeness to her meant anything other than a softening toward his friend's guest. And yes, perhaps he was friendlier with his older acquaintances, with people to whom he felt most comfortable. He was pleasant, and she did enjoy their conversations as well as his sharp mind. But these were trifling reasons to imagine anything more.

Of course, if Jane should eventually marry Mr. Bingley, she would not mind seeing Mr. Darcy again and perhaps meeting his sister of whom she heard so many lovely things. But that was an entirely different matter—something to consider in the future.

She went to bed determined to rest well and to put aside any disturbing thoughts. Yet she had little success, only drifting to sleep as she heard the servants move about the house at dawn.

"I HOPE, MY DEAR," SAID MR. BENNET TO HIS WIFE, AS THEY WERE AT breakfast the next morning, "that you have ordered a good dinner today because I have reason to expect an addition to our family party."

"Who do you mean, my dear? I know of nobody that is coming."

"The person of whom I speak is a gentleman and a stranger."

Mrs. Bennet's eyes sparkled. "A gentleman and a stranger! It is Mr. Bingley I am sure. Perhaps Mr. Darcy too? I really do not like that man, but I will force myself to be civil enough. After all, ten thousand a year is not something to neglect."

Elizabeth glanced at Jane, who had turned crimson and smiled shyly, and felt her own face burn. Surely, Mr. Darcy did not have any interest in dinner with her family. But soon enough, Mr. Bennet put them all at peace, informing them that he expected the visit of his cousin Mr. Collins, to whom Longbourn was entailed.

Nobody waited for the visit with any real pleasure, but some curiosity existed in everyone except Lydia and Kitty.

Mr. Collins was received into the Bennet home with great civility. From that moment on, Mr. Collins split his praises between complimenting Elizabeth or Jane and praising his noble patroness, Lady Catherine de Bourgh, a subject that elevated him to more than usual solemnity of manners.

Mr. Bennet's expectations of amusement were exceeded. He secretly declared to Elizabeth that his cousin was as absurd as he had hoped, but he could not bear him more than a couple of hours. Thus, Mr. Bennet retired to his library, and Mr. Collins was consigned to the care of Mrs. Bennet, who even engaged in a tête-à-tête with him.

Mr. Collins openly declared his intention to marry and expressed his hopes that a mistress of his heart might be found at Longbourn; then he offered his admiration for Jane. She cautioned him that her eldest daughter was very likely to become engaged soon. As to her *younger* daughters, she did not *know* of any prior attachments.

Mr. Collins left the conversation with great encouragement and changed his affection from Jane to Elizabeth, next to Jane in birth and beauty. He scarcely left Elizabeth's side and rarely drew breath in all his conversations.

Unlike her father, Elizabeth found little reason to be amused. She was tired after the sleepless night, irritated by her cousin's presence and by her mother's obvious approval, and only wished for some privacy as her thoughts grew more distressing. She found herself daydreaming more than once about the places Mr. Darcy might ride and whether Blackie would join him.

THE SECOND DAY OF MR. COLLINS'S VISIT, AT THE SUGGESTION OF MR. Bennet, who was happy to have his library to himself again, Lydia and Kitty insisted on walking to Meryton to visit with their aunt Phillips. Elizabeth and Jane eagerly accompanied them, but their enthusiasm diminished when their cousin joined the walking party as well.

The walk was rather short, their pace being more rapid than usual in order to put an end to Mr. Collins's continuous preaching about the benefits of exercising outdoors.

Once in Meryton, Mr. Collins was further ignored as the ladies' eyes were caught by a Mr. Denny and a few other officers strolling toward them. Among them, an unknown gentleman was singled out for his handsome features and elegant posture.

The groups met, and the introductions were made. The unknown gentleman was presented as Mr. Wickham, friend to Mr. Denny and ready to join the regiment immediately, a bit of news that was received with the greatest joy by Kitty and Lydia and with restrained smiles by Elizabeth and Jane. In all the flurry, Mr. Collins could not get a word in.

Mr. Wickham had a fine countenance, a good build, and a pleasing address. The introduction was followed with happy conversation, and the whole party was still standing and talking together when the sound of horses drew their notice.

Darcy and Bingley were seen riding down the street, and Elizabeth's heart raced while she struggled to keep her composure.

Distinguishing the ladies of the group, the two gentlemen came directly towards them. Bingley immediately addressed Miss Bennet, declaring he was on his way to Longbourn on purpose to inquire after her. Mr. Darcy bowed slightly without dismounting. Elizabeth's eyes met his, and she thought she noticed a trace of a smile, so she smiled back. Blackie appeared at the horse's side and hurried to Elizabeth, who patted him with great pleasure.

Only a moment later, however, Blackie started to growl and bark at the men in the group. Surprised, Elizabeth looked to Darcy, whose countenance had changed. He harshly called his dog, who hesitated but a moment before joining his master. Then Darcy turned his horse and returned the way he had come.

She was all astonishment. Jane was still talking to Mr. Bingley, and Lydia and Kitty with Mr. Denny, but Mr. Wickham had paled, gazing after the departing gentleman and his dog. He noticed Elizabeth's surprised look and responded with an awkward smile. Soon after, Mr. Bingley amiably took his leave and hurried after his friend.

Elizabeth's thoughts were in an uproar. How could she expect and wish for civility from a man like Mr. Darcy? Yes, he had been polite at Netherfield. And yet he could not be troubled to favor them with a single word! She had smiled at him like a silly girl, and he ignored her completely. It would seem he could not bear to be seen in public having a civil conversation with her and her sisters, who by his estimation were not as accomplished as his!

Everything he told her about his admiration of her was surely nothing but deceit and another attempt to toy with her for his amusement—just like his invitation to dance a reel to have the opportunity to despise her taste! Hateful man, indeed!

Her distress grew as she gazed after the horsemen departing at a gallop.

"Such irresponsibility to allow a dangerous dog to run unrestrained in the village," said Mr. Wickham.

Elizabeth wanted to respond that Blackie was only dangerous because he stood near such a cold and spiteful man, but she had no time to reply before Lydia loudly shared her opinion on the matter—as did Mr. Collins, who finally found a subject on which he might preach.

Mr. Denny and Mr. Wickham escorted the young ladies to the door of Mr. Phillips's house, and then made their bows, declining Miss Lydia's entreaties that they come in, despite Mrs. Phillips throwing up the parlor window and loudly seconding the invitation. At the gentlemen's polite refusal, Mrs. Phillips asked them to come the next evening for dinner, together with their fellow officers.

The Bennet sisters were all invited, and Mr. Collins managed to acquire an invitation too, which he received with much condescension and too many thanks.

That evening at the dinner table at Longbourn, the younger sisters continued to praise Mr. Wickham's merits to Mrs. Bennet, who listened with equal excitement. Mr. Collins remained in offended silence while Elizabeth spoke only a few words and ate even less.

THE FOLLOWING MORNING FOUND ELIZABETH NO LESS DISTRESSED THAN the evening before. She could not escape the sense of disappointment and fought with little success to raise her spirits. Several times, she answered Mr. Collins with a sharpness that sounded offensive even to her ears, but their cousin seemed unmoved in his decision to pursue her.

Around noon, Mr. Bingley called, and Elizabeth's heart skipped until she realized he was alone. He declared he came to inquire briefly after Miss Bennet. Both the object of his interest and Mrs. Bennet were beside themselves with happiness although they each expressed it differently.

Elizabeth was tempted to ask after Mr. Darcy. She wished for an opportunity to speak to him again if only to observe his behavior before making her final judgment about him. But she did not dare. Thus, she carried her frustration in silence while Mr. Bingley spoke with enthusiasm about his delight in seeing Jane so improved and his eagerness to host a ball.

"Is Mr. Darcy well?" Mrs. Bennet inquired in an obvious attempt to carry on a conversation.

"Yes, ma'am. He is taking care of some business. He is very dutiful with his estate."

Of course, he would do anything to avoid our company. While he writes letters, Miss Bingley will admire his writing and mend his pen, Elizabeth thought with bitterness.

"I hope he will not attend business during the ball too," Mrs. Bennet said.

"Well, considering how much he hates dancing, it would not make much difference," Elizabeth heard herself say. Then she apologized with horror for her own impropriety, claimed a headache, and retired to her room.

Later in the afternoon, still troubled and ashamed of her own behavior, Elizabeth started to prepare for the dinner at her aunt Phillips's house. She hoped she would meet Charlotte; perhaps her friend's steady company would settle her.

She also wondered briefly whether some of the inhabitants from Netherfield would join the dinner party, but she dismissed the thought immediately.

When the carriage stopped in front of the house, Mr. Collins demanded a seat near his fair cousin Elizabeth and, to the sisters' despair, began to expound on proper deportment at parties, at dances, and with officers.

As soon as they arrived at their uncle's house, Lydia and Kitty hurried to join the officers while Elizabeth and Jane joined their friend Charlotte. When he was introduced to Miss Lucas, Mr. Collins offered his profuse gratitude and an unctuous bow.

Fortunately, he soon joined Mrs. Phillips in walking about the room and complimenting the windows and the fireplace.

While Mary started to play at the piano, Elizabeth discreetly attempted to temper her younger sisters, whose boisterous mood was loudly expressed. She met with little success, and when she returned toward Charlotte and Jane, she was stopped by Mr. Wickham's charming smile.

"Miss Elizabeth, what a pleasure to see you again."

"Mr. Wickham, I am delighted to meet you too, sir."

"Mrs. Phillips was so kind as to invite me, and I could not be more grateful for such a warm reception."

"I am glad." She smiled while noticing the distinguished handsome features of the gentleman and his obvious attempt to deepen their acquaintance.

"Speaking of invitations, we, the officers, already received one from Mr. Bingley. I understand that he is hosting a ball at Netherfield in a few days. He is the gentleman we met yesterday, is he not?"

Elizabeth recoiled as she recollected the incident. "He is indeed. I hope you will accept the invitation. It would be a great benefit to have the presence of more charming gentlemen with an inclination to dance."

"I will most certainly do so. And I shall take this opportunity to ask for the favor of a set." His large smile matched hers.

"It would be my pleasure, sir."

"Excellent, thank you. I was wondering whether Mr. Bingley and his family will be here tonight."

"It is unlikely. He might have come, but his family and his friend are hardly fond of our company. We are very different from what they are accustomed to."

He laughed briefly. "You mean Darcy. Yes, I know that very well."

Elizabeth could not hide her surprise. "Do you know Mr. Darcy?"

"Indeed, I do, Miss Elizabeth. In fact, I know him more than I would have liked. You see, we grew up at Pemberley together, and his father was my godfather."

"Is it possible? But I thought... Yesterday you..."

"I understand your surprise, but for years Darcy and I have behaved like strangers. Are you *well* acquainted with Mr. Darcy?"

"I...not very well... We met several times, and I spent a few days at Netherfield, but Mr. Darcy is not an easy man to know," Elizabeth said with restraint. She wished to hear more of Mr. Darcy from Mr. Wickham but could hardly countenance such an improper conversation.

"Mr. Darcy? Oh, he is the most unpleasant of men," said Lydia to Elizabeth's embarrassment. "Nobody in the neighborhood likes him! He refused to dance with Lizzy one night, and he called her—"

"Lydia, stop!" a flustered Elizabeth interposed angrily. "This is not an appropriate conversation."

"Very well. But you must allow Mr. Wickham to dance with us later if Mary can be persuaded to play something. Oh—and will you come to the ball? You must come!"

With much reluctance, Lydia left, and Elizabeth apologized to Mr. Wickham.

"There is no need. Miss Lydia is a charming young lady. And her honesty does her credit. I recognize Darcy's behavior in her words. I have rarely seen him dance."

"You said Mr. Darcy's father was your godfather?"

"He was—and excessively attached to me. He helped me prepare myself for the church, and I was bequeathed the best living when it became available. After he passed away and the living fell vacant, it was given elsewhere."

Elizabeth was bewildered. "Good God, how could *that* be? How could his will be disregarded?"

"Jealousy. His father was deeply attached to me, and Darcy despised me for it. A man of honor could not have doubted the intention, but Darcy treated it as merely a conditional recommendation and asserted that I had forfeited all claim to it by extravagance, imprudence—in short, anything or nothing. The living became vacant two years ago, exactly as I was of an age to hold it, and then it was given to another man."

"This is quite shocking! I have always suspected Mr. Darcy of being a severe man, but I never imagined him being unfair and cruel."

"I can imagine your astonishment, Miss Elizabeth, because the world is often blinded by his fortune and consequence or frightened by his imposing manners and sees him only as he chooses to be seen."

"I hope I am not blinded by anything. It is just that, from what I observed, I could not have guessed such a terrible thing. He has not the warmest manners, but he did not seem a dishonorable man either."

"I know Darcy can be rather pleasant when he wants to, but he usually does not. He surrounds himself with those who are completely obedient and devoted to him. I am referring to Mr. Bingley or, at the opposite extreme, his aunt Lady Catherine de Bourgh, whom I heard your cousin mentioning with great admiration. Even his dog is ill tempered and unsociable as you saw for yourself. He almost attacked me yesterday. I would say it is a savage and dangerous beast."

"I was not under the impression that Blackie might be dangerous—quite the contrary." A moment later, the revelation struck her.

She recollected the previous day's scene moment by moment and realized how stupid she had been. Mr. Darcy did not depart in haste to avoid her but his old acquaintance. And Blackie barked at him too! Elizabeth wondered whether she had ever heard his dog bark other than when he played outside.

Countless questions spun in her mind while Mr. Wickham continued.

"This is because Darcy's pride and his willingness to be universally recognized as faultless make him control everything—and everyone. But I assure you that, in private, both he and his dog are rather uncivil. That animal attacked me before, quite badly I might say. If I had a pistol, I would have shot it right away."

Her eyes wide with shock, she said, "I am very sorry to hear that. I did not imagine…"

Elizabeth's distress only matched her increasing curiosity. "I cannot testify about Mr. Darcy's behavior in private of course, but I have heard quite the opposite—that he is more pleasant within his family circle than with strangers. And I know he is very fond of his sister."

"Yes, maybe with his close family. But I doubt any other gentleman in his position would dare disregard his father's dearest wish. Yet he did it. And it was only my luck and my friend Denny that brought me presently to a position about which I have no cause to complain."

Elizabeth had barely noticed Wickham's anger or his attempts at civility as she was too preoccupied with her own thoughts. In front of her was a gentleman with pleasant manners and comely features who trusted her enough to share a most astonishing story. His words were so harsh and his expression so affected that she had little else to do but express her sympathy. As for the other gentleman involved in the story, Elizabeth did not dare consider how that history spoke of his character.

Yes, she now realized that he was not avoiding her but Wickham. His rudeness had been in a different direction, but it was still there.

"And yes, he is fond of his sister, I imagine. She used to be a pleasant child.

I often spent time with her at Pemberley, trying to amuse her when she was young. Now she has turned out much as her brother likes: obedient to him and proud to the rest of the world. She has also treated me in an unfair manner."

"This is terrible, sir. My astonishment is beyond words indeed. I wonder—is there nothing to be done to reconcile you? Have you attempted to speak to Mr. Darcy recently? Perhaps you may find a way—"

"No, I have not spoken with either of them since Darcy refused me the living two years ago, and I have no intention of doing so. I cannot humiliate myself further. You observed Darcy's attitude yesterday. Surely, not even someone as generous as you can imagine him willing to reconcile. I even wonder whether I should attend the ball."

"I hope you will, sir. Mr. Bingley invited you, and he is the master of the house. And I am sure many others will be pleased with your company. Besides, I trust that two well-behaved gentlemen who happen not to be friends will behave with civility, especially in company."

"I may promise that although I am not equally certain of Mr. Darcy."

"I believe I may predict quite accurately that Mr. Darcy will not even entertain conversation with you, sir. We both know he has a clear displeasure in dancing."

Their conversation was interrupted, and Elizabeth was surprised to find welcome in Mr. Collins's appearance. She enjoyed Mr. Wickham's company, but the entire conversation was burdensome and deeply distressing.

She spent the rest of the evening in a muddle, recollecting each word that was said and reconsidering the revelation that she had accused Mr. Darcy—in her mind—of avoiding her without reason. Yet, what a terrible reason he had to avoid someone else, and was that not a shade in his character?

Why she would be so distressed by this recent intelligence about Darcy was a question she did not wish to answer yet.

In the privacy of their room, Elizabeth shared the story with Jane, expressing her abhorrence at Darcy's behavior toward Wickham.

"Jane, now it is no longer just my impression or my holding a grudge against him for calling me tolerable or about his uncivil manners. It is about a man who used his power against an old acquaintance, contradicting his father's wishes, and pushing a young gentleman into poverty. How can this be explained or even excused? I was so close to improving my opinion about Mr. Darcy, and I am so pained to know I was wrong."

"Dearest Lizzy, this is truly shocking. But should we believe someone we met only a day ago?"

"But why would Mr. Wickham deceive me? What could be his purpose?"

"I wonder about his presuming to share such a story with you on such a short acquaintance. This was risky and hardly proper. Just imagine if you were a friend of Mr. Darcy."

"In that I might have an answer. He asked me whether I knew Mr. Darcy, and I told him that I knew him a little, then suddenly Lydia intervened and said Mr. Darcy is an unpleasant man and nobody likes him and that he refused to dance with me... I really do not know what we should do to temper Lydia..."

"Oh, how rude. Dearest Lydia has questionable manners, and her charm can be greatly affected by this. So Mr. Wickham guessed you are not partial to Mr. Darcy...and then he told you the story."

"Yes."

"I see... Lizzy, please promise me you will be prudent in approaching this. I will also try to ask Mr. Bingley." She blushed. "Discreetly. If only to find whether he knows anything about Mr. Wickham."

"Very well... Just remember that Mr. Bingley will certainly be partial to his friend."

"I know that, dearest. But if we give so much credit to a mere stranger whom we knew for only one day, we should give equal courtesy to Mr. Bingley's objectivity."

"You are right, Jane. I promise I will avoid any prejudice before I have all the facts."

They embraced, and Elizabeth was left with her tumult of thoughts, wonderings, and distress.

She had barely fallen asleep when the wind blew in the windows, making Elizabeth jump as from a nightmare, and she woke Jane. "Lizzy, what happened?"

"Jane, forgive me for disturbing you, but I realized something very, *very* strange! Mr. Wickham said Blackie is a savage and dangerous dog that attacked him in the past. That might be true, as Mr. Darcy told me that the dog is rather protective, especially of his sister. But Mr. Wickham pretended that he had not met either Mr. Darcy or Miss Darcy in more than two years!"

"And?"

"And Blackie is not even two years old! Can you imagine? And it cannot be a mistake as he insisted that he last met the Darcys when the living became available—two years ago!"

"Oh, Lizzy, this is quite curious, indeed. What should we do? *Should* we do anything at all?"

"It is strange, Jane! I shall speak to Mr. Wickham again to repeat this question, and if he persists in his claim, I shall speak to Mr. Darcy himself!"

"Lizzy! You would surely not dare do that! You cannot speak about this with either of them!"

"I can and I will! I know I cannot be certain of Mr. Darcy telling me the truth either, but I shall give him the chance to tell me his side of the story."

"But he might be offended!"

"He might, but I must do something. I am starting to believe that Mr. Wickham is trying to besmirch Mr. Darcy's name and is using me to do it. He must take me for a fool! This I shall not accept!"

"Oh, Lizzy. You must calm yourself, dearest. Let us sleep now." When both were wrapped in blankets, Jane whispered, caressing her hair, "Dear Lizzy, why are you so excited about this story? Should we better not leave things as they are? Why would you put yourself into such a distressing situation?"

"I do not know, Jane. I cannot explain it to myself either. But I must do something." Elizabeth closed her eyes and retired in silence to her own tormenting thoughts.

EVEN BEFORE IT WAS DAYLIGHT, ELIZABETH DRESSED AND LEFT THE HOUSE for a walk. She could not sleep and had no strength to bear Mr. Collins's attentions without a proper dose of fresh air.

The paths were frozen, and the bracing cold cut her skin sharply.

She took the path towards Netherfield without even realizing her direction.

She startled and her cold cheeks heated when she heard the thunder of hoof beats and vigorous barking. Mr. Darcy was riding at a gallop, and in front of the horse was Blackie.

The moment he noticed Elizabeth, the dog ran toward her and sat at her feet. Laughing and affectionately patting the dog, Elizabeth watched as Darcy dismounted and bowed.

"Miss Elizabeth, it is a pleasure to see you."

"I am delighted to see you too, sir," she said with a glance, returning her attention to Blackie.

"I must take this opportunity to apologize that I left in a hurry the day before yesterday when we met in Meryton. I wished to talk to you, but—"

"Do not worry, sir, I imagine you are not very fond of our Meryton society. We rarely have the chance to see you in company and even less to actually speak to you."

"I confess it was an intentional gesture to avoid socializing in Meryton. However, it is not the inhabitants but rather a newly arrived person whose company I wished to avoid."

She held his gaze. "May I dare presume that you are referring to Mr. Wickham? We only made his acquaintance moments before your arrival."

He did not appear surprised. "You are not wrong. And I am pleased that you opened the subject. I know you have no reason to trust my words, but please be guarded against Mr. Wickham. He has charm and makes new friends easily but is not equally capable of keeping them."

"May I ask what you mean, sir? You must realize that Mr. Wickham may claim the same of you."

"I know, Miss Elizabeth, and I do not expect you to believe my words but to judge for yourself."

"I shall try although it is quite difficult when I only have a part of the story. But I can well understand your reluctance to trust a complete stranger with your private affairs."

"It is not a matter of trust but one of propriety and respect. Each of us has family burdens. It would be quite unfair to tax others around us, especially on such a short acquaintance. No gentleman who admires a lady would do so with an easy heart."

Elizabeth's breathing stopped for a moment as she struggled to decide whether she truly heard him declare again that he admired her.

"It is entirely your decision whether we should speak further." They were walking side by side with Blackie in front of them and Darcy's horse following. Neither of them looked at the other.

"I would be grateful if we did, sir."

"Very well. As you wish. I shall tell you as much as can be said and allow you to make your own conclusions. You already mentioned that you know only one side of the story, so I shall presume Wickham complained about my refusing his inheritance. However, he surely neglected to mention that it was entirely his responsibility to behave in a manner worthy of his inheritance."

Elizabeth glanced at him then turned her eyes to the road again.

"He was fairly rewarded for his inheritance—at his own request. He denied that he had any intention of entering the church and rather wished to study the law instead. While studying, he often asked me for monetary support. When the living became available, he attempted to claim it as if he had not refused it in favor the law! Of course, I refused him and demanded that he never bother me again. Since then, he has made it his goal to denigrate my name and my family. I do not know how he managed to obtain this commission, but no good can come of it, I can promise you that. Forgive me; I must sound unfair and harsh, but I can only give you my word that it is deserved. Despite my poor manners, my lack of conversational skills, your low opinion of me—and all my other failings—I hope you will believe that I am not a cruel man."

"I have no reason to disbelieve you, sir, but I must admit that Mr. Wickham seemed honest too. He offered facts and details that made his words credible. As for you: my opinion has changed many times. I am not sure what to believe of you. Anyone can see your qualities, your education, your taste in books and music, but as for your character, I still do not know what to believe."

"I thank you for your honesty."

"Is it honesty or impertinence?" Elizabeth laughed. "Perhaps our acquaintance has not been long enough to form a fair opinion of each other. I am sure your opinion of me is no better."

"In this, I must contradict you. In fact, even from the beginning of our acquaintance, my opinion was favorable and grew more so with each day."

"Surely, you are joking, sir."

"I am completely honest. You must know I am serous when I tell you that I confessed to Miss Bingley my admiration of you."

She turned to him in disbelief, unable to breathe, and would have slipped had he not caught her arm. "Surely you jest. I was certain of the contrary."

It was his turn to be surprised. "Really? What made you believe so?"

Her astonishment increased. They had stopped walking, and he was still holding her arm as their gazes met.

"Well, sir, perhaps the fact that you refused to dance with me and called me tolerable…"

He paled, and she laughed.

"Please do not distress yourself; I am teasing. That has long passed."

"Miss Elizabeth, I do not even know what to say or how to apologize. Regarding my rude comment and my appalling behavior the first night we met, my excuse is insufficient. The truth is, I came with Bingley at his instance after he leased the property, following a difficult summer for both my sister and me. I would have rather stayed with her, but she preferred to visit my aunt Matlock. I was in no disposition to dance, and I refused Bingley's insistence without even looking at you. The moment I did notice you—my opinion was nothing but admiration."

They resumed walking in silence.

"Sir, may I ask you another question?"

"Of course…"

"About Mr. Wickham. Can you tell me when the two of you met last?"

His face blanched

"I shall answer, but may I inquire why you ask?"

"He complained about how aggressive Blackie was and that he attacked him in the past—and also yesterday. Then he mentioned that he had not seen you and Miss Darcy in more than two years. But I know Blackie is barely two years old. I confess that was what aroused my doubts about his tale."

Darcy stopped and gently turned her to face him. "Miss Elizabeth, you are a remarkably clever young lady. I am not certain when we will see each other again, but there are few people whom I trust as much as I have come to trust you. Therefore, I shall tell you the rest of the story, asking this confidence not be shared with anyone else. Exposure would adversely affect the most important person in my life: Georgiana."

Elizabeth shivered from the gravity of his voice and countenance. "Sir, there is no need…"

"I think there is."

They continued walking, and without guile, Elizabeth took hold of his arm.

"Wickham is right; Blackie did attack him. It happened six months ago in Ramsgate when he attempted to elope with my sister who was but fifteen. She was staying there with her companion for the summer, and he went with the obvious purpose of trapping her in a most horrible scheme. His main target must have been Georgiana's dowry but also revenge on me. It was only fortunate that I came to visit her a day before and her noble heart could not bear to pain me, so she confessed their plan. You can imagine how I reacted. I tried to protect my young sister and to avoid scandal, so I demanded he leave and never cross paths with me again. He was rather impertinent and shamelessly blamed Georgiana for the attempt. I was angered and raised my voice. So did he, and Blackie jumped and pushed him to the ground. He was not hurt at all—only frightened."

"Dear Lord, how is this possible? And he dared to approach me with his awful story! He has no shame and no honor. What a horrible character! I wonder whether Colonel Forster knows what kind of man joined his regiment!" She looked at him again and, seeing his pained expression, said, "Poor Miss Darcy... I cannot imagine her suffering—nor yours."

"She is much improved now. I think she preferred to stay with my aunt to avoid sharing her mortification with me. No one else knows this story, except a cousin who is also her guardian. She seems to be more comfortable with those who are unaware of her misadventure."

"Your family does not know of this?"

"No."

"And yet you shared it with me?"

"Yes. And I am sorry if I burdened you, but I feel much better for having shared with you what Wickham really is."

"Mr. Darcy?"

"Yes?"

"Sir, may I venture to ask—had I not played with Blackie that day, and had we not spoken to each other at Netherfield, would you have told me this story?"

He hesitated only a moment, studying her intently.

"Most likely not. But, Miss Elizabeth, if Blackie had not come to play with you that day and we had not spoken to each other at Netherfield, would you have even troubled yourself to ask me about the story?"

"Most likely not," she answered boldly, and to her utter surprise, a smile twisted his lips.

"It seems Blackie made a perfect choice in friends that day. Now, please allow me to company you back to Longbourn. Then I must continue to Meryton; I need to speak with Colonel Forster."

THIS NEW INTELLIGENCE TORMENTED ELIZABETH'S BODY AND SOUL, AND she lost all appetite to break her fast. She toyed with the food on her plate then dragged Jane to their room to share her shocking news.

"Oh, Lizzy. Poor Miss Darcy! I can only imagine her suffering at such a young age. And poor Mr. Darcy! To be torn between his own conscience and his father's wishes! And to see his young sister so pained…"

"How could I allow a man to take me as a complete fool and force his dishonorable story on me? Is my behavior so poor as to encourage this? And Mr. Darcy—can you believe that he shared such a confidence that nobody from his family knows? Oh, Jane. Not a word to a living soul! Not even to Mr. Bingley. Not even after you marry!"

"Of course not, dearest. And there is no understanding. You mustn't say—"

"If not yet, there will be soon. I am certain. But I wonder what will happen. Mr. Darcy said he would speak to Colonel Forster. How will that affect Mr. Wickham? Can you imagine how furious he will be with Mr. Darcy?"

"I hope not! Surely, two civil men can handle a difficult situation without harming each other! Come, let us have some tea and calm ourselves. "

Half an hour later, Mr. Collins found them in the drawing room, and there was no room for other subjects the rest of the day. And to make matters worse, a cold, autumnal rain commenced and continued for the next three days, keeping Elizabeth quartered inside with her thoughts and Mr. Collins's unbearable discourse.

The twenty-sixth of November arrived, bringing blues skies along with the prospect of the anticipated ball at Netherfield. Although Elizabeth wished for nothing more than to enjoy a long walk, there was no time due to the fervent preparations.

Her mother and youngest sister burst into her room. "You are very pretty, Lizzy, very pretty indeed! I am sure Mr. Collins will be pleased with your appearance. Take care and be nice to him! I know you will dance the first set with him, so you must pay him kind attention."

Elizabeth rolled her eyes at her mother's speech.

Lydia laughed and said, "I hope you will not dance too much with Mr. Wickham! I want to have a set with him too."

"Lydia, I have no plans to dance with Mr. Wickham—and neither should you!"

"La! Such a merry evening ahead. I cannot wait!"

Nor I, thought Elizabeth.

The Bennets were among the first to arrive. Immediately, Mr. Bingley came to welcome them. Elizabeth smiled as he heard him complimenting Jane and asking for the first set, which was gratefully accepted.

Several officers were there, and Lydia and Kitty hurried to them.

Mr. and Mrs. Bennet, as well as Mary, joined them in the ballroom. Elizabeth remained behind with Jane. Then she felt a gentle touch on her arm, and from only a few inches away, Mr. Darcy bowed to her politely.

"Miss Elizabeth, may I escort you to the ballroom?"

"Yes, thank you." Her cheeks burned, no doubt because of the warmth in the room.

They walked silently a few moments before he leaned toward her.

"I hope you will not be disappointed by Mr. Wickham's absence, Miss Elizabeth. I was informed that he left Meryton yesterday. Apparently, a better commission was suddenly offered to him in the north, and he needed to present himself to the regiment directly. Colonel Forster readily accepted this news as Mr. Wickham had not officially joined the regiment here."

Elizabeth's hand tightened on his arm. "I thank you for telling me, sir. How fortunate for him to be offered such an advantageous position with no effort on his part. I wonder what he did to deserve such generous compensation."

"Fortunate indeed. But I would hope we shall find better subjects to discuss this evening. Would you do me the honor of dancing the first with me?"

Elizabeth was beyond astonishment with this new intelligence.

It would appear Mr. Darcy had solved the situation with Wickham—with haste but not without generosity. She wondered how it happened that he was so easily convinced to leave Meryton, how the commission was purchased so quickly, and how much Colonel Forster knew—but she did not presume to ask further.

And now he not only asked her to dance but requested the first set? Was he aware of the special attention he was conveying?

"I thank you, sir, it will be my pleasure," she said brightly. A moment later, she paled then felt her face color. "Please forgive me, sir. I already promised the first set to my cousin Mr. Collins. He is my father's cousin, and he came to visit and…" Mortified to have misspoken, she was now unable to find proper words and slowly withdrew her hand from his arm.

Moments later, she raised her eyes to meet his. He was smiling.

"Then another—whichever you have open?"

"Yes...thank you...I am not otherwise engaged."

"I thank you for the privilege, Miss Elizabeth. Would it be acceptable to—"

Before he could finish his thought, Mr. Collins approached her and bowed low to Darcy.

"Mr. Darcy, I heard the astonishing news that you are the nephew of my noble patroness, Lady Catherine de Bourgh. Indeed, sir, I cannot imagine a greater honor than to be in the same room with you and to inform you that her ladyship was in perfect health four days ago."

"I am glad to hear that. And you are...?"

"Mr. Darcy, this is my cousin Mr. Collins," Elizabeth said quickly, her cheeks warmed with shame. To her complete astonishment, Darcy's expression showed his surprise, then nodded in acknowledgement.

"I am glad to make your acquaintance, Mr. Collins."

"My dear sir, I cannot thank you enough for your kind reception and—"

"Mr. Collins, come. Have you met my dearest friend, Charlotte Lucas?" Elizabeth took her cousin's arm, prompting him away from Mr. Darcy. She looked over her shoulder to notice a hint of a smile on the gentleman's lips while Mr. Collins prattled on, praising Mr. Darcy's posture and condescension.

Soon after, Elizabeth found herself in the middle of the most humiliating half hour she had ever experienced. Her dance partner, Mr. Collins, barely knew the steps, bumped into several partners, and apologized to everybody in their set. And worse yet, when her eyes met Mr. Darcy's, his barely concealed amusement increased her distress.

The pause between sets was the sweetest music to Elizabeth's ears. Her cousin escorted her back to her friend, where he promptly asked Charlotte for the next set. After she graciously accepted his request, he bowed reverently and hurried to treat himself with a glass of wine.

"I am sorry you will have to bear the same torture. He is the poorest dancer I ever met," Elizabeth whispered to her friend.

"Do not worry for me, Lizzy. I am sure I can bear his lack of skills quite easily."

They smiled at each other, and soon the eldest Miss Bennet joined them. A few moments later, their little chat was interrupted by Mr. Darcy himself.

"Miss Elizabeth, would you do me the honor of dancing the next set with me?"

Her companions' eyes widened in surprise. "Of course, sir, it would be my pleasure." Elizabeth curtseyed, and he thanked her then stepped away. Behind her fan, Charlotte said, "This is rather unexpected, Lizzy. I hope you know what an honor Mr. Darcy is doing you by singling you out."

"Perhaps, Charlotte, but I am also doing him an honor by accepting his request," Elizabeth replied playfully, eagerly anticipating the music.

Darcy returned and gently took her hand while he directed her toward the top of the set.

Each time they moved closer and their hands touched, Elizabeth trembled.

She spoke nervously. "Thank you, sir. I am pleased you were not upset for my denying you the first set."

He smiled.

"Surely you have no reason to doubt I would ask for another since your first set was already engaged. I should have asked sooner to be assured I would secure it."

She bit her lower lip in amusement. "Well, sir, perhaps considering our previous common experience at a ball, you thought it unlikely my card would be filled and such a precaution was not necessary."

His eyes narrowed. "That was an unfair comment, Miss Elizabeth. I already apologized for my poor behavior on that occasion."

"I know, sir, but you must know a lady does not easily forget such remarks," she said archly.

"I will be more prudent in the future."

"Perhaps. I understand you will leave for Town tomorrow."

"Indeed." His steady gaze made her think he wished to say something more, but he remained silent.

Elizabeth was tempted to inquire about the length of his stay in London, but she refrained. What if he planned to never return to Netherfield?

No more words were spoken aloud. As the dance ended, he offered his arm and said, "I am very anxious to see my sister again. And I hope to have the chance to introduce her to you."

A warm wave tinged her face and neck. "I would like that very much, sir."

THE NEXT HOUR PASSED WITH LITTLE REASON FOR ELIZABETH TO FEEL ANY joy. Her family seemed determined to shame her. Lydia and Kitty flirted wildly with the officers, and Mary exhibited her skills on the pianoforte no less than three times. She knew Mr. Bingley's sisters were laughing at such untoward behavior and were pleased to find new reasons to criticize her family. She could hardly imagine Mr. Darcy's opinion, and when she observed him across the room several times, she could not meet his gaze.

Elizabeth looked to her father for assistance, but he was missing. She found him outside on the terrace.

"Please come and stop Mary. She has played long enough and not allowed anyone else to exhibit. And you know very well that her skills are much weaker than her will."

"Very well, my dear, let us try to lessen some of the disaster," Mr. Bennet said. "But you, Lizzy, seem to be enjoying yourself. I have rarely witnessed a spectacle as entertaining as your opening set with your cousin."

"Papa!"

"Then with Mr. Darcy himself! I was shocked that he asked you."

Elizabeth smiled. "I was surprised too, Papa. And I will tell you a secret. He asked for the first set, but I had to refuse him as I was already engaged with Mr. Collins."

"Now I am impressed. He offered for you again, eh? To be second after your cousin's performance."

"Papa!"

"So Mr. Darcy changed his opinion of how tolerable you are, has he?"

Elizabeth laughed with embarrassment. "Mr. Darcy and I have had the opportunity to speak several times lately, and our impressions of one another have changed."

"Is that so? Should we expect to see more of Mr. Darcy in your future? Does poor Mr. Collins have no chance of your favor?"

"Papa, please do not tease me about this. Mr. Darcy is a bright and well-educated man, and it is a pleasure to speak to him. But surely, I am not so naïve as to believe that he might regard our company in other ways than mere acquaintances. Perhaps, if Mr. Bingley were to propose to Jane, we might also see Mr. Darcy, being his close friend. But no more than that. And I beg you—do not make such jokes in the presence of Mama. You know how her imagination—"

"Very well my dear. I promise. The last thing I want is your mother chasing Mr. Darcy around Hertfordshire and beyond. She is busy enough encouraging Mr. Collins to propose to you. I hope you realize that you will have a trying next few days."

"I do...I am sorry to pain either Mama or Mr. Collins, but I see little chance of avoiding it."

Mr. Bennet laughed and patted his favorite daughter's hand, and they returned inside.

ENTERING THE HOUSE, ELIZABETH FURROWED HER BROW UPON SEEING Mr. Collins speaking with Mr. Darcy Their voices were loud enough to be heard from the door.

"Mr. Darcy, I thank you for your kindness toward my cousin Elizabeth. I shall take the liberty to interpret it as a gesture of approval of my choice, and I assure you that I value your condescension as much as I would if it came from Lady Catherine herself."

Elizabeth's eyes widened in horror.

Darcy scowled at the man bowing to him. "Mr. Collins, what on earth are you talking about?"

Mr. Bennet intervened by taking a few steps closer. Elizabeth's knees almost betrayed her as she observed the scene unfold before her. "Mr. Darcy, we often have difficulty in understanding Mr. Collins's excessive expression. I have rarely met anyone this skilled with rhetoric."

Darcy's amusement brought dimples to his cheeks while Mr. Collins's obvious pleasure at the compliment made him bow even deeper.

Mr. Bennet continued. "Mr. Collins, I was under the impression that Sir William was looking for you. He was interested to hear your opinion on several subjects. He seemed disappointed that he could not find you."

"Indeed? Mr. Darcy, I must beg your forgiveness. As a clergyman—"

"Indeed, go. Mr. Collins, I would never purposely detain you at the expense of others who might better benefit from your presence."

Mr. Collins departed, and Darcy looked from a silent and drawn Elizabeth to her father, who looked highly diverted.

She briefly excused herself, claiming she needed to speak to Jane. While she felt Darcy's eyes on her back, Elizabeth hoped that somehow a large hole might suddenly open in the floor and swallow her.

"SIR, I BEG YOUR FORGIVENESS FOR MY JEST AT MR. COLLINS'S EXPENSE BUT—"

"No need to apologize. I quite enjoyed it." Mr. Bennet smiled. "My cousin has a peculiar way of understanding only what favors him, and I am sure he is pleased with your attentions."

"Yes, well… Whatever could he have meant by my approval? Surely, he has no understanding with your daughter?"

Darcy noticed Miss Elizabeth's vexed expression across the room as she whispered in Miss Bennet's ear. Mr. Bennet took a seat and asked a passing servant for a glass of brandy—the third that evening.

"I would be happy to enlighten you, but I do not want to bore you at a ball."

"Please do, sir. I would be most obliged."

"Are you aware that Mr. Collins is my heir? He came to visit us a few days ago, and he has decided to choose one of my daughters as his future partner in life. It seems your aunt, Lady Catherine de Bourgh, has instructed him to marry, and he is anxious to obey. Equally amusing, it seems he has chosen Elizabeth."

Darcy's eyes opened in disbelief.

"Miss Elizabeth is engaged to Mr. Collins?"

"Dear Lord! Of course not. He has not yet proposed, but I expect it to happen soon."

"I did not imagine that Miss Elizabeth might be expected to marry Mr. Collins."

"And I did not imagine you might ever be interested in the marriage prospects of my daughters," Mr. Bennet said laughing.

"Forgive my impertinence."

Mr. Bennet waved his hand. "Elizabeth is expected to marry Mr. Collins. Any woman with very little dowry, no connections, no other means, four sisters, and their home entailed would. But I am certain she will refuse him. My poor cousin will have the surprise of his life, and I expect it to be a huge scandal in our house."

Mr. Bennet's voice was much lighter than the confession would require, and it astonished Darcy. Was the gentleman making sport at the expense of his daughter?

"Do not believe me indifferent to my daughter's well-being. It is true that I struggle to avoid the clamor of a household of women and prefer to keep my sanity in the solitude of my library." He raised the brandy to his lips again. "Nothing is more important to me than my daughters' happiness. But as a young man, I never took steps to make proper provisions for them after my death as I always intended to father a son, but when it appeared we were to have only daughters, the case seemed pointless."

Mr. Darcy responded uneasily at hearing such an intimate confession. "I understand very well; the library is also my favorite room. I often lock myself away there. I, too, avoid noise when I happen to find myself in the middle of it."

"Well, I am sure Mr. Bingley has a comfortable library. We could sneak off there and have a glass of brandy and some peace for an hour. I am not sure anyone would miss us."

Again, Darcy was astounded by Mr. Bennet's drollness.

Mr. Bennet smiled against his half-empty glass. "I see that I have surprised you once again, sir. It is only fair, as I was also surprised to see you dancing with my Lizzy. You seem quite skillful. Sir William repeatedly said that he has rarely seen such elegance."

Darcy was disconcerted, and he could feel a bead of sweat form above his lip.

"Indeed, I had the pleasure of dancing with Miss Elizabeth; however, I must confess, I enjoyed her witty company more.

"Mr. Darcy, you are full of surprises this evening! Surely, you must know that the gossiping matrons have remarked how you have only danced that single set."

"I imagined they might wonder, but I can provide no other explanation than it was my intention to assure myself some pleasant conversation with your lovely daughter."

Mr. Bennet laughed.

"It is your right to offer no explanation as it is your right to dance as little as you please. I myself am not fond of large gatherings. But as the father of five eligible daughters, I am unable to do what I please. I only hope that you are careful of what you are doing…in order to avoid raising expectations."

They stared at each other wordlessly with the sounds of the festivities surrounding them. Mr. Bennet smiled and took another swallow of brandy. "As for me, I would love to hide myself in the library, but of course, that would not do. I will have to content myself with *wondering* what books Mr. Bingley might have."

Darcy smiled anxiously. "It is a perfectly good library although rarely used. I find benefit there, and Miss Elizabeth also visited it several times during her stay. Generally, though, the room is disregarded."

"My library is not as large, but I may say that it is a worthy collection of which I am quite proud. I do try to improve it as I might wish, but I have noticed over the years that a fondness for books is not very beneficial to the management of one's estate and income, especially when one has five daughters and the property is entailed to one not-so-worthy cousin."

Darcy took a glass of brandy himself. "Mr. Bennet, it is my belief that the value of a library consists not in its dimensions or the number of its books but in the passion and care of those who value that library."

"Well, I dare say we are of like minds, Mr. Darcy."

Darcy smiled and nodded, slightly embarrassed. He speculated that Mr. Bennet was referring not only to the books and balls but also to Elizabeth.

Mr. Bennet emptied his glass. "If you happen to have time to join Mr. Bingley in his calls to Longbourn, it would be my pleasure to show you my collection."

"I would like that very much, sir. I am sorry that I did not take the opportunity during my stay here. Tomorrow morning, I accompany Bingley to Town, but I look forward to furthering the acquaintance on future visits."

Mr. Bennet seemed highly amused, possibly encouraged by Mr. Bingley's excellent brandy. "Well, well... Did you notice how many eyes we have attracted? It is no wonder, considering that, during your stay in Hertfordshire, you barely exchanged a few words with anyone. My neighbors might believe that I have become your second-favorite companion—after my Lizzy."

Mr. Darcy hid his smile behind his own glass of brandy, as he looked across the room at a pair of fine eyes on the face of a pretty woman, and said, "Sir, I yield to your superior knowledge of your neighbors."

Mr. Bennet's words turned into a storm in Darcy's mind. He remained where he was, staring out at the moving forms on the floor.

As his eyes rested on Elizabeth's figure as she danced with an officer, their eyes would meet. Her smile made him tremble though he knew not why a country maiden should have such an effect on him.

Darcy was a man of the world, but the emotions Elizabeth aroused in him by her smallest gestures—the brief touch of her hands while they danced, her mere presence—astonished and frightened him. Yes, her family was far beneath him. And yes, his family, his duty, and his own reason demanded that he select a woman worthy of the role as Mrs. Darcy. Miss Elizabeth Bennet, no matter how praiseworthy she might be, was still from an inconsequential family with no fortune or connections. And for that reason—and to avoid raising expectations, as Mr. Bennet just said—he had struggled not to show her any preference during the first weeks of his stay in Hertfordshire.

But his heart, his feelings could not be controlled. That was why he had been so hasty in convincing Bingley to leave for London and agreed so readily with Caroline and Louisa that Jane Bennet was not the proper wife for Bingley. That was the reason he planned to join Bingley in Town—to cowardly put distance between him and the only woman who had ever stirred his heart.

But as Fate would have it, driven by his dog, he lost his resolve, and instead of remaining silent and retreating from the scene, he chose to speak to her, to discover her opinion about him, her dislike of him—and tried to convince her otherwise. He imprudently admitted his admiration for her and let himself be attracted more by her charming company.

She proved her worthiness and intelligence when she doubted Wickham's story and then courageously approached him for his side of the tale. Thanks to her, he decided to speak to Colonel Forster, and together they forced Wickham to leave the neighborhood. Though it cost him the price of a new commission, it was worth the effort.

In these past days, he had discovered not only the truth about his feelings, as well as Elizabeth's, but also the true character of Jane Bennet. Thus, he decided he would offer no advice in matters of the heart, and as promised, he would accompany him to Town then back to Netherfield.

He recognized Elizabeth's own partiality to him, but his mind was still fighting his heart for the choice he had to make.

Then a revelation struck him: Fate, happiness, and life could not wait for him! Certainly, there would be other men who would pursue Elizabeth. That ridiculous, pompous clergyman was proof of that. And even if she were to refuse Collins now, she might accept another man. He knew he could make her happier than any other man would, but his wish meant nothing without his acting once and for all.

Darcy stared at Elizabeth again, then at Collins. On the other side of the room, he noticed Mr. Bennet studying him. Then suddenly, Darcy understood that he was no better than Collins—quite the contrary! He was worse, much worse.

As Mr. Bennet had said: he had wealth and complete liberty; he depended on no one else. And yet, like Mr. Collins, he, too, cared about what his aunts or uncles had to say and about what society would say. He did not deserve more respect. He would need to work relentlessly if he wanted to gain it.

And there, in the middle of the Netherfield ballroom, amidst loud music and laughter, Darcy chose his future and his destiny.

He walked toward her, holding her gaze, stepping closer and closer to the woman to whom he decided to offer his soul and his life. It was not the right time for that yet—he knew he had to do more to prove himself worthy—but once his decision was made, his mind and heart were both light and ceased fighting against each other.

When suppertime arrived, Elizabeth saw Jane walking to dinner on the arm of Mr. Bingley and behind them, looking displeased, were the Hursts and Miss Bingley. Her eyes were drawn toward the impressive presence of Mr. Darcy directly across the room from her—whose gaze was more intense and dark than ever.

Her throat tightened when she realized he was striding in her direction.

"Miss Elizabeth, may I escort you in to supper?"

"Yes, thank you." She put her hand on his arm, and they walked together while Elizabeth wondered what he was about.

"I had a very pleasant conversation with your father."

"Truly? My father can be very...eccentric."

"I dare say you take your spirit and tendency to tease from him." His voice matched his bright eyes.

"Shall I take that as a criticism?"

"By no means—quite the contrary. I have not forgotten so easily your lesson from earlier this evening." He paused before continuing. "Mr. Bennet kindly invited me to visit his library as soon as we return from London."

Her heart began to race. "We will be delighted to receive your call. But I was under the impression that your plans were not yet fixed— that you were uncertain as to how long you would be in Town."

"I am still uncertain about the precise date of our return, but now I am certain it will happen. As for my plans, I have only made the choice that has troubled me for many weeks."

"Oh? You seem pleased."

"I am. I have great hopes this will turn out to be the best choice I have ever made. May I ask—what is your opinion should I call on Longbourn?

I want to be certain of your welcome."

"I certainly would not—" She met his gaze. "Your presence will be most welcome. I was just thinking…I believe you have never visited Longbourn during your stay in Hertfordshire."

"It is true. Although I wished to."

"So may I ask what stopped you?" She put a smile in her voice to soften her question.

"My own foolishness. For many weeks I believed that it would be better for me to…spend most of the time at Netherfield."

Her hand resting on his arm trembled slightly, and she put the other one over it. She struggled to understand the meaning of his words, fearful to be either wrong or too hopeful. He put his hand over hers.

"Tonight, I realized I have been proud and selfish for most of my life, Miss Elizabeth. I am not a man without faults. Miss Bingley, as usual, was wrong."

Her heart was beating so strongly that she was certain he could hear it.

"I am glad that Miss Bingley is wrong. I am pleased to hear you are not a man without faults." Laughing, she said, "You were intimidating enough even without this label of perfection."

His smile mirrored hers. "Unlike Miss Bingley, you are correct again."

Elizabeth's heart was so light, so full of joy and excitement, that she felt she could fly.

As Mr. Darcy seated her at the table, Mr. Collins appeared.

"My dear cousin, I have been looking for you the entire evening." He prepared to take the seat at her side.

Elizabeth was crestfallen. Darcy turned toward her cousin and said decidedly, "Mr. Collins, come and sit on my left, sir. There are several things that I wish to discuss with you, and I do not want to disturb Miss Elizabeth."

Mr. Collins's excitement did not allow him time to wonder about Darcy's reasoning as he took the chair indicated. Elizabeth smiled to herself and met her father's amused smirk from the other side of the table.

During the entire supper, Elizabeth was torn between joy and the deepest embarrassment. Her mother did not lose a moment to share her hopes that she would have two daughters married soon. Lydia and Kitty had quickly forgotten about Mr. Wickham; they were in the middle of an animated and coarse conversation with some officers, and Mary intervened from time to time with words of wisdom.

Jane's face glowed as she and Mr. Bingley shared a quiet conversation, seemingly oblivious to the antics surrounding them.

On her left, Mr. Darcy made perfunctory remarks to Mr. Collins's copious conversation. She found that, when their hands would touch or his leg brush against hers, she glowed from within. Without many words, they reveled in each other's presence.

Elizabeth did not wish to think about the end of the ball as that meant that certain gentlemen would soon depart for Town. And there, in the middle of the din, surrounded by music and voices and laughter, Elizabeth realized that she dreaded his departure!

Before the end of the evening, Elizabeth danced several more dances but Darcy none. She was delighted to see his eyes follow her through the figures, and she returned his smiles with her own.

When the ball ended, and after a friendly and warm farewell from both Mr. Bingley and Mr. Darcy and a promise to meet again soon, the Bennets left Netherfield.

Looking once more over her shoulder to where the gentlemen were standing, Elizabeth felt a pain in her chest as her father handed her into the carriage.

She heard her mother and sisters discussing the ball animatedly, she felt her father's insistent gaze, and she knew she should be well pleased with the evening.

Happiness shyly enveloped her soul, but a strange sense burdened her heart. Later in the dark solitude of her bedchamber, she wondered when she might expect his return to Hertfordshire.

The morning after the ball, Mr. Collins (to no one's surprise) proposed to Elizabeth, and she (to no one's surprise but her mother and Mr. Collins) refused him. Mr. Collins insisted that he would patiently wait until her modesty passed, and her mother then began a campaign to change her mind, commencing with parental insistence to appealing to her sense of familial duty to loud cries of how they would all end starving in the hedgerows.

When Mrs. Bennet applied to Mr. Bennet, he declined any interest and locked himself in the library.

Mrs. Bennet implored Mr. Collins to have a little more patience and gave him her word that she would convince Elizabeth to accept him before he returned to Kent.

Though Mr. Collins appeared offended, with much condescension, he agreed to wait. In the meantime, to Mrs. Bennet's despair and Elizabeth's relief, he accepted two dinner invitations at Lucas Lodge.

Three days after the ball, Elizabeth's mind was no less troubled by questions without answers, the cause of her restless nights. The gentlemen from Netherfield had not returned. Worse yet, when the Hursts and Miss Bingley arrived in London, they sent Jane word that they would remain in Town for the winter as her brother was closely engaged with Mr. Darcy and his sister.

The news shocked both Jane and Elizabeth. Though the eldest's distress might have been expected, the second eldest daughter had to bear her pain alone as nobody imagined that Mr. Darcy's departure might affect her in any way. Elizabeth encouraged Jane not to believe in Miss Bingley's insinuations about a possible connection between Miss Darcy and Mr. Bingley. But her confidence in Mr. Darcy and Mr. Bingley's return diminished with every day, every hour, and every minute that passed.

She was angry at her folly, discomfited that she entertained hopes with no foundation and suffered so deeply for a man with whom she was barely acquainted. Why could she not have simply enjoyed his conversation as an agreeable and sensible young man without having a wish beyond it?

As expected, the news of Mr. Bingley's not returning made Mrs. Bennet more maddening than ever. She hounded Elizabeth relentlessly to accept Mr. Collins, repeating that, when her father dies, they all would be thrown out to fend for themselves.

Mr. Bennet's emotions were much more tranquil on the occasion, and he said, "My dear, do not give way to such gloomy thoughts. Let us hope for better things. Let us flatter ourselves that *I* may be the survivor."

On November 29, late in the afternoon, Elizabeth and Jane were called to the library. Mr. Bennet stood at his desk, looking as amused as ever.

"So, girls, I see you are still pale and suffering."

"Papa!" Elizabeth grasped Jane's hand in support.

"Ah yes, let us all be serious, cry over pillows, lose sleep and appetite. The joys of love."

Elizabeth rolled her eyes at her father's ill-timed humor.

"I have received a letter this morning that has astonished me exceedingly. It has a most elegant hand, which can only belong to a superior person, as my cousin would say."

Elizabeth's knees almost betrayed her, and she tightened her hold of Jane's hand.

"Mr. Darcy asks my permission to call tomorrow afternoon, together with Mr. Bingley, shortly after they arrive at Netherfield."

A shocked silence fell upon the library, but it was soon broken by Mrs. Bennet's shrill voice as she barged into the room in her dressing gown and with her hair finished, crying out, "Mr. Bennet! You are urgently wanted! Now! Oh, you are here too, Lizzy. Good. Just hear the disaster you are inflicting on our family." Dabbing her eyes dramatically with a lace handkerchief, she continued. "Mr. Collins will return to Kent tomorrow! He insists on an answer, as he cannot return to his patron without one! Further, he says he shan't go home before he is able to inform Lady Catherine that he is engaged! And now, he is speaking of Charlotte Lucas! Her qualities, her steady manner, her accomplishments in running a household. Oh, dear Lord, I cannot breathe. I shall die before my time. My poor nerves. And it is all your fault, Lizzy!"

"Well, my dear, you will at least be happy not to be thrown out of the house on my death. Now, what can I do under the present situation?" Mr. Bennet's mischievous smile lit his face.

"What? Force Lizzy to marry Mr. Collins, of course!" cried Mrs. Bennet. "He is in the hall, waiting to hear Lizzy's answer. I insist she accept him this instant!"

"My dear Mrs. Bennet, it seems we are in a delicate situation." Mr. Bennet cleared his throat. "I have received an express from Mr. Darcy. He informed me that he will return to the neighborhood on the morrow, together with Mr. Bingley, and he asked for my permission to call on Lizzy. It seems he is very fond of her company and finds her to be 'a spirited and bright young lady as he had never met before.' I confess I rather liked that fellow, and I will be sad to refuse him, but I see no other choice. I shall force Lizzy to marry Mr. Collins since you insist, and I will send Mr. Darcy away."

The effect on Mrs. Bennet was extraordinary. She blinked repeatedly then suddenly flopped down on the nearest chair, pressing her palms to her chest. She opened her mouth; then her face turned crimson. She glanced from her husband to her second daughter as if to make sense of Mr. Bennet's news. Then she unexpectedly ran out of the library, leaving the door open, and met Mr. Collins in the hall.

"My dear Mr. Collins, I can go no longer without apologizing for my error. It was my deepest wish to have you marry Lizzy, as we consider it a great honor to have you in our family. However, after recent discussions with my husband, I came to the conclusion that Lizzy would not be the right choice for you. It pains me to admit, but her spirit is too wild, and she is too stubborn for a clergyman's wife. I strongly believe you need a young woman with a steady character, accustomed to running a household, with temperate manners, calm and restrained. Nothing less would be acceptable for your right and honorable patroness!"

Mr. Bennet smiled at his astonished daughters while, through the open door, they heard their cousin.

"My dear madam, your generous wisdom honors you! I hope my fair cousin Elizabeth will not suffer her disappointment long, but for now, you must excuse me. I must hurry to Lucas Lodge. I am expected for dinner."

There was silence for a moment then again Mrs. Bennet's voice continuing towards the kitchen: "Hill, where are you? We must change the dishes for tomorrow's dinner. Hill! We need at least five courses! My poor nerves, how will I bear all these upsets?"

The library suddenly became too small for their joy, so Elizabeth and Jane kissed their father and hurried to share their excitement in their own room. Inside, Mr. Bennet returned to his book. There was no need to lock the door as he was certain nobody would disturb him for the rest of the day.

THOUGH ELIZABETH STILL COUNTED THE HOURS UNTIL MR. DARCY'S anticipated return the following day, she fell asleep with a happy heart, and for the first time since before the Netherfield ball, she woke rested.

Shortly thereafter, Lady Lucas and Charlotte arrived to share the news. To their guests' surprise, Mrs. Bennet received the news with genuine delight and declared that it was truly a perfect choice and that Charlotte had made an excellent match. Then she gushed that Mr. Bingley and Mr. Darcy were expected to come and dine at Longbourn.

Once the guests left, Elizabeth ventured out for a walk to gather her thoughts in anticipation of their dinner guests.

As she skipped along the leaf-strewn paths, she suddenly cried out in surprise when she was knocked from behind.

She turned around and let out another cry—one of disbelief and joy at discovering a zealous black Great Dane. She bent down to caress Blackie and barely turned her head, avoiding a wet kiss from the tall dog. She laughed, her eyes burning with unshed tears, and Elizabeth did not need to lift her gaze to know that Darcy had dismounted his horse only a few steps away from her.

"Miss Elizabeth! I did not expect to meet you here. We have only arrived at Netherfield, and as you see, Blackie and I are stretching our legs. We planned to call on Longbourn later—with Bingley, not Blackie. You are well, I hope?"

She laughed. "Yes, very well, thank you." She clutched her hands together to stop their trembling. "Such a surprise to see you, sir. We believed you would not return to Hertfordshire anytime soon—that you would stay in town for the winter." Emotions almost overwhelmed her. "Forgive me," she said, turning her back to him. She heard him step toward her.

"Miss Elizabeth, I told you that we would return. Are you displeased? Should I leave you?" His voice was revealing his distress.

"No...please do not leave. Of course, I am not displeased. Forgive me." She turned to him, forcing a smile and blinking repeatedly to stay her tears.

He took one more step, closing the distance between them.

"I hoped you would not be displeased by my return..."

"I am not unhappy. It is only...Miss Bingley wrote to Jane that you would all stay in Town for the winter." Her cheeks were red, and her eyes sparkled behind moist eyelashes. "I did not know what to believe when my father said you were to return today. I am not at all displeased—quite the contrary..."

The corners of his lips rose in a smile while his tender gaze felt like a caress. "I confess that a fortnight ago I was indeed decided to leave Netherfield with no intention of returning. Not because I wanted to be in Town but because I could not bear to be close to you any longer. I struggled to run from feelings that I had never felt before, to put distance between me and a woman who completely bewitched me and with whom I knew I could have no future... A woman that I believed to be beneath me and the expectations of my family."

Her lips trembled and she wondered why he would tell her such painful things. Could he not see that he was hurting her?

"Then why did you return now?"

"Because I have struggled in vain! Before I left, I had decided to return to you as soon as possible. Those few days, I spent every moment watching you, admiring your smiles and sparking eyes, and while I enjoyed your company and your glances, I suddenly faced the reality that I might lose you to someone else, and I could not bear it. During the night at the ball, your father pointed out how I am too wealthy to not do what I please! That I need not be accountable to anyone. That my duty must be to myself, to my heart, to my future. He is a wise man indeed."

Elizabeth burst out in nervous laughter, wiping her tear-stained eyes. "Yes, he is…"

He struggled to remove his riding gloves and then tucked them in his pocket. He stretched his hands to hers, and she found her fingers secure in his warm, strong palms.

"There is no one I need to ask to allow me to be happy—except you, who holds my happiness in your hands. Therefore, you must allow me tell you how ardently I admire and love you. I have returned to you until you ask me to leave Hertfordshire or you decide to leave with me."

He slowly brought their hands to his chest.

"I shall never ask you to leave," she whispered, her face lifted to his.

His tender look melted the tears frozen on her cheeks. He released her hands, and then his strong hands gently cupped her face. His thumbs brushed over her cheeks, barely touching the corners of her lips. She stopped breathing and closed her eyes. His lips lightly touched her cheeks, then traveled along her face and lingered a few moments over her eyelashes.

"It is too soon for anything more," he whispered, his moving lips tasting her skin, salty from tears. "I still have to put much effort into dissipating the poor opinion I have made during the last months. You were too generous to forgive me so easily, though I do not deserve it."

"That is true. I am generous and many other things that you are welcome to praise, sir," she teased him and released a nervous laugh. Her movement made her face lean against his and his lips touched hers. Neither breathed; neither moved. His lips withdrew an inch from hers then pressed again, warm and gentle as a breeze, and her own lips shyly dared to part.

They fell into each other's arms, and they united in an unexpected yet long desired kiss when Blackie tried to nudge between them, curious and vying for his share of attention.

They laughed with unleashed joy, now lighthearted and filled with hope for a bright future, and remained closely entwined as they patted the dog.

Darcy placed another gentle kiss on her forehead.

"I have missed you, Elizabeth."

Her name on his lips made her shiver, and her face and heart brightened. "I missed you too. So very much. I hope not to have to miss you ever again."

The cold December wind made the windows shudder, but the house was bursting with Christmastide visitors and activity, and no one seemed to notice.

Elizabeth stopped a moment in the halls she knew so well, then, instead of turning to the drawing room, she climbed the stairs, pushed open the large door, and then closed it behind her.

She saw Darcy at a small table, writing. Their eyes met, and she smiled. His hand stretched to her, and she placed her fingers in his large palm.

"I only need to finish these papers. Where are the others? How did you escape?"

"My father and uncle are in the library, and Blackie sleeps by the fireplace." She brushed a curl away from his brow. "Mr. Bingley is with Jane in the drawing room. Georgiana and Mary are playing duets, and Lydia is arguing over the new shawl I gave Kitty for Christmas. Mama is fussing with Cook over the sauces, and my aunt tries to temper them all."

"I have become very fond of the Gardiners."

"As they are of you. I thank you for the time you share with my family."

Her finger pushed the errant curl back again, and he caught her wrist. He brought his lips to her wrist. "Everything that gives you joy is a pleasure to me," he said hoarsely. "Do you return downstairs or shall you keep me company?"

"Propriety would require I return immediately." Hearing the squeals of laughter coming from down the hall, Elizabeth grinned. "But I think we can assume my presence will not be missed. My decision to secret away for a few more moments won't disturb you?"

"You always disturb me, even when you are not near. I can hardly do or even think of anything else." His lips slowly turned her wrists then rested inside her palms.

He rose from his chair, his eyes never leaving hers. His right hand gently caressed her cheeks, and his thumb brushed over her parted lips. She smiled, her eyes sparkling, and her hand mirrored his movements, caressing his handsome face.

Her arms encircled his waist, their bodies pulled together. His head leaned to her, and his lips captured hers, first tender and gentle, growing more eager, more demanding.

"Our guests are waiting for us," she whispered.

"I have no excuse for letting them wait but my ardent love and passion for you." Her eyes closed, and she felt countless kisses caress her face. "As it is our eight-month wedding anniversary"—she gasped as his lips trailed down her neck—"and thirteen months since I made the *perfect* choice for my life there in the middle of the Netherfield ball"—she sighed when his lips found the swell of her breast—"I believe we are entitled to not be *perfectly* proper."

His lips captured hers again, and he lifted her into his arms. He slowly lowered her to the bed and lay beside her.

"Nothing makes me happier than to make you happy, my beloved."

No more was said as his body almost crushed hers and his lips begged—demanded—the sweetness of her skin. She was breathless from his weight and from his passion, which matched her own desire. She could think of no better way to celebrate these little anniversaries that were significant to none but them, and she soon allowed herself to be conquered by her husband's passion and her own longing.

Elizabeth found her Christmastide visitors would simply have to wait for the mistress and master of Pemberley for a few moments longer. And in the end, it was the perfect choice.

. . . .

LORY LILIAN is a Romanian *Pride and Prejudice* aficionado with a background in business. She has an awesome daughter and the gentlest French bulldog ever. She fell in love with *Pride and Prejudice* when she was thirteen and has read it about a hundred times since. The A&E television mini-series in 1995 had a dramatic impact on her fascination with Darcy and Elizabeth and inspired her to read and then start writing countless variations about her favorite couple.

Lory is the author of five *Pride and Prejudice*-inspired books: *Rainy Days*, *Remembrance of the Past*, *His Uncle's Favorite*, *The Perfect Match*, and *Sketching Mr. Darcy*.

She is currently working on three more, all at the same time.

Acknowledgements

MY THANKS TO MICHELE REED AT MERYTON PRESS FOR GIVING ME THE opportunity to be part of another anthology project and for her additional eyes in the reviewing process—because it is a process.

Thank you to Ellen Pickels for working her "Ellen Magic" and making this an impeccable, elegant collection. I think she could write her own book— *Outtakes from Editing Other People's Books*—as her side commentary is not only an invaluable source of intelligence but sometimes just downright funny!

Thank you to Zorylee Diaz-Lupitou for creating another gorgeous cover that not only complements the anthology *Sun-kissed: Effusions of Summer*, but also seemingly effortlessly captures the spirit of this holiday anthology, *Then Comes Winter*.

Thanks to Jakki Leatherberry for promoting the book and for all the sound advice, and to the panel of bloggers, reviewers, readers, and authors who graciously read through MANY submissions, offering evaluative criticism to cull the search to the collection we have here. I appreciate their continued and enthusiastic support of this project, the writers, and me.

And thank you to the brilliant authors who are such pros to work with. It's not easy to submit a story, only to have initial edits returned and marked up in a bloodbath of red with entire paragraphs slashed or with suggested re-writes. I have found that only the most courageous professional can humbly accept and smartly defend the changes and then trust that this editor has their best interest at heart. I thank you for your confidence, dedication to your craft, and commitment to get this done right.

I thank my father, Dr. E. C. Angel, who taught me how to read. I well remember the day we finally broke the code and the world opened up to adventure and wonder. And thank you to my mother, Mrs. Donna Baker, who always has a book in hand, teaching me by example the love and escape of curling up with a good read.

As so often in real life, *last but never least*: my thanks to my dear Mr. B and busy Boydlings, who show me their love and support by not complaining too loudly when the laundry has piled up or the grocery list is lengthy, allowing me to spend hours a day at the computer to get "one more story" done. You sustain me.

About the Editor

CHRISTINA BOYD WEARS MANY HATS AS SHE IS AN EDITOR AT MERYTON Press, a contributor to Austenprose, and a ceramicist for the Made in Washington stores under her own banner, Stir Crazy Mama's Artworks. A life member of the Jane Austen Society of North America, Christina lives in the wilds of the Pacific Northwest with her dear Mr. B, two busy teenagers, and a retriever named BiBi. Visiting Jane Austen's England remains on her bucket list.

CPSIA information can be obtained
at www.ICGtesting.com
Printed in the USA
FSOW01n0406301115
13711FS

9 781681 310039